Lex Fai

PROLOGUE

REICH CHANCELLERY, BERLIN – OCTOBER, 1942

It was an unseasonably warm and sunny day as the gleaming, black Mercedes W150 convertible made its way along Voss Strasse past the new Reich Chancellery building that had been completed three years earlier. The limestone facades of the sprawling three-storey complex had been deliberately designed with a stern and authoritarian neo-classical appearance by the Nazi regime's favoured architect, Albert Speer, who had also been appointed Reich Minister of Armament and Ammunition. The spartan severity of the chancellery was modelled after the grand temples of ancient times but also designed to evoke awe as well as a sense of intimidation and fear of the power of the Nazi party.

Glinting in the midday sun, the limousine had been polished to a high sheen, and mounted on its front were two red flags with a white circle containing a black swastika within, which fluttered in the wind as the car drove along. With its sweeping curves, shining chrome radiator grille, large headlights and powerful engine, the Mercedes convertible represented the pinnacle of German automotive design and engineering, and Mercedes had built a handful of them specifically for the passenger in the back seat. When it arrived at the end of the street and reached the corner with Wilhelmstrasse, it turned left and immediately pulled over to park in front of the main entrance to the austere-looking chancellery building.

Flanking the entrance and standing guard in anticipation of the Führer's arrival were two armed soldiers from the elite paramilitary organisation, the *Schutzstaffel*, also known as the SS. They wore their characteristic black uniforms consisting of polished knee-high boots, black steel helmets with white swastikas, red-black-and-white swastika armbands, wide black leather belts with shiny steel buckles around their waists, and the intimidating white double victory runes on the lapels of their jackets that were often mistaken for two lightning bolts. They were both cradling black MP40 submachine guns, and they carried holstered 9mm Walther P38 pistols attached to their belts.

As the car came to a stop, a tall and smartly dressed chauffeur got out from behind the wheel and moved around to open the left-hand passenger door. He held it open as the two guards by the entrance snapped to attention, and then Adolph Hitler stepped out. As he had done since the beginning of World War 2, the Führer was wearing his usual double-breasted field-grey jacket with silver buttons, black trousers, a white shirt with a black tie and a black belt around his waist. Mostly shying away from wearing his military decorations, he wore only his swastika-adorned golden Nazi party badge on the left side of his chest, along with the black-and-white Iron Cross and the black Wound Badge that he had received during World War 1.

He gave a quick salute to the two SS soldiers as he walked briskly up a few steps and through one of the two seven-metre-tall doorways that led to the *Ehrenhof*, or Court of Honour. The two soldiers then filed in behind him to escort him inside the chancellery complex. The courtyard was approximately seventy metres long and twenty metres wide, and like the rest of the chancellery, it had been constructed from granite and limestone that had been quarried by forced labour from concentration camps in the south of Germany and in Austria. In particular, the granite had come from the quarries in the town of Flossenbürg near the border with Czechoslovakia. Here, the nearby Flossenbürg camp had become one of the main sources of construction materials destined for the many new grand buildings about to be constructed in the German capital.

On either side of the courtyard were tall and narrow multi-paned casement windows and Greek limestone columns. The columns were placed inside wall niches and reached the full height of the building, thereby giving the space a soaring temple-like appearance. At the far end of the courtyard was a set of ten steps leading up to a portico containing the main entrance to the chancellery's interior. Above it on the wall hung a two-metre tall bronze *Reichsadler* eagle with its wings outstretched, and in its claws, it was gripping a laurel wreath with a swastika. The entrance was flanked by two more Greek columns on either side that were set into the façade, and next to each of them in the corners of the courtyard were two gleaming male bronze statues reminiscent of Greek marble sculptures. Muscular and impressive, the shiny figures were four metres tall and cast in the idealised shape of an Aryan man. The much vaunted Nazi *Übermensch*. One was holding aloft a torch, while the other was holding a sword. They represented the *Partei* and the *Wehrmacht,* respectively. The Nazi Party and the German Army.

Saluting once more as he ascended the steps and walked past the two soldiers who snapped to attention, Hitler continued towards the tall double doors ahead of him. They were opened from the inside as if by magic, and he pushed through with his armed entourage following close behind. Once inside the building, he proceeded up a wide marble staircase to a 12-metre wide and almost 150-metre-long gallery that had been designed to emulate the famous Hall of Mirrors at the Palace of Versailles, except it was twice as long. Its polished floors were made of large slabs of veined red marble, as were the Greek columns on one side of it flanking the 9-metre tall windows that overlooked Voss Strasse. Halfway along was the door to the Führer's office, and outside it stood another pair of SS guards clad all in black. One of the guards opened the door for him, and Hitler swept inside.

Covering 400 square metres, the enormous office was one of the largest rooms in the entire chancellery, and it looked out across the peaceful chancellery gardens with their neatly kept lawns, colourful flowerbeds, footpaths and water fountains. The coffered wooden ceiling some six metres above the hardwood floor was heavily ornate, and the dark red marble walls and brown wood panels created a severe and sombre atmosphere amid the general grandeur of the space. Centred on the wall to his right was an open fireplace with a plush sofa placed in front of it, and in the corner by the window was a large globe roughly one metre across that was sitting in a wooden cradle.

The door closed behind Hitler, and he then strode diagonally across a huge rug that covered almost the entire floor as he headed for his desk. Made of hardwood and polished to a high sheen, it was placed in the far corner by one of the five tall windows in order for him to have as much natural light as possible. Every last detail of the chancellery complex, including the interior of the offices and meeting rooms within it, had been meticulously planned and designed by Albert Speer. The complex had been built in just one year by teams of labourers working in shifts day and night to meet and eventually beat the deadline.

Speer's unwavering attention to detail and seeming ability to work miracles on large-scale building projects such as this had played a significant role in him ending up being put in charge of the design and construction of many of the hundreds of concentration camps that were now spread across virtually every country in Europe. As well as functioning as chillingly efficient extermination camps for Jews, homosexuals, gypsies, communists, the disabled and all other undesirables, the camps served as a virtually inexhaustible source of free labour for countless construction and manufacturing projects that had utterly transformed Germany over just a few short years since the Nazis had taken power.

Hitler first met Speer before the spectacular 1933 Nuremberg rally. Speer had joined the Nazi Party in

1931, and Rudolf Hess had sent him to Hitler's apartment in Munich to present his ideas for the rally. The Führer had been so impressed by the young architect that Speer soon became a member of his inner circle, and he saw in the young man a kindred spirit. This in turn led him to appoint Speer as Berlin's General Building Inspector and the man in charge of the construction of the Reich Chancellery. And every time Hitler walked through the long, spectacular gallery to his office, he knew that he had made the right decision.

As he headed for his desk, he glanced over to one side to a large dark green marble table sitting by one of the huge windows facing the gardens. Placed on top of it was a spectacularly detailed white gypsum model of the city of 'Germania', which Speer was also designing for him. Once the war had been won, this would become the new *Welthauptstadt* or World Capital.

Not for the first time, Hitler stopped for a moment and then moved to stand next to the display. The scale and ambition of the project was nothing short of breathtaking, and changing the capital's name from Berlin to Germania was emblematic of those ambitions. Once completed, it would utterly transform the German capital into a city much more impressive than London or Paris, although its layout and many of the buildings, squares and avenues were modelled on those older but soon-to-be lesser capitals. Germania would become the centre of German power and culture as those were spread to all corners of the world.

The centrepiece of the white model on the marble table was the truly gigantic domed and colonnaded *Volkshalle*. The 'Hall of the People'. Based on a drawing sketched by Hitler himself seventeen years earlier in 1925, its design was reminiscent of the Capitol Building in Washington D.C., or the Pantheon in Paris, except it was to be much bigger. The dome alone would be 250 metres across and rise to almost 300 metres, making it capable of easily fitting two entire St Peter's Basilicas on top of each other or the entire Capitol Building inside it. The relatively small 46-metre oculus sitting at the very top of the Volkshalle dome was intended to let in light, and it would be large enough to hold the dome of the famous basilica in Rome.

Hitler marvelled once more at his soon-to-be-constructed architectural masterpiece. It had been designed to have a capacity of 180,000 people, and in a matter of years, its interior would be filled with several tiers of concentric rows of seating, modelled on the Colosseum in Rome. Here would eventually sit tens of thousands of Nazi party members as well as thousands of representatives from the many countries of the world that the Third Reich, leveraging the superiority of its race and technological advances, would soon conquer and subjugate as it established a New World Order across the globe. However, true power would continue to reside right here in this sumptuous office in the chancellery, resting safely in the hands of Reich Führer Adolph Hitler.

Another central Germania structure to be built at the opposite end of a seven-kilometre-long avenue cutting through the capital from north to south would be the 170-metre-tall Great Arch. Hitler envisioned it as a memorial to Germany's defeat in World War I, and it was going to be engraved with the names of the almost two million Germans who died in that war. As he gazed at the model, Hitler felt pride swell up inside him at what he and his people were able to accomplish once they all worked together, got rid of the people holding the Fatherland back, and freed themselves of the suffocating chains that had been placed on them by the victors of World War 1.

The only item with any colour on the otherwise entirely white gypsum model was a small Nazi flag hanging from the Great Arch. The visually striking swastika flag had been designed by Hitler himself for the National Socialist German Workers' Party. Based on an ancient Hindu symbol for well-being and prosperity, which itself was based on symbols from as much as ten thousand years ago, it had come to symbolise Nazi power both inside and outside of Germany. As he had once explained to a group of eager listeners, the flag's red background signified the social movement of the party, the white circle represented the nationalistic idea of a united German Reich, and the rotated black swastika at the centre was meant to embody the struggle of the Aryan race for victory, as well as the idea of creative work to achieve those ends. If Germany could build all of this, then it could surely conquer the whole world.

It had now been three years since the German invasion of Poland that had started the war. Since then, Germany had expanded far beyond its borders like never before, taking over almost all of Europe, dominating huge areas of northern Africa and the Middle East, and reaching far into Russia and the Caucasus. The precursor to these events in his country's quest for *Lebensraum*, space for life and growth of the Aryan people, had been the taking back of the occupied and resource-rich Saarland on the border with France in 1935 following a plebiscite. In 1936, German troops marched into the heavily industrialised Rhineland, which, after the end of World War 1, had also been occupied by the Allies. Then came the peaceful *Anschluss* in 1938, when Austria was annexed into the German Reich. Finally, the annexation of the German-speaking *Sudetenland* territories of Czechoslovakia was realised in 1939, and soon the entire country was under his control.

During all of this, the British and the French both talked tough, but they ultimately acquiesced and even facilitated his ambitions, so when those two nations threatened to declare war if Germany also invaded Poland, he decided to ignore them. To his surprise, they came good on their promise and issued a declaration of war once the invasion had happened. However, ever since then, Germany had done nothing except expand across Europe in all directions, and he was now confident that it would be a question of time before the deluded British would succumb to the raw power and superior weapons technologies of his armies.

As he sat behind his desk and looked out at the garden where staff were milling around in the sunshine busily tending to the flowerbeds, he reflected on how far he had come since his days as a child in the small town of *Braunau am Inn* in the Empire of Austria-Hungary near the German border, where he had been born on the 20th of April, 1889. He and his younger sister Paula were the only two out of a brood of six children to survive childhood. At a young age, he decided that he wanted to become an artist, but this gave rise to a highly antagonistic relationship between him and his father Alois who wanted him to follow in his footsteps and become a customs officer. He was sent to a secondary school in the city of Linz in Austria, where he would later recall that he had deliberately performed poorly in order to prove that a conventional education was not for him.

When Alois died suddenly in 1903, it had allowed him to move to Vienna where he applied to join the Academy of Fine Arts. However, he was rejected twice and told that his talents would be more conducive to a career as an architect. In 1907, his mother died of cancer. He was 18 years old at the time, and her death had a devastating impact on him. He soon ran out of money and resorted to working as a day labourer and sleeping on park benches, but he was also able to sell some of his watercolour paintings of various Viennese sights. When the final tranche of his father's estate was released to him in 1913, he moved to Munich, Germany.

In late 1914, World War 1 broke out, and he volunteered to join the Bavarian Army where he served as a dispatch runner in the trenches. Respected by his fellow soldiers, he was soon decorated for his bravery, being awarded the Iron Cross, Second Class. In 1916, during the Battle of the Somme, he was wounded in the left leg by an exploding shell, which put him out of action for two months. As soon as he was able, he returned to his unit, continued as a runner and was awarded the rare Iron Cross, First Class, on the recommendation of his Jewish superior. In late 1918, he was temporarily blinded by mustard gas and spent weeks in a hospital bed. It was during this time that he learned of Germany's defeat, and it left him numb and disillusioned.

Returning to Munich after the war, he was appointed as an intelligence officer and told to join the German Worker's Party as a spy. However, discovering his talent for public speaking, he soon ended up taking over the party's leadership and renaming it the National Socialist German Workers' Party, or 'Nazi Party' for short. Discharged from the army in 1920 after which he became a full-time politician, his rousing speeches began to attract large crowds, and the Nazi Party soon grew significantly in size. The fledgling party promoted the ideas of overt ultranationalism, antisemitism, opposition to both capitalism and Marxism and a burning resentment of the implementation of the Treaty of Versailles that had formalised Germany's defeat. It was during this time that his fellow travellers, Rudolf Hess and Hermann Göring, had become part of his inner circle.

Having been inspired by the rise of fascism under Benito Mussolini in Italy, and with the help of the famous World War 1 general Erich Ludendorff, he attempted a badly planned coup in 1923. Along with his supporters, he interrupted a large public meeting in a Munich beer hall, fired his gun in the air and declared the formation of a new government with himself and Ludendorff at its head. He and his supporters subsequently marched to the Bavarian war ministry to overthrow the state government by force, but they were quickly dispersed by the police. Sixteen Nazi Party members were killed, and two days later, he was arrested for high treason and eventually sentenced to a term of five years in prison. However, he used the trial as a political platform to promote the Nazi Party's ideas, along with his sense of grievance over what had befallen Germany after the First World War. By all accounts, it seemed to have a rousing effect on those present in the courtroom.

It was during his time in the Landsberg Prison, where he was incarcerated in relative luxury due to his political status and the widespread sympathy for his cause, that he had dictated his book, *'Mein Kampf'*. It was partly an autobiography and partly a political program for the Nazi Party. It was also a call to arms for revanchist World War 1 veterans like him who were embittered by the humiliating loss in that war and a denunciation of the German mass media. However, more than anything, it was an uncompromising vilification of the Jews of Europe and a call for them to be exterminated. The book, which eventually sold more than 10 million copies since it was first published in 1925, extolled the virtues of German blood. In it, Hitler used the notion of Germanic superiority as justification for the forceful colonisation of much of Central Europe. In his mind, such a colonisation would finally bring about the long-desired reunification of the German peoples that had been scattered across the fledgeling states of Central Europe following the carving up of the continent after the First World War.

Gazing out at one of the gardeners who was tending to a flowerbed, he contemplated how his views on Jews had evolved over time. In some ways, the hatred that he now felt for them had been inculcated in him from birth via his deeply conservative Catholic parents, his doting mother Klara and his violent and alcoholic father Alois. As had been taught from the pulpit by the

Christian clergy across Europe for over a millennium, the Jews were the cause of evil in society. But worse than that, according to the Church, they were guilty of nothing less than deicide. The literal killing of God. Not only had they rejected Jesus Christ as the Messiah, but they had then gone on to engineer his death on the cross at the hands of the Romans in Galilee. For this, there could be no forgiveness, and in the minds of Hitler and many other German Catholics, that act alone justified the extermination of that whole race of people. On top of that, Hitler was convinced that the Jews were behind a global cabal that secretly manipulated and controlled world affairs. They were clearly behind the Bolsheviks in Russia as well as the government of the United States, which was almost entirely controlled by Jewish financial interests. What he, with the help of his most loyal compatriot Heinrich Himmler, was now doing to the Jews was in fact an inevitable outcome. In his mind, it was simply the natural order of things. A way to finally resolve the centuries-old Jewish problem once and for all throughout both Germany and the world. It was the *Endlösung*. The Final Solution.

However, dealing with the Jews and what he considered to be the other sub-human groups of people that by their very existence were undermining the quest for Germany to become a shining beacon of progress, technology and racial purity in the world, was not foremost on his mind. His main concern was to develop the means with which to win the war. He and Germany were now engaged in what could only be described as total war. A civilisational struggle where all of the resources of the nation were directed towards defeating the enemy, and where individual human beings meant nothing. The only thing that mattered was how to win by any means necessary. Whether it cost a million lives or a hundred million lives, victory had to be achieved.

The twin ideologies of racial purity and German land were brought together in the slogan, *Blut und Boden*. Blood and Soil. Through this intertwining of German land with German blood, the Nazi Party had sought to instil in the German people a sense that the purity of their blood was bound to the land in a near-mythical fashion, and that rural peasants served as the heroic backbone of the people and the state. The conservative rural values of self-reliance and hard work found in the noble farmers who tilled the earth were to be emulated throughout society. In order to promote this notion, the slogan 'Blood and Soil' had even been incorporated into the official logo of the Reich Ministry of Food and Agriculture.

But ideas about racial purity and new lands for growth were far from all that had appealed to the German electorate. With its call for the abolition of the class system and for placing the interests of the state above all else, the Nazi party had eradicated the old aristocratic system that had run the governments of Germany and Prussia for centuries. However, in the SS, it had created a new elite based on racial purity, and it was now the core of the future of German governance.

Hitler poured himself a glass of water from a carafe and sipped it as he recalled with fondness his time in prison with Hess as the two of them crafted and shaped 'Mein Kampf'. It had proven to be a watershed in his life, and it had provided him with the time and focus required to write his opus magnum.

He put down his glass and thought back to December of 1924 when he had been released from prison just over a year into his sentence. He had been pardoned by the Bavarian Supreme Court, likely because of the court's sympathy for his anti-Marxist and antisemitic views, both of which were widespread across Europe in the 1920s. Two months later in February 1925, after a meeting with the Bavarian Prime Minister during which he promised to respect the state's authority, he had secured a lifting of the ban on the Nazi Party that had been in place since the attempted beerhall coup. However, soon after, he was again banned from public speaking following an inflammatory speech, and this led him to appoint others, including Joseph Goebbels, to be the face of the party.

For several years after that, and as Germany's economy began to recover and improve after the war, he and the Nazi Party had failed to win over enough Germans to take power. However, when the global stock markets crashed in October of 1929, it devastated the world economy, including the German economy, which was still fragile after World War 1. Millions were plunged into unemployment almost overnight, losing all of their possessions and being quickly forced into homelessness. This environment had proved fertile ground for his particular brand of grievance-based, revanchist, and ethnocentric politics. In fact, had it not been for the Great Depression, he considered it doubtful that he would have been able to rise to the position of power that he now enjoyed.

The turmoil and general desperation of those days had left huge swathes of the population yearning for order amidst all the chaos and misery. A firm hand to right the sinking ship. A strong leader to finally take control and deliver the wretched masses to a brighter future. And in that environment, the Nazi Party suddenly seemed like an attractive option to many. It brought with it a message of German superiority under the guidance of a strong leader, and it pointed at sinister forces, foreign and domestic, that were working together to suppress the German people, preventing them from rising up to achieve greatness once more. It was just what the electorate needed to hear, and with his unrivalled oratory skills, he had tapped into this sentiment to great effect. Soon, people were flocking to the Nazi Party's rallies like never before.

The more moderate democratically minded political parties kept talking about consensus and compromise, but they simply could not compete with the simple but effective tactics of the Nazi Party, and it went on to win almost twenty percent of the votes in the general election of 1930. However, much to his frustration, the election had resulted in a fragmented parliament with a weak and ineffective minority government, and it had left the president, the aristocrat Paul von Hindenburg, having to rule by decree. In 1932, he himself had attempted to become president, but he came in second behind Hindenburg. However, it had cemented his position as a one-man political force in Germany.

Two more elections were called in 1932 to try to arrive at a majority government, but they too failed. Under intense pressure from influential industrialists, Hindenburg finally and reluctantly agreed to appoint

Hitler to the position of chancellor in January 1933. Less than a month later, the parliament building, the *Reichstag*, was burned to the ground through arson, and Hitler and Göring immediately blamed a communist plot. In the ensuing turmoil, President Hindenburg agreed to sign an emergency decree suspending basic rights of the country's citizens and allowing detention without trial.

The next month in March, the Enabling Act was brought to parliament. Officially named the 'Law to Remedy the Distress of People and Reich', it gave Reich Chancellor Hitler the power to make and enforce laws without the involvement of parliament or the president. Using the democratic institutions that he had railed against in *Mein Kampf*, the goal of this law was to eliminate democracy. And it had succeeded. Its passage through the Reichstag was facilitated through the support of the Catholic Centre Party, as well as by the detention of dozens of communist parliamentarians who were consequently unable to vote. The law was passed, and from that day forward, democracy was effectively abolished. The two positions of Chancellor and President were merged into one, creating the new position, '*Führer* and Chancellor'. And now here he was. Omnipotent dictator, ruler of the Fatherland, and one day soon, the entire world.

In his own mind, he was convinced that in some inexplicable way, it was ultimately Germany itself that had brought him into life in order for him to lead it to a great future. For centuries, Germany had been little more than a collection of small competing kingdoms and even smaller principalities held loosely together in an empire. But his destiny was to unite all of those disparate entities that were spread across much of Central Europe into one united and all-powerful country. After the catastrophe of World War 1, and the resultant collapse of Germany's power and the loss of much of her territory, his country had given birth to him. Germany had given him life, and his destiny was to again lift up the Aryan race to its rightful place above the other races. Consequently, all other things, including people, were merely tools given to him to accomplish this exulted task. He would raise this once-great nation from the depths of humiliation brought about by the end of World War 1. A humiliation that had been inscribed into the Treaty of Versailles. This treaty had been crafted by the treacherous French, the cowardly British, the barbaric Russians and the arrogant Americans. But worse than that, its creation had been aided by the loathsome Jews of the decrepit German political class, and it had served to impose a so-called 'peace' on his beloved Fatherland. With its demands for crippling war reparations and the limiting of the size of the German army to just 100,000 men, it was a peace so onerous and humiliating as to be nothing more than enslavement and servitude. But this enslavement had engendered resentment among his countrymen so deep as to make them flock to him and the Nazi Party.

Now, ten years on from taking power, he had already ensured that France had been brought to its knees and had paid the price for what it had done. Russia was putting up a fight on the Eastern Front, but it would almost certainly collapse soon under the onslaught of the German war machine. And then Britain would be next. With the development of a whole suite of new *Wunderwaffen*, or 'wonder-weapons', it would merely be a question of time before the Brits would be brought to their knees. And after that, an invasion of America would follow. It might take five, ten or twenty years to accomplish, but with German technology and ingenuity on his side, time was immaterial. Armed with these devastating new weapons, there was no doubt in his mind that it would all come to pass.

Once his great project was complete and Germany had conquered the entire world with him at its head, his own place in history would be secure. But more importantly, Germany would have taken its rightful place as the greatest power the world had ever known. And as he had dreamed of since he had been a young man during World War 1, Germany would become the *Tausendjähriges Reich*. The thousand-year Reich.

Hitler's reverie was brought to an abrupt end by the ringing of the phone on his desk. It rang three times before he brought himself back to the present, reached for the black handset, and brought it up to his ear.

'Mein Führer,' said a male voice. 'Doctor Kammler is here to see you.'

'Send him in,' said Hitler, replacing the handset in its cradle and leaning back in his chair to wait for his guest.

As the head of Office D in the SS Main Economic and Administrative Office, *Obergruppenführer* Hans Kammler was in charge of planning and construction of the main concentration camps throughout the German Reich. However, he was also the official administrative head of the Nazi wonder-weapons programs, and as such, he usually reported directly to

Hitler's old friend and loyal confidant, Interior Minister and head of the SS, Heinrich Himmler. One of the reasons that Himmler had put Hans Kammler in charge of all of Nazi Germany's advanced secret weapons programs was his keen eye for raw scientific talent. An example of this was Wernher von Braun, who was currently heading up the new V-1 and V-2 rocket programs. Although still in their infancy, Kammler was convinced that von Braun would be able to perfect the new ballistic missile weapons and eventually scale up production to make a real difference in the war. Especially if the planned two-stage intercontinental A-9/10 rockets, which were designed to reach the United States, could be successfully developed. All he needed were adequate resources and time. Resources could be arranged with the stroke of the Führer's pen. Nazi scientists, unlike their counterparts in the rest of the world, had a virtually unlimited supply of funding and slave labour in the form of political and ethnic 'undesirables' as well as POWs at their disposal, and this allowed them to initiate production programs at huge scale in a short amount of time. Adequate time was less certain, and it depended on the eastern front stabilising in the face of the Russian onslaught. However, Wernher von Braun was just one of several young and gifted scientists whom Kammler had identified and appointed to lead some of the most advanced weapons development programs the world had ever seen. In all the major science institutes and private corporations throughout Germany, highly gifted young men were developing a whole host of new weapons that, combined, had the potential to ensure victory for Germany within just a few short years.

These scientists were all vying for the attention and funding that the Nazi Party lavished on the most promising projects, and Kammler was the gatekeeper of those funds.

The double doors out to the gallery opened, and a tall man with a lean face who was wearing a smartly tailored olive green SS uniform stepped inside. He was holding a thin leather document folder under one arm, and as the doors closed behind him, he strode briskly across the floor to Hitler's desk, where he came to an abrupt halt, snapped his heels together and extended his right arm in the ubiquitous Führer salute.

'Heil Hitler!' he said as his arm shot out in front of him.

Hitler gave a small wave and motioned to the chair in front of his desk.

'Kammler,' he said. 'Please sit down.'

Kammler's arms came back down, and he stepped sideways to sit on the chair with the document folder on his lap.

'Tell me how the Vengeance projects are proceeding,' said Hitler.

'Yes, *mein Führer*,' said Kammler, opening his folder and extracting a set of documents accompanied by notes and schematics. 'As you know, the first V-2 launched successfully in March, reaching an altitude of about 1,6 kilometres. The second launch unfortunately resulted in the rocket exploding, although it reached 11 kilometres. However, I am glad to tell you that we have just completed the third test launch on the 3rd of this month, and the vehicle functioned perfectly. It followed its planned trajectory, reached an altitude of 83 kilometres, and landed very near the intended impact site 193 kilometres away. All in all, it was a great success.'

With a pensive look on his face, Hitler leaned forward, placed his elbows on his desk and steepled his fingers in front of himself.

'And the warhead?' said Hitler. 'How large?'

'At the moment,' said Kammler, 'the V-2 can deliver a warhead containing 725 kilos of high explosives. Enough to flatten a large building or factory in England.'

'Very good,' nodded Hitler. 'And does this then mean that the weapon is now ready to be deployed?'

Kammler shifted in his chair.

'In theory, yes,' he said. 'But we will need to expand our production capacity significantly. We already have several concentration camps dedicated to this, but we will need more.'

'That's fine,' said Hitler, producing a dismissive wave with his hand. 'Allocate as much as you require. And make sure von Braun has everything he needs.'

'As you wish,' said Kammler with a deferential nod.

'And the *Uranprojekt?*' said Hitler. 'What progress can you report?'

The Uranium Project was launched in April of 1939, just three months after the discovery of nuclear fission by Otto Hahn and his team at the Kaiser Wilhelm Institute in Berlin. Initially, the project revolved around efforts to construct nuclear reactors for energy production. However, once the scientists realised the potential for military applications, the nuclear project also acquired an important weapons development component. Specifically, it was theorised that a rapid chain reaction inside a uranium core could produce a powerful explosion that would be many orders of magnitude that of conventional explosives like TNT. An effort had therefore been launched to separate radioactive isotopes for use in a bomb.

Kammler knew that the Führer's natural inclination was towards more conventional weapons, and that he particularly liked the idea of carpet-bombing London and New York with ballistic missiles such as the V-2. But Kammler's instincts told him that if the nuclear weapons program could be brought to fruition, then there was a very real possibility that the war could be won one in a single day.

'Some of our very brightest scientists are working on this,' he said, extracting a sheet of paper with a list of names which he handed to the Führer. 'Hahn, Diebner, Geiger, Heisenberg and others. As you may already be aware, they have established a solid theoretical framework for nuclear fission, and they are busy building several reactors to demonstrate its energy production potential. And we believe that we have secured enough supply of heavy water from Norway to make it work.'

'Energy,' said Hitler dubiously as he scanned the names on the sheet of paper.

'Yes,' nodded Kammler, sensing the Führer's reticence. 'Imagine a world where we have access to an unlimited supply of energy. This alone will make Germany the most powerful nation on Earth.'

'What about weapons?' said Hitler impatiently, a slight note of irritation creeping into his voice. 'I need weapons to win this war.'

'I understand,' said Kammler, extracting another sheet from his folder. 'We are working hard to construct our first atomic bomb. We call it Project Alpha. But we need to produce enough uranium-235 to succeed. The separation of isotopes is a significant challenge, but we are making progress. We could have a test device ready in a matter of months.'

'I see,' said Hitler, sounding somewhat mollified. 'Very good. Keep me updated. The sooner we can perfect these weapons, the better. Whoever can make the first bomb will conquer the world.'

'I agree, *mein Führer*,' said Kammler, pulling a manilla envelope from his documents folder. 'And to that end, I have initiated a new development program that I believe could make that happen. It is not a weapon as such, but it could revolutionise warfare.'

Hitler's eyebrows crept up as Kammler handed him the envelope. On its front, it had the *Reichsadler* printed in black above the words '*Projekt Omega*', and underneath that was a stylised logo that appeared to be a circle with a spiral shape inside it.

'Projekt Omega,' said Hitler as he regarded it. 'I vaguely remember you mentioning this last year.'

'Yes,' said Kammler, pointing to the spiral logo. 'The logo represents a particle accelerator used in nuclear physics research. The project is headed up by Doctor Otto Drexler, and he and his team have just completed the construction of their upgraded machine. It should be operational within weeks. If it works as we hope, it could change everything, and I believe it has the potential to win the war.'

'Otto Drexler,' said Hitler pensively. 'I remember the name.'

'Yes,' said Kammler. 'He is one of our best theoretical physicists. And he has also proven himself to be a very gifted engineer. With him at the helm of this project, we have a good chance of success.'

Hitler opened the envelope and extracted a set of documents stapled together in the top left corner. While Kammler waited silently in his chair, the Führer began to read. As his eyes swept across line after line of text and examined the included diagrams and schematics, they grew hard, and his mouth fell slightly open. When he had read the final paragraph on the last page, he lifted his gaze towards Kammler.

'*Mein Gott*,' he said, looking momentarily stunned. 'Hans, is this really possible?'

'We believe so,' said Kammler. 'Doctor Drexler and his team of theoretical physicists all say that the mathematical proofs are unassailable. They will, of course, need to build the device, and that will almost certainly present very significant technical challenges. But they are throwing everything they have at this. With some luck, they might have a working prototype within a few months. Perhaps a year.'

Hitler sat silently for a moment, looking down at the documents. Then he shifted his gaze dreamily to the garden outside.

'Alpha and Omega,' he said. 'What fitting names.'

He had always been somewhat sceptical about what he considered esoteric physics, favouring instead the more conventional rocket weapons. Especially since the former appeared to be dominated by Jewish scientists such as that weasel, Albert Einstein. However, now that it appeared that Drexler's device was at least technically feasible, he was rapidly changing his mind. If this device could be made to work, then it could change everything. It could become a clear path to victory and a gateway to almost instant world domination. A weapon against which the allies would have no warning, no defence and no other option but to immediately lay down their arms and capitulate.

When he turned back to look at Kammler once more, the SS-Obergruppenführer saw a steely determination in the eyes of his Führer that made him sit bolt upright in his chair.

'Spare no expense,' said Hitler resolutely, fixing Kammler with an intense gaze. 'This project must be given the highest possible priority. With Alpha and Omega both successful, we will conquer the entire world. Nothing will be able to stand in our way.'

★ ★ ★

UPPER AUSTRIA - FEBRUARY 1943

The sun had set over the mountains several hours ago, and dark leaden clouds now hung low over the narrow alpine valley as a distant rumbling of thunder came from somewhere to the south. The mountainous region was blanketed with a dense forest of pine trees reaching straight up at least 30 metres, and along the valley floor ran a narrow paved road that travelled roughly towards the north. Mixed in with the rain were large snowflakes that descended over the forest like fluffy bits of cotton wool, and they drifted to the ground, where most of them melted. As others settled on the tree branches, an MI6 agent codenamed Sparrow crept along underneath them at the top of a rocky escarpment above the valley floor.

Below him was a German checkpoint manned by four soldiers, but only one of them was outside by the lowered boom blocking passage to the research complex inside the mountain. The other three guards were sitting inside the guardhouse. Using his binoculars, Agent Sparrow could see them huddled around a small table where they appeared to be playing cards and drinking steaming hot coffee. The lone helmeted soldier outside by the boom had a rifle slung over his shoulder, and his hands were thrust deep into the pockets of his long leather coat. He was smoking a cigarette whose ember glowed orange every time he took a puff, and its grey smoke was carried up and away by a gentle breeze. Shifting from side to side on his feet, he regularly stomped his boots onto the road surface in an attempt to stay warm as he waited to be relieved by one of his colleagues after his one-hour stint on boom duty.

From the top of a large moss-covered boulder among the trees up on the ridge, Agent Sparrow had a clear view of the valley. To his right, some fifty metres below was the guardhouse, and on either side of it had been placed several large Czech hedgehogs made of steel designed to block vehicles. Behind them was a row of pyramidal dragon's teeth made from concrete and capable of stopping tanks from moving through. There was also a concrete pillbox next to the guardhouse, inside which was a machine gunner's nest. From here, the soldiers on guard could spray approaching vehicles with heavy fire should that become necessary.

To his left, roughly two hundred metres further along the valley floor, Agent Sparrow could see the point where the road disappeared into a dark tunnel that had been dug deep into the mountain. A large concrete structure had been constructed around the entrance, and at this moment, the tunnel mouth was almost a pitch-black void. But based on his observations during the past few nights, he knew that when vehicles moved in or out of the complex, a set of lights would be switched on inside, and he would then be able to see it stretch deep into the mountain.

More soldiers stood guard by the entrance where another guardhouse with an accompanying pillbox had been built, and he knew that these men would perform a cursory inspection of any arriving vehicles, unlike the soldiers at the guardhouse, who only ever seemed to inspect the shipment documents that the truck drivers brought with them.

Agent Sparrow's real name was Edward Harding, and he had worked as an analyst for MI6 since 1937, back when it was still most commonly referred to as the Secret Intelligence Service, or SIS. A Cambridge graduate with a degree in history and philosophy, he had been recruited to MI6 by his tutor during the time when he had been writing his thesis on continental European geopolitics leading up to World War 1. The thesis had focused on the military technologies of the great powers of that time, with special emphasis on Austria-Hungary's development of innovative new weapon designs like rotary-magazine bolt-action rifles, anti-aircraft machineguns, smooth-bore mortars, and some of the first flamethrowers ever to be deployed in infantry warfare. This expertise had then attracted the attention of the foreign intelligence department, and he had soon found himself in an office in Whitehall where his job was to gather and analyse as much information as possible about the weapons development programs inside the Third Reich.

During the early 1930s, he had watched the newsreels covering the rise of the Nazis in Germany, including the massive and spectacular rallies at Nuremberg, where hundreds of thousands of Germans had come to worship the Führer as he railed against his enemies from the podium. Most people in England at that time had not taken the Austrian firebrand seriously, or they had thought of him as merely a rabblerousing clown similar to the Italian dictator Benito Mussolini. This attitude had even been pervasive within the top ranks of the intelligence services, and Harding had found himself the object of mockery and even derision over his attempts to draw attention to the developing threat. He had been branded loopy and even paranoid, but he had sensed very clearly that this man, Adolph Hitler, was a profound threat to world peace with his talk of territorial expansion and racial superiority.

Harding's deep and extensive knowledge about the new weapons programs that the Nazi scientists were developing only served to reinforce this view. Having only been allowed a small defensive army and no air force after the First World War, Germany had rapidly expanded its capacity to wage war, and the Allies had done precious little about it. Harding was of the view that the powers that be had their heads firmly buried in the sand about what was unfolding on the continent. They seemed to prefer to pursue a policy of denial or appeasement about what Nazi Germany was preparing to do. With thousands of tanks, aircraft and submarines, as well as more than a million soldiers now in the German army, there could be no doubt about Hitler's true intentions. As far as Harding was concerned, these weapons were not merely meant to intimidate. They were meant to be used. And so it had eventually turned out. The whole world was now embroiled in war, and if the Nazis succeeded in developing the so-called 'wonder weapons' that Harding had been investigating, then there was a real risk that the Nazis could win the war in Europe and then go on to dominate the rest of the world.

Gathering intelligence about German weapons programs from London had often proven to be a very difficult task, but Harding had developed a small network of contacts inside the German weapons industry, including an administrative clerk in the Reich Ministry of Armaments and War Production that was headed up by one of Hitler's favourites, Albert Speer. Through this particularly valuable contact, Harding had learned of the existence of a top-secret effort designed to leverage the power of nuclear fission, which had only just been discovered a few years earlier.

According to Harding's source, Nazi scientists were now pouring immense resources into twin efforts codenamed 'Alpha' and 'Omega'. As far as he had been able to ascertain, Project Alpha was the development of a nuclear bomb, and it had become clear that many of Germany's top scientists were involved in the effort. Project Omega was somehow related to the nuclear bomb project, but Harding had been unable to discover precisely what it entailed. The secrecy surrounding the project had been so tight that he had only been able to uncover a few facts about it. One was that it was headed up by a man named Doctor Otto Drexler, who appeared to have been personally appointed by Hans Kammler, the head of Nazi Germany's secret advanced weapons program. Another fact, which he had only learned very recently, was that a top-secret weapons project was being developed inside a mountain in Austria somewhere east of the city of Linz. A project that he believed could be Project Omega.

There were several circumstantial pieces of evidence to suggest that something very big was going on inside the mountain, not least the fact that a concentration camp was located just a couple of kilometres away. This camp would be capable of supplying the required free labour, and Harding knew that this was part of a pattern across Germany and the occupied territories in Europe. Wherever there was a large-scale Nazi production facility, there was invariably also a concentration camp nearby.

Harding already had clear evidence indicating that this particular location housed a production site for the new state-of-the-art Messerschmitt Me-262 turbo-jet fighter aircraft. This revolutionary plane was the world's first operational fighter jet, and it was widely viewed as being years ahead of allied fighter designs. However, he had also been able to obtain a copy of a shipment document that listed a range of different types of equipment that had been sent to the subterranean facility. It included advanced electronic parts for the assembly of the Me-262 aircraft, most likely for their instrument panels. But there were also other pieces of equipment on the list, which indicated to him that something much more advanced was being developed inside the facility. Equipment that, as far as he could ascertain, could only be related to the Nazi nuclear weapons program. This included components that he was sure were for the construction of a particle accelerator. This type of device, which had only been developed a few years earlier, was a clear sign that some sort of nuclear research was going on there. In addition, the list included miles of heavy-duty power cables and hundreds of switches of a type indicating that huge amounts of electricity were being consumed.

Because of the location of the mountain deep inside the Third Reich, aerial reconnaissance of the valley would be impossible, even if he had been able to convince his superiors, and that in itself would be an uphill battle, to say the least. In addition, MI6 had no local assets on the ground that might be able to verify the information he had received. This left him with only one option, which was to travel to Austria himself to investigate. He had put in a request to his section chief for permission to go to Switzerland. The plan was to use a fake passport and enter Europe under the cover of being a Swiss banker by the name of Karl Holtz, and then he would make his way across the border into Austria, where he would head for a small town near the site indicated by his source. Here, he would take up temporary residence in a local inn while he investigated the area.

However, much to his surprise and disappointment, his section chief had turned down his request, citing that the MI6 needed to have its best people working hard in London rather than galivanting off on some wild goose chase behind enemy lines inside the Reich. Harding had attempted to explain what he knew about the German efforts to harness the power of the atom, but it had soon become apparent that he was hitting a brick wall. His section chief was of a generation to whom Newtonian physics was the final answer to all things in the universe, and the old man's eyes had glazed over when Harding had attempted to explain the recent theories about the nature of atoms and nuclear fission as well as its possible applications in the field of weapons development.

He had eventually given up trying to explain Project Alpha, and he had not even bothered to mention the even stranger and more mysterious Project Omega. However, the lack of interest displayed by his superiors did not lessen the actual risk of these programs coming to fruition, and if they ever did, everyone in MI6 would be out of a job. Worse still, everyone in England would soon be scrambling to learn how to speak German. After much consideration, Harding had decided that there was only one thing to do. He had to leave for Austria, with or without permission. This was simply too important to shelve and ignore.

The trip into that Alpine country had been fraught with danger, and on several occasions, he had found himself face-to-face with German soldiers demanding to see his identity documents. He happened to be naturally proficient in foreign languages, and his research into Austro-Hungarian history had prompted him to learn German. After joining MI6, he had also taken a slew of additional courses to enable him to access all available information and to communicate seamlessly with his contacts inside Germany. By now, he was fluent in the language, albeit with a slight accent that didn't seem to attract undue attention, and he was able to pass himself off as a Swiss citizen. This had proved a lifesaver on more than one occasion, and by the time he arrived in the small mountain village near the mountain complex, he felt calm and confident about his ability to remain undercover.

As it turned out, it had not taken him long to discover the location of the secret facility. Every day, there were heavy military trucks moving through the village, and from his window in the inn, he had been able to observe them all taking the same turn out of town as they headed north. It also appeared that several high-ranking SS officers had taken up permanent residence there, and most mornings, he would be able to observe black Mercedes limousines taking those officers up towards a nearby valley.

Leaving the inn wearing heavy boots and a backpack, he had headed up into the mountains with his camera every early afternoon. It was a small and compact Kodak 35 camera loaded with 35mm film capable of 24 shots. The camera's outer casing was made from black Bakelite and aluminium which made it relatively light to carry and use, and he had hand-painted the metal sections black to ensure that they would not reflect any light. To add credibility to his cover, he had made sure to ask the innkeeper to point him to the best local walking trails, even asking him to make notes on a map of the area indicating waterfalls and spectacular mountain peaks.

The village and the surrounding mountainous area appeared calm and idyllic, and when the sun was shining and the valley presented itself at its most beautiful, it was difficult to imagine that somewhere nearby was a concentration camp where the wretched souls of forced labourers were being detained. More than once, he had spotted a truck carrying those labourers through town, and each time, they appeared to be heading further up into the valley above the village.

On his third day there, he had left a walking trail that curved up into an adjacent gorge. He then crested the ridge and made his way down through the forest towards the valley floor on the other side. It was here that he had identified a perfect observation spot overlooking both the guardhouse and the entrance to the mountain. Observing the movement patterns of trucks and soldiers, he made sure to take several pictures using his camera. The next day, he returned and did the same thing again, and then he decided to come back late at night and attempt to enter the mountain.

And now here he was, sitting up on the escarpment watching the lone soldier by the boom below through his binoculars. He suddenly began to feel a sense of trepidation that he had not experienced before. Up until this point, it had all been like a research project. An attempt to gather information and to try to make sense of it. Now, however, he was about to enter a facility that was crawling with heavily armed Nazi soldiers. He had no backup whatsoever and no way of communicating with London, and he knew that if he was caught, he was almost guaranteed to meet a sticky end.

He lowered the binoculars and took a deep breath to calm himself. Now was no time for cowardice. He had come this far, and he simply couldn't turn back. This was too important, even if the higher-ups back at MI6 HQ in London thought he was a paranoid fantasist.

But with photographic evidence, they would be unable to remain in denial any longer. If he could get pictures of the inside of the mountain facility back to MI6, then they would have to take him seriously. All he had to do now was wait for another truck and then execute the plan he had made for how to get into the mountain undetected.

He reached inside his brown leather jacket and extracted his top-break Webley Mk. VI revolver from its holster. It was loaded with six rounds of .455 ammunition, and it packed a real punch. However, since it did not have a silencer, it was to be used only in extreme circumstances where there were no other options. He broke it open, inspected the cartridges and spun the cylinder. Everything seemed to be well-oiled and working smoothly. He snapped it shut and engaged the safety. Then he smeared his face and hands with crushed-up charcoal that he had got from the fireplace at the inn and waited.

An hour went by with no activity other than the expected guard change. The snow was now coming down hard, depositing a blanket of white across the whole valley, and visibility was less than a hundred metres, but that would mostly work in his favour. He waited for another hour and was about to give up for the night when he heard the distinctive sound of a diesel engine in the distance. Moments later, he spotted the headlights of a military vehicle through the falling snow. It was a heavy, six-wheeled truck with a large canvas-covered cargo bed. As soon as he saw it, he moved from his position along the top of the escarpment and proceeded down the slope towards some thick bushes about twenty metres from the pillbox.

Concealed behind the vegetation, he remained still while the truck approached. It slowed down as it passed him, and as it drew nearer to the checkpoint, the soldier by the boom raised a hand to shield his eyes from the bright glare of its headlights. This was Harding's chance. Taking advantage of the fact that people tend to focus directly on bright lights which then causes temporary vision impairment, he ran stooped over towards the pillbox where he crouched down out of sight. He was now only about five metres from the truck, and he could smell the sharp diesel exhaust as its engine idled while the soldier approached the driver's side door.

Harding heard the voices of the soldier and the driver as they greeted each other in German, and he risked peering out from behind the pillbox to look. As expected, the driver was leaning out of the window and handing the soldier a clipboard with what Harding assumed were details of what was being transported into the subterranean facility. And as had happened on every other occasion the MI6 agent had witnessed, the soldier gave the driver a quick salute, took the clipboard and turned around to walk back towards the guardhouse, presumably to check the documents. For Harding, it was now or never. This was the only opportunity he was going to get, and he had to take it.

While the lone soldier was walking in the opposite direction, Harding rushed forward while crouched low, dropping to the ground as he reached the truck and rolling swiftly under its large fuel tank and into the middle of the space below the vehicle. Once he had positioned himself, he extracted a wide leather belt from his coat pocket and looped it up and over the truck's main axle. Pulling himself up, he wedged his feet in place, lifted himself up and tightened the belt around his waist. With the truck's engine still idling and producing exhaust fumes that drifted under the vehicle, he clung on motionlessly and waited. About a minute later, he heard the soldier come back to have another brief exchange with the driver, and then the soldier opened the boom and the truck drove past the checkpoint towards the entrance to the mountain a couple of hundred metres away.

Harding breathed a sigh of relief, and he made sure to fill his lungs with the cold, clean air that now rushed past him. As he hung there, feeling like a spit-roasted pig, a wave of doubt suddenly washed over him. He had never done anything remotely like this before. Perhaps his section chief had been right. Perhaps this was all a mistake. Nothing more than a spectacularly stupid way to get himself killed. If caught, he would most likely be interrogated, tortured, shot and then dumped in the forest. Food for the wolves. And if he died tonight, no one would ever know how or why. It would all have been for nothing.

He managed to grab himself by the proverbial scruff of the neck and calm himself down. He was committed. There was no way back now. He had to go on. However, he wasn't out of the woods yet. About a minute later, the truck slowed down again and came to a stop in front of another boom that blocked the entrance to the mountain. This time, several soldiers emerged from a small hut, and while one of them spoke with the driver to inspect his documents once more, two others moved to the back of the vehicle where they snapped open the two metal latches on the tailgate and pulled the gate down to inspect the truck's cargo. One of them climbed up onto the cargo bed, and Harding felt the vehicle's suspension system shift slightly under the man's weight. He could then hear the sound of the soldier's heavy boots on the wooden boards in the cargo bed as he moved around to check the contents of the delivery. Harding didn't move a muscle, and after about a minute, he realised that he had been holding his breath the entire time. Exhaling slowly and attempting to calm himself down again, he then heard the soldier jump back down to the ground, the tailgate being slammed shut and the metal latches being secured.

'*Alles in ordnung!*' shouted one of the two soldiers as they headed back towards the front of the vehicle.

'*Zehr gut*,' said the soldier who had been speaking to the driver as he tapped the door twice in quick succession, giving the driver the order to continue. '*OK. Weitermachen.*'

The boom was raised, and the driver put the truck into gear once more. Seconds later, the heavy vehicle disappeared into the tunnel with Harding still clinging to its underside. As they continued ever deeper inside, the noise from the truck's engine seemed to amplify and reverberate inside the concrete-covered space, and Harding realised that they were proceeding down a gentle yet clearly noticeable slope. The facility appeared to have been constructed deep under the mountain.

After about a hundred metres, the two sides of the tunnel that had raced by as Harding clung on for dear life suddenly swept outwards to reveal a large open subterranean area. Attached to the truck's underside, he couldn't see much of what was there, but he could hear that it had to be a very large, cavernous space. The truck driver turned slightly and purposefully drove the vehicle over to one side where he stopped and then began reversing back into a loading bay. It was clear from the way he handled the vehicle that he had done this before.

Once the truck had come to a halt, the engine was turned off and the driver got out, slamming the cab door behind him. He shouted something in German that Harding couldn't make out, and then he heard several other voices in the vicinity. Once again, there was the sound of the tailgate being opened, and then of several men mounting the cargo bed and beginning to carry goods off the truck. This went on for several minutes, and from their groans and heavy breathing, it sounded like a large number of heavy items were being offloaded. Eventually, the transfer was complete, and Harding felt the men dismount the truck. Then he heard the sound of their receding footsteps. This was his chance to get clear of the truck before it left the facility again.

Clinging on with one arm, he untied the leather belt looped over the axle and lowered himself to the dry and dusty concrete floor below. Then he rolled out from under the truck towards the nearest wall where several wooden pallets loaded with oil drums had been placed. He swiftly got to his feet and slipped behind the barrels just as the driver returned to the truck and climbed up into the cab where he started the engine. The truck moved out of the loading bay and headed for the tunnel to go back outside, and as Harding leaned out slightly to watch it leave, he got his first clear glimpse of the enormous, high-ceilinged artificial cave that had been excavated inside the mountain. It was at least a hundred metres across with a dome-like ceiling, and several more tunnels of varying width stretched away from it in different directions. Some were wide enough for two people to walk through, and others looked like they had been constructed to accommodate small vehicles. There was even one in the centre, which appeared to have been fitted with rail tracks. Above each tunnel were large, white-painted metal signs with black lettering. One read '*Befeelsraum*', which meant Command Centre. Another one read '*Kraftstofflager*', or Fuel Storage. There were several more, but one of them made Harding's heart skip a beat. It read '*Omega Testkammer*'. Omega Test Chamber.

'Bingo,' he whispered to himself as the red taillights of the cargo truck disappeared up the long tunnel and the cave fell relatively quiet.

From his hiding place, he could see and hear several Nazi soldiers moving around the area, and there were also a couple of what appeared to be technicians who were wearing white lab coats. They were holding clipboards and inspecting a large, boxy and complicated-looking electrical device on the other side of the open space of the enormous cavern. With its cables, ceramic coils, wires and analogue dials, Harding thought it might be some sort of generator, but he couldn't be sure. Suddenly, a loud disembodied male voice came over a hidden speaker system, and the sound echoed around the cavern.

'*Achtung*,' it said in an automaton fashion that still managed to sound stern. '*Zwanzig minuten bis der nächste Omega-gerätetest. Alle techniker auf ihre posten.*'

The next Omega device test was happening in twenty minutes, and all technicians were being ordered to their posts. The voice repeated the message. At that, the two technicians standing across the cavern left the equipment they were inspecting and began walking briskly towards the tunnel leading to the Omega test chamber.

'Blast,' whispered Harding.

He had to get there without being seen, and he had to move fast. But there was a serious problem. He couldn't simply walk casually into the tunnel that led straight there. Firstly, he didn't know what he was going to find at the other end. Secondly, with a test of the device now imminent, he was bound to run into Nazi soldiers and scientists, and it would only take them a few seconds to realise that he was not supposed to be there. And then he would soon be dead. He had to find a different way in.

He looked up towards the domed ceiling of the cavern where dozens of flat industrial-looking lamps hung from metal netting illuminating the huge space. But there was also something else. Squinting past the many lights, he noticed large rectangular metal vents that all emanated from a central point near the main tunnel to the outside and then spread out and snaked their way along the cavern's interior to each of the smaller tunnels that led deeper into the complex. These were part of the ventilation system, and they were his only chance. Somehow, he had to get inside the vent that led to the Omega test chamber.

Next to the main tunnel exit directly under the nexus of the many individual vents, he spotted a narrow metal door sitting in the concrete wall. This was almost certainly the engine room for the equipment powering the facility's ventilation system. If there was a way into the shafts, it had to be in there.

Making a mental note of the layout of the vent shafts and their multiple forks as they snaked their way from the engine room across the ceiling to the various tunnels, he then leaned out to make sure the cavern was clear of personnel. Then he moved swiftly and quietly along the wall while attempting to stay concealed behind the many large pieces of equipment arranged inside the cavern. When he reached the main tunnel exit, he paused to check for movement again and then proceeded to cross over to the metal door. Turning to look behind him one final time, he extracted his revolver and flicked the safety off. It suddenly felt heavy in his hand. He steeled himself for a brief moment, gripped the door handle and pushed inside with the weapon up. To his relief, the large engine room was empty. Had he been forced to use his weapon, he might have been successful in fighting off a couple of machinists and engineers, but within a few seconds after that, the whole place would be swarming with soldiers, and then he wouldn't stand a chance.

He quickly closed the door behind him and produced a sigh of relief as he shoved the Webley back under his jacket. The room was about the size of an average living room, and it had smooth concrete walls and a row of bright lights mounted along the ceiling. Along the entire length of the wall to his right was a huge machine that appeared to be driven by a diesel engine that he assumed sucked in fresh air through a big tube that extended up through the ceiling. At the other end, the machine was connected to a large cylindrical unit, inside which he figured that a set of fans was located. This unit was connected to a single large horizontal main ventilation shaft that soon angled up and out through the concrete wall to the cavern. On the side of the shaft, roughly around chest height, was a maintenance panel that could be removed simply by turning two small thumbscrews. This was going to be his way in.

For a moment, he eyed the whirring cylinder with disquiet as he imagined the metal fan blades spinning at hundreds of revolutions per minute inside it. If, for some reason, he lost his footing, he might be sucked back into the fans and end up as minced meat. He shook his head to clear it of that image and began turning the thumbscrews. They came out easily, and he gripped the maintenance panel. As soon as he pulled it free, a blast of air shot out of the vent as the overpressure inside it attempted to escape. He then realised that the fans were actually blowing fresh air into the facility rather than sucking old air out, and that it might end up helping him climb up through the shafts and through to the test chamber.

With no time to lose, he clambered up through the hatch and into the horizontal vent shaft where a forceful wind immediately began to pull at his clothes. The vent shaft's interior was about a metre tall and roughly as wide, so he had to crouch low and waddle to move anywhere. Behind him, the spinning fan blades whirred noisily, and looking back at them sent a shiver down his spine. He wasted no time and pulled out a small torch from a jacket pocket, and then he began to move up the incline so that he could pass through the wall and find the right fork for the Omega test chamber. Unable to close the maintenance panel behind him, he simply left it open and hoped for the best. There was nothing he could do about it.

Scaling the first incline was easy, and within seconds he was inside a short level section, which he knew would be the part of the vent system passing through the wall into the cavern. Once there, he proceeded along a slightly curved section that followed the interior wall of the cavern. This section was about twenty metres long, and by the time it split into two smaller vents, he knew from memory that he was directly above the tunnel to the Omega test chamber. However, the path that he now needed to take was straight up for about two metres, and he was unable to reach the edge where the vent levelled out again and continued inside the rock and parallel to the smaller tunnel.

He wedged himself with his back against one side of the vent and his feet against the other, and then he half walked and half wriggled his way up to a point where he could grip the edge of the next horizontal section. As he pulled himself over the edge and onto the flat metal, his right foot smacked against the wall, and it made a noise that felt loud enough to him to attract every single soldier in the complex. He lay still for several seconds, but he could hear no voices or commotion to indicate that he might have been detected.

The next section of the vent system was much narrower than before, and he found himself worming his way along with his torch lighting the way as he held it between his teeth. Breathing heavily, he began to feel the sides of the shaft closing in on him, although he knew it was only in his mind. He took a short break and breathed slowly in and out several times to calm himself down and fight off the encroaching claustrophobia. Then he continued along a straight and level section that was at least thirty metres in length.

Halfway along, he realised that there was a large grille directly in front of him to his right. As he approached it, he could hear voices, the whirring of generators and the clanking of metal equipment, and there was a strange ozone-like quality to the air. It tasted of metal and electricity. There also seemed to be a low humming emanating from deep within the mountain.

He switched off his torch and inched slowly forward until he could peek through the grille and down into what he deduced had to be the Omega test chamber. It was a large square space, roughly thirty by thirty metres in size, and the ceiling was at least five metres above the floor. It looked to have been carved straight out of the granite and then rendered with concrete on the inside to make smooth walls.

Technicians were moving purposefully around the space, and the entire area was crammed with large pieces of equipment that bore no resemblance to anything Harding had ever seen before. There were huge ceramic coils sitting in arrays of eight, heavy electrical cables snaking their way everywhere, and intense buzzing noises emanating from the equipment. The only thing that looked vaguely familiar was a control station where a group of men in lab coats sat monitoring banks of gauges and dials and other forms of telemetry. Pacing between them was a tall and lean man with a gaunt face wearing a lab coat over a dark suit. With short, blond but greying hair and rimless glasses, he appeared to be in his mid-fifties. His dark eyes peered intently at the multitude of instrument panels in front of him and his team of technicians. Every so often, he would lean forward and appear to direct one of his subordinates to perform one task or another.

Watching the man through the slits in the grille for a few moments, there was no doubt in Harding's mind. This had to be the Doctor Otto Drexler that he had read about. Harding had never been able to acquire a photo of the man before, but he was sure that this was the chief of Project Omega. The brilliant Nazi scientist, who, if Harding's intelligence was correct, had been personally appointed by *SS-Obergruppenführer* Hans Kammler.

Soon, however, Harding's attention was drawn to the centre of the chamber where a strange, tall contraption had been erected. Harding had never seen anything like it. Constructed on a concrete platform about a metre tall and five metres across, it was circular in shape and roughly three metres across. Looking vaguely like a plain engagement ring, it had been placed horizontally on the platform where it was elevated further onto a metal support structure. It appeared to be studded with many dozens of smaller, intricate-looking electrical devices that looked to Harding as if they might be sensors and detectors of various kinds. With multiple wires and cables sticking out of them, the devices were crammed tightly all the way around the edges of the ring-shaped contraption. Several power cables as thick as a man's arm connected to the base of the ensemble from a central point at the back of the chamber.

Next to the ring was a clear area of the smooth concrete floor where a white square had been painted, and in the middle of the square was a yellow 'X'. Surrounding the white square were banks of what appeared to be detectors and measuring equipment, as well as two large cameras sitting on tripods. Behind the large ring was a somewhat smaller disc-shaped machine that, upon closer inspection, suddenly looked vaguely familiar to Harding. He was almost sure that he had seen pictures of one of these machines taken inside the Kaiser Wilhelm Institute in Berlin in 1937. Yes, there was no doubt in his mind. He was looking at one of the new groundbreaking particle accelerators that German scientists had used to bombard uranium atoms with neutrons, thereby creating nuclear fission. Five years ago, for the very first time in human history, these machines had proven themselves capable of splitting the atom. A truly revolutionary technology that now showed every sign of ushering in a new paradigm for both energy production and weapons applications.

A small crane stood next to the circular contraption, and at the end of a steel wire suspended over the centre of the ring, was a metal cube that was about twenty centimetres on all sides. As Harding gawped at the futuristic vista below him, a loud claxon suddenly went off. The voice from earlier came over the speaker system once more, and Harding's fluency in German allowed him to translate it seamlessly in his mind.

'One minute until start of test sequence,' the voice said. 'Initialise cyclotrons.'

Immediately, what had previously been a low humming sound began to rise in intensity until the air itself inside the chamber felt as if it was vibrating, and he then began to hear crackling electrical noises coming from the various pieces of equipment.

'Engage auxiliary power couplings,' the voice called out. 'Increase power to maximum.'

The humming was now so intense that Harding could feel it inside his chest.

'Cyclotron output stable,' the voice called out. 'Initiate proton transfer.'

Harding suddenly realised that the inside edge of the ring was fitted with small blue lights, and they were now turning on and off in a strange rippling sequence that seemed to accelerate in tandem with the rise of a piercing whirring noise. The lights kept accelerating until they were a hazy blur, and the whirring coming from the ring kept on climbing in pitch until it produced a sharp whine that seemed to mingle and overlap chaotically with itself inside the confined space of the test chamber.

'Particle transfer in progress,' the voice called out. 'Calibrate magnetic field stabiliser arrays 1 through 6.'

The light from within the ring now seemed to intensify dramatically, and only then did Harding realise that he had yet to take any pictures with his camera. He clumsily yanked the camera out from inside his jacket, removed the lens cover and brought it up in front of one eye to point the viewfinder towards the centre of the test chamber. He took a single picture. With only 24 shots on the roll of film, he had to conserve them.

'Cyclotron proton output at maximum,' the voice said. 'Magnetic field stable. Proton mass accumulation in progress.'

Below him on the chamber floor, all the technicians, including Doctor Otto Drexler, put on large dark eye protectors that looked like bulky futuristic sunglasses. Moments later, brief flashes of bright white light came from the centre of the ring, and small blue arcs of electricity flashed through the air around them. The light was now so intense that Harding found it difficult to look straight at the ring, but he took another two photos.

'Curvature detected!' the voice suddenly called out, for the first time betraying a hint of excitement. 'Curvature expanding. Monitoring gradient.'

The noise inside the chamber grew even more extreme, and Harding could sense strange and powerful vibrations in his chest, and he also began to feel a piercing ache inside his skull.

'Curvature approaching critical,' said the voice. 'Hold energy input at current level. Monitor field fluctuations. Prepare for release.'

The entire chamber was now lit up by the bright light from the ring as well as the brilliant flashes coming from its centre. Combined with the immense noise from the various pieces of equipment, which sounded like they were about to tear themselves apart, it was an unnerving scene that made Harding wonder if the experiment was properly under control. His intuition was soon screaming at him to get out of there. He was sure that there was now so much power being pumped into the contraption at the centre of the chamber that if anything went wrong, everyone inside it, including him, would end up being vaporised in a brilliant man-made flash of lightning.

'Opening detected!' the voice called out in what was a near shout. 'Opening stable at 0.3 metres. Initiate drop.'

Harding brought up the camera again and took several more shots. As he watched through the viewfinder, the small metal cube suspended above the ring was suddenly released. It fell as if in slow motion, through the air towards what looked like a spinning otherworldly vortex of light below, and time seemed to slow down.

'Opening unstable!' the voice suddenly called out, and Harding could have sworn that it contained a hint of fear.

A searingly bright flash of light exploded from the centre of the ring amid a loud burst of intense electrical noise as the cube reached the vortex, and for an instant, the entire subterranean facility was bathed in pure brilliant white light that blinded Harding and forced him to close his eyes and turn away with a grimace. But even through the noise of the test chamber, he heard the distinct clonk as the heavy metal cube hit the concrete floor.

'Test complete,' the voice called out, and the chaotic soundscape suddenly waned rapidly as all the equipment in the test chamber was spun down and power levels were cut back.

Harding blinked several times in an effort to recover his vision after the blinding flash. When he turned his head back to peer out through the grille, he could barely believe what he was seeing. The metal cube that had been dropped a few seconds earlier was lying on the concrete floor, and thin tendrils of white smoke were slowly rising from it. However, by any measure of normal physics, it was not where it should have been.

'What the devil is this?' he whispered breathlessly. 'This can't be.'

Composing himself, he brought the camera back up again and took several more photos as a pair of technicians approached the metal cube, and several others began inspecting the ring that was now powered down and seemingly idle, dark and inert. He also angled the camera to allow him to take a picture of the control station where Drexler and his team had removed their goggles and seemed to be pouring over telemetry logs from the experiment. It was then that he spotted what appeared to be an enclosed, raised viewing platform near the chamber's exit. This had probably been constructed to allow VIPs to witness the device in action once the technology had been perfected.

He then also realised that an elevated metal walkway some three metres above the concrete floor wrapped around most of the inside of the chamber's wall, and that it ran directly underneath the section of ventilation duct where he was hiding. The walkway also connected to the viewing platform some fifteen metres further along, and that gave him an idea. Instead of attempting to crawl slowly and awkwardly backwards through the narrow vent system to the engine room by the large cavern's exit tunnel, he might be able to detach the grille, lower himself onto the walkway and get out that way. But he would have to wait until the test chamber was empty.

Looking down onto the chamber floor, he could see that most technicians were leaving and that two of them were transporting the metal cube out on a small trolley. The men at the control station also looked as if they were packing up, and he just caught a glimpse of Drexler as he left the area through the tunnel, seemingly deep in conversation with a colleague. After several minutes, the only other remaining personnel were two uniformed soldiers standing by the exit, and soon, one of them left via the tunnel, leaving only one person in the entire chamber. Harding watched him for a few moments, but the soldier did not appear to be moving from his post. He did, however, pace lazily back and forth in front of the exit some thirty metres away, and every half minute or so he had his back turned for about ten to fifteen seconds.

Harding examined the grille and realised that it had been mounted with four sets of nuts and bolts. The bolts had been screwed in from the outside, so the nuts were on the inside. Using his fingertips, he managed to loosen and unscrew all four of them, and then he held the grille in place while he waited and watched the lone soldier intently. He was only going to get one chance at getting this right.

The soldier turned his back once more and reached inside a coat pocket for a packet of cigarettes. While he extracted his lighter and lit the cigarette, Harding gently pushed the grille free and then turned it so that he could pull it back inside the duct where he placed it quietly on the floor. The soldier was now back to pacing, and he did not appear to have noticed that one of the grilles in the duct system mounted under the ceiling was missing.

Waiting for the right moment, Harding pushed his legs out through the hole and then squeezed himself through so that he ended up hanging by his fingers, his feet less than half a metre from the walkway. When he let go, he was able to use his legs to absorb enough of the energy from his fall to make barely a sound. He landed in a crouched position and immediately went prone to stay out of sight of the pacing soldier.

Moving forward in a low crawl, he inched his way quietly along the walkway towards the viewing platform. It took him several minutes to get there, and by the time he was able to squeeze himself up against the structure near its thin metal door where he was out of sight of the soldier, he was sweating profusely from the effort and the fear of being spotted.

What he needed to do now was open the door, enter the viewing platform, and then try to come up with some way of attracting the soldier's attention. If he could get him to enter the enclosed platform unawares, he might have a chance of overpowering him. He couldn't use his pistol since it would make too much noise, but he did also have a knife. He had never even contemplated the idea of killing someone, let alone with a blade, but it was almost certainly going to be the only way out of there that didn't draw undue attention.

He silently got to his feet, placed a hand on the door handle and pressed it down. Opening the door quietly, he was faced with something he had never expected. A couple of metres away by a large window stood a technician with his back turned. The man was wearing a white lab coat and a grey cap, and he was tinkering with a large film camera that was mounted on a raised metal support structure. It was pointing out through the window and down into the test chamber, and it was clear from the roll of film still sitting in it that the technician had been filming the entire test of the device. When Harding opened the door, the man's head turned slightly to one side, but he did not appear to be alarmed. Perhaps just slightly surprised at hearing a colleague enter from the walkway at this time.

Barely realising what he was doing, Harding moved on pure instinct and rushed forward towards the technician. Reaching him in less than a second, he wrapped one arm around the man's neck and placed the other over his mouth. Then he pulled him roughly onto the floor of the room and placed himself astride his victim. The technician grimaced and opened his mouth to cry for help, but Harding again clamped a hand over it. The man began pushing feebly at Harding's body and moving his head in an attempt to call for assistance. Harding used both his hands to grip the man's throat, and then he began to squeeze as hard as he could.

The technician's hands closed around Harding's wrists as he began to choke, and he strained wide-eyed as he tried to tear his attacker's hands from his throat while the veins on his temples bulged and he produced a strained croak. But it was no use. Above him, Harding's face had now taken on a desperate, almost maniacal expression, and he grimaced wildly as he squeezed with all his might. His eyes were watering from the effort and from the knowledge of what he was in the process of doing, and spittle flew from his mouth as he wheezed and strained to bring to an end the diabolical predicament he had suddenly found himself in. The simple reality was that he couldn't let the man live. It was either him or the technician. Only one of them would be leaving this room alive.

The technician gave up trying to wrestle Harding's hands from his throat, and instead, his arms flailed as he clawed desperately at Harding's face. Harding pulled his head up and away while baring his teeth and redoubling his effort to choke the man underneath him to death. There was no other way.

Finally, after what seemed like minutes, the man's movements became slow and uncoordinated, and then he suddenly seemed to pass out. His arms flopped down onto the floor, and his whole body ceased moving. Harding kept squeezing in case it was all a ruse, but after another half a minute or so, he finally released his grip on the man's throat. When he tentatively removed his hands, there was purple bruising all around the technician's throat, especially near the voice box. His eyes stared vacantly up past Harding's face to the ceiling.

Harding panted, and his heart was beating out of his chest. The truth was that he had never killed a man before. He had received basic firearms training upon joining MI6, but he had never fired his weapon in anger, much less used his bare hands to harm anyone. He sat open-mouthed for a moment, turned over his hands in front of his face and stared at the tools he had just used to take another man's life. Yes, the man had been a Nazi, and he was working on a device that threatened to win the war for Germany and lay waste to Britain. But he was still just a man. He might have a family waiting for him at home. Harding shook his head and forced those thoughts from his mind.

'Bloody hell', he whispered to himself as he slumped back to sit on the floor next to the dead technician. 'What have I got myself into?'

He got up on his knees and rolled the technician onto his front. Then he stripped him of his lab coat and put it on himself, along with the cap. His only chance of escaping the facility was to attempt to walk casually to the exit under the guise of being a technician. There seemed to be no shortage of people in that attire, so he just might be able to pull it off. And with a bit of luck, he might be able to hijack one of the vehicles that were parked in the large cavern near the exit. The only thing that mattered now was for him to get the film out of the facility and back to London. That suddenly gave him an idea. He glanced up at the film camera. The film roll was large and sitting inside a disc-shaped metal case, but it would just about fit inside his leather backpack. And if he were able to present moving images rather than poorly focused single shots from inside a vent, his message would be infinitely more convincing to the heads of MI6.

He reached up, detached the film case from the camera and shoved it inside his backpack next to his own small handheld camera. Then he moved towards the opposite door which would take him down a set of steps to the test chamber's exit. He couldn't quite believe how the soldier had managed not to hear the commotion inside the enclosed viewing platform, but when he gently opened the door and peeked outside, he realised that the soldier had now gone.

Breathing a sigh of relief, Harding steeled himself, adjusted his lab coat and his cap, grabbed a clipboard from a table next to the window and then opened the door to descend the steps to the chamber floor. Walking briskly and purposefully with his back straight and his shoulders back, he tried his best to appear as if he belonged in the facility. Inside, however, he was almost coming apart at the seams with fear.

Proceeding along the tunnel back towards the large cavern, he soon spotted two soldiers moving towards him. His cap was pulled down low in front of his face, and he cradled the clipboard in front of his chest and pretended to be studying some documents. The two soldiers were walking along silently next to each other, and as he passed them, he could have sworn that one of them was eyeing him suspiciously. Risking a quick glance over his shoulder, he realised that the two men had kept walking and appeared to have taken no interest in him. A few seconds later, a technician in a lab coat swung out in front of him from a narrow side passage, and Harding almost bumped into him.

'*Entschuldigung*,' he mumbled apologetically as he brushed past.

Hoping that the technician would accept his apology and that he hadn't seen his face, Harding picked up the pace and kept walking without looking back.

'*Vorsicht*,' said the man, clearly unhappy, but he had seemingly not spotted the unfamiliar face under the cap.

Harding kept walking briskly ahead, praying that the technician wouldn't chase after him to remonstrate about the collision. To his relief, no such altercation ensued, and after a few seconds, the technician kept going about his business, muttering something under his breath.

As Harding approached the large cavern, he spotted two pairs of soldiers marching past the tunnel exit, and he could hear voices and the sound of vehicle engines. Now that the test of the Omega device had been completed, normal activity inside the facility had clearly resumed. Clenching his jaw, he had to force himself to continue walking forward, and he suddenly felt convinced that as soon as he entered the large, well-lit cavern, he would be spotted and caught.

As he exited the narrow tunnel, his attention was immediately drawn to the opposite side of the cavern where a couple of soldiers were talking to what looked like an officer. They were right next to the door to the engine room containing the ventilation machines, and the door was open. A cold shiver ran down Harding's spine. Had someone discovered the missing vent panel? Did they realise that there was an intruder in the facility?

At that moment, a dark grey motorcycle with a sidecar followed by a small green military jeep emerged from the tunnel and pulled over to park up in a designated parking area near one of the larger main tunnels that led deeper into the mountain. The motorcycle rider dismounted, and the two men in the jeep, both of whom appeared to be officers, exited the vehicle and began walking through the large tunnel that had a rail track running down its centre. The motorcycle rider took off his goggles and helmet, placed both of them on the seat of the bike, and walked briskly to catch up with the two officers. Harding's eyes focused on the motorcycle. This was his opportunity to escape.

As inconspicuously as possible, he swerved towards the motorcycle and kept his head low as he pretended to be studying the clipboard. When he reached the bike, he discarded the clipboard, strapped the goggles and the helmet onto his head and swung a leg over the seat to mount it. The bike was one of the BMW R75 models that had been mass-produced for the German Army since the late 1930s, and it had been fitted with large saddlebags and a spare wheel. This would make it relatively slow and much less nimble, but with its 750cc engine producing 26 horsepower, he stood a good chance of getting away, as long as he had a clear run out of the cavern.

He turned the key and pressed the ignition button, and the two-cylinder engine sprang to life. Clicking the bike into gear with his left foot, he then twisted the throttle with his right and turned the handlebar to steer out of the parking space. At that moment, he heard a voice calling out from somewhere to his left. Glancing over, he spotted the officer who had been standing near the door to the engine room now marching towards him and waving an arm. Harding ignored him, gunned the engine and made for the exit.

As soon as the officer realised what was happening, he drew his pistol from his side holster and took aim. The two soldiers behind him unslung their rifles and did the same, but by then, Harding had picked up speed and was almost out of the cavern. As he disappeared into the tunnel leading back up to the outside, the officer fired. The bullet smacked into the concrete wall about a meter from Harding's torso, but then he was gone. To his relief, there were no other vehicles coming in or going out at that moment, and he twisted the throttle all the way back to feed the engine as much fuel as possible. As he sped along towards the exit up ahead with the lab coat flapping and flailing behind him, a flash of light appeared in his side mirrors. It was a vehicle. He quickly turned to look behind him, and at the far end of the tunnel near the cavern was a pair of headlights that appeared to belong to the jeep. And then another pair of lights appeared.

'Bollocks!' Harding swore inside the helmet.

This was bad. He didn't think that he would be able to outrun a jeep riding a motorcycle with a sidecar, and things were now suddenly looking decidedly dicey. As his bike roared up through the tunnel towards the forested valley, his mind was racing as he tried to decide what to do among a rapidly shrinking range of options. He had planned for this type of scenario, but he had hoped and prayed that it would never come to that. But here he was, and he now had very little choice. With escape all but impossible, he had to try to make his way to his designated drop point. And then all he could do was hope that his colleagues back in London would eventually read his notes and be able to put two and two together.

Stooping low over the motorcycle to reduce drag, Harding shot out of the tunnel exit and crashed through the wooden boom blocking the way. The boom splintered as the front of the bike slammed into it, and the small group of soldiers appeared too overwhelmed to raise their weapons and fire. Within seconds, Harding was approaching the other checkpoint, but here a couple of the soldiers were dragging one of the large Czech hedgehogs out into the middle of the road, blocking his path. Behind him, the two pursuing vehicles roared out of the tunnel and raced along the road after him.

The soldiers by the hedgehog were now kneeling next to the riveted steel contraption and aiming their weapons towards the oncoming motorcycle. However, they hesitated in firing for fear of hitting the two vehicles behind it, and this gave Harding the time he needed to close the distance. When he was about twenty metres away from the checkpoint, he suddenly swerved out to the left and drove up the incline. He shot through a gap between several trees next to the concrete dragon's teeth, and then he drove back down to rejoin the road on the other side of the checkpoint, where he then twisted the throttle and accelerated away. While the two soldiers pulled desperately at the hedgehog to clear the way for the pursuing vehicles, their remaining colleagues began spilling out of the small guardhouse, raising their rifles and opening fire.

Harding swerved from side to side in an attempt to throw off their aim and evade the bullets, but as a result, the motorcycle almost lost its grip on the snow-covered road. He wrestled the bike back under control and raced along in a straight line, and this gave the soldiers the window they needed. Within the space of a couple of seconds, several bullets smacked into the back of the sidecar and shattered the small glass windscreen at the front. Another bullet felt like it went into the rear of the bike itself. An instant later, Harding felt as if someone had slapped him hard on his left shoulder, knocking him forward, and he knew immediately what had happened. A split second later, another bullet caught him in the ankle. He cried out in pain, realising that his chances of getting away alive were now becoming vanishingly small. He had to get to the drop point, even if it killed him. He could feel a burning sensation in his shoulder, and he wasn't sure whether it was from the impact of the bullet or from warm blood escaping his body. Wincing through the pain, he turned to glance over his shoulder, and it was now clear that his pursuers were gaining on him.

The motorcycle's engine suddenly sputtered. It must have taken some sort of damage from one of the bullets, and he soon felt the revs beginning to reduce. He looked down at the engine to see that black oil was spewing out and covering his trousers. By the time he looked back up, he realised that he was heading into a tight bend in the road. He turned the handlebar, but it was too late. He was going too fast and the road was too slippery. Within seconds, the bike skidded off the road and hit a mound of dirt that launched it into the air. In mid-flight, he managed to kick himself clear of the motorcycle before it slammed into a large tree trunk. The sidecar was sheared off, and the bike was sent cartwheeling into another tree where its fuel tank ruptured and enveloped it in a bright orange fireball. Harding landed hard on the forest floor, but the impact was softened slightly by leaves and a blanket of snow. Still travelling at high speed, his body spun and rolled as he hit the ground, and it took several seconds for him to come to a stop in a cloud of fine snow. His lab coat was in tatters and covered in blood and dirt, and one of his trouser legs had been ripped open from the knee down.

Momentarily disorientated, he lay there blinking as he looked up at the snow-covered pine trees towering over him, trying to make sure that he could still feel all of his limbs. Bringing his right hand up to his forehead, it came away covered in blood from a large gash. He coughed and spluttered as he got up onto all fours, but he knew that he had to keep moving. Recalling his map of the area, he knew roughly where he was and in which direction he needed to go.

With blood dripping from his face, he got to his feet and immediately felt a sharp pain shooting up through his leg from his shattered ankle, and his left arm was dangling uselessly by his side. As he stood there for a moment, he couldn't quite believe that he was still alive, but being alive meant that he was still in the game. He might not live for much longer, but there was still a chance that he could make a difference.

Staggering forward, he headed down the slope between the trees, leaving a red trail of blood behind him in the snow. Gritting his teeth, he pushed through the intense pain and soon spotted a clearing ahead. There was a large grove down below, and he now knew exactly where he was. He kept going. Not long now.

When he reached the edge of the grove, he heard the engines of the pursuing vehicles behind him. Then he heard voices shouting in German, and then he heard a sound that he had dreaded more than anything else. Dogs. Barking and growling, they were clearly keen to be let loose so that they could hunt down their prey and rip it to shreds.

Harding stumbled forward and almost fell several times as he began making his way across the grove towards a small mountain chapel sitting by a narrow road on the other side. Off in the distance, he could see the lights from the small town further down the valley, but he knew that he would probably never be going back there. As he staggered ahead, he left a messy trail of blood dripping from his head as well as from his shoulder, down his left arm and off his fingertips.

The shouting and barking grew louder, and as he turned to look back to where he had come from, he saw a handful of soldiers with torches descending the incline and arriving at the edge of the grove with at least two dogs. They looked like they might be German shepherds, and they were straining against their leads, forcing their handlers to hold on tight. Harding stopped and turned around, pulled out his gun and fired five shots in their direction without expecting any of them to hit their mark. All he was trying to do was buy himself some time. He left one round in the cylinder for the unthinkable. He knew that he couldn't allow himself to be caught alive. Death at the hands of Nazi interrogators was quite possibly the worst way to die. If only he could make it to the chapel.

Somehow managing to ignore the pain and muster hidden resources that he had never realised he possessed, he picked up speed and walked to cover the final stretch to the chapel. As he reached the wooden door and pulled it open, the soldiers behind him opened fire and released their dogs. Several bullets smacked into the chapel's brickwork and its door, but by then, Harding was through and out of sight. He could hear the dogs barking and rasping for breath as they sprinted across the grove in his direction, and he managed to pull the door closed behind him.

Turning around, he found the small chapel as he remembered it from several days earlier. It was about four metres across and eight metres long, and at the far end of it, directly opposite the entrance, was a stone altar sitting in front of an intricately carved reredos depicting several scenes from the Bible. The wooden altarpiece was framed in gold, and its detailed motifs had been decorated and hand-painted with great care. He stepped forward unsteadily. He could feel himself becoming weaker as the loss of blood began to take its toll, and it kept dripping onto the flagstones as he staggered up to the altar, unslung his backpack and reached inside. Then he looked up at the altarpiece. If there was going to be any kind of salvation for his mission into Austria, this would be it.

Outside, the dogs arrived at the chapel and began jumping up against the door while barking and growling menacingly. Soon after, their handlers and the other soldiers arrived, led by the officer who had first spotted the intruder stealing a motorcycle inside the cavern. The dog handlers recalled their ferocious beasts and put them back on their leads as the officer stepped up to the door surrounded by his team of soldiers. Each one of them was carrying a submachine gun, and they seemed eager to use them. There could be no escape for the intruder now.

'I need him alive,' shouted the officer. 'Understood?'

The gun-wielding soldiers reluctantly murmured their acknowledgement, and then the officer extracted his pistol from its holster and raised it before ripping open the door. With their weapons up, the group spilled into the small chapel to find their prey on the floor in front of the altar, facing away from the door. He was slumped and resting on his knees, with his head hung low in front of his chest. Blood was dripping from his right arm, and he was panting heavily.

'*Hände hoch!*' shouted the officer, ordering Harding to raise his hands.

'American?' he continued, taking a step towards the kneeling man. 'English?'

Harding nodded weakly.

'Yes,' he said. 'English.'

'Stand up!' yelled the officer in heavily accented English. 'Now!'

Harding raised his right hand, but his left arm refused to obey him. He somehow managed to get back onto his feet, but as he stood there, he swayed and looked as if he was about to fall over any second.

'Turn around,' ordered the officer.

Harding complied and turned to face his pursuers. His face was covered in blood, and there was a steady trickle from the gash on his forehead. A whimsical expression seemed to be playing on his face, and blood was dripping onto the stone floor where he stood. Looking exhausted, he lowered his right arm to his sides and dropped his head to his chest.

'Hands up!' shouted the officer again.

Harding ignored him, but the officer did not fire his weapon. It was clear to him that they would rather capture him alive for interrogation than shoot him where he stood. Standing there for a few moments, Harding finally sighed and then looked up from under his blood-crusted eyebrows.

'Sorry, chaps,' he said wearily. 'I'm afraid I won't be coming with you this evening.'

His right hand moved slowly up towards his chest. It then suddenly shot inside his coat and came back out holding his revolver. He had just had time to reload before the soldiers entered the chapel, and he raised the weapon and managed to fire off several shots, two of which struck a soldier in the chest and caused him to collapse. But then the remaining soldiers opened up and peppered him with bullets. Harding slumped to the ground and lay immobile in an expanding pool of blood. With rasping breath, he lay there for a moment as the soldiers rushed him, removed his backpack and searched his body for more weapons. He blinked a couple of times as he looked up at them.

'At least I managed to take one of you Nazi bastards with me, eh?' he whispered feebly.

His expression froze in a sardonic smile as he locked eyes with the officer. He then exhaled for the final time, his eyes staring straight up at the chapel's ornately decorated ceiling. Agent Sparrow was dead.

ONE

LAKE NANTUA, FRANCE – PRESENT DAY

Adam Holbrook was far from his native England, but he felt perfectly at home. Living in the small, picturesque commune of Nantua in the beautiful and mountainous *department* of Ain in the Auvergne-Rhône-Alpes region of France, he had rarely been happier. He was in his early sixties but thought he had managed to keep in decent shape considering his age, even if a small paunch now sat above his belt and his posture was somewhat less straight than it had been in years gone by. With mid-length wavy grey hair, a short grey beard and pale blue eyes behind thin-rimmed glasses, he looked like the quintessential scientist, and in many ways, that was exactly what he was. He was wearing his usual leisure-time attire consisting of light beige slacks, dark blue trainers and a light green linen shirt, and it was only recently that he had realised that he had begun to dress like the locals. But that suited him just fine. Never particularly gifted with foreign languages, he had now spent enough years in France to master the language somewhat. And as his French language proficiency had grown, he had noticed the friendliness and inclusiveness of the local villagers grow with it.

Sitting in his small white wooden rowing boat on the emerald green glacial lake, he had decided to spend the afternoon fishing after having seen the weather forecast earlier that day. As it had promised, it had turned out to be full sun all afternoon, and with balmy temperatures and hardly any wind, it was perfect for a day out on the water. It was also one of his favourite things to do when he was not working. Above him was a clear blue sky with an airliner cutting a thin contrail from east to west, and he could hear the pleasant chirping of birds in the birch trees on the lakeshore.

The elongated lake, which was nestled between low but steep, tree-covered mountains on either side was rich in carp and trout, and after many dozens of fishing trips over the past several years after buying the boat, he had yet to row back to shore and leave the lake without having first secured his dinner for the evening. Being out on the lake by himself also afforded him time to think. He would mostly use this time to himself to ponder all manner of things, large and small, as he sat there with the fishing rod in his hands, sipping coffee from a thermos. But an afternoon in the boat was also ideal for contemplating aspects of what was at the centre of his life. His work.

A professor specialising in high-energy particle physics, he worked at the enormous CERN complex that straddled the border between France and Switzerland roughly 25 kilometres away from his home. Renowned throughout the world mainly for its Large

Hadron Collider, the particle physics research centre possessed the world's largest and most powerful particle accelerator, and it had shot to fame during its operation by accelerating and smashing subatomic particles into each other. This had allowed scientists to discover and study the smallest elementary building blocks of the universe known as quarks and gluons, from which protons and neutrons are made.

However, the LHC was not the only piece of equipment at CERN. Far from it. The research centre comprised many other facilities that were equally important for pushing the boundaries of modern particle physics. One of them was the CERN Proton Synchrotron, which was the very first particle accelerator to be built there in 1959. Just like all the other accelerators at the research complex, it was a circular ring buried underground, and Holbrook had now served as its chief science engineer for over a decade. With a circumference of just over 600 metres, it was relatively small and now many decades old, but in some ways, it was still the backbone of the complex. Its function was to serve as the initial step in the LHC research process. It did this by using powerful magnetic fields to accelerate protons to very high speeds, after which they were fed through a series of further acceleration steps until they finally entered the 27-kilometre-long LHC ring, where they would be guided to precisely slam into other particles at near lightspeed. The resultant radiation emissions and breakup of the accelerated particles and their targets into smaller constituent parts had given the particle physicists a deep understanding of the sub-atomic world, although many more experiments were still planned for the future.

When Holbrook closed his eyes, he could vividly imagine the inside of the particle accelerator as the magnetic fields were engaged and the raging torrent of protons began hurtling around its circular high-energy pathway, reaching almost unimaginable speeds. Holbrook knew as well as anyone that the technology was now almost a century old, having first been developed by scientists at the Kaiser Wilhelm Institute in Berlin in the late 1930s, but the basic design principles of a particle accelerator had changed very little since then. There were, however, some essential differences between the first basic cyclotrons and CERN's modern and powerful synchrotron. Unlike a cyclotron, which uses a constantly oscillating magnetic field to accelerate particles as they spiral out from its centre, the synchrotron also adjusts the magnetic fields dynamically to keep the accelerated particles moving in a circular orbit until they are released into a particle collider such as the LHC.

When the first cyclotrons were built in the 1930s, this aspect of the science was not well understood, and even if it had been, it was not possible at that time to adequately control and modulate the magnetic fields. In contrast, the modern proton synchrotron at CERN had as much computing power available to it as it needed, and Holbrook's control of the powerful magnetic fields was virtually perfect, down to vanishingly small fractions of a second. This allowed the synchrotron to maintain firm control of the particles even as their speeds came close to the speed of light.

With a large team of highly skilled scientists working for him, Holbrook's job was to ensure that the proton synchrotron worked perfectly to deliver streams of protons on demand into the much larger LHC. In essence, his job was to fine-tune the synchrotron and make sure that it operated at peak performance all the time. And as such, his responsibilities were far removed from the high-profile, cutting-edge science of CERN's most famous particle accelerator. Away from the limelight of his more famous celebrity colleagues, Holbrook was quite happy to remain unseen and just get on with things. However, everyone understood that without him, his team and the synchrotron, the entire CERN complex would be unable to function.

As much as Holbrook loved and took pride in his work, there was one thing that he loved even more and felt even more proud of. His daughter Alice. From an early age, she had shown genuine fascination with her father's work, and as soon as she had been able to, she had gone off to university to get a degree in particle physics. This had been when Holbrook's wife Eleanor was still alive. Before she had lost her battle with cancer. The devastating affliction had seemed to arrive out of nowhere, and less than a year later, Holbrook found himself forced to adjust to the life of a widower.

During this time, he and Alice had become closer than ever, and they had both used their work as a way to maintain some sort of purpose during those difficult months and years following Eleanor's death. However, using each other as support, they had somehow managed to cope and eventually move on with their lives, and Holbrook could not have been happier than the day Alice had announced that she had applied for a position as a high-energy physicist at the LHC. When she eventually got the job, Holbrook had been beside himself with pride, and there was barely a soul in Nantua that he had not told. Alice had soon moved from London to the Swiss capital, where she had settled by herself in a flat overlooking Lake Geneva, and the two of them now saw each other several times a week, either at CERN or when meeting up for lunch in the city. Now in her early thirties, Alice was his pride and joy, and as much as he loved his science, like any father, he would have given it all up for her in a heartbeat.

As he sat there in the gently bobbing boat, listening to the wavelets lapping softly against its wooden sides, Holbrook suddenly felt a slight tug on the fishing line. He gripped the rod and held it tightly in his hands in anticipation of a fish swallowing his bait and attempting to swim away. Like so many times before, the tug came, but it was much more powerful than he expected. This had to be a big one. Perhaps it was one of the large pike that moved lithely under the surface of the lake, looking for food in the form of smaller fish or sometimes even other pike. Suddenly, there was a violent tug that almost wrestled the rod out of his hands, and then the line went slack. Holbrook began to reel it in, but he could immediately feel that the hook and the lure were no longer attached. Whatever creature had swallowed them had also managed to snap the nylon line, despite it supposedly being able to withstand a strain of up to three pounds. Holbrook was genuinely surprised. This had never happened before. Not once in all his time in Nantua. As he reeled in the final bit of fishing line, he pondered whimsically if this might mean that his luck had now finally changed. Perhaps this blessed life here in southeastern France was about to change. He smiled to himself and shook his head. He didn't hold with any kind of superstition, either in the form of black cats crossing the road or ancient Middle Eastern mysticism. This was simply bad luck or a fishing line with some sort of manufacturing defect. Or perhaps he had simply managed to come across the oldest and largest fish in the lake. A fish that would now live to swim another day.

Deciding to accept defeat and head back to shore, Holbrook placed the fishing rod at the bottom of the boat and gripped the oars. Then he turned the boat towards the small sailing club on the western side of the lake and began rowing. Finding an easy cadence, he repeatedly sank the oars gently into the water and propelled the small vessel stroke by stroke across the calm lake towards the shore. The sailing club was usually never busy, and today was no different. A single person on the pier had just come back from the lake in his small fifteen-foot daysailer boat, and behind him was a group of three people having a conversation next to their cars in the parking lot.

Coming to a stop in his usual berth, he used a hemp rope to secure the boat to a wooden pylon supporting the pier, and then he gathered his fishing equipment and climbed out. As he walked back to his car, which was an old and unglamorous but very dependable blue Ford Mondeo, he noticed a vehicle in the parking lot that somehow seemed out of place. It wasn't because he was unfamiliar with the make or model or that he had never seen one before. It was simply that it was an unusual car for this area. This wasn't a rich area by any stretch of the imagination, and most people here drove older and more utilitarian vehicles like vans or estates in which they could transport their dogs. This car was a top-of-the-line, white Mercedes saloon that looked brand new, and its dark windows were so heavily tinted that it was impossible to see inside, even on this sunny day. Holbrook eyed it as he walked past, and he noticed that on the right-hand side of the numberplate next to the registration number was printed '69M', which he knew to mean that the car was registered not in the local département of Ain but in the large city of Lyon to the southwest. Perhaps this was just a day-tripper having come to enjoy the peace and tranquillity of Lake Nantua.

Walking past the Mercedes, he unlocked the boot of the Mondeo and placed his equipment inside. Then he closed the boot, got in behind the wheel, rolled down the window and started the engine. He drove slowly across the crunching gravel that covered the parking lot, and then he turned left onto the road to head back towards the centre of town just a couple of hundred metres away. His house was perched up on one of the elevated streets that overlooked the lake, and he was about to turn right and head up there along the winding, characterful streets when he suddenly changed his mind. Instead of going home and digging around in the freezer for his dinner, he would instead head over to the Restaurant Belle Rive. It was situated on the opposite side of the lake from the sailing club, and it had unparalleled views towards the west as the sun began to sink lower in the sky, bathing the wooded eastern bank in golden light. On top of that, it served some of the best food anywhere in the whole département.

Less than three minutes later, he pulled off the road and into the parking lot. The restaurant was a long building constructed right on the lakeshore about twenty metres above the water, and its peach-coloured exterior render glowed warmly in the late afternoon sun. At the back facing the lake was a large outside terrace with tables and parasols where patrons could enjoy the view as they ate their meals.

Holbrook parked up and exited the car, and then he walked inside while checking his clothes to make sure he didn't have patches of dirt stuck to him. He was not exactly a vain man, but his sense of old-fashioned propriety meant that he didn't want to show up at a restaurant looking like he didn't care about his appearance. That would just be disrespectful.

'*Bonsoir, Claude,*' he said as he entered and nodded at the head waiter.

'*Bonsoir, Monsieur Holbrook,*' said Claude with a smile as he recognised one of his regulars.

'*Encore la terrasse ce soir?*' asked Claude, motioning to the outside, where a couple of other diners were already seated.

'*Oui, s'il vous plaît,*' replied Holbrook. '*Merci.*'

Claude nodded and smiled, and Holbrook followed him to the terrace outside, where he was shown to his usual table by the railing nearest the lake. The sun was gleaming as it reflected in the small ripples of the water, and he sat down and began to peruse the menu. With his lost catch still on his mind, he ordered roasted pike steak with *Vin Jaune* sauce, rice, tomato compote and fresh vegetables from the local market. He also asked for a glass of the house white wine, which he knew to be excellent for the price.

As he sat there enjoying the pleasant warmth of the late afternoon sun on his face, he felt his phone vibrate in his trouser pocket. It was a brief message from Alice, asking how his fishing trip was going. He replied and told her of his failure to catch anything, and of his planned revenge at Restaurant Belle Rive, and she replied with an emoji that was one of the seemingly endless variations of smiley faces. Another brief message from her then pinged in asking him if he was still able to meet up for dinner the following day, and he replied in the affirmative. Another variant of the smiley face arrived, this time alongside an emoji showing a pair of wine glasses. He put the phone away just as the wine arrived, and as he leaned back and enjoyed his first sip, he looked out over the lake and smiled to himself. Life was good.

After a couple of hours, and with a belly full of fish and wine, Holbrook paid the bill and left the restaurant. When he walked outside and headed for his car, he immediately noticed the white Mercedes he had spotted at the sailing club. It was now parked in one of the restaurant's few parking bays along the road, and he cast his mind back to the terrace to try to guess which of the guests it might belong to. There had been a few locals that he recognised, but there had also been a stylish young couple who looked like city dwellers who might be on a day trip here from either Geneva or Lyon or perhaps even Grenoble. Still, he couldn't quite shake the feeling that something was out of place with that vehicle. He frowned. It wasn't like him to be paranoid or suspicious. It was time to head home, watch some TV and then go to bed. As he got into his car and joined the road back towards town, he glanced in his rearview mirror, but the Mercedes remained in its parking bay.

He drove through town for a couple of minutes and then swung onto a small, narrow road that wound its way up through a small part of Nantua located about a hundred metres above the lake. The climb was short but fairly steep, and the curving road was lined with trees and bushes partly obscuring the view. He finally turned left into a short cul-de-sac, where a low automatic metal gate with vertical bars blocked the way to the driveway in front of his house. As he pulled up to it, the sun seemed to be balancing on the mountain ridge behind him to the west.

The modest two-storey building was nestled on the hillside with its front facing out towards the lake below, and behind it was a small garden surrounded by trees. Then the terrain steepened and continued up towards a large rocky escarpment high above the town. It was an idyllic place to live, and Holbrook never took it for granted. Not a single day went by when he didn't appreciate his lot in life, and he was sure that this tiny corner of France would remain his home for the rest of his days.

He fished the key fob for the gate out of the chest pocket of his shirt and pressed the button. The gate squeaked and rattled aside, and then he parked up and headed for the front door. Just as he put the key in the lock, he heard the sound of what sounded like a noisy diesel engine out on the road, and when he turned to look, he saw a white van with the logo of one of the regional telecoms providers emblazoned across its side.

The van pulled partly into the cul-de-sac, but then swung around and stopped. Perhaps the driver was lost. The narrow roads and streets of Nantua could be a bit of a warren in some places, and the road signs were often lacking.

Holbrook continued inside and went to the kitchen where he put the kettle on to make himself a cup of coffee. He then dug into a cupboard for a piece of chocolate. As the kettle began to boil, he could have sworn that he heard the rattle of the automatic gate outside, but there was only one fob, and it was in his pocket. He paused for a moment and listened, but could hear nothing now. It must have been in his imagination. Just as he picked up the kettle to pour the boiling water into a cup, there was a knock on the door. He turned his head and put the kettle back down. Who could be knocking on the door now? And how had someone come to his front door?

He walked out into the entrance hall and peered through the spyhole. Outside were two large men of similar height and build wearing blue overalls with the telecom provider's logo stitched onto the left side of their chests. They were both wearing blue caps that partly obscured their faces, but Holbrook could see that they sported what appeared to be identical short, black goatees.

Holbrook creased his forehead as he looked out. Why were these men here? He had not asked for any telephone engineers to come and visit, and he had no need for it. Everything was working perfectly. As he watched, the man at the front reached up and knocked on the door again, and Holbrook then decided to open it. This had to be some sort of mistake that could easily be cleared up.

As he unlocked the door and pulled it open, the two men both raised their heads and looked straight at him, but there was no warmth or politeness in their eyes. With their olive skin and dark eyes, they both had a vaguely Latin appearance, and as they stood there, they looked like predators regarding their prey. As he looked at them more closely, Holbrook noticed that the two men looked like they could be brothers. In fact, the only way he could tell them apart was that the one at the back appeared to be slightly taller, and the one at the front had a small black tear tattooed under his left eye. Holbrook immediately began to feel uneasy.

'Adam Holbrook?' said the man at the front with an accent that Holbrook couldn't quite place, except that he knew it wasn't French.

'Yes?' said Holbrook. 'What's going on? Why are you here?'

'Good,' said the man at the front, taking a slow step forward. 'We need to have a word with you.'

'I'm sorry,' said Holbrook. 'First, you'll need to tell me...'

He never got to finish his sentence. In one fluid movement that was so fast as to take Holbrook completely by surprise, the man moved forward, extracted a small metal cylinder from his pocket, grabbed Holbrook around the back of the head with a large hand, and jammed the cylinder against the side of his neck. He immediately pressed the button on its side, and the spring-loaded jet injector clicked as its internal piston compressed the liquid inside and shot it at high speed out through a tiny nozzle. The high-pressure burst of the liquid tranquillizer cut through the skin of Holbrook's neck, and the effect was dramatic and almost instant. Within a couple of seconds, during which time both men rushed inside and grabbed Holbrook, his body began to sag as he became unsteady on his feet, and to his horror, he realised that he was suddenly unable to speak. As his vision constricted to a dark tunnel, he tried to cry out but only managed to move his jaw and lips uselessly. No sound came out. His pupils then dilated, and he passed out and collapsed into the arms of his assailants. Two minutes later, he was lying bound on the floor of the fake telecoms van, heading towards a small civil aviation airfield eight kilometres west of Nantua, where his still unconscious body was loaded onto a private jet that took off, climbed to cruising altitude, and then began heading southwest for its first stop before going on to embark on its long journey to its final destination.

Two

Three kilometres west of Gibraltar

The sun was about to rise above the watery horizon in the western Mediterranean as the black dinghy raced out across the water towards its floating target due east of the British overseas territory. At the front of the small but fast vessel sat Andrew Sterling. With his muscular build, short black hair, strong jaw and piercing blue eyes, he was a handsome man in his late thirties, and he was almost as fit as he had been during his time with 22 SAS, despite now spending much of his time behind a desk.

Earlier that morning, he and his old friend and former colleague Colin McGregor had put in an hour of shooting practice at the headquarters of the British Forces in Gibraltar. The roughly ten-acre site, which went by the name Devil's Tower Camp, was located just south of Gibraltar's international airport, and it had first been established as an RAF base in 1942.

Among a host of different facilities, it also included an underground shooting range where Andrew and McGregor had practised their skills with what was the preferred firearm of both men, the compact 9mm semi-automatic Glock 17 pistol. Andrew in particular had enjoyed the feel of the composite pistol grip in his right hand once again, and he had emptied six magazines at paper targets hung at various distances.

As the pistol kicked repeatedly in his hand, spent brass cartridges popped sideways out of the ejection port, and the bullets zipped downrange at just above the speed of sound, and he relished the sensation of every shot. Not because he enjoyed the idea of killing, but because every dry report and every rapid recoil that kicked into his hand and travelled through his wrist, up through his arm and into his shoulder was a reminder and a reaffirmation of who he was. For all his suit-wearing, desk-driving, hand-shaking investigative work at his special unit's HQ building on Sheldrake Place in Kensington, deep down he was a soldier. A warrior and a fighter who felt most at home with a weapon in his hand, a mission to accomplish, and a brother like McGregor by his side.

Andrew had asked the Scot, who was a few years younger than him and still with the Regiment, to join him on today's unusual exercise. And McGregor had only been too happy to oblige when he discovered that it would involve a trip from rainy England to sunny Gibraltar. At the back of the boat, controlling the powerful outboard motor, was a Royal Navy sub-lieutenant named Stevens, who was steering them confidently across the water.

While Andrew was now attached to the investigative unit in central London and tasked with finding and eliminating terrorists preparing to use weapons of mass destruction, McGregor was still in active service with 22 SAS. Several years back, Andrew had been McGregor's instructor at the Regiment's home in Hereford, and the two men had clicked as well as any two soldiers could. During numerous overseas operations with the Special Air Service, the pair had completed countless missions behind enemy lines together, either in a pure reconnaissance capacity or as the tip of the spear in covert operations to take out high-value targets, most often in various unstable countries in the Middle East and North Africa.

However, today's activity was slightly different. Special forces boardings of marine vessels and oil rigs were something the SAS trained extensively for, and they usually involved either a covert approach using scuba diving equipment or a fast-action direct assault using either helicopters or dinghies. Today's training mission was conducted using the latter approach, and the target was the Royal Navy patrol boat HMS Trent, which was one of the British Navy's forward-deployed vessels stationed in Gibraltar. The patrol boat was playing the role of a commercial vessel that had been taken over by a group of terrorists, and the two-man SAS team were preparing to board the ship using a novel piece of equipment that the UK special forces were in the process of testing and evaluating.

Under normal circumstances, the fast-moving dinghy would approach the target ship and attempt to draw closer from the rear, typically under cover of darkness. The boarding team would then use hooks and rope ladders to scale the side of the ship, quickly form up as a unit, and then enter the superstructure to subdue whoever was in control of the vessel using the three cornerstones of an assault. Speed, aggression and surprise.

However, there was one crucial difference between today's exercise and a standard shipboarding task. Using hooks and rope ladders was a tried-and-tested technique, but it was notoriously tricky to rapidly pull alongside the boat, attach the hooks and begin to climb up the ship's side, especially in choppy waters and at night. The equipment Andrew and McGregor were wearing today was designed to solve that problem. Both men were strapped into a jet suit consisting of a harness, a powerpack worn on the back, and two dual jet nozzles that they were gripping firmly, one in each hand. The concept was already proven to work in a controlled environment on land, but the higher-ups had decided to test whether it might serve as a faster and simpler way to conduct ship boardings. The two men were also wearing a full kit of weapons and body armour under the harnesses, and part of the exercise was to determine whether they could quickly strip out of the jet suits and proceed with the mission in the highly dynamic marine environment.

Behind them, at a distance of just over three kilometres across the water, was the Rock of Gibraltar sticking high up into the air and ready to catch the first rays of sunlight for the day. Up ahead was the rear of the HMS Trent, silhouetted against the brightening orange morning sky. The ninety-metre-long vessel looked huge from the small dinghy, and it was churning up the water in its frothy swirling wake as it cut across the sea.

'Keep moving up!' Andrew shouted above the noise of the outboard motor as he turned back as much as the suit would allow him in order to address sub-lieutenant Stevens. 'Another fifty metres closer.'

The wind ruffled his short black hair, and as the small dinghy bounced across the waves, there was the occasional salty spray coming over the front of the vessel and landing on his face and his lips.

'Ready?' he said, turning back to McGregor.

'Ay,' said the stocky Scot with a nod. 'I hope these things can cope with a bit of salt water. Otherwise, you and I are going for a wee swim.'

'Wouldn't be the first time,' said Andrew with a wry smile. 'Let's fire them up.'

The two SAS men released the safety catches on the suit controls and allowed them to begin spooling up. As they did so, the high-pitched whine from the miniature jet engines began to climb ever upwards, and both men moved to stand up in the boat. Despite now being inside the wake of the patrol boat, the water was still somewhat choppy, and they had to make an effort to remain upright on their feet. Only then did it occur to Andrew that falling overboard now might well present a serious problem. The jet pack weighed about thirty kilos, and it would quickly drag him down unless he could free himself and swim back up to the surface. He glanced down at the display on the control unit attached to his left wrist to see that the thrust gauge indicator was now almost full. He then turned back to McGregor once more.

'On my mark,' he shouted over the noise. 'I'll go first. You follow after three seconds.'

'Roger,' shouted McGregor.

Andrew squeezed the throttle mechanism inside the casing holding the dual jet nozzles attached to both hands, and the four small jet engines screamed as they went to maximum power. Tensing his shoulder muscles to keep his arms locked in place while moving his body to shift his centre of mass slightly, he began to rise up into the air. It felt precarious for the first few seconds while he was still close to the bouncing dinghy, but as soon as he was up and away by around five metres, he suddenly felt in full control as he rose into the air and began to accelerate forward towards the ship up ahead. Three seconds later, McGregor launched from the dinghy, and soon the two men were moving at around 80 kilometres per hour towards the ship at an altitude of roughly twenty metres. With their arms extended downward and their bodies leaning forward into the wind at a roughly 45-degree angle, it was a smooth ride, and it turned out to be surprisingly easy to maintain control even out over the open ocean.

As they came closer to the Royal Navy vessel's large rear deck, they could feel the swirling vortex that was being created by its tall superstructure as it cut across the water, and they had to compensate using their nozzles to maintain their course. At almost the same time, the two men touched down on the rear deck, where they hit the quick-release button of the suits and wriggled out to stand with their submachineguns up and ready. Then they moved swiftly towards the door to the interior, taking up positions on either side of it. Keen to demonstrate a full start-to-finish boarding exercise, including the use of weapons and the neutralising of enemies, they continued with the boarding as planned and pushed inside the tall superstructure. Here they proceeded up the stairs to the bridge, where they performed a simulated breach using a dummy flashbang and blank rounds.

Mere seconds after entering the bridge, all the 'terrorists' had been neutralised, and the commanding officer of the HMS Trent then stepped forward and raised a hand.

'End of exercise!' he shouted, turning to Andrew and McGregor as the ship's crew got back onto their feet. 'Well done, chaps. That all seemed to go quite well, wouldn't you say?'

'Much better than I expected,' nodded Andrew, glancing at McGregor as he secured his weapon. 'I am starting to regret not taking part in active missions anymore.'

'I don't blame you,' said McGregor in his broad Scottish accent as he grinned. 'I need to get myself one of those suits. I hope the top brass will sign off on them. I could definitely see them coming in handy.'

'No doubt,' said Andrew. 'But I guess that's all up to the bean counters now. I hear those things are expensive.'

'Alright, gentlemen,' said the commanding officer, clasping his hands together. 'Thank you for your time. If you would like to make yourselves comfortable in the mess hall, breakfast will be served there in about ten minutes. We'll then be finishing our patrol, and we should be back in Gibraltar in just over three hours.'

Andrew and McGregor headed for the mess hall and were handed a full English breakfast on a tray, which they wolfed down with a cup of strong tea. Then they went back up onto the deck and stood by the railing, looking out over the ocean as the patrol boat began making its way back towards the Rock. After all the time they had known each other and everything they had experienced together, the two of them were comfortable in each other's company, and they talked little as they stood there. Sometimes, the best way to spend time was to say nothing.

As HMS Trent rounded the southernmost tip of the overseas territory and made its way into the port, heading for HM Dockyard Gibraltar, Andrew's phone buzzed in his pocket. He extracted it and saw that he had received a text message from his girlfriend, Fiona Keane, whom he lived with in a house in Hampstead in London. She was a gregarious, feisty and to him absolutely gorgeous blond Irish historian and archaeologist who was working at the British Museum. They had met several years earlier during his efforts to solve the mystery of an enigmatic missing cargo that had secretly been transported out of Nazi Germany aboard a U-boat. Among many other talents and abilities, Fiona was an authority on the Second World War, and she had been instrumental in finally uncovering the nature of the lethal cargo and ultimately preventing nefarious forces from using it against civilians. The two of them had soon got on like a house on fire, quickly developing more than just a professional relationship, and they had gone on to complement each other's skillsets during a series of adventures over the past several years.

As was typically the case, Fiona liked to bury herself in her studies, and her text message today was brief.

"Hi, Andy. Hope the test went well. Looking forward to seeing you later. I've discovered something really interesting!"

'Let me guess,' smiled McGregor. 'Fiona's keen to see you again?'

'Something like that,' replied Andrew, shooting his old friend a glance and a smile. 'She's been busy with a new project lately, and I think she might have made some progress.'

'She's a clever las,' said McGregor, giving Andrew a quick nod and a wink. 'I never could understand what she's doing with someone like you.'

'That's cute,' scoffed Andrew good-naturedly. 'What about yourself? Isn't it time you settled down?'

'What, me?' said McGregor, feigning incredulity and smiling broadly as he spread his arms out to his sides. 'And deprive the world's women of this fine specimen? I think not. That would be a crime!'

Andrew shook his head and chuckled.

'Sorry,' he said, deadpan. 'I momentarily forgot that you're the ideal man. The best a woman could hope for.'

'Well, you said it. Not me,' shrugged McGregor with a grin as he gazed out over the harbour. 'But you just might be on to something there. Anyway, please give her my best.'

'I will,' said Andrew, putting the phone back in his pocket. 'Alright. Let's go back downstairs, pack up our gear and get ready to disembark. I have a plane to catch back to London.'

* * *

LONDON – LATER THAT DAY

After the flight from Gibraltar to Heathrow, Andrew arrived back at his home in Hampstead around mid-afternoon. Walking up to the front door of the house and letting himself in, he noticed classical music playing in the living room. He proceeded into the large open-plan kitchen, where he dropped his bag on a bar stool by the kitchen island, and then he continued into the bright, sunlit living room, where Fiona was curled up on the sofa with a cup of coffee. Wearing light blue jeans and a pink shirt, and with her fine features and blond hair, Andrew thought she looked as effortlessly gorgeous as always. She appeared to have been engrossed in reading a stack of documents that were now splayed out on the sofa next to her, and on the coffee table were more piles of paper and a few books.

'Sorry,' she smiled, looking up at him with her emerald eyes as if emerging from a dream. 'I didn't even hear you come in. I've been so engrossed in this stuff ever since you left.'

'That's alright,' smiled Andrew, walking over to bend down and give her a kiss. 'How is it going?'

Fiona sat up on the sofa, checked the time on her wristwatch and rubbed her eyes.

'It's going well, I think,' she said, giving a yawn as she placed the documents on the coffee table and ran her fingers through her shoulder-length hair. 'I never knew about any of this stuff. I'm considering a collaboration with the Imperial War Museum. I think we could make quite an interesting exhibit about this whole thing.'

'Remind me again,' said Andrew. 'Something about some World War 2 tapes?'

'That's right,' said Fiona. 'Or rather, transcripts of tapes from a place called Farm Hall. It is a Georgian manor house near Cambridge that had been used by MI6 as a staging area for various resistance groups who were then air-dropped into occupied Europe during the Second World War. Immediately after the war ended, a whole bunch of Nazi scientists were interned there for months. They were some of the best scientific minds of the Third Reich, physicists mainly, and they had been snatched by the Allies during the final days of the war as part of what was called the Alsos Mission. It was basically an effort to hoover up as much information about Nazi Germany's advanced science and weapons projects as possible, especially with regards to nuclear research.'

'Nuclear?' Andrew said, sitting down next to her on the sofa and reclining. 'As in, nuclear weapons?'

'Nuclear power and nuclear weapons,' nodded Fiona. 'Before the war, the Nazis had been far ahead of the rest of the world in both fields of research. It was German scientists who first discovered nuclear fission in Berlin in December of 1938, which I am sure you probably understand a lot better than I do.'

'The process of splitting the atom,' Andrew nodded. 'Yes, it's the basis of all nuclear reactors and most nuclear bombs. You take a fissile material like uranium and enrich it using centrifuges that separate fissile Uranium-235 from the much more abundant Uranium-238. And then you bombard it with lots of neutrons.

The neutrons split the uranium atoms, releasing energy along with even more neutrons, and then you have your chain reaction. With enough fissile material, the so-called critical mass, the process continues exponentially. That's the simple version, anyway.'

'You make it sound so simple,' smiled Fiona.

'It is actually a fairly straightforward process,' said Andrew. 'At least, theoretically speaking. But it does require a lot of expertise and high levels of energy to kickstart. But once it gets going, it can release energy on a scale that is orders of magnitude larger than what simple chemical processes such as fire can produce. Several million times more. As a rule of thumb, a single kilo of uranium can release energy equivalent to about ten thousand tonnes of TNT.'

'Right,' smiled Fiona. 'This is clearly more your field than mine. Anyway, the Alsos Mission was looking for reactors and centrifuges that could be used to create that weapons-grade enriched uranium you just mentioned.'

'I vaguely remember reading about that,' said Andrew. 'The Manhattan Project had already developed the bomb for the Americans, so I suppose the people working for the Alsos Mission knew exactly what they were looking for.'

'That's right,' said Fiona. 'But as I have discovered over the past few days, this whole field of research was obviously in its infancy back in the late 1930s. After the German scientists had discovered fission in 1938, it took another few months for them to theorise that splitting the atom would release particles that could then cause a nuclear chain reaction in other atoms. And once they realised this, it became clear to them that this technology could have some pretty groundbreaking consequences, both in civilian and military applications.'

'But wait a second,' said Andrew, holding up a hand and regarding Fiona with an intrigued look. 'Are you saying that the Nazis were researching nuclear power and weapons as early as 1938 or 1939?'

'That's right,' nodded Fiona, reaching for one of the documents on the coffee table. 'And in the spring of 1939, they were already planning to build nuclear reactors that could use turbines to generate electricity capable of powering ships and submarines.'

'World War 2 nuclear submarines,' said Andrew, looking impressed as he contemplated the seemingly ludicrous idea. 'That's mindboggling to think about.'

'And then there was the weapons research,' said Fiona, tapping her document with her index finger. 'Look at this. This is a copy of a letter written by one of the scientists who was later held captive at Farm Hall. An Austrian chap by the name of Paul Harteck. In late April 1939, he wrote the following to Erich Schumann, who was the head of the *Heereswaffenamt,* which was the German Army's weapons research agency:

> "We take the liberty of calling to your attention the newest developments in nuclear physics, which, in our opinion, will probably make it possible to produce an explosive many orders of magnitude more powerful than the conventional ones. That country which first makes use of it has an unsurpassable advantage over the others."

'Interesting,' said Andrew. 'I had no idea. It sounds like they already understood the full potential of nuclear weapons. And this was in early 1939?'

'That's right,' said Fiona. 'This was six months before the war even began with the invasion of Poland, and they were already at a point where they were discussing military applications for this research. At that time, of course, they still only had the theoretical framework. But as far as I can tell, they pretty much immediately set about trying to build both a reactor and a bomb.'

'A costly exercise,' said Andrew. 'Even today, that sort of thing requires some serious hardware and a lot of money and resources.'

'It was,' said Fiona. 'It was all conducted under the codename 'Uranprojekt'. The Uranium Project. It was basically a whole bunch of prominent German scientists who were all involved in developing nuclear fission technology centred around uranium. The goal was for them to construct nuclear reactors for power generation and nuclear weapons for winning the war. And this Paul Harteck chap was far from the most celebrated or influential scientist in that enterprise. He was a pale shadow of people like Werner Heisenberg, who was one of the primary forces in the nuclear research program.'

'Heisenberg,' said Andrew. 'I've heard about him.'

'Yes,' said Fiona. 'He was a Nobel Prize-winning physicist and one of the pioneers of quantum mechanics, and he also went on to become a very influential physicist after the war. Anyway, in 1942, after the Germans had already been pushing ahead with nuclear research for several years, Heisenberg held a lecture at a Uranium Project conference in Berlin, which we know was attended by high-ranking SS dignitaries such as Heinrich Himmler and Albert Speer. Also in attendance was a certain Carl Friedrich von Weizsäcker, who was another prominent nuclear physicist and one of the main proponents of developing nuclear weapons for the Nazis. With regards to a prototype uranium reactor that was under construction in the Black Forest in southern Germany at the time, Heisenberg said this:'

> "As soon as such a machine is in operation, the question of the production of a new explosive takes a new turn, according to an idea by Von Weizsäcker. The transformation of uranium in the machine produces a new substance, Element 94, which is most probably, just like Uranium-235, an explosive of the same unimaginable effect."

'Note that this was three years after the scientists had realised the weapons potential of nuclear fission,' said Fiona. 'So, you would have to assume that they had already made significant progress in actually building a reactor and designing a bomb. By the way, this new substance, Element 94, which Heisenberg mentioned, was plutonium. As you know, it is another radioactive element that can be used to create an explosive chain reaction. So, Heisenberg clearly understood the entire process very well at this point. And Von Weizsäcker had already described the process of "plutonium breeding" inside a uranium reactor as "the open road to the bomb" as early as July 1940.'

'Wow,' said Andrew. 'Amazing. I had no idea they were that far ahead.'

'And here's the real kicker,' said Fiona, pulling another document from a pile. 'This bit just blows my mind. In 1941, Von Weizsäcker drafted a patent application to the German patent office, which states the following:'

> "The production of Element 94 in practically useful amounts is best done with the uranium reactor. It is especially advantageous – and this is the main benefit of the invention – that Element 94 thereby produced, can easily be separated from uranium chemically. With regard to energy per unit weight, this explosive would be around ten million times greater than any other existing explosive, and comparable only to pure uranium-235."

'He then goes on to say this about his invention,' continued Fiona.

> "This is a process for the explosive production of energy from the fission of Element 94, whereby Element 94 is brought together in such amounts in one place, for example, a bomb, so that the overwhelming majority of neutrons produced by fission excite new fissions and do not leave the substance."

'Now, this might sound a bit convoluted,' said Fiona, 'but this document written by Von Weizsäcker is in effect nothing short of a patent claim for a plutonium bomb using a nuclear chain reaction. And this was in 1941.'

'Crikey!' Andrew said, looking surprised and slightly unsettled. 'They really meant business, didn't they?'

'Clearly,' said Fiona. 'I never realised quite how advanced their efforts actually were until I started looking into these Farm Hall transcripts.'

'Imagine if they had got there first,' said Andrew. 'Imagine if they had developed the bomb before the Americans did. It would have changed everything. They would most likely have won the war.'

'Exactly,' said Fiona. 'It's very sobering to think about. Anyway, getting back to Farm Hall. Between July 1945 and January 1946, the brilliant Werner Heisenberg was one of ten Nazi scientists being interned there, along with Von Weizsäcker, Harteck, Hahn and several others. And the really interesting thing about the whole affair is that they weren't just being held as prisoners in that particular location for no good reason. They enjoyed quite comfortable living conditions, which they seemed to take as a mark of respect for their scientific value to the Allies, and they were allowed to mingle freely with each other.'

'But?' smiled Andrew, raising one eyebrow. 'There's a catch, right?'

'Yes, there is,' said Fiona. 'The catch was that the entirety of the manor house was wired from top to bottom with hidden microphones. The whole thing was part of what was known as Operation Epsilon, which was set up with the express goal of capturing and detaining Germany's nuclear physicists and then recording every single word they said to each other for the next six months. And that's exactly what happened at Farm Hall.'

'Interesting,' said Andrew. 'I suppose the Allies were keen to find out how far the Nazis had come with their nuclear weapons research.'

'Precisely,' said Fiona. 'Towards the end of the war, before the Americans developed the Manhattan Project and eventually dropped the bomb on Hiroshima and Nagasaki, the Allies were petrified about the prospect of the Nazis acquiring a nuclear bomb first. In fact, the British government was so concerned about Germany developing nuclear weapons that they examined all V-2 impact sites in London with Geiger counters. The idea was that the Nazis were likely to construct a so-called dirty bomb prior to using actual fission bombs. But no trace of uranium was ever found in any of the impact sites.'

'I guess we would have known about it if that had been the case,' said Andrew.

'Probably,' said Fiona. 'Anyway, another point of Operation Epsilon was to make sure that the Soviets didn't get their hands on Germany's nuclear research. As you know, the Second World War had barely ended before the Cold War began, and everyone could already see the schism between Western capitalism and Eastern communism shaping up in the near future, so both sides were keen to obtain any advantage they could. And then there was the fact that the Allies simply weren't quite sure what to do with those scientists after the war. There was a pervasive fear that they still represented a potential risk if they were released back into Germany, and so their internment was also a way to stall for time while the British and American governments decided what to do with them.'

'That's an incredible story,' said Andrew. 'I had never heard about it. Do you actually have the Farm Hall transcripts?'

'I do,' smiled Fiona. 'Ben Ambrose sent them to me. You remember Ben, right?'

'The name sort of rings a bell,' said Andrew, rubbing his jaw. 'Remind me again?'

'He works at the University of London's Institute of Historical Research,' said Fiona. 'I think you met him at that drinks party last summer. You know, the one at that rooftop bar in Mayfair.'

'Was he the guy driving that 1960s MGB?' said Andrew. 'The silver one.'

'That's him,' nodded Fiona.

'Right,' smiled Andrew. 'Bit of an unusual choice of car for an academic like him. Nice chap, though. I liked him.'

'Well, he has access to all the original material,' said Fiona. 'And he let me have a copy of the transcripts when I told him I was thinking about maybe setting up an exhibition at the Imperial War Museum about them. I think it would do really well. A lot of people would be interested in this stuff.'

'I'm sure that's true,' said Andrew. 'It's fascinating. Do you know if the original tapes still exist?'

'Oh, yes,' said Fiona. 'Ambrose told me that they are locked away in a secure vault somewhere. But the written transcripts are supposedly accurate.'

'I see,' said Andrew. 'So, just how close did the Nazis actually get to making a nuclear bomb?'

'Well, there is still some debate about this,' said Fiona. 'After the war, Heisenberg, von Weizsäcker and all the other scientists were obviously keen to distance themselves from the whole thing. They claimed that they were actively trying to dissuade Hitler from building a nuclear weapon, even going as far as to say that they were trying to sabotage its development. But that clearly runs counter to some of the written records from that time.'

'How can there still be any debate about this?' said Andrew. 'I would have thought that it was all perfectly clear by now.'

'You'd think so,' said Fiona. 'But it isn't quite as simple as that. There are still new documents surfacing regularly from various places, casting new light on the whole thing. The official history will tell you that the Nazis never got close to developing either a working atomic reactor or a nuclear bomb. The Alsos Mission found a prototype uranium reactor in a research centre in the town of Haigerloch in the southwest of Germany. What they had found was essentially Heisenberg's research and development lab, which had been relocated from Berlin, including the Nazi attempt at building what they called the 'Uranium Machine'. But it was supposedly deemed by the Alsos Mission to be barely operational, having possibly suffered some sort of malfunction during its operation. But the Alsos Mission personnel still disassembled the whole thing and took it with them out of Germany. With regards to the bomb, there has never been any definitive proof that the Nazi scientists ever managed to build one. But there is some anecdotal evidence that they may have come much closer than the history books would have you believe.'

'What do you mean?' said Andrew.

'Well,' said Fiona, leafing through some of her other documents before extracting a sheet of paper. ' In November of 1944, an agent of the Soviet Army's foreign intelligence agency, the GRU, produced a report indicating that he had discovered evidence that the Nazis were constructing a nuclear device. That report has now been retrieved from the GRU archives, and it says this:'

> "The Germans are about to test a new secret weapon. One with enormous destructive power. The already constructed bomb has a diameter of 1.5 metres and consists of interconnected hollow spheres."

'Interesting,' said Andrew. 'That design actually sounds about right. That's more or less what the Manhattan Project's designs looked like.'

'Well, there's more,' said Fiona. 'The GRU concluded immediately after the war that the Germans had indeed managed to produce a nuclear bomb. Their archives also recount how the head of the GRU personally briefed Joseph Stalin in March of 1945 about how Nazi scientists had carried out two tests of a new device near the town of Ohrdruf in the central German state of Thuringia. The devices supposedly proved immensely powerful, and according to the reports, they flattened trees out to a distance of 600 metres. Reports in the archive also recount how hundreds of Polish POWs who were chained up near the device were vaporised, with no trace of them remaining after the blast.'

'Bloody hell,' whispered Andrew. 'Did that really happen?'

'Apparently so,' said Fiona. 'And the surrounding area supposedly exhibited significant radiation levels immediately after the explosions. There were also soil samples taken decades later, and an analysis of those samples indicated the presence of radioactive elements not found in nature, such as caesium-137 and cobalt-60. So this seems to point to some type of nuclear device having been detonated there. Interestingly, it is known conclusively that the head of Nazi Germany's secret weapons program, *SS Obergruppenführer* Hans Kammler, met with Heinrich Himmler the very next day after the second of the two tests. This would seem to indicate that Kammler had something very important to report to the *SS Reichsführer* and Minister of the Interior, and that he therefore decided to go meet him in person in Berlin.'

'That's quite something,' said Andrew. 'I remember reading about Kammler. He was in charge of all the top-secret programs, right? The wonder-weapons.'

'That's correct,' said Fiona. 'Only Himmler was between him and Hitler in the Nazi hierarchy, and he was heading up the development of the V-1 and V-2 rockets. He also oversaw the development of new fighter jets like the Messerschmitt 262 and the so-called 'Amerika Bomber' which was a plane intended to fly across the Atlantic to drop bombs on New York. And he and Wernher von Braun worked closely together to develop an advanced two-stage rocket designed to reach the US. I believe they were called the A9 and A10, and when von Braun was being interrogated after the war, he spoke of plans to mount new types of warheads to his rockets with "much more powerful explosives". So it seems von Braun was aware of the efforts to develop a nuclear weapon.'

'Alright, said Andrew. 'So, in other words, if the Nazis actually had an advanced nuclear weapons program, then Hans Kammler would have been involved somehow.'

'Absolutely,' said Fiona. '100 percent. In fact, he would probably have been personally overseeing its development.'

'Right,' said Andrew. 'And if those GRU reports about the two weapons tests are accurate, then it seems like the Nazis were almost there with the bomb, if not actually ready to deploy it. That's quite staggering.'

'It is,' nodded Fiona, picking up another document from her pile. 'And there is one more very interesting piece of anecdotal evidence from August of 1944. At that time, the Romanian Prime Minister, Marshal Ion Antonescu, visited Germany. Up until then, he had fully supported Hitler's vision of creating a greater thousand-year Reich. But by 1944, he had apparently got cold feet and was desperate to get Romania out of the war, since the Soviet army was bearing down on his country. And according to official notes taken during his meeting with Hitler, the Führer did his best to impress Antonescu and keep him onside with talk of a soon-to-be-completed V-4 rocket capable of carrying what he referred to as "a weapon that could kill anything within a 3 km radius". I think it is pretty obvious that this could only have been a nuclear device. And if all of this is true, then it demonstrates beyond any doubt that Nazi nuclear scientists were much closer to fulfilling their ambitions than most history books would have you believe. Just imagine intercontinental ballistic missiles with nuclear warheads in 1945. If the Nazis had been able to secure another few more years, or possibly even just months, to develop these weapons, then the war could have turned out very differently.'

'Yes,' said Andrew thoughtfully. 'And you and I would probably have been speaking German right now.'

'To be honest,' said Fiona ruefully, 'I think it is more likely that we wouldn't even be here.'

'But hang on,' said Andrew. 'If the Nazis did actually develop these technologies, either a nuclear reactor or a weapon, then why have we not heard about it? Surely, the Alsos Mission would have uncovered clues to it, and it would all be public knowledge by now. It's not like those scientists discovered anything that hasn't been surpassed many times over since then, right? There would be no reason to continue to keep it all a secret.'

'It's simple,' shrugged Fiona. 'When the Nazis realised they were losing the war, the scientists did everything they could to remove all traces of their most advanced technologies, in the same way that the Nazi leadership hid all the gold they had stolen from the occupied countries. Many of them were convinced that the end of the war was just a temporary setback. In fact, very detailed plans have been found for a Fourth Reich that was meant to rise from the ashes of World War 2. There were whole cadres of Nazi party members and military officers who were expecting to simply bide their time in anticipation of the right moment to remobilise. So, either they managed to hide their most advanced research and equipment, or the Allies decided not to tell anyone about it.'

'That's an interesting thought,' said Andrew. 'And a little bit disconcerting. I wonder if some of those weapons and technological discoveries remain hidden even now.'

'Well,' said Fiona, 'Think about this for a moment. As I am sure you probably know, the RAF conducted bombing raids on the V-2 launch sites at Peenemünde in northern Germany in August of 1943, and as a result, Kammler ordered most of the top-secret programs to be relocated to various Alpine underground sites in southern Germany and Austria. So, when the Alsos teams swept through those areas in 1945, they found lots of places where research and production of advanced war materiel had taken place, but many of them had been cleaned out by the Germans before being abandoned. The bottom line is that the Alsos Mission probably didn't find everything there was to find. Much of it was either spirited away or hidden somehow. For all we know, there could still be hidden sites out there that no one knows about.'

'That's really fascinating,' said Andrew. 'A bit like that Nazi gold train that is rumoured to still be hidden inside a tunnel somewhere in the mountains of southern Poland.'

'Exactly,' said Fiona. 'During the war, there were dozens of secret projects all headed up by different scientists who all reported directly to Kammler, and there is no guarantee that the Allies ever uncovered every single one of them.'

'That all sounds reasonable,' said Andrew. 'I have another question, though. If the Nazis were close to being able to construct a nuclear weapon, why did the Americans and the British claim after the war that Germany was nowhere near making a working bomb? Even today, that still seems to be the official version of events.'

'I think that's pretty obvious too,' said Fiona. 'I am sure they were convinced that it might cause serious unease among the civilian population to find out that the Nazis almost acquired those weapons and that victory for the Allies was a close call. But there is another important aspect to this. You see, while the Alsos Mission was racing through Germany and Austria from the west, trying to find as many scientists and as much research equipment as possible connected to the various advanced Nazi weapons programs, the Soviets were doing the exact same thing from the east. Both the Allies and the Soviets knew that Germany had been working on nuclear weapons. They both wanted to capture the research and the scientists and then fold them into their own programs, in the same way that the Americans effectively whitewashed Wernher von Braun and some of his team members and put him in charge of the United States lunar space program Apollo. Germany was far ahead of both the US and the Soviets in a whole range of areas, particularly with regard to jet engines and rocket technology, so the German scientists represented huge value to those two countries. And with that in mind, if the Alsos Mission actually recovered working reactors or possibly even some components from a Nazi nuclear weapon, then they would have quietly spirited them away under the noses of the Soviets and never revealed this fact publicly. The best strategy, whether there really were

Nazi nuclear bombs or not, would have been to deny their existence and concoct a plausible story about how Nazi scientists never came close to making a bomb.'

'That makes a lot of sense,' nodded Andrew. 'For all we know, the Soviets could have found a whole bunch of things too.'

'We actually know that they did,' said Fiona. 'A good number of captured German scientists ended up working for the Soviet Union's space and aeronautics programs after the war. So this happened on both sides. It might also be why the US and Soviet nuclear weapons and military jet engine designs turned out to be so similar over the following decades. It was essentially all based on the same German technology.'

'I can see why the West or the Soviets would have wanted to downplay all of this,' said Andrew. 'It would have looked better to say that those new technologies were homegrown. The less said about the Nazi scientists, the better, right?'

'Bingo,' said Fiona, smiling and jabbing a finger at him. 'As soon as the war ended, everyone was keen to move on. And the Cold War arms race made that whole process a lot easier to accept. No one wanted to talk about the past anymore. All that mattered was winning the race to make next-generation fighter jets, nuclear weapons, ICBMs and space rockets capable of going to the moon.'

'Very interesting,' said Andrew. 'Anyway, have you had a chance to look at those Farm Hall transcripts?'

'Yes, I have,' said Fiona, lifting up a stack of documents. 'I have them right here.'

'Ok,' smiled Andrew, leaning forward. 'So, tell me what was on the tapes. I'm dying to know now.'

'To be honest,' said Fiona with a shrug. 'They are interesting, but a bit disappointing.'

'Really?' said Andrew. 'How so?'

'Well,' said Fiona. 'They do provide a glimpse into the minds of these brilliant men as they talk about nuclear physics and all sorts of other things, and there is an especially interesting section after they have been told about the Americans dropping the bomb on Japan. They also keep working on their own theories, discussing the properties of radioactive materials and the practicalities of building nuclear reactors, and they present all this stuff to each other in biweekly lectures.'

'How quaint,' said Andrew. 'Almost as if they think they're on a holiday?'

'That's sometimes the impression they give,' said Fiona. 'But I have to say that most of them come across as quite entitled and self-satisfied. They seem to perceive themselves not as prisoners but as highly valuable assets with lots of options after the war, and they often talk as if they will soon be in a position to decide who to offer their sought-after services to. They even talk about the possibility of going to Argentina, to where a lot of former Nazis fled, and working for universities there. It is all a bit naïve and mercenary, actually. It is as if they haven't quite grasped that they are entirely at the mercy of the Allies, who could have them shot at any moment, which is actually what one American general suggested at one point.

'Really?' said Andrew.

'Yup,' said Fiona. 'There were a lot of Americans that didn't trust any German any further than they could throw them. So putting them to the wall was considered as a serious option. Anyway, these scientists seemed to see themselves as exceptional, and they talked about how they would soon be released to carry on with their work either for the British, the Americans or some other highest bidder. But either way, there is very little in the transcripts to suggest that the Nazis were close to developing a nuclear weapon. And this is quite strange since we know that they understood the physics of it. Both the theoretical side and the practical side. In fact, people like Heisenberg and Von Weizsäcker had been instrumental in discovering how to do it, and we know that several of them had been heading up separate nuclear reactor and bomb projects that had been running for years. But when you read the Farm Hall transcripts, you come away with the impression that they barely understood how to build a reactor, never mind a weapon. And that simply wasn't true. It all just seems really odd to me.'

'So what are you saying?' said Andrew. 'Are the transcripts not accurate?'

'I really don't know what to think,' said Fiona with a small shrug. 'What is clear from the transcripts is that the scientists were very concerned with how they would be perceived after the war. It seems to me that they understood how their work for the Nazis might look, and that they were keen to put a spin on it that did not make them appear complicit. So, perhaps they weren't being entirely honest in their conversations.'

'Do you think they might have suspected that they were being recorded?' said Andrew.

'I assume that is the case,' said Fiona. 'We're literally talking about some of the brightest minds in the world at that time. I have to believe that they would at least have suspected that they were being listened to. And that means that the Farm Hall transcripts might not give us the full picture.'

'Yes, I tend to agree,' said Andrew.

'Anyway,' said Fiona. 'I am meeting up with Ben Ambrose tomorrow for lunch, so I guess I can ask him about it then. Do you want to come along?'

'No thanks,' said Andrew with a small shake of the head as he got to his feet and headed for the kitchen. 'I would feel like a third wheel. Plus, I would have no idea what you two were talking about half the time. I am just a simple soldier, remember?'

He gave her a grin as he glanced over his shoulder.

'Yeah, right,' she said, her voice laced with irony.

'Coffee and some chocolate?' he asked.

'Oh, yes, please,' she said as she stretched out on the sofa. 'Let's watch a movie together. A comedy or something. I need to take my mind off all this stuff. My brain is tired.'

'Sounds good,' said Andrew. 'I'll be right back.'

THREE

Across London, south of the Thames in his home in a leafy part of Wimbledon, Ben Ambrose was sitting at his desk in his study which overlooked the small but neat and well-cared-for garden at the back of his modest terraced house. He was a tall and unassuming man in his early forties, and some might say that he was handsome in a bookish sort of way. His hair was brown and receding slightly at the temples, and his short full beard had acquired a few flakes of grey over the past few years. An affable character with kind, dark brown eyes behind thin-rimmed black rectangular glasses, he could easily have passed for a GP or an accountant.

He worked at the University of London's Institute of Historical Research, and having remained in his work clothes after coming home from his office in Senate House in the heart of Bloomsbury near the British Museum, he was still wearing blue jeans and his trademark beige corduroy blazer over a light blue open-collar shirt. Next to his desk in a wicker basket lay his dog Toby curled up on his favourite blanket. The beagle was almost two years old, and to Ambrose, who was single and rarely went on any dates, Toby had been a faithful companion ever since he had been picked up at the breeder at the tender age of eight weeks. Being a sociable dog, as most dogs are, he preferred to be in the same room as his owner, and when Ambrose was at his desk for hours, as he often was, Toby would simply lounge and sleep next to him until something more interesting happened.

The mild-mannered senior research fellow was sipping Earl Grey tea from a mug emblazoned with the Union Jack while preparing to write another chapter of his upcoming book entitled 'Wonder Weapons of the Third Reich'. Over the past several years, many new sources had emerged from private sources as well as official British, American and Russian archives. They were now shedding new light on the advanced weapons being developed by Nazi Germany towards the end of World War 2, many of which were years, if not decades, ahead of those of the Allies. Ambrose had written his PhD on the wonder weapons programs, but that was almost a decade ago, and he was now in possession of so much more new and fascinating material that he had decided to compile it all and write a whole book about it.

Initially, his focus had been on some of the more traditional military hardware such as the huge Maus tank, which weighed almost 200 tonnes and was several times larger than the already impressive, mass-produced Tiger II. He had also dedicated a chapter to the even bigger *Landkreuzer P. 1000*, which was essentially a fully tracked land battleship. Forty metres long and weighing in at over 1000 metric tonnes, it was bristling with anti-aircraft guns for self-protection, and it was designed to carry a set of enormous 280mm battleship guns, which would have made it the most powerful mobile weapons platform ever built. Other topics for the book were the 800mm *Schwerer Gustav* railway gun, which was capable of firing high-explosive shells weighing 7 tonnes as far as 50 kilometres. Another weapon whose development Hitler had asked Albert Speer to accelerate was the V-3 Cannon. This was a multi-charge gun designed to fire large projectiles at London from underground bunkers near Calais in northern France. Unlike conventional guns, which propel a shell using a single controlled explosion inside a barrel, the V-3 used several staged explosions from multiple separate chambers to continuously accelerate the shells, allowing them to cover the 150-kilometre distance across the English Channel to the British capital. There were dozens of examples of such seemingly outlandish weapon designs, but whatever else could be said about the Nazi scientists and engineers, one couldn't accuse them of being unambitious.

A few weeks ago, however, spurred on by his friend Fiona Keane from the British Museum, Ambrose had stumbled across something much more esoteric. On the back of her recent work on the Farm Hall transcripts, which he himself was very familiar with, he had once again decided to take another look at them to get a full understanding of just how close the Nazis might have come to developing a functioning nuclear bomb.

Ambrose had spent years accumulating as many original sources as he could, and those had proven to be a treasure trove of information about the enigmatic wonder weapon program. His collection of sources included a recently acquired ledger that had been recovered from Albert Speer's Reich Ministry of Armaments and War Production in Berlin during the final days of the war. The ledger had been part of a set of documents he had acquired several weeks earlier. The highly organised and comprehensive ledger listed funds and other resources that had been allocated to various military projects throughout the Reich during 1942 and 1943. It contained an entire separate section dedicated to the secret projects overseen by *SS-Obergruppenführer* Hans Kammler, and Ambrose was familiar with almost all of those. However, at the bottom of the list were two projects that appeared to be grouped together in the ledger, but they had separate amounts allocated to them, suggesting that they were in fact separate research projects. One was called Project Alpha and the other was called Project Omega, but by their choice of names and the way they were listed in the ledger, it seemed obvious to Ambrose that the two were somehow connected.

There was no mention of the exact nature of the two secret projects, but Ambrose had seen a reference to Project Alpha before, and it had seemed to be related to what the German scientists had called Element 94, which was later to be named 'Plutonium'. It had also appeared to involve some of the same scientists that he already knew were involved in Nazi Germany's Uranium Project. This had led Ambrose to wonder if the name Project Alpha had simply been an actuarial name used for accounting purposes to designate the nuclear weapons program. And if that was the case, then what was Project Omega?

Over the next few days after receiving the box of documents, Ambrose had meticulously examined each one in turn. Most of them had turned out to be information that he was already aware of, but then he came across a set of documents captured by the Alsos Mission from the Munich home of a Dr Otto Drexler in 1945. Ambrose had not come across this name before, even though he believed himself to be familiar with all of the main scientists in Kammler's advanced weapons programs. Drexler was apparently a physicist and electrical engineer who had been personally appointed by Kammler to head up a new top secret project somewhere in a location in Austria codenamed 'B8'. The tranche of documents also included a faded manilla folder with the words '*Streng Geheim*' stamped in the top left corner. 'Top Secret'.

When Ambrose had opened it, he was met with the name 'Omega' written in large, bold letters across the top of the first page above the *Reichsadler* eagle of the Third Reich, and he had immediately felt a jolt of excitement. As he began to read through the documents in an attempt to glean the project's nature, the hairs on the back of his neck stood on end. As he had suspected, Project Omega was in fact related to the nuclear weapons effort codenamed Project Alpha, but it did not appear to be directly related to the construction of a fission bomb, which Ambrose knew had been the focus of the Nazi nuclear research efforts.

Unfortunately, the documents contained scant information on the project's precise nature, except to go into significant detail about energy calculations and hardware specifications for the construction of a very large cyclotron that seemed to be at the centre of it all. From the various appendices included in the folder, it had also become clear to Ambrose that whatever Project Omega was intended to achieve, it had been an extremely energy-intensive undertaking, which had required the delivery of large amounts of electrical power generation equipment to an undisclosed location somewhere in northern Austria, possibly the mysterious site designated 'B8'. He would have to look into this more closely at some point.

Now sitting at his desk in his study, Ambrose was re-reading the documents that had arrived along with the ledger. He had received them weeks ago, but he was only now beginning to be able to wrap his head around all the information they contained. He had also been trying to find more information about the mysterious Dr Otto Drexler, but so far without any luck. There were no references to the scientist in any of the historical research that he had come across, which was in itself decidedly odd. Interestingly, the Alsos Mission had seemingly failed to apprehend him after the war, and so his fate remained unknown.

Ambrose decided to leave the Omega mystery aside for now and instead focus on the Farm Hall transcripts in preparation for his lunch meeting with Fiona the next day. The charming Irish historian and archaeologist was about as bright as they come, and since he was supposed to be an authority on Operation Epsilon and the transcripts, he wanted to make sure he didn't end up embarrassing himself. However, after a short while, the seemingly endless transcripts of the thousands of conversations between the German scientists at the Cambridge manor house began to merge into one, and he closed his eyes for a moment as he rubbed his temples. Then he glanced at the clock on his laptop and yawned. To his surprise, it was already ten o'clock at night. His tea was now stone cold, and since he was suddenly beginning to feel very tired, he decided to go to bed. His research would still be there in the morning, and perhaps his meeting with Fiona might give him some new inspiration about how to proceed.

* * *

Adam Holbrook felt as if he was emerging from the deepest drunken sleep he had ever had. It was like the days of old, many decades ago, when he would wake up in his student digs early on a Saturday morning after a particularly raucous Friday night in a local pub near his university. His head felt like it was full of cement, and it seemed to weigh a tonne, and his entire body was yelling at him to stay asleep for a few more hours.

But he hadn't been drinking. In fact, he rarely drank more than a glass of wine these days, so what had happened, and where was he? He realised that he appeared to be reclining somewhere, and in addition to the muffled, distant-sounding humming of an engine, he could feel a faint vibration through his seat. Then there was a small jolt and the familiar squeal of rubber tyres. He was on a plane, and it had just landed. Had he fallen asleep on the way to a holiday? The plane was now braking, and he could feel the deceleration and the slight swerve as it seemed to leave the runway and curve away onto a taxiway.

Amidst the overwhelming dizziness and the strange sense of detachment from his own body, he tried to open his eyes, but he remained in darkness. Focusing all of his attention on his eyelids, he finally managed to prize them open. To his surprise, he was not looking at the back of the passenger seat in front of him. He appeared to be strapped to a plush light grey leather seat inside a small private jet, and he was looking directly at a face that was now both familiar and frightening in equal measure.

Across from him, leaning forward in an opposing seat with his elbows resting on his knees and a cold look in his eyes, was one of the men who had rung the doorbell at his home in Nantua. It was the one with the teardrop tattoo in addition to the short and neatly trimmed black goatee that Holbrook seemed to remember they had both sported. His eyes were hard and probing, and he sat as still as a statue while regarding Holbrook with an expression that was disturbingly predatorial. No longer wearing his blue cap, his head was clean-shaven and slightly reflective in the overhead lights mounted in the plane cabin's ceiling. He had also changed out of the blue overalls from the telecoms company, and it was obvious that he and his companion had merely been using those as a disguise. Instead, he was now wearing a dark grey suit and a white open-collar shirt.

The memories of that shocking and terrifying event suddenly rushed back into Holbrook's mind, and he pressed himself back in his seat as his eyes opened wide, looking at his attacker. He involuntarily raised his left hand to feel the sore spot on his neck where he had been injected with what must have been some form of a powerful sedative, only to discover that his wrists had been placed in rubberised handcuffs. He looked down at them, and his first instinct was to wriggle his hands to try to get out of them. However, as soon as he moved, the man spoke.

'Please don't move,' he said coldly in what Holbrook felt sure was a slight Spanish accent. 'I don't think you want me to use this again.'

The man reached inside his suit jacket and extracted the silver cylinder he had used once before, dangling it in front of his prisoner. Holbrook froze and slowly lowered his hands back down to rest them on his lap. The jolt of surprise and fear at seeing his assailant again now seemed to have cleared his fuzzy mind somewhat, and he looked at the man across from him and blinked a couple of times as he tried to put together a sentence.

'Who... Who are you?' he finally managed, his voice sounding weak and hoarse. 'What's going on?'

'You will find out,' said the man coolly. 'Just do as I say, and you will not be hurt.'

'But where am I?' Holbrook pressed on, resulting in a flash of irritation in the eyes of his captor.

'No more talking,' said the man icily. 'Understand?'

Holbrook nodded and leaned back in his seat. He turned his head to look out of the small window at the taxiway rolling past outside, and when he lowered his head slightly, he was able to see yellow grass growing on sun-bleached soil along the taxiway, and behind it was what appeared to be a set of ramshackle aircraft hangar buildings.

'Look straight ahead,' said the man gruffly.

Holbrook straightened back up and once again leaned back in his seat. He attempted to stretch his legs, but they had been restrained by a metal chain about thirty centimetres long, and when he tried to move them, they felt as heavy as lead. Holbrook tried to lean forward in his seat but was immediately pushed back forcefully by his captor's hand.

'Sit back,' the man sneered as he gripped Holbrook by the collar. 'Don't move.'

'Or what?' said Holbrook, suddenly finding courage that he didn't know he had. 'You've kidnapped me, you bastard. Let me go.'

'That's not going to happen,' said the man.

Before he knew what he was doing, Holbrook had spat in his captor's face, and after flinching and turning his face away, the man tilted his head to one side, pressed his lips together and glared icily at Holbrook while seemingly making an effort not to punch him in the face and break his nose.

'You are very lucky the boss wants you unharmed,' he finally said menacingly as he wiped the spit from his face. 'Otherwise, you'd be in a lot of pain right now.'

'Who?' said Holbrook. 'Who is your boss?'

'*Ernesto*,' said the man, now ignoring Holbrook and looking past him to a seat behind him. '*La capucha.*'

It was only then that Holbrook realised that his other assailant had been sitting in another seat a couple of metres behind him on the other side of the cabin. Evidently, the man's name was Ernesto, and as he rose, he extracted a black hood from a pocket and pulled it down over Holbrook's face. Holbrook was now in almost complete darkness, but the hood's fabric appeared to be perforated enough for him to breathe without any trouble. After a few seconds, his eyes adjusted to the darkness, and he realised that he could make out the rough shapes of his surroundings through its tiny holes.

'Any more trouble,' hissed the man, 'and I will hurt you in places that can't be seen.'

The private jet continued along the taxiway until it came to a smooth stop, and the pilot turned off the engines. A few seconds later, the door to the outside was opened. Holbrook was then manhandled out of his seat and down the steps to the tarmac, and he could only just make out where he was going as the jet engines were spooled down and the high-pitched whine receded to a low hum. With the tattooed captor gripping the back of his neck firmly and guiding him forward, he shuffled along as much as the chain attached to his ankles would allow. About ten metres from the plane was some sort of vehicle, which, from its length and shape, Holbrook assumed might be a large black sedan. Standing next to it, he could just about make out the outline of a tall man. As the trio approached him, he appeared to raise a hand in greeting, and Holbrook could smell cigarette smoke in the air.

'*Hector. Ernesto,*' he said as he calmly greeted the two kidnappers in turn. '*Todo bien?*'

'*Si,*' grunted the man with the tattoo, evidently named Hector. '*Vamonos. El jefe nos espera.*'

'*Muy bien,*' said the tall man casually, moving around to the driver's side door.

Holbrook had never taken Spanish lessons, but his proficiency in French allowed him to glean the meaning of the exchange. Hector was keen to get moving. Their boss was waiting for them. But who was their boss, and where were they?

Now outside under the open sky, Holbrook sensed that it was close to sunset. He looked up and turned his head around in an attempt to see what was nearby, and before he was pushed towards the rear passenger door, he managed to see what looked like flat and verdant countryside in one direction and distant snow-capped mountains in the other. This did not look like anywhere he was familiar with, but it could be somewhere in northern Spain except for the fact that the mountains seemed very high, and he wasn't sure there would be snow on any of the Spanish mountain ranges at this time of year. His last impression before being bundled into the back of the car was the deep orange sun sinking behind the mountains to the west.

The car's passenger cabin appeared unusually large and smelled of leather, and Holbrook thought that perhaps he might be in some sort of limousine. Whoever was responsible for detaining him was clearly not short of money. As the doors slammed shut, he sensed that one of his two captors had got into the front passenger seat while the other had slid onto the seat next to him. Holbrook then leaned back in his seat and noticed pleasantly cool air flowing over him from the car's AC system.

As the vehicle began to move, he turned his head ever so slightly to one side. It was clear that his captors had failed to realise that the tiny holes in the black hood allowed him a faint but just about discernible view out through the heavily tinted window next to him. The car appeared to drive along a small concrete road next to a large hangar, and Holbrook caught a glimpse of some text emblazoned across it. In large white letters, it appeared to read '*IV Brigada Aérea*'. Then the car turned left and then right to exit the airfield through an open gate in a chain-link fence. After that, the driver took them onto a main road and then quickly joined some sort of highway. None of his captors spoke.

The light outside was now fading fast, but Holbrook did his best to try to identify and take note of as much of what was passing by as he could. On occasion, he would spot landmarks such as tall buildings or a water tower, but soon they were surrounded by general urban sprawl that slid by in one barely discernible mass of grey. This continued for about ten minutes until he sensed a change. Buildings were now giving way to the odd open plot and several sparsely built-up areas, and then they found themselves continuing on a two-lane road that cut through a verdant area with hardly any houses. Another few minutes later, as the darkness closed in, Holbrook sensed that they were now travelling on a straight road across a large open expanse of flat countryside. There were bushes and the occasional tree on both sides, and beyond those, he could make out row after row of what might have been low fruit trees or bushes. This seemed to go on forever, and by the time the driver slowed down and turned onto a smaller road, it was completely dark outside. Holbrook could only make out the rough shape of the road ahead, which was lit up brightly by the car's headlights, but at this point, he had no clear sense of his surroundings.

Eventually, the car came to a stop in front of what looked like a tall metal gate through a high wall. The driver waited patiently for a few moments, after which the gates opened and they drove through. Holbrook noticed trees with light-coloured bark planted on either side at regular intervals, and he could feel the slight unevenness of the road surface through the car's suspension. They appeared to be on someone's private road, presumably now close to their destination, and after continuing along the avenue for several minutes, they appeared to finally have arrived. Through the perforated hood, Holbrook could make out the end of the avenue that opened up onto a wide gravelled drive in front of a very large house that sat raised a couple of metres about its surroundings.

The car crunched its way across the gravel, and the driver pulled up at the bottom of a set of steps. Then Hector and Ernesto got out. Hector, who Holbrook was pretty sure was the one who had sat next to him during his unwelcome road trip, stepped around to Holbrook's side of the vehicle and opened the door. Then he gripped his prisoner by the arm and shoulder and extracted him roughly from his seat, and Holbrook could feel the man's raw strength as he did so. With a swift tug, Hector yanked the hood off of Holbrook's head. Then he crouched to remove the chains from his prisoner's ankles.

As he stood there, Holbrook blinked repeatedly and inhaled what at that moment seemed to him like the cleanest air he had ever breathed. And despite the fact that it now had to be about an hour after sunset, the air was still warm and slightly humid. Then he looked around himself. He was standing at the foot of a set of stone steps leading up to the tall black front door of a big and impressive house built from large sand-coloured stone blocks. The general impression was of a manor house built in a rustic Mediterranean style, but with its large windows sitting in heavy black-painted metal frames, it was clear that this was the modern and relatively recently built home of someone of exceptional means.

The house and its large drive were tastefully lit by warm uplights placed to create a soothing and elegant ambience, and they were surrounded by trees that whispered in the gentle breeze. Holbrook could also hear birds chirping happily, and there were the sounds of cicadas in the bushes and the gentle splashing of what sounded like a water feature nearby. With its distinct air of affluence and carefree tranquillity, the house felt more than anything like a luxury boutique hotel.

'*Vamos*,' said Hector, planting a large hand between Holbrook's shoulder blades and giving him a shove forward. 'Move. Up the steps.'

With stiff limbs, Holbrook walked wearily up the steps towards the front door. Still feeling under the dizzying influence of whatever drug he had been injected with back in Nantua, and with Hector and Ernesto filing in behind him, the door appeared to magically open as the trio approached. Inside was a man wearing a black butler's suit and sporting a short grey beard. He was dressed like a servant, but like Holbrook's two unsolicited companions, he was well-built and probably more than capable of physically ejecting unwanted guests from the premises.

'*Buenas noches, Caballeros*,' he said with a small nod. '*Ven por aquí.*'

Then he turned around and led the new arrivals across a large foyer that had auburn wood flooring laid in a fishbone pattern and whose walls were all clad in dark wood panelling. The ceiling was at least five metres above them, and an enormous silver chandelier was hanging from a large, ornately carved wooden ceiling rose. On the walls on either side were large oil paintings in gilded frames, most of whose motives were snow-capped mountains with green pastures in the foreground. To Holbrook, who would be the first to admit that he was no expert in the arts, they all looked distinctly Alpine. However, the most eye-catching features of the foyer were the two large suits of armour that had been arranged on either side of the solid double doors on the other side, directly opposite the front door. Their shining metal armour plates appeared to have been polished to a mirror-like sheen, and they both had large and heavy-looking broadswords at their sides. In addition, they each held a hefty wedge-shaped shield that was painted white with what appeared to be a large black Maltese cross in the centre. The mark of the medieval Teutonic Order.

The suited butler pushed through the double doors and made a left turn along a wide corridor that was equally opulently decorated, and Holbrook began to feel like he had been transported back in time several centuries. At the end of the corridor was another set of double doors, and here the butler stopped and knocked gently. Holbrook did not hear anyone reply, but the butler must have heard someone respond because he gripped the two door handles and pushed the doors open. Then he stepped aside and waited for the trio to proceed past him into a large living room on the other side. As soon as Holbrook and his two captors were inside, the butler closed the double doors behind them.

The living room had two large, white comfortable-looking sofas arranged in a V-shape on a big rug in the centre of the wooden floor, facing away from the double doors. Across from them on the wall was an enormous TV showing a newscast, and it somehow seemed at odds with the room's general decor. Above them was a large plaster ceiling rose and another silver chandelier, and the room's walls were covered in wood panelling painted a soft white colour. A large mirror with a silver frame hung over a wide marble fireplace, but it appeared not to be in use, installed only for decorative purposes.

Only then did Holbrook realise that a man had been reclining in one of the high-backed sofas, and as he got to his feet and began striding towards his visitors, Hector and Ernesto both took a step back, demonstratively leaving the room in the control of what Holbrook assumed was the owner of this house.

'Mr. Adam Holbrook,' said the man, smiling aloofly and using a tone that gave the impression that he had been awaiting Holbrook's arrival for a long time. 'How nice to make your acquaintance.'

The man's voice was silky smooth and perfectly controlled, and Holbrook thought he detected a hint of a German accent, although he couldn't be sure. The man was short in stature with a slightly portly and jowly appearance, and he carried a noticeable paunch. He looked to be in his mid-sixties, and his mid-length grey hair had been slicked back from his heavily receding hairline. With bushy eyebrows and a Roman nose upon which rested a pair of glasses, he had the appearance of a European aristocrat, not that Holbrook had much personal experience with the type. He was wearing a mustard-coloured tweed suit jacket over a pale pink shirt with a flowery blue tie, and in his suit's breast pocket was a matching folded handkerchief. He also wore a pair of dark navy blue trousers and shiny black shoes that looked more appropriate for a cocktail party than anything else. All in all, his mysterious host gave the appearance of someone exceedingly wealthy who lived a very comfortable life, wanting for nothing and having his every need tended to by an army of diligent servants.

As the mysterious man approached him, holding a glass of white wine in one hand, Holbrook remained where he was, his mind racing to understand what on earth was happening and where he was.

'I am very pleased to finally meet you,' said the man, conspicuously not introducing himself. 'My team had you at the top of their list of candidates, so I am glad you're here.'

'Where is "here"?' Holbrook scowled from under his brow. 'I am here against my will.'

'Well, yes,' said the portly man with a wan smile. 'That is unfortunately the nature of things, at least for the moment. You are now in Argentina, and this is my humble abode. We make wine here. Red, mostly. Do you enjoy wine?'

'Who the hell are you?' demanded Holbrook. 'What do you want from me? Money? Are you mad? Do you even realise what someone like me gets paid?'

'Mr. Holbrook,' the man chuckled patronisingly as if speaking to a child. 'No. I am not interested in your money. I am interested… in your mind.'

'What?' Holbrook said, looking confused. 'What are you talking about? Enough of these games. I demand to be told what the hell is going on.'

The well-dressed man gave a silent nod before taking a sip of his wine.

'Mr. Holbrook,' he said, looking thoughtful. 'You have been invited here to assist me and my team in a most important venture that will bring profound change to this world. And I am sure that it will also bestow enormous wealth on anyone involved.'

'And this could include you,' he added reasonably, placing his glass on a small side table next to the sofa. 'Just as long as you do as I ask.'

'Why don't you get stuffed?' Holbrook blurted out. 'I am not going to do anything for you. And I don't care who you think you are or what this is all about.'

'Right,' sighed the man, ignoring the insult and sounding disappointed but not entirely surprised. 'I was hoping to avoid this, but I suppose that was somewhat naïve on my part. Hector, please show Mr. Holbrook the photos.'

Hector moved silently to another small side table and flipped open a slim laptop sitting there. After a few seconds, he swivelled it around so that its screen was facing Holbrook.

'Take a look,' said his mystery host. 'I think you might recognise this person. I believe it is someone very dear to you.'

Holbrook felt his stomach drop and his windpipe constrict as he stared through what felt like a long, dark tunnel at the screen in front of him. It was a picture of his daughter Alice, and it appeared to have been taken recently on the grounds of CERN. He could see that it was recent because she was wearing a new pair of trainers that he knew she was particularly enamoured with and that she had bought only a few weeks ago.

'She's a lovely young lady, I must say,' the man said blithely. 'It would be such a terrible shame if something nasty happened to her.'

Holbrook felt as if he needed to steady himself, wondering for a moment if he was about to faint, but then a burst of fury suddenly erupted inside of him.

'Who the bloody hell do you think you are?' he shouted as spittle flew from his lips. 'If you touch my daughter, so help me God, I will tear your heart out. I swear I will.'

Holbrook's cuffed hands were now clenched in front of him so that his knuckles had turned white, but just as he was about to launch himself at the cretin in front of him, he felt a large and heavy hand being placed on his right shoulder. Hector stepped up behind him and whispered menacingly.

'Calm yourself,' he hissed, sounding to Holbrook like a viper about to strike.

'Come now, Mr. Holbrook,' said the man, apparently unperturbed by his guest's rising anger. 'Please settle down. Your daughter is perfectly safe. At least for the moment. How she fares in the future is entirely up to you.'

Holbrook worked his jaw as he struggled to control himself. He looked down at the floor and took a deep breath. Then he raised his gaze to look at the man in front of him.

'Tell me who you are and why I am here,' he said as calmly as he could manage, although his trembling voice gave away the strain and anguish that he felt.

'All in good time, Mr. Holbrook,' said the man. 'All in good time.'

He picked up the wine and took another sip before placing it back on the side table next to the laptop.

'Please follow me,' he then said.

Turning around, he then headed for a door to his right, and as his shiny shoes clacked audibly across the heavily varnished wooden floor, Hector gave Holbrook a slight push from behind.

'Come along now,' said the man over his shoulder. 'I would like to show you something. Something marvellous.'

Four

Around noon the next day, Fiona packed up her things and placed them in a black leather shoulder bag. Already wearing white jeans, trainers and a light blue top, and with her hair tied up into a ponytail, she donned her short green leather jacket, slung the bag over her shoulder and left the house for the tube station. It was a pleasant sunny day, and as she made her way through the narrow streets of Hampstead, she was excited to discuss her findings with Ben Ambrose, whom she was meeting at a Starbucks Coffee on Wimbledon Hill Road, just across from the tube station. Ambrose had offered to come to Hampstead, but she had insisted on meeting him near his home. After all, he had graciously arranged for her to access a significant amount of his research material, and she was keen to cause him as little inconvenience as possible.

When she emerged onto Wimbledon Hill Road, she spotted the coffee shop across to her right. She jogged over to it, flashing a smile at the driver of a white van who had slowed down to let her cross safely. Checking the time as she entered their intended meeting place, she realised that she was a few minutes early, but when she looked back up from her wristwatch, she spotted Ambrose already sitting at a table for two by the window to the busy street. She gave him a quick wave as she approached.

'Hey Ben,' she said, offering him her hand. 'Have you been here long?'

'Just a few minutes,' said Ambrose, taking her hand in his as he moved two paper coffee cups out of the way to make space on the table. 'I took the liberty of getting you a latte macchiato. I remember you liked that last summer.'

'Wow,' smiled Fiona as she took off her jacket and sat down opposite him. 'And here I was thinking that *I* have a good memory.'

'People's habits rarely change,' he said, gesturing at the froth-covered coffee. 'Is this alright?'

'Yes,' she beamed. 'Thank you. I do love my coffee.'

'I'm in the same boat,' smiled Ambrose, leaning forward conspiratorially. 'I might seem like a nice guy, but I can be an absolute fiend if I don't get my morning coffee.'

'I know the feeling,' said Fiona. 'How is Toby?'

'He's very well,' said Ambrose. 'He's coming up on his second birthday now. He likes his sleep and his food, so as long as he gets those, he is about as happy as can be.'

'Sweet,' smiled Fiona. 'Anyway, how are you? How's it going with the transcripts?'

'I've read through all of them twice now,' said Fiona, 'and there are a couple of things that stood out to me.'

'Shoot,' said Ambrose, sipping his cappuccino.

'Firstly,' said Fiona. 'I simply can't wrap my head around the degree to which these supposedly top-level physicists seem to have no understanding about how to build a nuclear reactor or how to make a bomb. It's just not credible to me. I mean, think about it. One of those scientists, this Weizsäcker character, literally tried to take out a patent on a plutonium bomb in 1941. Secondly, and this is a related point, I only just realised that only 10 percent of the tape recordings were ever transcribed and committed to paper.'

'Yes,' nodded Ambrose. 'Both of those thoughts have crossed my mind, and in that order.'

'I mean, listen,' said Fiona, now in full flow. 'Don't you think it is just a little bit strange that only 10 percent of the tapes were ever transcribed?'

'I don't know,' said Ambrose. 'I am sure that most of what they talked about was of no interest to anyone. For all I know, they were probably arguing and bickering most of the time or moaning about the wonderful English weather.'

'Perhaps,' said Fiona. 'Still. I can't help thinking that there is something more going on here.'

'So, what do you make of it all?' said Ambrose.

'Honestly?' said Fiona. 'I think Heisenberg and the others were trying to conceal just how advanced the Nazi nuclear program really was. I am sure they realised that they were being recorded at Farm Hall, and they were clearly hiding what they knew.'

'That's certainly possible,' said Ambrose. 'And I tend to agree.'

'On top of that,' said Fiona, raising an index finger. 'If it is really true that only 10 percent of the tapes were transcribed, then what about the other 90 percent? Where are they? And what's on them? Why, after all these years, hasn't someone made the effort to transcribe all of it? We're talking about hundreds, if not thousands, of hours of recordings. They are almost guaranteed to contain some new, interesting and informative conversations. Conversations that could give historians a much better understanding of this whole thing.'

'Very good point,' said Ambrose. 'I don't have the answer to those questions, but I think the original tapes are still somewhere in the National Archives. It might be worth putting in a request to access them.'

'And if they won't release them,' said Fiona, levelling an even gaze at Ambrose, 'then we'll know why.'

'What do you mean?' Ambrose said, placing his cup back on the table.

'Well,' said Fiona. 'Not to be a conspiracy theorist here, but I have been wondering if those tapes actually contain a lot more about the secret Nazi weapons programs than what is in those transcripts.'

'Really?' Ambrose said, looking slightly sceptical. 'You think there was some form of coverup?'

'Why not?' said Fiona, turning her palms upward. 'It wouldn't be the first time the government has withheld information from the public. And this information was related to some of the most closely guarded secrets of any nation at any time in history.'

'But why would all this be suppressed even now?' said Ambrose.

'I'm not sure,' shrugged Fiona. 'There could be all sorts of reasons that we are not aware of. But how about the simple fact that Weizsäcker's younger brother Richard, having served in the *Wehrmacht* as a captain during World War 2, ended up as nothing less than the President of Germany? If it became known that his older brother was on the cusp of eagerly wiping out London with a nuke and that he actually almost succeeded, then that might be a bit embarrassing, right? And that's just one aspect of this that is partly public knowledge. Imagine all the things related to this that we *haven't* been told about and that could be regarded as a national security issue and therefore never made public.'

Ambrose nodded thoughtfully.

'I must admit, I never really thought about it in those terms,' he said. 'Essentially, you're saying that the original tapes contain a lot more than what has been released.'

'Precisely,' nodded Fiona emphatically. 'And I'd bet you anything that they would give us a much more accurate picture of what those scientists were really up to. I wouldn't be surprised if they reveal that they almost had the bomb. And then there is the prospect of insights into other advanced projects that have never been disclosed. It's not like the Nazis lacked imagination when it came to dreaming up new weapons.'

'Hmm. Yes,' muttered Ambrose, stirring his coffee pensively. 'Funny you should mention that. I was going through some documents last night, and I came across something called Project Omega, which was headed up by someone named Otto Drexler. Have you ever heard his name?'

'No,' said Fiona, slurping her coffee.

'Me neither,' said Ambrose. 'Anyway, from what I could gather, Omega seemed to be connected to another endeavour called Project Alpha, which I am pretty sure was the Nazi nuclear bomb project. But I can't figure out what Omega might have been, except that it involved a particle accelerator called a cyclotron, and that it was incredibly resource-intensive. As far as I can tell, the Nazis threw huge amounts of money and resources at this thing during the last year or so of the war. And I have discovered that Hans Kammler was overseeing it, which means that it was a top priority for Hitler and the Third Reich.'

'You see what I mean?' said Fiona, raising her eyebrows and cocking her head to one side as she looked at him meaningfully. 'If this Project Omega was in any way related to Nazi nuclear research, then at least some of the scientists at Farm Hall would have known about it, right? Those transcripts come in 24 separate reports covering 240 pages, yet there isn't a single word about anything called Omega in any of them. At least not in the 10 percent that has been released.'

Ambrose paused as the penny dropped.

'But what about the other 90 percent?' he finally asked, rhetorically.

'There,' Fiona nodded with a wink. '*Now* you're getting it. There's no telling what else those tapes might contain, but I am convinced that they contain things that are much more interesting than what we already know.'

'Perhaps even including details about Project Omega?' Ambrose said, allowing himself to be carried along by Fiona's infectious enthusiasm. 'You know, you might be on to something here.'

'No one has ever discovered anything new by sitting on their hands,' said Fiona, picking up her coffee to take another sip. 'So, I think we should keep digging. This could be really big.'

Ambrose picked up his own cup and paused for a moment while looking out through the window at the passing traffic. Then he took a sip and placed it back on the table.

'Since we're talking about all this,' he said, as a few creases formed on his forehead. 'I might as well tell you about something else that has happened recently that is related to this whole thing. Perhaps I could have your thoughts on it.'

'Sure,' said Fiona, folding her hands on the table and leaning forward attentively.

'As you know,' said Ambrose, 'I have been trying to get my hands on as much new material for my upcoming book as possible. This obviously includes things from archives and museums across this country and Europe. I even put in specific requests for files from our intelligence services who have their own archives, some of which aren't actually classified anymore.'

'Yes, I remember,' said Fiona.

'I have also dabbled in various auctions,' said Ambrose. 'Mainly of heirlooms and things coming out of private collections, especially old documents and diaries that might help throw a bit of light on a small corner of my field of research.'

'That's interesting,' said Fiona. 'I didn't realise that there is a market for those things.'

'Oh, it's quite a big thing, actually,' said Ambrose. 'For some reason, original Nazi memorabilia like medals, weapons and uniforms are quite sought after by collectors, and often the museums get involved as well. And then there's the separate area of documents, which also attract a fair amount of attention. Usually, the most headline-grabbing items are things like hand-written notes by Hitler or even draft speeches that can easily fetch tens of thousands of pounds. But every so often an auction lot comes up for sale that includes more boring things like old archive materials, random documents from the Nazi party or from various ministries, or even private letters between members of the top of the Third Reich. And these are the ones I have been focussing on.'

'So, tell me,' said Fiona. 'How has it been going? Any luck lately?'

'Yes,' nodded Ambrose. 'In fact, I have been able to get some interesting documents about the logistics surrounding these various Wonder Weapons projects, as well as several letters written by some of the main players involved. This has helped throw some light on how it all happened and who was in charge of what and when, and all of it will be really useful for finishing my book. But several times during these various auctions, I have also found myself in what I suppose can best be described as a bidding war.'

'Really?' said Fiona, with an intrigued look. 'With whom?'

'That's the thing,' said Ambrose. 'For a long time, I only knew what the bidder looked like, and I was sure that he was not actually the buyer. He is just working as an agent, bidding on selected items up to some prespecified limit. But every single time he shows any interest in an item, he keeps raising the bid until he wins. Every time, without exception. There appears to be no limit. And he only ever bids on items that might have some vague relation to the Nazi nuclear research program. Both the stuff related to a uranium reactor and everything related to the nuclear weapons program, and a mysterious Dr Otto Drexler, who appeared to be heading up the whole thing under the direction of Hans Kammler. The bidder has never shown any interest in any of the other stuff for sale unless it is somehow related to the nuclear program, no matter how spurious the connection. He also hoovers up anything to do with the Alsos Mission or Operation Epsilon. I haven't been able to win a single auction against him since my budget is limited and his appears not to be. It's quite bizarre.'

'That does sound strange,' said Fiona. 'Any idea who he is?'

'Well,' said Ambrose. 'This is where it gets a bit interesting. You see, I have now been in the room with this chap on several occasions, and I have to admit that it has been frustrating. There have been several lots of documents up for sale that I knew for certain would be useful for finishing my book, but I have never been able to get my hands on them. So, one day a few weeks ago, I decided to strike up a conversation with him, but he wasn't exactly forthcoming. He was perfectly pleasant and told me that he is working as an independent agent for a single client from Argentina, but he declined to divulge any more information. In fact, I think he felt that he had already said too much, so he quickly made his excuses and left. I didn't even get his name.'

'All very cloak and dagger,' said Fiona, raising an eyebrow. 'So, was that the end of it?'

'No,' said Ambrose, giving a small shake of the head. 'I found that I simply couldn't just let it go.'

'So what did you do?' said Fiona.

'I'm ashamed to say that my curiosity got the better of me,' said Ambrose with a sheepish look.

'How so?' said Fiona.

'I followed him,' replied Ambrose. 'I just really wanted to know what was going on. And there's no law against sitting near someone in a restaurant, right?'

'So is that what you did?' she asked.

'Yes,' nodded Ambrose with a shrug. 'I followed him into a steakhouse just off Bond Street. You know, one of those that has booths for four people along the windows out to the street? Anyway, he didn't notice me come in after him, and I sat down in a booth just behind him, minding my own business.'

'I didn't know you had such spy craft in you,' smiled Fiona.

'Me neither,' said Ambrose, returning her smile self-consciously. 'I was quite out of my comfort zone. But at the same time, it was also quite exciting. So, I just sat there and waited, until he eventually did exactly what I had hoped he would do. He phoned up his client, and I was able to listen in on the whole conversation. Or at least, his half of it. It was still early, and there were only a couple of other diners there, so I could hear everything he said quite clearly.'

'Ok,' said Fiona, now sitting forward on the edge of her seat. 'So, what did he say then, and who was he speaking to?'

'Well,' said Ambrose. 'First of all, he seemed very deferential and fawning when he spoke, and when he first greeted whoever was on the other end of the line, he used a name that I think was 'Mr Rittenhausen'. Or at least, that's what it sounded like to me.'

'What did they talk about?' said Fiona.

'First, the agent went through a long list of items that he had acquired,' said Ambrose. 'Then he asked whether he should have them sent to the same address as last time once the auction house releases them. And it seemed like the client wanted him to do that. Then the agent asked some questions about money transfers to cover the purchases and commissions and so on. Nothing that stood out. And then the call ended. It probably lasted less than five minutes.'

'Any idea who this Rittenhausen character might be?' said Fiona.

'No,' said Ambrose. 'I did a quick internet search, but all I could come up with were some references to old German nobility. Nothing that allowed me to even take a guess at who this particular person is.'

'Right,' said Fiona, leaning back in her chair. 'I guess that's the end of that, then.'

'Uhm…, well,' said Ambrose haltingly. 'Not quite.'

'Really?' said Fiona with a curious look.

'Well, I thought it was over too,' said Ambrose. 'But then a few days ago, I got an email from the very same agent that I had stalked about a week earlier.'

'Crikey,' said Fiona. 'That's unexpected.'

'Precisely,' said Ambrose. 'He introduced himself as Christopher Bateman, and he began by mentioning the chat he and I had at the auction house. So, I don't think he realised that I had followed him to that steak house. Anyway, he asked if I would be able to join him for a drink and a chat about our mutual interest in World War 2 artefacts and perhaps enter into some sort of collaboration. At first, I wasn't sure what to reply, and I felt a bit foolish having engaged in all that skullduggery, but then I thought I might as well meet up with him and hear what he had to say. You never know, right?'

'Of course,' said Fiona. 'So did you meet him?'

'Yes,' said Ambrose. 'Two days ago. We met up in the afternoon at a pub in Mayfair, and he actually turned out to be a perfectly nice chap. At least initially. Well-dressed and well-spoken. But I also got the sense that he had a clear agenda that wasn't actually his own.'

'How do you mean?' said Fiona.

'Just a feeling,' said Ambrose. 'He seemed as if he had a list of questions for me that he was working his way through. Most of them were about my work and which documents related to the Nazi nuclear program I had been able to collect. But he never actually gave much away about himself or his client. It was all a bit odd. And in the end, I must say, I became quite frustrated. It was as if he was proposing a collaboration, but what he really wanted was for me to divulge what I knew without giving anything in return. And that's when I think I may have messed up a bit.'

'Messed up?' said Fiona.

'Well,' said Ambrose. 'I met up with him in good faith, and I know for a fact that he has secured a whole bunch of interesting documents that I could certainly use for my book, but every time I tried to discover precisely what he had in mind in terms of a collaboration, he just obfuscated and ended up trying to get me to divulge what I had in my possession. I ended up becoming so irritated that I let slip that I knew the name of his client. This Rittenhausen character, whoever he is.'

'Wow. So what happened next?' asked Fiona, now thoroughly captivated.

'It was quite strange, actually,' said Ambrose. 'I saw surprise and perhaps even fear flash briefly across his face. And then it was as if his personality had changed completely. He clearly wasn't prepared for me to drop that name, and he began to clam up and fiddle nervously with his cufflinks. I could practically hear the cogs turning over in his mind as he was trying to decide what to do, and within a few minutes, he seemed to have decided that he had to end the meeting. It was quite an extraordinary change.'

'Weird,' said Fiona, pursing her lips. 'Did he ever mention anything specific, such as the Omega project or maybe that Otto Drexler you mentioned?'

'No,' said Ambrose. 'Nothing that allowed me any sense of what information he had himself.'

'So what happened next?' said Fiona.

'He just made his excuses and left fairly abruptly,' said Ambrose with a shrug and a slight shake of the head. 'No apparent interest in taking things further and actually working together on anything. I ended up sitting there thinking to myself, 'What on earth was this even for?' Why did I just waste an hour of my time with this guy? The whole thing was just completely bizarre.'

With a pensive frown on her face, Fiona leaned back in her chair while regarding her friend across the table as she tried to make sense of what he had just told her.

'Whatever this Bateman guy's plan was,' she finally said, 'it seems pretty clear that he never actually had any interest in working with you on anything.'

'Exactly,' said Ambrose.

'In fact,' she continued, 'it is almost as if it was just some sort of scouting mission to find out if you had access to anything that his client might be prepared to pay for.'

'That is my feeling as well,' said Ambrose. 'It was a bit insulting, really. Like I said, I entered into this with an open mind, but that was clearly naïve of me. And the way he became so visibly uncomfortable when I mentioned his client's name was a bit unsettling. I really don't know what to make of that. What if his client is some sort of gangster artefact collector with a penchant for Nazi memorabilia?'

'If that's the case,' said Fiona with a cautious smile, 'then perhaps it is better that it turned out this way.'

'I suppose,' shrugged Ambrose.

'I wouldn't worry about it,' said Fiona genially. 'At the end of the day, it makes no difference to you or your book, right? Whatever Bateman and his client are up to, you're probably better off having nothing to do with them. Even if the whole thing is really peculiar.'

'Yeah,' said Ambrose thoughtfully as he gazed out of the window. 'I'm sure you're right. Anyway, I should get going. I have a few things I need to do this afternoon.'

'Alright,' smiled Fiona. 'No problem. Thank you for taking time out to meet up. And thanks for the coffee.'

'You're very welcome,' smiled Ambrose as he got to his feet and extended his hand. 'I'm sure we'll see each other again soon. And give my regards to your man. Andrew, was it?'

'Yes,' said Fiona, taking his hand in his and giving it a brief shake. 'I will do that. He remembers you, and he really liked your car.'

'Right,' chuckled Ambrose as they left the coffee shop and paused on the pavement outside. 'I never get to drive the damn thing these days. I can't park anywhere. Maybe I'll take it for a spin down to the South Coast this weekend. I am sure Toby would have a great time on those beaches chasing after seagulls.'

'Oh yes,' smiled Fiona, who had met the dog soon after Ambrose had got him when he was just a small puppy. 'Please ruffle his ears for me. He's such a lovely little dog.'

'I will do that,' said Ambrose. 'Anyway, very nice to see you again, Fiona.'

'You too. Take care,' she said, and then the two of them went their separate ways.

As she jogged back across the busy road to Wimbledon tube station, Fiona could never have known that this would be the last time she would see Ben Ambrose alive.

Five

For the first time since landing the lucrative job as a dedicated agent for what was now his only but very wealthy client, Christopher Bateman was apprehensive about making the weekly call to update him. For months now, he had been supplying the enigmatic Ferdinand von Rittenhausen with everything he could get his hands on related to the work of Nazi nuclear scientists, specifically a Dr Otto Drexler. Bateman had no idea why Rittenhausen was so keen on acquiring these paper relics, but as long as the large fees kept rolling in, he wasn't really interested in the whys and wherefores. Discretion seemed to be the name of the game, and Bateman was only too happy to oblige.

Today, however, he would also need to convey what he had reluctantly come to accept might have been a serious misstep. He considered keeping quiet about it, but given the apparent reach and resources of his client, he had decided to come clean. Rittenhausen was likely to find out at some point anyway. All he could do was apologise and hope that his benefactor would be prepared to let it slide.

Sitting in his small home office with his thumb hovering over the call icon on his phone screen, he hesitated for a moment, but then he pressed it. It rang twice before being picked up.

'Von Rittenhausen,' said a voice casually with a German accent.

'Mr. von Rittenhausen,' said Bateman. 'It's Chris. Chris Bateman. Do you have a few minutes? I'd like to run you through what I have managed to acquire this past week.'

'Christopher,' said Rittenhausen. 'Yes, of course. Please go ahead.'

Bateman then proceeded to go through a list of items that he had secured at auction and which he would be sending to Rittenhausen's private address in Argentina. It included, among other things, the personal notes of a functionary in Heinrich Himmler's Ministry of the Interior and a set of physics books owned by a colonel attached to the Uranium Projekt. There were also some technical documents from a private collector in the United States. These appeared to have been taken back to the US by an army colonel who might or might not have been connected to the Alsos Mission, and they were supposedly related to the German 'Uranium Machine' program. Bateman had no idea if this was in fact the case, but he had been given a free hand to buy up as much material as he could find, so that is what he had done.

'Very good,' said Rittenhausen, sounding moderately pleased. 'I shall look forward to receiving them. And of course, your payment will be sent later today.'

'Thank you,' said Bateman deferentially.

Sensing himself flushing with anxiety, he hesitated nervously for a moment before proceeding.

'There's one other thing,' he said. 'If you don't mind.'

'Yes?' said Rittenhausen. 'What is it?'

'It's just that,' began Bateman, 'there may be a slight problem.

'Go on,' said Rittenhausen, sounding as if he already thought that he wasn't going to like what Bateman had to say.

'Well, it's about Ben Ambrose,' Bateman said. 'The researcher that we agreed I should approach.'

'Yes, I remember,' said Rittenhausen somewhat impatiently. 'What about him?'

'He appears to have discovered your name,' said Ambrose, realising that he might just have jeopardised his relationship with this client.

'What?' said Rittenhausen sternly. 'How?'

'I am not sure precisely how,' said Bateman nervously, already regretting having brought it up. 'He mentioned it during our meeting at a pub. I think he felt frustrated and was perhaps trying to put pressure on me. I'm not sure. I've been wondering if I accidentally mentioned it during our talk at the auction house, but I feel quite confident that I didn't. Although, I guess I can't be 100 percent certain. Anyway, I'd like to apologise. I understand that privacy and discretion are of the utmost importance to you. But I thought I should tell you.'

There was a long pause, during which time Bateman sensed that Rittenhausen was thinking about how to proceed. And then his client said the words that he had dreaded the most.

'Right,' Rittenhausen began, sounding calm but cold. 'Thank you for telling me, Mr. Bateman. I would like to ask you to proceed as normal and send the items you listed earlier to me as soon as possible. I also need you to pause your work as my agent until further notice. I need to decide how to move forward in light of what you just told me. This is a quite sensitive issue to me, and I need a bit of time to decide how to move forward.'

'Right,' said Bateman as he felt the blood drain from his face at the prospect of losing what had become a highly profitable client. 'I see. Once again, I can only apologise.'

'Not to worry,' said Rittenhausen. 'I am sure we can solve this somehow. I will call you back once I have decided what to do, alright?'

'Alright,' said Bateman, squeezing his eyes shut. 'Fine. Ok. I will wait for your call then.'

'Very well,' said Rittenhausen affably. 'Have a good day.'

The line was cut, and Bateman tossed the phone onto the desk in front of him. Then he ran his fingers through his hair.

'Fuck!' he spat, wincing and shaking his head. 'You idiot.'

He should never have told Rittenhausen about his slipup. If he had just kept his stupid mouth shut, everything would probably have continued as normal. But now, he had almost certainly been cut off from what had been his most lucrative run as a private agent.

Why hadn't he just kept schtum? He sighed. So much for honesty.

* * *

Across the Atlantic, Hector and Ernesto Navarro entered Ferdinand von Rittenhausen's large and opulent office inside the main building of the sprawling winery estate named Villa Magdalena in the mountainous province of Mendoza in eastern Argentina. The two hulking, musclebound men were giants next to their diminutive boss, and as they walked in with their clean-shaven heads, small black goatees and shiny grey suits, they looked more like a pair of nightclub bouncers than anything else. The two mostly mono-syllabic brothers, who were both in their early thirties, had worked for Rittenhausen for a handful of years now. Before being hired as his personal protection squad and general fixers, the two of them had spent most of their lives running with the criminal cartels of Mendoza City and serving various prison sentences for drug dealing and violent crime.

Through connections that still remained opaque to them to this day, Rittenhausen had tracked them down and offered them jobs on his luxury estate. And for some reason, the head of their former crime family had agreed to let them go. It had soon become clear that Ferdinand von Rittenhausen somehow had connections in Mendoza City's criminal underworld, although the two brothers had no idea how or why. However, to them, none of that mattered. They had always lived in a dog-eat-dog world where certain people held power while others didn't, and as far as they were concerned,

Rittenhausen, despite his harmless appearance, was now the top dog. He had brought them in and treated them like valued members of his entourage, and they in turn had done what they did best, which was to intimidate people and solve problems with their knuckles, knives and guns. Despite the deep chasm that existed between the two men and their benefactor in terms of background and social status, a level of mutual respect had developed over the years. Now, several years later, the duo would do just about anything for the man who had pulled them out of poverty and given them a life of comfort and relative prosperity that they could only have dreamed of growing up in one of the most deprived neighbourhoods in Mendoza City.

'Gentlemen,' said Rittenhausen. 'Come in. Sit.'

The two large men ambled silently over to a sofa by the window and sat down, the sofa creaking under their weight. Rittenhausen then joined them and reclined in an armchair.

'There's something I need you to do for me,' he said affably, taking off his glasses and polishing them on a handkerchief. 'And it is rather urgent this time.'

The two goons said nothing. They knew better than to interrupt the boss, so they simply waited for their instructions.

'I need you both to go to London,' he continued, lifting an envelope from the side table next to him. 'Tidy up a few... loose ends. Maximum discretion. This file will tell you everything you need to know, but you must destroy it before setting out. I myself will be flying to Berlin for a few days to meet an old friend from Moscow. I'll be staying in my apartment, and I'd like you to remain in London until further notice. It is quite possible that I might need you again. And after my meeting in Berlin, I intend to pay another visit to the site in Austria.'

The two men glanced briefly at each other before looking at Rittenhausen and nodding.

'Okay, boss,' said Hector as Rittenhausen handed him the envelope. 'No problem. We'll take care of it.'

'Excellent,' said Rittenhausen. 'Your flight leaves in two hours. You should pack up and get moving.'

★ ★ ★

Coming home from his meeting with Fiona, Ben Ambrose felt reinvigorated. Writing a book like the one he was in the process of finishing often involved hundreds of hours of research, and sometimes it could get on top of him and he would temporarily struggle for a direction to head in. But Fiona's insistence that there might be much more to the Farm Hall tapes than had been made public had kindled a new flame of excitement in him. What if she was right? What if the Nazis really had been close to making the bomb and it had been kept a secret all these years? That would be hugely significant, and it was bound to make waves in the literary world once his latest work had been published.

He walked up to his front door, put the key in the lock, and was about to step inside when he heard a man's voice calling from behind.

'Excuse me,' he said. 'Mr Ambrose?'

Ambrose turned around to see a courier standing at the end of the front garden path carrying a heavy-looking cardboard box.

'Yes,' said Ambrose. 'That's me.'

The courier hurried up to him with the box and placed it on the ground in front of him. Then he stood back up and handed him the delivery scanner.

'Sign here, please?' said the man, glancing at his wristwatch.

'Who's it from?' said Ambrose.

'No idea, mate,' said the courier as Ambrose returned the scanner. 'Cheers.'

Without further ado, the courier turned and hurried back to the pavement where he turned left and headed for his van, which was parked a bit further along the street. Ambrose looked down at the box. He didn't remember ordering anything, and certainly nothing of that size and heft. It was only when he bent down to look at the delivery label that he realised what he was looking at.

'Wow,' he muttered to himself, somewhat surprised. 'They actually did it.'

Several weeks earlier, after much lobbying and attempts at leveraging his position as a senior fellow at the Institute of Historical Research, he had put in a formal request to the director of legacy archives at MI6 for any documents pertaining to the Farm Hall transcripts, as well as any written reports related to the German Uranium Project written up by Her Majesty's Secret Intelligence Service during the Second World War. Even as he had formulated the letter, he had realised that it was a long shot, and he had fully expected to receive a refusal or to be told that no such reports existed or to be ignored. Yet, here was what appeared to be a whole tranche of material.

Feeling as excited as a small child on Christmas morning, he picked up the box and brought it inside where Toby soon arrived with his tail wagging with excitement. When he went to his office and opened the box, he found a cover letter wishing him good luck in his research and instructing him to return the material no more than three months later. Once he began to look inside, he realised that the contents of the box turned out to be more than he could have hoped for.

There were several reports written ahead of the Alsos Mission and Operation Epsilon, laying out what the British had been speculating about the German nuclear program during the latter stages of the war. There were annotated summaries of the Farm Hall tapes, which Ambrose would have to go over in detail at some point, and there were also minutes from a number of meetings between senior British army officers discussing what had been brought back by the Alsos Mission from the reactor complex in Haigerloch. It was a veritable treasure trove of recently declassified documents, and Ambrose suddenly found himself wondering if he might end up having to split his book into two volumes.

Lifting the documents out of the box one by one, he came across something that soon made everything else pale in comparison. It was a report prepared for the head of MI6 in the spring of 1943 by one of its section chiefs. On the front of its faded cover, written in large red letters were the words 'TOP SECRET', and underneath in a smaller black font was written 'SIS EXEC. EYES ONLY'. This was a report written specifically for the head of the Secret Intelligence Service at a time when Nazi Germany was at its maximum extent, having subjugated almost all of continental Europe and fighting deep inside the territory of the Soviet Union. With a sense of excitement and anticipation now swelling up inside him, Ambrose pushed the cardboard box aside, placed the report on his desk, and carefully flipped open the cover. Then he began to read.

The report was regarding a British intelligence agent codenamed Sparrow who had been working for MI6 during the war. His real name was Edward Harding, and since 1942, he had been attempting to uncover evidence about two highly advanced German weapons research projects called Alpha and Omega. Harding, although highly intelligent and capable, had been regarded as somewhat paranoid and had apparently come close to being fired for what the section chief referred to in his report as his "irrational and all-consuming obsession" with the idea that the Nazis were on the cusp of developing both a nuclear bomb and a device that he was certain represented an even greater threat to the United Kingdom, her allies and their joint efforts to win the war.

According to the section chief, Harding had become convinced that Project Alpha was the nuclear bomb.

'I knew it', whispered Ambrose excitedly as he read on. 'I bloody knew it.'

Only then did he realise that it was very likely that the only reason he now had these documents in his possession was that he had included the words Alpha and Omega in his search query with MI6 archives. They had then simply run his query through their computer systems and delivered to him whatever was in the archives related to those words.

The report went on to say that Harding had also become convinced that Project Omega revolved around some sort of highly esoteric particle physics involving a cyclotron, which the section chief frankly admitted to struggling to understand. Harding was convinced that, as part of Project Omega, the Nazi scientists were pushing ahead with the development of a device or weapon that was unlike anything the world had ever seen before, and that there was a risk that this device could give the Germans a decisive advantage in the war.

Interestingly, the report said that all of Harding's assessments were the result of inferences he had made from information gathered by a loose network of low-level spies placed inside the Third Reich. This network had proven invaluable in providing insights into the inner workings of the Nazi advanced science and weapons programs. However, this was unfortunately also a double-edged sword. It was precisely because the spies were placed low down in the Nazi hierarchy that Harding had struggled to arrive at very firm conclusions about the two secret projects. He had often found himself pursuing hints and vague references to the true nature of Project Omega, and according to the section chief's report, he had on several occasions referred to this frustrating pursuit as "chasing shadows.".

The section chief then recounted how Harding's apparent sense of dread and urgency about the whole affair, combined with the fact that he lacked any hard evidence, had eventually led him to conclude that he himself should travel to a site in Austria where he suspected the twin projects were being undertaken. The section chief had denied his request to leave for the continent, but Harding had seemingly ignored this and left on his own accord. His last message had been sent from Zürich in Switzerland, but after that, he seemed to have vanished without a trace, and nothing was ever heard from him again. Out of an abundance of caution and possibly wanting to avoid any career fallout should Harding's theories prove to be correct, the section chief had then decided to notify the head of MI6 directly and in writing about the missing agent.

'Crikey,' muttered Ambrose as he finished reading the report and leaned back in his office chair.

This was an amazing scoop. If he could find corroborating sources, then this quite literally had the potential to open a whole new chapter in the history of the wonder weapons. But even if this turned out to be the only direct source, it still provided an intriguing glimpse into the MI6 bureaucracy during the war.

Ambrose then spotted another item sitting at the bottom of the cardboard box, and this time it wasn't a document folder. It was a small, slim box the size of a cigar case made of dark varnished wood with brass edging. Ambrose took it out, removed the sticky tape that was sealing it shut, and opened it. Inside were what appeared to be the personal effects that had been removed from Harding's desk at MI6 once it had been determined that he was likely to have died in the service of Her Majesty's Government. Why these had never been handed over to his next of kin, Ambrose could only speculate about. Perhaps they had been locked away for security reasons after his presumed death, at least until the war had ended, and then simply forgotten.

The small, ornate wooden box contained only a few items. A silver Ronson petrol lighter, three 10 Shilling bank notes, a black fountain pen, and several 1 Penny stamps carrying the profile portraits of Queen Victoria and Edward VI. Glancing at the stamps, Ambrose idly wondered if they might be sought after by collectors, but then another item caught his attention. Underneath the stamps was a small brass key, about an inch long, with a faint patina of greenish corrosion. He picked up the key and turned it over in his hand. Across the head of one side was embossed the text 'YALE & TOWNE MFG CO', and on the other side was stencilled what appeared to be a small, stylised yet ornate crown. The small metal key was cool to the touch as he shifted it gently in his hand and inspected it closely, but there was nothing to indicate which lock it might fit.

He placed it back in the wooden box and closed the lid. Smiling to himself as he glanced across the various documents and items he now found himself in possession of, his first instinct was to share news of his latest acquisition with someone. He picked up his phone and composed a short email to Fiona laying out his discoveries. After their conversation earlier that day, he knew that she would probably find this as intriguing as he had, and he was hoping that she would eventually help him sift through it to determine what new information they might contain. Two minds were always better than one. He sent the email and replaced the phone on his desk.

Then an idea came to him. He was going to load the cardboard box with its contents into the boot of his MGB and drive down to Brighton. One of his friends owned a small B&B near the beach, and he had offered

Ambrose first dibs there at a reduced nightly rate. If the small rural annexe was free, he would spend the weekend there going over the contents of the box in detail. He couldn't wait.

★   ★   ★

The next morning, Ambrose had loaded up the sleek, vintage silver MGB with everything he needed for a weekend away, including the MI6 archival material that was now safely stored in the boot. He was ready to go. However, he decided to delay slightly in order to avoid the worst of the traffic and instead go for a walk on Wimbledon Common before setting out for the South Coast around midday. The nearby common was a regular destination for him when he needed to clear his mind and get some fresh air after too many hours hunched over in front of his PC, and he always enjoyed walking there, even on a day like today when a spell of light rain was moving across the capital.

'Come on, Toby,' he said, picking his coat off a hook by the front door. 'Let's go for a walk.'

The inquisitive beagle was immediately on his feet, knowing exactly what was about to happen and making his way excitedly towards the front door.

Half an hour later, Ambrose and Toby were making their way along the footpaths to their favourite spot in the very sizeable public park in South West London. Queensmere was a large pond, although Ambrose tended to think of it as a lake. At roughly 160 metres in length and deeper than any of the other ponds, it lay secluded amongst dense woods by the northern edge of the common near a large cemetery. All around the concrete-edged circumference of the pond was a wide footpath, and at one end it widened further to a large open area covered in fine gravel where several benches had been placed.

It was never very busy in this part of the common, especially at this time of day, and he often found that he could spend half an hour there just sitting on a bench without seeing anyone else. And so it was today where the light rain also kept some of the common's visitors away. Strolling along the edge of the pond with Toby on a lead beside him, Ambrose peered out from under the umbrella at the leaden sky overhead. He stopped by the edge of the pond and looked out over the water, watching the raindrops hit the surface and listening to the gentle pitter-patter as they did so. In the distance, near the other end of the pond, a man wearing a cap was walking along the footpath with his hands dug deep into the pockets of his black leather jacket.

'Lovely weather today,' said Ambrose with cheerful sarcasm as he glanced down at Toby with a smile. 'Do you want a snack?'

Toby looked up at him and wagged his tail, seemingly oblivious to the rain. Ambrose reached into a pocket and fetched a small dog treat, which he handed to the cheerful pet. Barely chewing it, Toby wolfed it down and then looked up at his master again while doing his best to seem as if it had been days since he had last been given a dog treat.

'I'll get you another one when we get home,' said Ambrose.

Toby wagged his tail again, and his tongue shot out and licked his lips. Then he took a step closer and sniffed Ambrose's hand, licking it for good measure.

'Good dog,' smiled Ambrose, stroking Toby's head.

To one side, the man with the cap was now about to pass behind him, and Ambrose turned his head to look at him. He was stocky with dark eyes and a small goatee, and as their eyes met, the two of them exchanged the polite smiles of strangers, merely acknowledging each other's presence, knowing that they would probably never see each other again.

Ambrose turned back to look out over the water just as Toby produced a low and very uncharacteristic growl. Surprised, Ambrose barely had time to look down at his dog before he heard the sound of gravel crunching under the twisting feet of the man behind him. With no time to react, Ambrose felt a powerful arm wrap around his neck and the sensation of something cold being pressed against the side of his neck. A fraction of a second later, just as Toby produced a loud bark, he felt a stinging pain as the liquid inside the jet injector punched through his skin and entered his bloodstream. The effect was almost instantaneous. He felt as if liquid fire had been injected into his veins. A couple of seconds later, while the man held him in place with terrifying strength, the massive dose of high-strength anti-depressant, mixed with a few other rapidly degrading chemicals, reached his heart. It immediately began to falter, beating erratically several times and with such force that a panicked Ambrose thought it was going to burst out of his chest. Then it seized up. He had gone into cardiac arrest. The pain was excruciating, but only for a few seconds. Then the compound mixture reached his brain, and his vision turned to shades of grey before finally disappearing entirely at the end of a long, dark tunnel. Then he passed out.

Hector Navarro kept his left arm locked tightly around the neck of the researcher as the man's legs suddenly gave way under him. Hector held him there as the small dog growled, barked and moved around frantically at his feet, but it didn't bite him. After another ten seconds, satisfied that the injection had done its job, Hector shoved Ambrose forward. Limp like a ragdoll, Ambrose fell face-first into the dark waters of the pond. Floating there with his arms and legs splayed out to his sides like a fully dressed mannequin, he slowly drifted away from the concrete edge as the waves from the impact travelled silently across the surface of the water.

Hector quickly scanned the footpaths on both sides, and once he was sure that no one had seen what had happened, he bent down, gripped Toby's collar and jammed the injector into his neck. The young dog was so confused and distressed by his master's sudden fall into the water that he barely reacted as the injection happened. Seconds later, he flopped onto the ground with a last feeble attempt at a growl. Hector then picked him up by his hind legs, wrung his neck with a bony crunch, and flung him into the water where he splashed down next to his dead master.

As Hector pulled the cap back down in front of his face, thrust his hands into his pockets and began walking away along the edge of the pond, the light breeze pushed Ambrose and Toby along, and their dead bodies floated gently out onto the lake. Once he had disappeared into the woods along a footpath leading back towards the edge of the common, he reached inside his jacket pocket and extracted a phone. He swiped his way to the number he needed and tapped the call button. It rang only once.

'Hector,' said Rittenhausen. 'Give me the latest.'

'Boss,' said Hector. 'It's done.'

'Good,' said Rittenhausen. 'Clean?'

'Yes,' replied Hector. 'No witnesses. He was leaving the house with his dog when I arrived, so I followed him to a park and took care of business. What about the house?'

'Go back there right now,' said Rittenhausen. 'Take whatever documents you can find and then torch the place. Burn it to the ground.'

'Understood,' said Hector. 'Consider it done.'

Six

Fiona had been heading home from Wimbledon when, on a spur of the moment, she decided to get off the tube at Earl's Court and catch the District Line to Kew Gardens tube station. From there, it was a brief ten-minute walk along pretty, tree-lined streets through the well-to-do Richmond to the National Archives. The enormous complex, whose brutalist architectural style seemed like a throwback to the 1960s, was situated a stone's throw from the Thames. Housed inside its roughly eighty thousand square feet of internal space were countless collections of official government records, maps, wills and other legal documents, Foreign and Home Office records, as well as service and operational records of the armed forces, including historical documents from the War Office, the Admiralty and several other branches of the military.

Fiona had visited the archives on numerous occasions in connection with her own research into World War 2, and she knew several of the staff by name. She walked past the square artificial pond that was embedded in concrete in front of the main entrance and headed inside. She made her way to the reception and asked to see Helen Winkworth, who had been working there for almost a decade as a so-called collections and engagement manager. Her job was to liaise with external researchers and facilitate their access to the archives for research purposes.

The receptionist picked up the phone and placed a call to Winkworth's office, and a couple of minutes later, the woman appeared from a lift near the reception area. She was in her early forties with a round and cheerful-looking face, a slightly heavy build and light brown hair reaching down past her shoulders. She was wearing a light pink blazer over a loose flowery top, as well as black trousers and a pair of ergonomic white trainers. Around her neck, on a blue nylon strap, hung a plastic employee badge that also functioned as an access card to the various archives inside the building.

'Hi, Helen,' Fiona smiled as she spotted the familiar face.

'Hello, Fiona,' she said effusively, producing a wide smile as she grasped Fiona's hand and gave it a squeeze. 'What a pleasant surprise. How lovely to see you. What brings you here today?'

'Nice to see you too, Helen,' said Fiona. 'I could use some help with a project I've been working on. It has to do with the war. MI6 records about secret German science programs, to be specific.'

'Ooh,' said Winkworth conspiratorially as she smiled and raised her eyebrows. 'Very exciting. How can I help?'

'I have been working with Ben Ambrose at the Institute of Historical Research,' said Fiona, 'and we've been going over the transcripts from a place called Farm Hall.'

'Oh yes,' said Winkworth, nodding as she retrieved the information from the back of her mind. 'That's where they detained those German scientists, right?'

'That's right,' said Fiona. 'The thing is. Only 10 percent of the transcribed conversations have ever been released, and Ben and I have managed to convince ourselves that the other 90 percent could hold valuable information that could help in our research.'

'I see,' said Winkworth. 'And I am guessing that you'd like me to see if all those transcripts are kept here?'

'Yes,' nodded Fiona. 'In fact, we've been wondering if perhaps the original tapes still exist.'

'I see,' said Winkworth, nodding pensively. 'That's an interesting idea. I don't know why they would ever have been disposed of, so I suppose they would be kept here somewhere. Although I must say that I have never had anyone ask for them before. I'll tell you what. Let me just go and check on the computer.'

'Thanks,' smiled Fiona. 'I'll wait here.'

Winkworth turned and headed for one of the two desks placed behind the reception area. She sat down and pulled the keyboard towards herself, and Fiona could see her fingers flying across the keys as she searched the archive's database. At one point, she leaned forward with a slight frown on her face, and after a moment, she pushed out her lower lips. Then she shrugged and got to her feet.

'I just checked on our system,' she said, as she returned to Fiona, 'and it does seem that we have them. At least they are logged as having been placed in the War Office collection back in late 1945 when it was located on Chancery Lane. But strangely, I can't get the system to provide me with a current location. Let me just go and speak to my manager.'

Winkworth disappeared off again, and a couple of minutes later she returned, walking behind a short and portly man with glasses, a comb-over and purple suspenders over a beige shirt.

'Ms. Keane?' he said as he greeted Fiona with a handshake. 'I'm Brian Moyles. I'm the head of archives research. Would you mind coming with me for a moment?'

'Sure,' said Fiona, surprised by the somewhat odd turn of events. 'Is there a problem?'

'I'll explain,' said Moyles as he began walking towards a set of stairs. 'If you'll just follow me to my office, please.'

Fiona dutifully filed in behind the man, and soon they were sitting on a couple of armchairs arranged around a small coffee table inside his cramped office.

'I'm sorry,' he said apologetically. 'I didn't mean to make a fuss about this, but there's something I need to tell you about your request for the original Farm Hall tapes.'

'Oh yes?' said Fiona, unsure of where this was going.

'We don't have them anymore,' said Moyles almost sheepishly. 'They were stolen.'

'What?' said Fiona. 'When? How?'

'1961,' said Moyles. 'They were part of the classified MI6 war records kept inside the War Office collection on Chancery Lane, but they disappeared.'

'Disappeared,' Fiona repeated, as if trying out the word for the first time. 'Do we know who took them?'

'In fact, we do,' said Moyles, shifting uncomfortably in his chair. 'It was all highly embarrassing, which is probably why you've never heard about it. What I am about to tell you has never been publicly acknowledged, but I am telling you since I am aware of your professional reputation and I think you deserve to know.'

'This sounds serious,' said Fiona.

'Well, yes and no,' said Moyles. 'It's all a long time ago now, but we still try not to shout it from the rooftops, if you know what I mean. Anyway, as you might know, in the decades after the Second World War, there was a lot of spying going on between Britain and America on one side and the Soviet Union on the other. As it turned out, the Soviets had managed to place a double agent inside MI6. A chap named Pierce Latimer. Unfortunately, it turned out that Latimer had been working for Moscow ever since his recruitment during his time as a student at Oxford. Apparently, he was motivated by some sort of idealistic notion that world peace could only be ensured if neither of the two sides in the Cold War possessed the technology to wipe out the other. Which makes sense, in a naïve sort of way.'

'Pierce Latimer,' said Fiona. 'I've never heard of him.'

'That's because he defected and disappeared behind the iron curtain in the autumn of 1961,' said Moyles.

'And the powers that be made sure to keep it hushed up for a long time. But he took with him a whole bunch of documents that appeared to have been carefully selected. In essence, he stole everything he could get his hands on that was related to Nazi Germany's atomic weapons program, as well as any of its spin-off projects. And this included the original Farm Hall tapes and their full transcripts.'

Fiona could barely believe what she was hearing, and she thought back to her conversation with Ambrose about the two projects codenamed Alpha and Omega.

'So you're saying that we no longer have the original tapes or the transcripts?' said Fiona incredulously.

'Unfortunately, that is correct,' said Moyles, pressing his lips together. 'We only have the limited transcripts that I gather you've already seen.'

'The 10 percent that was made public,' said Fiona.

'Correct,' nodded Moyles.

'And no copies were ever made?' said Fiona.

'No,' said Moyles. 'Copying that sort of sensitive material was deemed a security risk since it effectively doubles the chance of it ending up in the wrong hands. Although, in this case, that clearly didn't seem to make a difference.'

'So, there's no way for me to get my hands on those transcripts?' said Fiona.

Moyles shrugged.

'Not unless you plan to go to Moscow and ask the Russian nicely,' he said with a non-committal shrug. 'Those tapes are probably somewhere deep in the archives of the Russian intelligence services. And I suspect the answer from them will be a very emphatic 'Nyet'.'

'Well, that's disappointing,' said Fiona. 'I was really hoping to get a chance to get access to them. Does anyone know what happened to Latimer?'

'I'm not sure,' said Moyles. 'I've never seen any reference to him since he was smuggled across the border into East Germany. He must be long dead by now, of course, but as far as I know, no one knows when or how it happened.'

'Right,' said Fiona, clasping her hands together. 'Well, that's the end of that trail, then. What a shame. Anyway, thank you very much for taking the time to explain this to me.'

'That's quite alright,' said Moyles as he got to his feet and moved towards the door. 'Just keep it to yourself, please. As I said, this is not exactly our intelligence services' finest hour. In fact, it is all a bit awkward, even today. Countries usually don't go around advertising having been embarrassed by a hostile nation, even if it was something that happened many decades ago. And I think that MI6 would prefer it if you or I didn't go around giving this sort of thing a lot of publicity.'

'Alright,' nodded Fiona. 'I understand. Thank you for your time. I really appreciate it.'

'You're very welcome,' smiled Moyles. 'And give my regards to Ben. He and I have spoken a few times. And good luck with your research.'

★ ★ ★

It was late in the afternoon when Christopher Bateman left the impressive family office of the earl to whom he had just offered his services. He had not met the principal himself, of course, but he had instead spent an hour with his taciturn personal secretary. The man, a bearded and disturbingly well-groomed and fragrant individual, had asked a surprising number of questions, mostly related to Bateman's knowledge of ancient Roman jewellery, of all things. The earl appeared to have a penchant for those, and he was keen to expand his private collection. Bateman had felt somewhat out of his depth, and he had not expected to be interrogated about such a niche area. He had been hoping that the sum of his past work for similar high-net-worth clients would have been enough to impress the earl's secretary, but that had not appeared to be the case.

He swore under his breath as he left the townhouse on Grosvenor Square in London's Mayfair. The meeting had been another flop. He could do with a bit of luck after almost certainly losing Rittenhausen as his client. And rather than wait for the letter to arrive, he had decided to hit up some old contacts and see if he could get himself a new client or maybe even several. Perhaps it was wiser not to have all of his eggs in just one basket but instead spread the risk a bit.

He walked to Hyde Park, past Speaker's Corner, and headed for Marble Arch tube station where he allowed himself to be swallowed up by the rush hour surge as he made his way down several dilapidated stairwells and past the ticket barriers towards the tracks. As he emerged onto the platform inside a throng of people from all walks of life wearing all manner of clothing, he had to use small steps to avoid placing his shoes on the heels of the person in front of him.

He eventually managed to find a spot on the yellow line near the edge of the platform where the mass of commuters could pass behind him in their quest for a place to stand. Then the screeching sound of the next train began to build from the black void of the tunnel at the far end of the platform, and finally, the headlights of the next train appeared. Bateman watched as it shot out of the tunnel and moved at speed along the platform where the impatient crowd now began moving forward towards the edge. Doing everything they could to appear nonchalant, each one of the commuters around him was already surreptitiously jostling for position, hoping to be the first to squeeze onto the crowded carriage before the person next to them did so. Bateman sighed. He could barely wait to be pressed up tightly against a commuter with questionable personal hygiene while having his face buried in someone else's armpit. The joys of the London tube.

As the train approached and began to brake, he felt someone pressing uncomfortably close up against his back, and when he turned his head to look behind him, he only managed to catch a glimpse of a light blue denim jacket before he suddenly found himself shunted forward, travelling through the air and falling onto the tracks. The last thing he heard were the screams of bystanders and the wail of the train's horn, and then he landed heavily in the rail trench. The left side of his head connected with one of the metal rails, knocking him out instantly. A second later, the train rushed over him, mangling his body and sending the crowd surging back from the edge of the platform amid screams of distress and panic. Commuters scrambled to get away from the grisly, blood-soaked scene, and there was a rush of people back up the stairwell nearest to where Bateman had been standing.

Inside the shocked and terrified crowd of people rushing for the exit, Ernesto Navarro, now carrying his denim jacket under his arm, allowed himself to be carried along up the stairs to the ticket hall. When he got there, it had been a couple of minutes since he had shunted the defenceless Bateman onto the tracks, and the tube staff had already opened the barriers to allow the crowd to exit the tube station unimpeded. It was clear to Ernesto that no one had seen him push his victim to his death, and all he had to do now was make his way to the hotel room in Marylebone, where he would meet up with Hector who he assumed had carried out his own task. The two brothers would then quietly make their way to London St. Pancras station and catch the Eurostar over to the continent to meet up with Rittenhausen in Berlin.

* * *

Early the next morning, the weather was sunny and pleasantly warm, so Andrew decided to go for one of his regular runs on Hampstead Heath. With Fiona still sleeping, he snuck out of the bedroom and put on his light grey running kit and black trainers. Then he left the house and walked casually towards the East Heath Road entrance to the huge public space. As he passed the gates, he broke into a jog and began making his way into the huge, undulating and wooded common. The sun had only been up for about an hour, and the heath was almost empty, save for a few dog walkers and a couple of fellow runners. Following one of the gravel paths, he picked up the pace as he passed the mixed swimming ponds and continued up to the top of Parliament Hill, from where he could see much of central London in the distance. Then he headed east down a gentle incline across a large open area before turning north and continuing on until he reached the impressive stately home, Kenwood House. From there, he followed the path west and then back down south to where he had started. The entire circuit was about three miles long, and his body was now working at peak performance, so he decided to go for another lap.

On his second approach to Kenwood House, his arms and legs were pumping hard as he pushed the pace even higher, and then he decided on a whim to cut across the heath and head through a more densely wooded area towards the park exit by the 16th century Spaniard's Inn public house, where he and Fiona had enjoyed countless lunches and dinners over the years.

Maintaining a high pace as he followed the narrow, winding footpath through the gnarled old trees, he suddenly heard a female voice cry out up ahead with what sounded like surprise and fear. He kept going and rounded a sharp corner curving around a large tree to see a woman about thirty years of age who was wearing a blue halter neck top, black running tights and pink trainers. But she was not alone. On either side of her, blocking the footpath in both directions, were two young men who, judging by their appearance, were not there for a run or a walk. They both sported tousled, unkept hair and were wearing baggy jeans and dark hoodies, and one of them had a large tattoo on the side of his neck. The men appeared to have been lying in wait behind the large trees, watching the early morning runners while waiting for a suitable victim to pounce on. Now, they were trying to corral the woman between them, spreading their arms out to their sides and slowly approaching her from both sides. She stood frozen to the spot, holding her hands up as if to try to ward off her attackers as she looked frantically from one to the other.

'No,' she said, her voice full of fear. 'Please, just let me go.'

'Calm down, luv,' said the tattooed one casually in a thick London accent. 'We just want your phone, innit?'

'Yeah,' said the other in a husky voice. 'Relax. Give us your phone and we'll let you go.'

'You don't want no trouble with us,' said the tattooed one. 'Trust me. Just hand it over. Now.'

'Don't!' said Andrew loudly, projecting his voice forcefully across the roughly ten metres between him and the trio. 'You two. Leave her alone. Right now.'

The two men turned their heads towards him in surprise and hesitated for a moment. Then the tattooed one, who was closer to Andrew, broke into a sneering grin, turned fully towards the new arrival and reached inside one of the pockets of his hoodie. When his hand came back out, it was holding a steel switchblade, which he snapped open with a well-practised flourish.

'Back off, mate,' he said coldly, locking eyes with Andrew. 'This ain't nothing to do with you, a'ight.'

'Yeah,' said the other. 'Piss off, fella. Or we'll cut you up. You get me?'

Andrew's heart was still pounding in his chest after his high-intensity run, but he felt perfectly calm as he faced the two muggers. Looking at their eyes and their demeanour, he knew instinctively that they were all bark and no bite, and as he stood there watching the two of them try to act tough, he felt no fear whatsoever. During his time in the Regiment, he had mastered almost every type of modern weapon ever designed, but he was equally capable in raw hand-to-hand combat. Compared with him, the two muggers were utter amateurs. They just didn't realise it yet.

'Last chance,' he said coolly as he took a couple of slow steps towards the men. 'Let her go, and I might not even call the cops. Just leave now and don't come back here again. Your choice.'

The tattooed one glared frostily at Andrew for a moment, seemingly taking a moment to register that this newcomer wasn't just going to stick his tail between his legs and run away. Then he chortled and glanced briefly back at his friend.

'Oy! Can you believe this fucker?' he said, after which he thrust the knife forward in a show of aggression as he raised his voice. 'Are you blind, mate? I'll fucking stab you, d'ya hear me?'

The woman had stood frozen in fear during the exchange, but she was now hugging herself and beginning to take small tentative steps backwards to get away from the knife-wielding thug. Andrew took another two steps forward with his arms hanging loose at his sides, and there were now only a couple of metres between him and the man with the knife.

'Just remember,' said the hoodlum menacingly as he took a step forward. 'You asked for this.'

Andrew barely listened to his bluster. Instead, he was watching his every movement, assessing the man's heft, balance and likely speed while looking for the opening that would allow him to take him down.

Without warning, the man suddenly lunged forward with his arm extended and the knife slicing through the air in front of Andrew. It almost looked as if he had been trying to emulate some sort of fencing move, but as an attack, it was next to useless. Andrew whipped his head to one side and took a quick step forward while bringing his lower arm up to deflect the stab. He was now inside the man's reach, and the knife cut uselessly through the air next to his shoulder. An instant later, Andrew's right fist came up from below and slammed into the man's jaw, knocking him out cold. His limp body had barely begun its ragdoll slump towards the ground before the other man threw himself forward. He had now also produced a knife from somewhere, and he was holding it in his right hand like an icepick as he came towards his target.

The attacker reached Andrew just as the tattooed man crumpled onto the footpath. With a shrill war cry, he sliced the blade in a wide arc in front of himself, hoping that it would cut across Andrew's face, but once again, the move had been telegraphed in advance, and Andrew saw it coming a mile away. With his clumsy lunge and the movement of his arms and legs, the man had betrayed his intent several seconds ahead, and Andrew had plenty of time to move back just enough for the knife to scythe through the air in front of his face. Using the man's own momentum, Andrew gripped his wrist and pulled him forward while at the same time twisting hard. He felt a bone snap in the thug's wrist, and as the man fell forward with a cry of pain, the knife clattered onto the hard ground and spun into the grass next to the footpath. Somehow, the man managed to remain on his feet, but an instant later, Andrew was on him again. He grabbed him by the hoodie, spun him around and brought his head back. With one quick, powerful thrust, he drove his forehead into the man's nose where it connected cleanly amid a wet crunch. Then Andrew slung him onto the ground where he curled up, moaning and clasping his broken and bleeding nose with both hands. Andrew approached him again and stood over him.

'Please,' the man whimpered. 'I'm done, a'ight. I'm fucking done. Please stop.'

Andrew took a couple of breaths as he stood there before commanding his body to calm down, and then he took a step back. The two men were no longer a threat, and he could now safely switch out of combat mode. He took another few seconds to calm himself, and then he turned to the flabbergasted woman who stood slack-jawed with her hands in front of her mouth as she gazed down at the two incapacitated assailants.

'Are they going to be alright?' she said in a near whisper, sounding both shocked and confused.

'They'll be fine,' said Andrew calmly. 'They might even get a couple of weeks of free bed and board to recuperate. Don't worry about them. Are you hurt?'

'No,' said the woman as if snapping out of a trance as she patted herself down and made sure she wasn't injured. 'I think I'm fine.'

'Alright. Could I borrow your phone, please?' said Andrew. 'I need to call the police so they can come and take these two away.'

'Of course,' said the woman, extracting her phone from the elasticated holder on her arm. 'Here you go. And thank you.'

Half an hour later, four uniformed police officers had arrived and taken the muggers into custody. After taking statements from both Andrew and the woman, they frogmarched the two thugs away from the wooded footpath and across the heath towards a couple of waiting police cars. Another fifteen minutes after that, Andrew arrived home and walked into the kitchen where Fiona was making tea.

'You were out there a while,' she said. 'Did you go for a long one this morning?'

'Oh,' said Andrew. 'I just got a bit sidetracked. I decided to help a lady get rid of some rubbish.'

'That's very nice of you,' said Fiona, and smiled. 'What a gentleman.'

Andrew said nothing but just smiled and shrugged. There was no need to let Fiona know that someone had just tried to stab him with a knife. It would only make her worried about the next time he decided to go for a run, but he was sure that the two men would never show up on the heath again.

'Early lunch at the Holly Bush?' he said, keen to go back to one of his favourite pubs. 'It's been a while.'

'Sounds good,' said Fiona, grabbing her phone. 'Let me try to book a table. How about eleven o'clock?'

'Perfect,' said Andrew contentedly as he headed for the bathroom to take a shower. 'I'm already looking forward to bangers and mash and a pint of Doom Bar.'

Seven

With the sun now hovering high over leafy Hampstead, Andrew and Fiona left the house and walked the short distance along cobbled streets up the hill to the characterful pub that Andrew had always had a weakness for. As they entered, the barman shot him a quick nod by way of greeting, and then he and Fiona turned left and entered the front room facing the street, where they sat down in one of the booths by the window.

They ordered their food and drinks, and when they arrived, Andrew made short work of the sausage and mash with gravy. Then he leaned back and sipped his ale while Fiona told him about the email she had received from Ben Ambrose the night before regarding his cache of documents from the MI6 archives, including the intriguing story about Agent Sparrow. She then also relayed what had happened during her visit to the National Archives.

'I don't think Mr. Moyles would be very pleased with me telling you about this,' she said. 'But if the government is prepared to trust you with our nation's secrets, then I think I can get away with telling you about this. It's not like it's the keys to our nuclear submarines. It's practically ancient history by now.'

'Still,' said Andrew, placing his glass on the varnished table between them. 'I can see why MI6 would be a bit embarrassed by having one of their people turn out to be a Russian double agent, even now after all this time.'

'I am just really disappointed that I won't be able to get my hands on those Farm Hall tapes or their full transcripts,' said Fiona. 'I am dying to know what is on the missing 90 percent. What were those German scientists discussing that was kept out of the official transcripts?'

'It's a very good question,' said Andrew thoughtfully. 'There has got to be something important on them, right? And if that is the case, then they would almost certainly have been transcribed in their entirety.'

'Pierce Latimer,' said Fiona with a small wince and a shake of the head. 'Stealing things like that is treason, isn't it?'

'Very much so,' said Andrew. 'But he clearly didn't intend to ever come back after he defected. I wouldn't be surprised if the Soviets gave him a medal for it.'

'Right,' snorted Fiona derisively. 'And a ten-square-foot flat in some crappy concrete apartment block somewhere in a run-down suburb of Moscow. I'll never understand those people, even if they thought they were doing it for a good cause. Although I am sure a lot of them did it for money and excitement.'

'You're probably right,' said Andrew. 'There have been dozens of cases like that over the decades. Even today, the Russians have people working for them inside our government and almost certainly also the military. That's just the way they operate. Find some gullible, misguided idealist with an important job, appeal to their greed or spin them a story about how they can help the world by handing over information, and before you know it, the Kremlin is reading the latest updates from No. 10, Downing Street.'

'It sounds cynical,' said Fiona, 'but I fear that you're probably right. Russia is as much an adversary today as it ever was.'

'Absolutely,' said Andrew. 'Anyway, regarding those transcripts that Latimer stole. He must have thought they were worth his defection. Or perhaps Moscow ordered him to defect. Either way, the very fact that they were stolen by a double agent who then blew his cover and defected to Moscow carrying those transcripts should tell you that their contents were considered extraordinarily important.'

'Evidently so,' said Fiona. 'The question is, what was on them? Was it recorded conversations about the Nazi nuclear weapons program, or was it something more than that?'

'Like what?' said Andrew. 'You think Nazis with nuclear weapons weren't bad enough?'

'What if this Agent Sparrow, Edward Harding, was really on to something?' said Fiona. 'What if the Nazi scientists were developing something even more dangerous than a nuclear weapon?'

'I have to say I struggle to imagine what that might have been,' said Andrew. 'Even now, all those years later, those are still considered the most dangerous weapons ever devised.'

'I know that,' said Fiona. 'But what if? I've seen enough plans for outlandish Nazi weapons designs not to rule anything out. And Harding was clearly so convinced that he was prepared to risk his career as well as his life to prove it to his superiors. That has to count for something, right?'

'I suppose,' said Andrew. 'When you put it like that.'

'I can barely wait for Ambrose to show me those documents from the MI6 archives,' she said with a look of excitement in her eyes. 'They sound fascinating.'

Just as she finished speaking, an email pinged in on her phone. She picked it up and looked at the display.

'It's from Helen Winkworth,' she said with a slight frown. 'Why is she emailing me on a Saturday?'

The subject header of the email read, 'Ben Ambrose – Have you heard?', and at that moment, she felt a cold chill run down her spine. It was like a premonition that something bad had happened. When she opened the email, her mouth fell open, and she felt lightheaded. As if the bottom had just dropped out of her stomach. As she gasped and brought her hand up to her mouth, Andrew leaned forward and took her other hand in his.

'What's the matter,' he said, concern etched into his face. 'What's happened?'

'It's Ben,' Fiona said weakly, her eyes fixed on the display, before looking up at him with horror. 'He's dead.'

'What?' said Andrew. 'When? How?'

'Someone found him floating in a pond on Wimbledon Common,' she said, tears now forming in her eyes. 'Him and Toby. Both dead.'

'That's shocking,' said Andrew. 'Do they know what happened?'

'Suicide,' sniffed Fiona, biting her lower lip. 'That's what the police say. Some sort of anti-depressant overdose, at least according to a toxicology report they released about an hour ago. I can't believe this.'

'Did he seem depressed when you met him?' said Andrew. 'He really didn't strike me as that kind of guy.'

'No,' said Fiona with a small shake of the head. 'Not at all. In fact, he seemed really excited about his research. Couldn't wait to get stuck in.'

'So, he didn't seem concerned about anything?' said Andrew.

'No,' said Fiona, wiping a tear from her cheek before hesitating. 'Well. He did mention one thing. But that was just something minor that he had been slightly perturbed by.'

Fiona went on to tell Andrew about the bidding wars for World War 2 documents that Ambrose had suddenly found himself involved in. When she had finished, Andrew tilted his head to one side as he made a pensive face.

'Wait one second,' he said. 'What did you say the auction agent's name was?'

'Bateman,' replied Fiona. 'Chris Bateman. Why?'

Andrew gazed across at Fiona as the cogs turned over rapidly inside his head, and then he suddenly realised where he had seen that name before.

'Holy crap,' he whispered, reaching inside his jacket for his phone. 'I need to show you something. Give me a second.'

He opened a browser and navigated to a news article from earlier that morning. Then he froze and looked up at Fiona.

'What?' she said, perplexed.

He placed the phone on the table, spun it around and pushed it over to Fiona.

'Look at this,' he said. 'It happened this morning. Read it.'

She picked up the phone and began reading as creases formed across her forehead, and when she reached the second paragraph, she read it out loud in a whisper with apparent shock and astonishment.

> "The man, who has now been identified as 38-year-old auctions agent Christopher Bateman, appears to have committed suicide by jumping in front of a tube train at Marble Arch. Rescue services arrived within minutes, but he was pronounced dead at the scene. Police are not treating the incident as suspicious."

Her mouth fell open as she finally took her eyes off the phone to look up at Andrew.

'What the hell is going on here?' she said quietly, her voice filled with burgeoning unease.

'I don't know,' said Andrew thoughtfully after a beat. 'But what I *do* know is that these two events are connected. Two men supposedly committing suicide in London on the same day, and they both just happen to be connected to the Farm Hall tapes and the top-secret Nazi weapons programs. There's absolutely no chance that this is a coincidence. You understand that, right?'

Fiona nodded faintly.

'So they were both murdered?' she whispered incredulously as she struggled to wrap her head around the idea.

'Yes,' said Andrew. 'I am sorry. I know this must be hard to accept. But there is simply no way this happens to both of those two men at virtually the same time. It is obvious that they were both killed. There's definitely something very dark going on here.'

'Like what?' said Fiona, letting the phone slide from her hand onto the table. 'Who's behind this? Why would anyone do this? Farm Hall happened a lifetime ago.'

'I'm not sure,' said Andrew. 'But what is certain is that whatever those old documents contain, and whatever those Nazi scientists were working on, people are still prepared to kill for them, even now. And we have to find out why.'

★   ★   ★

A little over an hour later, Andrew parked his Aston Martin DB9 about a hundred metres down the street from Ambrose's terraced house. Despite the emotional turmoil she felt after learning of her friend's death, Fiona had insisted that they go there as soon as possible to force entry and recover whatever Ambrose had left behind, just in case someone might come looking for his research later on.

However, when they arrived, they found the road blocked by a cordon. The road was drenched in water, and a fire engine was just leaving as they stepped out of the car. They immediately sensed a strong smell of smoke in the air, and when they walked up to where

Ambrose's house was supposed to be, they were greeted by the sight of a burnt-out husk that was still smoking. Parts of the front wall had crumbled, and the roof structure was a mangled mess of charred and blackened timbers jutting up like ribs on a rotting carcase.

'Shit,' said Fiona under her breath as the two of them arrived to stare at the smouldering ruin. 'I don't believe this.'

'Stay here,' said Andrew, giving her hand a quick squeeze. 'I'll be right back.'

He made his way over to a man wearing a dark uniform who was standing by a small BMW sedan painted in the livery of the London Fire Brigade. The man was holding a tablet in his hand and appeared to be in the middle of filling out a form. Along with a long strip of police tape, his vehicle was blocking the road where water still trickled from the property over the pavement and into the drains.

'Excuse me,' Andrew said as he approached the man, whose shoulders were adorned with what he presumed to be station officer badges. 'Hello. Could you tell me what happened here? We're friends of the owner.'

'Oh, right,' said the man, greeting Andrew with a curt nod. 'Sorry, Sir. We've yet to investigate this properly, but if you ask me, it's a gas leak. There was a small explosion late last night, apparently, and within a few minutes, the whole thing had gone up in flames.'

'I see,' said Andrew. 'Does that sort of thing happen a lot?'

'It happens,' shrugged the officer. 'It's rare, but it does happen. Luckily, no one was home, as far as we've been able to establish. I guess your friend was out.'

'Yes,' said Andrew, realising that the officer had yet to discover that the owner of the house had been found dead in a nearby park. 'I guess so. Alright. Thank you.'

'No problem, mate,' said the officer, returning to his electronic tablet.

Andrew returned to Fiona, and the two of them began walking back towards his car.

'They think it's a gas explosion,' said Andrew, 'but I'm not buying it. This was arson.'

'They probably broke in and raided the house for documents before setting fire to it,' said Fiona. 'Bastards.'

'Most likely,' said Andrew. 'Probably an attempt to throw investigators off the scent. Or they were making sure no one else was able to take anything else of value out of there.'

'His car seems to be okay,' said Fiona, pointing back at the silver MGB that was still parked outside.

'I guess that's a small silver lining,' said Andrew, glancing over his shoulder at it.

'Oh crap,' said Fiona suddenly, stopping and placing a hand on Andrew's arm. 'Wait. I've just remembered something.'

'What?' said Andrew.

'Ambrose mentioned he was going down to the South Coast this weekend,' she replied. 'He was going to bring along Toby and his latest research to pour over for a few days. It might be in his car.'

Andrew looked at the vehicle once more.

'It's worth a shot, I guess,' he said, glancing back at the fire brigade officer. 'Let's wait in my car. It looks like the fire brigade has done all they can, so this chap will be on his way soon.'

Fifteen minutes later, the fire brigade BMW left the scene, and Andrew and Fiona stepped out of the Aston Martin. Andrew then opened the boot of his car and extracted a flathead screwdriver from the small toolbox inside the spare wheel compartment. The two of them then returned to what was left of Ambrose's house and walked over to stand by the rear of the silver MGB.

Casting a quick glance around him to make sure no one was watching, Andrew placed the head of the screwdriver on the old-fashioned wafer lock on the MGB's boot. He lifted his hand up and then slammed the heel of it down hard onto the screwdriver's handle. The screwdriver's flat steel head punched down into the lock, which immediately disintegrated and fell to the bottom of the boot with a dull clonk. Andrew then wriggled the screwdriver free, shoved it into his pocket, and popped open the boot.

Inside was a large cardboard box and what looked like a hamper with supplies for the weekend. Next to those was a bag of dog food and a white plastic bowl with the name 'Toby' printed on its side. When Fiona saw the items, she silently pressed her lips together and gave a small shake of the head, as if she still couldn't quite grasp that Ambrose was no longer among the living.

'Focus,' said Andrew gently, sensing her distress. 'Quick. Let's grab the box and get out of here.'

He reached inside and lifted the cardboard box out. As he turned and headed for his car, Fiona closed the boot and clicked it shut, and then the two of them headed back to the Aston Martin. Once back in Hampstead, they placed the box on the coffee table in the living room, sat down on the sofa and opened it up.

'Whatever is in here might point us to who killed Ben,' said Fiona with a pained look on her face. 'And if it's here, we need to find it.'

'Agreed,' said Andrew sombrely. 'Let's go through it all.'

Fiona reached inside it and extracted the documents and the small wooden box that Ambrose had mentioned in his email. While she sat down and began leafing through the yellowed old pages of the formerly classified tranche, Andrew flipped open the lid of the box and inspected each item in turn.

'Agent Sparrow, or Ed Harding, might have been a bit loopy,' he said, turning over the Ronson lighter in his hand. 'But he certainly had good taste. These are quality items.'

He then picked up the fountain pen and held it between his fingers. From its modest weight, it appeared to be empty of ink. Either that or the ink had dried out many years ago, even after having been locked inside the body of the pen. Curious, he took off the cap and unscrewed the top of the pen where the gold nib was attached. Turning it over to look inside the pen's main body, he could see the small cylindrical ink ampule. But there was something else inside too.

'Hang on,' he said. 'What's this?'

As Fiona lifted her gaze from the pages she was scanning through, Andrew extracted a small but relatively thick piece of paper that had been wrapped around the ampule. He put the pen on the coffee table and used the tips of his fingers to spread the curled-up slip out onto the table. In what appeared to be typed print in the centre of the slip was what he assumed was an acronym followed by a word.

DSSD: 8714

'DSSD 8714,' said Fiona pensively as she leaned forward and studied the faded print on the small slip. 'I wonder what it means.'

'There's no way of knowing,' said Andrew. 'It could mean anything. Without knowing more about Harding, we'll never guess.'

He put the slip down on the table and picked up the small, lightly corroded brass key from the bottom of the wooden box.

'Same with this,' he said, holding it up in front of his face and peering at it as he turned it over. 'Yale & Towne Manufacturing Company. I wonder if that even exists anymore. And what about this little crown stamped on the back? Does that mean anything to you?'

Fiona took the key in her hand and studied it closely.

'No,' she said after a moment. 'I don't recognise that. It might be some sort of emblem belonging to whoever the key was made for.'

'What about the documents?' said Andrew, as Fiona put the key back in the box next to the lighter and the other items. 'What do you make of them?'

'Well, it's clearly the documents Ambrose emailed me about,' she said. 'The stuff he received from the

MI6 archives. I'll need a lot more time to go over it. There might be things here that he didn't tell me about or that he hadn't got around to examining. It will take some time. But there are also some brief notes that Ben must have jotted down ahead of his trip down to the South Coast. It's mainly speculation about the B8 site that he mentioned in his email. Nothing concrete, though. I don't think he had any clear sense of what it was or where it might have been.'

'Looks like we'll need to do some more digging,' said Andrew. 'If we're going to have a shot at getting to the bottom of this whole thing, then we need to get to grips with the details of what Ambrose was working on.'

'Yes,' Fiona nodded glumly. 'If you're right that Ben and Chris Bateman were both murdered, then we have to do everything we can to find out who did it.'

'I agree,' said Andrew, getting to his feet. 'Anyway, as Napoleon once said, "An army marches on its stomach," so I think I will run down and get us something to eat. Are you hungry?'

'I'm not really hungry,' said Fiona glumly.

'Doesn't matter,' said Andrew insistently. 'You have to eat something. Pizza?'

'Alright,' Fiona sighed with a reluctant smile. 'If I must.'

★   ★   ★

By the time early evening arrived, Fiona had barely left the living room where documents, books and maps were now spread out over the floor and the two cream-coloured three-seater sofas. Aside from poring over the pages, old and new, she had also made frequent use of her laptop to access information on the internet, not least through the special access logins that her position as historian and archaeologist with the British Museum afforded her. She was now hunched over the laptop which was sitting on the coffee table in front of her, and as Andrew walked in, having just come back from a local pizzeria with two large boxes of fragrant dinner, she looked up and managed to produce a faint smile despite the anguish she felt at the loss of her friend.

'I think I have made some progress,' she said wearily. 'I've worked out what B8 was.'

'Tell me,' said Andrew as he joined her and placed the pizza boxes on the coffee table.

'B8 was a huge secret subterranean complex under a mountain in Austria,' she said. 'Remember how I told you that the Nazis moved all of their most advanced weapons programs underground after the RAF performed bombing raids on the V2 launch sites at Peenemünde?'

'Sure,' said Andrew, flipping open the pizza boxes and grabbing a piece.

'Well,' continued Fiona. 'B8 was one of the largest of those complexes. Its full name was 'B8 Bergkristall', which means 'Mountain Crystal'. And it was massive. In fact, it was so big that it had its own train station inside the mountain, and it had several kilometres of large tunnels. I am quite sure Ben was familiar with this place since it is one of the main underground Nazi facilities that the Allies located after the war. But he probably only knew it as Bergkristall.'

'I see,' said Andrew. 'What was it for? What did the Nazis do there?'

'They built weapons,' Fiona said. 'V-2 rockets and Me262 fighter jets. And they had plenty of free labour to do it.'

'What do you mean?' said Andrew.

'It was located just outside a picturesque little village in Upper Austria called Sankt Georgen an der Gusen, just east of the city of Linz,' she said. 'And the Gusen is a small river that runs through the village and empties out into the Danube. Anyway, a couple of kilometres from Sankt Georgen was a large Nazi labour camp called Mauthausen, where somewhere in the region of two hundred thousand prisoners were kept. More than half of them died in that camp working for the Nazi war machine.'

'Crikey,' said Andrew. 'That's a huge number.'

'I know,' said Fiona, shaking her head. 'Most of them were worked to death in the granite quarries that served all the major construction projects in Germany. The steep steps up from the quarry pit at Mauthausen were called the Stairs of Death, and I don't think I need to tell you why it acquired that name. However, a large number of the prisoners were assigned to the weapons production lines inside the Bergkristall facility. They were pumping out V-2 rockets and Me262 aircraft as fast as possible, especially towards the end of the war, and it became one of the Reich's most crucial manufacturing facilities for advanced new weapons. In fact, it is now known that Hans Kammler himself lived in Sankt Georgen for several months during the latter part of the war.'

'Interesting,' said Andrew. 'I guess that tells us how significant that complex was.'

'Yes,' said Fiona. 'It must have been exceptionally important to the Reich for him to actually live there himself instead of what would have been a life of luxury back in Berlin.'

'So, in other words,' Andrew said. 'Edward Harding was really on to something when he became convinced that something special was going on there.'

'I think so, yes,' nodded Fiona. 'And this is where it all gets interesting. You see, Bergkristall came under the control of American forces on the 7th of May 1945. This was just three days after it had been abandoned by the Germans. Soon after that, the Alsos Mission and Operation Paperclip swooped in to recover anything valuable from there.'

'Paperclip,' said Andrew. 'That was the effort to catch and bring German scientists back to the US, right?'

'That's correct,' said Fiona. 'The Alsos Mission in particular would have been on the hunt for anything related to the wonder-weapons projects, especially the nuclear program. This would have included advanced materials, various weapons components, blueprints and research papers. This was all fairly standard operating procedure for those units, but when they arrived at Sankt Georgen and made their way into the Bergkristall complex, they couldn't believe the size of that place. All told, it had almost nine kilometres of massive tunnels, most of which were 13 metres high and 8 metres wide. In other words, large enough for the production of Me262 aircraft and V2 rockets.'

'Nine kilometres?' said Andrew with amazement. 'That's about six miles.'

'It was absolutely huge,' said Fiona. 'You can easily imagine just how many planes and rockets could be produced there at any one time. And there were thousands of workers working in shifts around the clock. Anyway, in August of 1945, control of the site was then handed over to the Soviets because it fell within their zone of occupation. They supposedly dismantled the remaining hardware and took it back to Russia, and then they finally blew up the entire complex, believing that they had recovered everything of value.'

'Right,' said Andrew. 'So, if the Nazis left anything behind, it would have been taken either by the Allies or the Soviets.'

'That's right,' said Fiona. 'And today, the site is actually a tourist attraction. Visitors can go on a tour of a small section of the complex, but most of it has been walled up and sealed.'

'Alright,' said Andrew thoughtfully. 'But how is this connected to what Ambrose was looking at? Have any signs been discovered pointing to nuclear weapons research being conducted there? And what about Harding? He clearly thought that Bergkristall was engaged in some sort of revolutionary research.'

'Well,' said Fiona, opening a book and flicking her way to the page she was looking for. 'First of all, it is interesting to note that in mid-1944, a directive from the Reich Ministry of Armaments and War Production was issued stating the following:'

"All scientific research on weapons in Germany will cease, except that which concerns itself with weapons of 'revolutionary' character, which in themselves might be battle winners, if not winners of war for Germany."

'This is a direct quote,' said Fiona, 'and if Harding was right, then this directive likely meant that from then on, all activities at Bergkristall were focused on the development of either a nuclear bomb or perhaps something even worse.'

'What could possibly be worse?' mused Andrew.

'I don't know,' said Fiona, 'but either way, there is a real possibility that Hans Kammler and his scientists, including Otto Drexler, were pushing furiously ahead with advanced weapons development. Either in order to win the war or in order to make themselves valuable to the Allies in case Germany lost. This sort of thing became a widespread phenomenon, and it is probably best exemplified by rocket scientist and developer of the V-1 and V-2 rockets, Wernher Von Braun, who handed himself over to the Americans and then went on to play a crucial role in getting the US to the moon ahead of the Soviets a couple of decades later. I mean, just look at the Saturn V rocket that took US astronauts to the moon in 1969. It is a giant booster rocket with a smaller rocket on top carrying a payload of astronauts. It is essentially a scaled-up A9/10, except it carried astronauts instead of a giant warhead. This was all Wernher von Braun's work. Without him, the US would never have got to the moon as fast as they did. Nazi Germany was years ahead of everyone else in a whole range of technologies. Even decades, in some areas.'

'Makes sense,' said Andrew.

'Now,' continued Fiona. 'An important upshot of this line of thinking is that the Nazi scientists might well have hidden away their most advanced working prototypes as the Allies closed in. If nothing else, then simply because they wanted to use them as bargaining chips for themselves and their futures. This could have happened in Sankt Georgen as well. As for whether anything has been found there pointing to nuclear weapons research, several things have been found that point in that direction.'

'Such as?' asked Andrew.

'Various components from high-voltage power supply systems,' said Fiona. 'And the ledger with shipment information that Ben found confirmed that. But there are also other things. Tangible things that have been found at the site, including a ceramic coil, which has been confirmed by experts as being a component for a cyclotron.'

'Really?' said Andrew. 'So, they constructed a particle accelerator inside that mountain?'

'Apparently so,' said Fiona. 'And if that is true, then that points to the Nazis having conducted some type of nuclear research there.'

'Holy crap,' said Andrew, raising his eyebrows. 'That sounds like something out of a movie.'

'Yes,' nodded Fiona. 'But there are strong indications that it could be true. Enormous resources were poured into the Bergkristall complex, and given the potential for Kammler's various projects to turn the tide of war, I am convinced that he was given virtually unlimited access to funds and highly skilled scientists and engineers. Not least this Otto Drexler character.'

'That is fascinating,' said Andrew. 'But are you suggesting that the Nazis managed to hide some of their research there?'

'I believe that's at least possible,' said Fiona.

'But you just said it yourself,' Andrew pressed. 'The Alsos Mission and the Soviets cleaned that place out, right? So they would have taken everything of value.'

'Supposedly so,' said Fiona. 'But what if there are still some clues left? Like that ceramic coil that was found not that many years ago.'

'Right,' said Andrew. 'But it still doesn't really help us move forward with finding out who killed Ambrose. There must be more to this than old ledgers and stories of underground weapons factories. Something that has some sort of relevance to today.'

'You're probably right,' said Fiona, leaning back on the sofa and rubbing her eyes. 'But I think I need a break now. I am bushed.'

'Alright,' said Andrew. 'Let's take a break. Have some of the pizza, and I'll get us a bottle of white wine from the fridge.'

'Thanks,' said Fiona, flipping open the other pizza box and picking up a piece. 'I really need this now.'

Eight

An hour later, having both devoured a large pizza accompanied by a glass of chilled Sauvignon Blanc, they leaned back silently on the sofa, staring at the contents of the cardboard box taken from the boot of Ambrose's vintage car. After a long moment, Fiona sat forward and picked up the small brass key.

'Where does this fit?' she said, thoughtfully. 'And what secrets might it unlock?'

'Could it be for a small chest?' said Andrew. 'Or how about a safe deposit box?'

'No idea,' said Fiona.

'What do you make of the small motif on the reverse side?' said Andrew.

Fiona turned it over and once again studied the small crown stencilled into the metal.

'It's just a crown,' she said, but then she looked closer at the ornaments.

'Wait,' she said. 'This one has three small leaves on the front and two on each side. That's a total of eight all the way around. Those are strawberry leaves, and that makes this a coronet.'

'A what?' Andrew said, reaching for his wine glass.

'A coronet,' Fiona repeated. 'It's the headpiece worn by a duke.'

'Right,' said Andrew. 'What does that say about the key?'

'Well, nothing,' said Fiona, frowning and tilting her head to one side. 'Unless…'

She grabbed her laptop and opened an internet browser.

'You just said it might be for a safe deposit box, right?' she said.

'Yes,' said Andrew, leaning over to look at the laptop's screen. 'So?'

'The paper slip you found inside the fountain pen had 'DSSD: 8714 written on it,' said Fiona. 'What if the first D is for 'Duke', and the SD is for 'Safe Deposit'?'

'Right,' said Andrew, not quite following.

Fiona's fingers flew across the keyboard, and then she turned the laptop's screen to face him.

'I knew it,' she said, looking pleased. 'Look. Duke Street Safe Deposits. It is one of the oldest safe deposit companies in London. Founded in 1873. I'd bet you anything that this key used to fit the safe deposit box there bearing the number 8714.'

'Holy crap,' said Andrew, staring at the key. 'You know, you just might be right about this. And what if the box that fits the key is still there?'

'It's possible,' said Fiona. 'In fact, it probably is. That company still exists at the same address at No. 3, Duke Street in Mayfair.'

'Are you thinking what I'm thinking?' Andrew said, giving her a look with one eyebrow raised.

'Yes. We need to get into that box,' said Fiona. 'That was Edward Harding's personal safe deposit box, and there's got to be something important in there, right? I mean, why else would he have had one?'

'You're right,' said Andrew. 'Let's go there first thing tomorrow morning. Good work, Fiona.'

'Thanks,' she said, reaching for her wine glass and flashing him a coy smile. 'It's hard work being the clever one *and* the pretty one all at the same time.'

'Not to mention modest,' said Andrew with a wink.

★   ★   ★

It was early evening at the idyllic winery in the low mountains near Mendoza City in eastern Argentina, and Adam Holbrook was in the room to which he had been confined since his arrival at the sprawling estate. He wasn't sure if he had been there for two or three days. He had been so confused, angry and disturbed by his drugging, kidnapping, and the veiled threats to his daughter's safety that he had lost track of time. And the jet lag didn't help either. But at least they had fed him well, and his host had come good on his promise to serve him some of the locally produced wine. At first, he had rejected out of hand the idea of drinking his captor's wine, but then he had decided that he might as well try to make the most of the situation. As long as he didn't rock the boat, Alice would be safe. Or so he hoped. The wine, as it turned out, had been excellent, and it had helped calm his nerves.

The room was basic but of a decent size and stylishly decorated. More than anything, it was akin to a very comfortable hotel room with a large bed, a writing desk and an ensuite bathroom. It also sported a kitchenette and a large window overlooking an expansive and beautiful garden beyond which stretched neat rows of grapevines as far as the eye could see. However, the window was locked, and so was the door to the corridor outside, and both were fitted with heavy-duty latches and locks that he would never be able to break open without some sort of metal tool. Not that he had seriously considered doing so. Whether his mysterious host was truly prepared to harm Alice was unclear, but Holbrook was not ready to take that chance. At least not until he had a better sense of what his options were.

The man had eventually introduced himself as Ferdinand von Rittenhausen, but he had provided no further information that would allow Holbrook to get a sense of who he really was or what he wanted. Shortly after Holbrook's arrival at the winery, Rittenhausen had taken him on a stroll through the estate's gardens, closely shadowed by what he could only assume were the two brothers who evidently served as Rittenhausen's personal protection squad.

During their walk, his always well-dressed host had casually explained that he needed Holbrook's particle accelerator expertise for a project he had been working on for almost a decade. Precisely how a winemaker with German ancestry living in Argentina had ended up attempting to build such a complicated and expensive device was still a mystery. However, when Holbrook had been shown the large subterranean facility where its construction was already well underway, it had become clear to him just how serious Rittenhausen was about the project.

The facility's main chamber was circular and spanned roughly fifty metres across, and its ceiling curved up towards an apex some twenty-five metres above the smooth white-painted concrete floor. Inset into the roughly fifteen-metre-high walls were three levels of walkways circling all the way around and built one above the next, providing a clear view of the device from all angles. At the centre of the cavernous space was a bulky, ring-shaped metal device that was at least ten metres across and placed in a vertical position. It was smothered in cables and wires of varying sizes, as well as dozens of additional pieces of complex equipment that were attached to it every few metres. When Holbrook had first been shown to the facility, there had been several teams of engineers working on it, and Rittenhausen had told him that those men would all be under his direct leadership from now on.

Surrounding the device were banks of other high-tech equipment, as well as a control station where computers and terminals were set up, presumably to run the experiments. The device looked familiar to him from his decades-long work at CERN, yet at the same time, it was subtly different. It was more substantial somehow, and the numerous bulky arrays of what he recognised as electromagnets were much larger and more powerful than what he had been used to. In fact, their output seemed to him to be complete overkill for a cyclotron.

The underground facility could only be reached by a small train riding along a tunnel stretching from the villa. Holbrook speculated that the research complex was located under a nearby mountain, and judging from the time it took the lift from the winery to reach the rail tracks below, he estimated that the facility was as much as fifty metres underground. As Holbrook knew better than anyone, a particle accelerator such as a cyclotron needed to be constructed deep underground in order to shield it from cosmic radiation, which could play havoc with the sensitive equipment, especially at very high power outputs. And as far as Holbrook could determine, this cyclotron was an extremely power-hungry beast, which was part of the reason that he had been taken here against his will. Rittenhausen evidently needed someone to help build the intricate arrays of powerful electromagnets that would guide the stream of particles as they tore around the circumference of the device. He also needed someone who was capable of calibrating and fine-tuning the accelerator in order to maximise its capacity to produce and then retain a large flow of protons travelling at close to the speed of light.

All of this was well within Holbrook's field of expertise, but there was one thing that he did not understand. Every single particle accelerator that he had ever worked on had the sole purpose of producing and accelerating sub-atomic particles that could then be fed into a particle collider such as the one he had been working for at the LHC in Geneva. However, this cyclotron was a closed loop, and it was not connected to any particle collider. In fact, it appeared to be the case that Rittenhausen was simply aiming to produce as powerful a stream of protons as was possible, and that he wanted to confine that torrent of particles inside the cyclotron, building it to levels that Holbrook had never seen done before, and about which he had serious safety concerns. The ultimate purpose of the device still escaped him, but he was sure that he would eventually find out. After all, if Rittenhausen wanted the best out of him, he would need to be told precisely what the project was trying to achieve.

Throughout their limited number of interactions, Holbrook had sensed that Rittenhausen seemed to carry an absolute conviction that it would be a question of time before Holbrook was won over. He seemed to think that once the true nature and potential of the project were relayed to him, Holbrook would welcome the opportunity to work on it. All in all, Rittenhausen came across as someone who never ever took no for an answer, and who always got what he wanted in the end.

His host had now apparently travelled to Europe for a business meeting, and in a few minutes, someone would be along to escort him down to the subterranean research facility, where he would spend the next ten hours. After that, he would be taken back to his room and served a decent meal, if precedent was anything to go by. He was very comfortable here, but there was no denying that he was inside a prison. Having gathered the courage a couple of times to ask Rittenhausen what the mysterious device was for, he had been met with an indulgent smile and a shrug accompanied by the now familiar refrain.

'All in good time, Mr. Holbrook. All in good time.'

★ ★ ★

The next morning, Fiona once again found herself weighed down by the sadness and numbness caused by the murder of Ben Ambrose. Andrew did his best to console her and attempt to cheer her up, although he knew there was nothing he could say to take away the pain she felt. The best he could hope for was to try to take her mind off the tragic events in Wimbledon and instead steer her razor-sharp intellect towards more constructive thoughts that might help them in their quest for the truth about his death.

When they left the house at just after nine o'clock and took the tube from Hampstead towards central London, Fiona seemed to have regained some of her sense of purpose, and they headed for central London, hoping to be able to return home with more clues to the deepening mystery. Stepping out of Bond Street tube station just shy of twenty minutes later, it was a short walk from there to Duke Street. The Duke Street Safe Deposit company was at the northern end, just off Manchester Square, and Fiona had already called ahead to make an appointment for 9:30.

The old building at No. 3 was a wide, four-storey Georgian townhouse with tall, narrow windows. It had been built with London stock bricks that had long since faded from their original pale yellow to a dark greyish brown. The façade had two smaller windows with iron bars on either side of a wide and sturdy-looking oak door with large square brass studs, no doubt chosen to lend credence to the resident company's ability to offer both safety and security to its prospective client.

When Andrew and Fiona entered, they were met by the duty officer, Mr. Davis, who was a smartly dressed middle-aged man with neat grey hair and a charcoal suit. He greeted them courteously at the reception, checked the small brass key that Fiona was carrying, and then took them down the stairs to the basement level and the vault inside, where all of the company's safe deposit boxes were kept safely locked away. The vault's large polished steel door was opened with a hand-cranked wheel, and behind it was another security measure in the form of a door made of heavy steel bars. Through the bars, Andrew and Fiona could see several rows of brushed metal floor-to-ceiling deposit boxes lined up neatly on a carpeted floor that was a deep burgundy colour. Spaced equidistantly inside the room were four support columns that had been clad in heavily veined beige marble.

'This way,' said Davis, turning left once he had unlocked both doors. 'The legacy deposits are over here. We had a major refurbishment in the 1970s where the vault was expanded with this new area, so all the old deposit boxes from before that time remain where they have always been. In fact, they are in the strong room that was used when this company was first started by my great-great-grandfather.'

He unlocked another door and led them into a much smaller space that was similar in design but looked noticeably older. The floor was covered by a faded dark blue carpet, the doors on the deposit boxes were all painted a pale green, and they all had brass locks placed at their centre. Next to each lock was a small polished brass plate with a four-digit number engraved into it.

'Here we are,' said Davis. 'What number was your box again? 8714?'

'That's correct,' said Fiona, suddenly feeling nervous in case the key didn't fit the lock.

'Eight. Seven. One. Four,' Davis repeated slowly as he homed in on the correct location. 'Right here. Now, please insert your key and turn it anticlockwise.'

With some trepidation, Fiona did as he had asked, and she was relieved to feel the small brass key slip into the lock smoothly. When she turned it, there was a satisfying sensation of tiny metal parts clicking aside and then of the lock disengaging.

'Wonderful,' said Davis matter-of-factly. 'Let me retrieve the box for you.'

As Andrew watched, Fiona stepped aside to let Davis pull the steel box free of the shelving unit and put it on a small varnished wooden table nearby. The box was roughly half a metre long, thirty centimetres wide and about ten centimetres tall.

'Would you like some privacy?' Davis said politely as he clasped his hands together in front of his chest.

'Thank you very much,' said Fiona. 'That would be appreciated.'

'Certainly,' said Davis with a small bow, and then he backed away one step, turned around and left the vault room.

Andrew and Fiona huddled around the steel box, and Fiona then lifted open the lid. Inside was a single item that appeared to be a leatherbound notebook. The dark brown leather was worn and faded, and it was held together by a wide leather strap with a small buckle like that on a belt.

'What have we here?' said Andrew as Fiona gently picked it up, undid the buckle and opened it.

'It looks like a diary,' said Fiona, intrigued. 'It must be Edward Harding's personal diary.'

She carefully leafed through the first several pages of the old and yellowed, lined paper. They contained a large number of handwritten and dated entries, along with what appeared to be sketches of various technical plans and schematics. Some showed the layouts of buildings, while others were of different pieces of equipment.

'Look,' she said, turning the pages gently and pointing at individual paragraphs. 'Page after page of this stuff. And I am already seeing the name 'Omega' appearing on several of them. This could turn out to be a real gold mine. But I need some time to go over all of this.'

'Alright,' said Andrew. 'Looks like we got lucky. Let's get out of here.'

★ ★ ★

An hour after their visit to Duke Street, Andrew and Fiona were back in Hampstead. Soon after that, Andrew had to head for his office at Sheldrake Place, where the special investigative unit of the SAS he worked for was located. His boss, Colonel Strickland, had asked for a meeting and a debrief on the jet suit test in Gibraltar. Leaving Fiona to pour over Edward Harding's diary, he left the house, got into his Aston Martin and drove to Kensington.

Upon his return roughly three hours later, he found Fiona ensconced on the sofa with a notebook and a pen, and the diary lying open on the coffee table next to her.

'How's it going?' he asked as he sat down. 'Anything interesting?'

'It's fascinating,' said Fiona. 'Harding lays out his whole line of thinking in these pages, right from the beginning where he notes that the very purpose of the diary, as well as the reason for keeping it under lock and key in a safe deposit box, is that he had come to suspect that MI6 might have had a German mole somewhere within the organisation. He never wrote anything specific about who it might have been, but he was clearly concerned that the Germans might catch wind of his efforts. And that would obviously have burned his entire intelligence network inside the Third Reich.'

'So, was he as paranoid as his superiors thought he was?' asked Andrew.

'I don't know,' said Fiona, placing a hand gently on the diary. 'It's hard to say. And even if he was, that doesn't mean that there *wasn't* a spy inside MI6. There were almost certainly several at that time. Anyway, what is clear from reading this thing is that he had indeed uncovered some sort of major project being developed inside the Bergkristall complex. But according to his sources, it didn't appear to have anything to do with either the V-2 rockets or the Me262 fighter jets. Project Omega was something entirely different, and it had something to do with a particle accelerator, just as Ambrose said it did.'

'What does the diary say about Project Omega?' said Andrew. 'Any specifics?'

'It talks about it in loose terms,' said Fiona, 'but there's nothing very tangible. Harding actually seemed to be fumbling in the dark, trying to work out what it might be. At least to begin with. Listen to this entry.'

December 18th, 1942.
"The reports I have been receiving via radio from inside Germany over the past few weeks are increasingly giving me cause for concern. The Omega project, whatever it might be, appears to be making rapid progress, although it is wrapped in an impenetrable veil of secrecy. From what little I have been able to glean, it appears to be an advanced technology stemming from the German cyclotron research, but I have yet to discover what its true nature or purpose is. However, what is clear to me is that Hitler, Kammler and Speer are pouring vast resources into it. The latest encrypted dispatch from Berlin indicates enormous amounts of military and industrial materiel being transported by train to the site codenamed B8, located somewhere in the Austrian Alps. The reports mention deliveries of enormous amounts of electrical power generation equipment capable of producing tens of millions of watts. Enough to light up most of London. What could possibly require such power?"

'Wow,' said Andrew. 'Power generation equipment capable of powering most of London?'

'It is an enormous amount of energy,' said Fiona. 'Anyway, in this entry from a few weeks later, he seems to have closed in on what Project Omega might be all about. Listen.'

January 9th, 1943.

"All of the material I have been able to gather over the past two years now leads me to the inescapable conclusion that what the Germans are developing is some sort of advanced weapons delivery system, possibly for Project Alpha and the atomic bomb. A system that is infinitely more capable and dangerous than the V-2 rockets. The precise nature of the system still eludes me. However, everything I have received from my network inside Nazi Germany during the past two months hints at a technology that is unlike anything that currently exists, and that will prove truly revolutionary. I must make my superiors take heed."

Andrew looked pensive and rubbed the stubble on his chin for a moment before speaking.

'So, according to Harding,' he said. 'Project Omega was not a weapon but rather some sort of weapons delivery system?'

'That's what it sounds like,' said Fiona. 'And it seems as if he was beginning to think that he had to take drastic measures to prove it. Listen to this next entry just a few days later.'

January 12th, 1943.
"The weapons delivery system appears to be making steady progress, and according to my sources, several tests are about to be conducted imminently. I have now finally discovered where B8 is located, and I know what I must do. The only course of action left for me is to travel to the site near Sankt Georgen in Austria where I will rent a room at the inn called Gasthaus Reinthaler. I must get inside the B8

complex, see it for myself, and bring back photos proving to my superiors that I haven't lost my marbles, but that something of the utmost importance to Her Majesty's Government is taking place inside that mountain."

'And guess what,' said Fiona, looking up at Andrew. 'The inn, Gasthaus Reinthaler, is still there. Right in the middle of Sankt Georgen, which happens to be a very pretty little village, even if it is only a few kilometres from a Nazi concentration camp.'

'I guess this is proof that Harding actually ended up going to look for the Bergkristall site,' said Harding. 'He was a brave man travelling into the Reich by himself like that.'

'He was,' said Fiona, 'although he was clearly worried about what might happen to him. Listen to what he wrote next.'

February 6th, 1943.
"This may be my last entry. Tomorrow evening, I will travel to Austria via Switzerland against the wishes of my superiors, and then I will attempt to locate and enter the B8 complex. In truth, I do not know whether I will ever return, but if my suspicions about what is happening there are correct, then perhaps my own life will prove of trifling significance. A German scout and collaborator has managed to send me a photo of a possible drop site designated KDB, in case I should need it. Its nature appears strangely apt, given that I may not return. May it be guarded by the shepherds of the mountain dead if I fail to make it

back to London alive. I pray it doesn't come to that. May the Lord watch over me."

'That all sounded very ominous,' said Andrew as creases formed on his forehead. 'The mountain dead? That has a particularly menacing ring to it. But I guess he was right in fearing that it might end up costing him his life.'

'That's how it appears,' said Fiona. 'He never made it back, and to this day, no one knows what happened to him.'

'Any idea what KDB might mean?' said Andrew.

'None,' said Fiona, shaking her head. 'It could mean just about anything, but it is clearly some type of location near Bergkristall.'

'I'd love to know what that weapons delivery system might be,' said Andrew. 'And precisely what technology were they developing there that was supposedly so revolutionary?'

'Me too,' said Fiona. 'But given that it seemed to be inextricably linked to Project Alpha, which we now know was the quest for a nuclear weapon, I think it is safe to say that Omega was most likely a delivery system for an atomic bomb.'

'Yes, I agree,' said Andrew. 'That's the only logical conclusion. But it still doesn't get us any closer to discovering what that system actually was or precisely how it worked.'

'I know,' said Fiona. 'But if it was unrelated to the V-2 or any of the later, more advanced rockets, then what could it be? It is difficult to imagine a delivery system that could be more impactful than the A-9/10 rocket system designed to reach New York. But

Harding was clearly convinced that Project Omega somehow involved a particle accelerator. A cyclotron, which, as far as I understand it, was a very new technology at that time. But I am at a loss as to how such a device might be employed.'

'Well, I'm no particle physicist either,' said Andrew, 'so I'm afraid I can't contribute much here. Perhaps we should try to reach out to someone who is an expert in that field.'

'That's a good idea,' said Fiona. 'That might be our next step. It would be useful to get a much better understanding of those things. I think we should definitely look into it.'

'By the way,' said Andrew, pulling his phone from his pocket and opening the email app. 'I managed to pull some strings with our intelligence services earlier today and called in a favour.'

'Cloak and dagger stuff,' said Fiona.

'It's more like keyboard and hacking these days,' said Andrew. 'But anyway, based on information found in the internal transaction databases at various major auction houses both here in this country and abroad, they managed to pin down exactly who Chris Bateman was working for. And they have very kindly provided me with a quick info sheet on the guy.'

Andrew slid a sheet of paper across to Fiona with two photos of a distinguished-looking middle-aged man. One looked to have been taken by a security camera inside a bank, and the other appeared to be his official passport photo. When she looked at them, it seemed to her that the portly, middle-aged man in the photos, with his grey mid-length backswept hair, his narrow eyes and his aquiline nose, had an indefinable aristocratic quality to him. Or perhaps it was just the way he looked into the camera in the passport photo.

'Who is he?' she said, intrigued. 'And how did you get these?'

'The less I tell you about the source, the better,' said Andrew. 'Anyway, he is a dual German and Argentinian national, and he has residences in both countries. It turns out that he is registered at a number of major international auction houses under the name Ferdinand von Rittenhausen. He is apparently descended from a line of minor German nobility on his mother's side. Currently, he appears to split his time between his winery in Mendoza in the south of Argentina and a large apartment in central Berlin's diplomatic quarter.'

'So, is he just some old-timer looking for the past glory of his fatherland?' said Fiona.

'He might be,' said Andrew. 'But there's more to him than that. A lot more, actually. You're going to love this next part.'

'What?' said Fiona with an expectant smile. 'Come on. Tell me.'

'The full name on his Argentinian birth certificate,' said Andrew, as he raised an eyebrow conspiratorially, 'is Ferdinand Drexler von Rittenhausen.'

Andrew produced a sly smile as he watched Fiona, waiting for the penny to drop.

'Drexler?' she said, astounded. 'Really? You mean to say that he is a descendent of Otto Drexler?'

'That's right,' said Andrew. 'It turns out that Otto Drexler married into a German noble family before World War 2. A young noblewoman by the name of Magdalena von Rittenhausen. They had a son called Maximillian and a grandson called Ferdinand.'

'Holy crap,' said Fiona. 'That puts a whole new spin on this.'

'I know,' said Andrew. 'As I am sure you're aware, a lot of the leadership of the SS were German nobility, and in a roundabout way, Otto was no different. And so his grandson Ferdinand was also born a noble, such as they come in Germany.'

'And yet, he seems to have hidden the name Drexler,' said Fiona. 'Why would he do that?'

'Perhaps he preferred the posh name,' said Andrew. 'Or perhaps he didn't want anyone to know who his grandfather was as he was busy hoovering up anything related to his work.'

'Fascinating,' said Fiona. 'Although it doesn't really bring us any closer to what Otto Drexler was working on in that Bergkristall complex. But it is certainly an intriguing aspect to this whole thing. All of this somehow seems personal to this Ferdinand von Rittenhausen.'

'Exactly,' said Andrew. 'His motivations seem to extend beyond science, money or whatever else might be involved here. I've asked the chaps on our intel desk to see what else they can dig up. So, there might be more coming.'

'Great,' said Fiona.

'Anyway,' said Andrew. 'Knowing what we know so far, what do you think should be our next move?'

Fiona smiled. Then she shifted in her seat and folded her hands on her lap as she contemplated how to phrase what she was about to say.

'I have an idea for something that I think could really help us move this forward,' she finally said with a disarming smile. 'But I don't think you're going to like it.'

NINE

It was approaching noon when Ferdinand von Rittenhausen left his apartment on the top floor of a corner block on Friedrichstrasse in Berlin. The historic old building, which now had a coffee shop on the ground floor and apartments on the floors above, was painted a sandy yellow, and it had been constructed in the highly ornate, late 19th-century *Gründerzeit* architectural style, which drew heavily on different time periods, including gothic, renaissance and baroque, all mixed into one. It was located right next to the infamous Checkpoint Charlie, which had served as the main crossing point between East and West in the divided city during the Cold War when the Berlin Wall had cut through the capital, thus separating two distinct realities from each other for around three decades. The checkpoint had seen several exchanges of spies between the East and the West. It had witnessed daring escapes from the East to freedom, and it had been the scene of an armed standoff between columns of

American and Russian tanks in 1961. An episode that had very nearly escalated into an exchange of live fire.

Rittenhausen, who considered himself a renaissance man as well as a historian, had chosen this place for its historical significance, and with money being no object, he had bought the entire top floor and converted it into a large modern apartment. He had always had a keen interest in history, even as a child growing up in Argentina, and especially that of the Third Reich. When his father had revealed to him the story of his illustrious grandfather, Dr Otto Drexler, his heart had surged with pride at being the descendant of such a brilliant scientist and patriot.

His father had told him that '*Opa*' Otto had managed to escape Germany to Argentina at the end of the war along with his young wife Magdalena. Ferdinand had never met his grandfather since he died from a mysterious illness not long after arriving in South America. However, his position in the top echelons of Nazi science had become a source of pride for the young man. And when he had begun delving into precisely what Otto had been attempting to build for Adolph Hitler, he knew then that he had to pursue it himself. This eventually led him to study physics at university, although he had soon realised that he did not possess his grandfather's brilliance. But this was far from an insurmountable obstacle. Money, of which his family had plenty because of the riches it brought with it from Germany, could solve any such problem. All he had to do was find the right experts to pursue his project, and he had become quite adept at this over the years.

With his German Shepherd named Blondi kept on a lead, Rittenhausen left his apartment, walked down the stairwell and exited onto the street via the private entrance on Zimmerstrasse. Blondi had been named after Hitler's dog of the same breed, but no one ever seemed to realise its origin when he called out its name in the nearby park. He turned left and walked along the pavement until he reached Wilhelmstrasse, where he took a right. A couple of minutes later, he stopped and looked across to the corner of Wilhemstrasse and Voss Strasse, picturing in his mind the imposing Reich Chancellery the way it had looked after its construction in 1939. It had now been replaced by a dull, nondescript and downmarket block of flats. What an insult.

As far as he knew, his grandfather had never set foot inside the chancellery himself, nor had he ever met the esteemed Führer. However, Otto Drexler's superior, Hans Kammler, with whom he had worked closely for several years, had been a frequent visitor to Hitler's office where the two men had pushed forward funding and support for some of Nazi Germany's most impressive scientific endeavours.

Rittenhausen's own historical research had led him to conclude that much of that groundbreaking science had been brazenly absorbed into the science programs of the Allies after the war, including the rocket program headed up by that turncoat, Wernher von Braun. The man who had shamelessly left the broken post-war Germany behind to live a comfortable life working for the enemy in the United States while developing moon rockets and ICBMs. Some of the allied science and weapons programs had never acknowledged actually having German origins, which Rittenhausen saw as an affront to the brilliance of German science. But he also knew that several of the other advanced Nazi projects had been cleverly hidden before Germany's defeat, and that they had never been discovered by the Allies. This included the project spearheaded by his exceptionally gifted grandfather, who had managed to flee south to Italy, and from there had escaped the clutches of the Allies and their Alsos Mission.

As far as Rittenhausen was concerned, Otto Drexler had never been given the recognition he deserved as a pioneering nuclear physicist, but with his own large-scale project in Mendoza in Argentina now taking shape, he was about to right that wrong. And once that had been achieved, he would become unimaginably rich by licensing this new and paradigm-shifting technology to governments and multinational corporations alike for eyewatering sums of money. He had no doubt that entire countries would be prepared to almost bankrupt themselves to acquire it, and he would shortly become the wealthiest person in human history. And with great wealth would come great power. Power to influence the world. However, this dream could only be fulfilled if he could perfect the device and make it operational, and much of the success of that endeavour rested on Adam Holbrook's shoulders. In other words, Rittenhausen had to make sure that Holbrook was well-motivated. There was literally nothing he would not do to make sure that happened, and he had no doubt that Alice Holbrook was the perfect leverage.

He bent down to ruffle Blondi's ears, and then he continued along Voss Strasse to Ebertstrasse where he took a right and walked almost due north past the huge, wooded Tiergarten Park. Halfway along, he passed by the vast memorial to the Jews who had been murdered across Europe during the Second World War. It covered an entire city block, roughly five acres, and it consisted of 2,170 vaguely coffin-shaped grey concrete blocks arranged in a maze-like grid. It was meant to serve as an indelible reminder to the citizens of Berlin and the world of the atrocities committed by Nazi Germany during the war. But to Rittenhausen, it was merely an eyesore designed to keep the German spirit cowed, and to ensure that his proud fatherland would continue to submit and prostrate itself at the feet of whichever president happened to occupy the White House in Washington DC. He was quite convinced that the number of Jewish victims of the war had been hugely exaggerated by the Allies, and that most of the so-called evidence from the concentration camps had been fabricated in order to shame Germany after her defeat. But even if many of the prisoners in those camps had indeed died, Rittenhausen saw their demise as necessary for the rise of the Third Reich, and they had at least been productive for as long as they were still alive.

Rittenhausen was well aware that in today's political climate, his views would be seen as abhorrent by most people. But as far as he was concerned, that just reflected a lack of perspective and appreciation for the ebb and flow of history on their part. Granted, the world had experienced brief periods of relative peace throughout the long arc of history, but as a rule, groups of human beings with different ideologies and different cultures have been warring furiously ever since the first ape picked up a rock and worked out how to hit the ape next to him over the head with it in order to take his food.

Despite what the soft, weak-minded elites of today might think, peace was the exception, and war was the norm. It was the natural order of things. The natural state of man. And to Rittenhausen, Homo Sapiens had never truly moved on from those basic impulses, despite appearances. It had only ever managed to convince itself that it had done so. But from his perspective, only one rule was truly valid across time and space. Conquer or be conquered. Hitler had understood this, and perhaps someday, one of his erstwhile countrymen would see the light and lead the nation to glory once more.

Ignoring the memorial to his right required some effort since it was more than 150 metres long on the side facing the street, so he instead turned his gaze across the road to the pleasantly green Tiergarten Park as he walked along with Blondi by his side.

A few minutes later, he was standing in front of the imposing Brandenburg Gate, which, more than anything else, had been a symbol of the divided city during the Cold War. In fact, the Berlin Wall had run just yards from it on the eastern side, and it had been here that people from both East and West had converged to climb on top of it in November of 1989 when the wall finally fell.

All of that, however, was of little interest to Rittenhausen. When he looked up at the ornate, 26-metre-tall neo-classical monument, he saw in his mind's eye huge red banners with a white circle and a black swastika at their centre hanging from it. This was how the gate had been decorated on numerous occasions during Nazi Germany's heyday. He then peered up at the bronze statue at the top of the monument. It depicted the ancient Greek victory goddess Nike riding in a chariot pulled by four horses and holding aloft a standard, with the German eagle sitting atop a laurel wreath encircling the easily recognisable iron cross. The statue, which was covered in a thin layer of green corrosion, had been there since its installation in 1791, and since then it had looked down upon a series of very different time periods in Germany's history. But regardless of time and circumstance, its symbology was as clear as it was unequivocal to Rittenhausen. The German spirit was irrepressible, and one day it would rise again to dominate the world. And if his work could have a small hand in achieving this goal while he also made sure to enrich himself in the process beyond his wildest dreams, then he would be both happy and proud to follow that path.

'Come on, Blondi,' he said, ruffling the dog's ears once more. 'Let's go. Our friend is waiting.'

Blondi wagged her tail, and then the two of them crossed the road and walked under the imposing Brandenburg Gate towards the planned meeting point.

★ ★ ★

Ten minutes later, Rittenhausen entered the swish restaurant where he was scheduled to meet up for lunch with his friend of many years from Moscow. The man's name was Grigory Komarov, and he was a Russian oligarch who owned a penthouse in one of Berlin's most expensive high-rise buildings, and whom

Rittenhausen has done financial business with numerous times. Most recently, Komarov, who, like all oligarchs, was well connected in the Kremlin, helped Rittenhausen secure a stake in a Russian private bank that had been listed on the Moscow stock exchange. Komarov also had connections at the successor to the KGB, the FSB, since he had worked there as an intelligence officer before going into private business. And it was this avenue that Rittenhausen had now become keen to pursue.

Komarov was a corpulent, barrel-chested man in his early sixties. His physique told the story of his indulgence in culinary pleasures and a lack of impulse control, but his solid frame, hard suspicious eyes and leathery bearded face hinted at his days as a fit and formidable active field operator for the KGB. His thick grey hair was slicked back over his head, he wore a dark pinstriped suit with a purple tie, and several of his fingers were adorned with hefty gem-studded rings matching his glinting cufflinks. On his left wrist was a large, limited edition Gucci watch, and the fingers on his right hand gripped a long Cuban cigar from which rose a thin wisp of grey smoke.

'Komarov, my friend,' said Rittenhausen as he joined the Russian at a table where two crystal shot glasses filled with premium vodka were waiting. 'Very good to see you again.'

Komarov did not get up to greet Rittenhausen, but he instead smiled broadly and gestured at the chair opposite before speaking in heavily accented English.

'Ferdinand,' he said, as always making a habit of only ever using someone's first name. 'I would never say no to a meal with an old friend. How are you? Still making wine?'

'Yes,' said Rittenhausen as he handed his jacket to a waiter and sat down. 'And the wine is getting better every year. I will send you a case after this growing season. The weather has been perfect in Mendoza this year, so it should be excellent.'

'Good,' said Komarov, drawing out the vowels. 'I'll look forward to it. Now, tell me. What can I do for you? Something about some old documents, yes?'

'Indeed,' said Rittenhausen. 'If you remember, we spoke a long time ago about Operation Epsilon and the Farm Hall transcripts.'

'Ah, yes,' nodded Komarov sagely. 'Brought to Moscow by comrade Pierce Latimer, yes?'

'That's correct,' said Rittenhausen. 'At the time, I said to you that I didn't think they contained anything of value to my research, but I have since changed my mind.'

'I see,' said Komarov sagely. 'You have discovered something new?'

'I have,' said Rittenhausen, deciding that it was better not to tell Komarov everything.

Several years earlier, he had spent some time looking into the transcripts and deciding that they were worthless to him since none of the scientists interned at Farm Hall had been directly involved with Project Omega. However, after Christopher Bateman had sent through a tranche of documents hinting at the notion that perhaps some of the scientists had provided input in the form of theoretical models for the construction of a large-scale particle accelerator, Rittenhausen had then decided to go back to trying to acquire the transcripts.

'I think they might prove useful to me after all,' he continued. 'And I remember you mentioning that you thought Latimer had defected with more than what has been officially acknowledged by the British.'

'I believe so,' nodded Komarov. 'These things are never as they appear.'

'Right,' said Rittenhausen, reaching for his glass of vodka. 'So, I would be most grateful if you could assist me in getting hold of those transcripts from the KGB archives. I thought that a man with your connections might be able to make it happen.'

Komarov put on a vague frown and seemed to consider the idea for a long moment, but then he nodded slowly, picked up his own glass, lifted it from the table and put on a contemplative face.

'Naturally, it will come at a price,' he said, reasonably. 'I'm sure you understand. It's just business.'

'Of course I do,' said Rittenhausen. 'I understand completely. And I am more than happy to pay.'

'Good,' said Komarov with a wide grin as he leaned forward and moved his glass towards Rittenhausen. 'It's a deal then. I will see what I can do.'

'Thank you,' said Rittenhausen graciously. 'That's all I ask. *Prost!*'

'*Nazdorovie!*' grunted Komarov contentedly. 'To our health!'

The two men clinked their glasses together, and then they downed the expensive vodka in one gulp.

'Now, my friend,' said Komarov, placing the shot glass on the table and picking up the leatherbound à la carte menu. 'Let's eat.'

★ ★ ★

Back in Hampstead, Fiona had just returned from the kitchen with two steaming mugs of freshly brewed coffee along with some chocolate cookies served on a tray.

'I've been thinking,' she said as she sat down. 'I really think that we should keep pursuing those Farm Hall tapes. The only possible reason for Pierce Latimer to be ordered by the KGB to steal them and then defect to the Soviet Union is if they contained something really important. Something of genuine value to the Soviet scientists and their weapons programs. Why else would the KGB have ordered Latimer to burn his cover and defect with the tapes and the transcripts? He would have been an extremely valuable asset to them, yet they effectively outed him to get their hands on the Farm Hall stuff. I am absolutely convinced that the tapes must have included recordings of the German scientists discussing projects Alpha and Omega.'

'Alright,' said Andrew, sipping his coffee. 'Let's say you're right. But those tapes and transcripts are now in the old KGB archives in Moscow. How do you propose we get to them? Are you suggesting we get on a plane, knock on the front door and ask nicely?'

'No,' said Fiona. 'Not exactly.'

'Then what?' said Andrew haltingly, already sensing that Fiona was putting together a plan in her head that was either brilliant, utterly hare-brained or a bit of both.

'Alright,' said Fiona, showing him her palms as if to placate him preemptively. 'Just hear me out on this. We know for a fact that those tapes made their way to Moscow, courtesy of Pierce Latimer.'

'Yes,' nodded Andrew.

'We also know that immediately after entering Berlin in April of 1945,' she continued, 'a special unit raced straight to the Kaiser Wilhelm Institute, where they took possession of all the research documents they could find that were related to the Nazi nuclear program. And in other areas of the country, the Soviets took control of as much German uranium as they could find and immediately shipped it back to Moscow.'

'Right,' said Andrew. 'I am sure they had their own version of the Alsos Mission.'

'Exactly,' said Fiona. 'They were just as keen to get their hands on the Nazi scientists and their research as the Allies were, and many German scientists did in fact end up working for the Soviets after the war. Several hundred of them, if I remember correctly. And so, it stands to reason that some of them just might have been involved in either Alpha or Omega.'

'Yes,' nodded Andrew. 'I suppose that's a fair assumption.'

'And finally,' said Fiona. 'It is also a known fact that the Soviets successfully infiltrated both the Manhattan Project and the British nuclear project codenamed 'Tube Alloys'. And this brings me to an important conclusion. I think that there is every reason to believe that the Soviets also managed to infiltrate the German nuclear research program, including Alpha and Omega.'

'Okay,' said Andrew. 'I guess that's a possibility. But where are you going with this?'

'If everything I have just said is true,' said Fiona, 'then there are almost certainly original documents, technical schematics and blueprints about projects Alpha and Omega hidden inside the KGB archives along with the Farm Hall transcripts. And none of it has ever been released.'

'That's a perfectly logical conclusion,' said Andrew. 'Although obviously a bit speculative. But what do you suggest we do to get hold of that material?'

'We go to Moscow and break into the archives of the Lubyanka building,' said Fiona, deadpan.

Andrew looked at her expressionless for a moment while trying to work out if she was pulling his leg, but the look in her eyes told a very different story. This was no joke. She really meant it.

'Please tell me you're not serious about this,' he finally said. 'You want us to break into the headquarters of the Russian secret service? The FSB? In the middle of Moscow?'

'I'm deadly serious,' said Fiona emphatically. 'No one in their right mind would even consider doing that, right?'

'Damn right,' said Andrew.

'And that's exactly why it just might be doable,' she insisted. 'The Russians will never expect anyone to try something this crazy, and that just might mean that there are ways of doing it that they haven't even thought of or prepared for.'

'Listen, Fiona,' said Andrew, reasonably. 'That place is built like a prison. In fact, it *is* a prison. Thousands of people have walked in there and never come out again, at least not while still vertical. I'm telling you, any sane Russian would do just about anything to never set foot in there.'

'Exactly', said Fiona emphatically. 'And that's why this could work. They have spent all of their attention designing that building to be impossible to get out of. I bet no one has ever thought of making it just as difficult to get into it. If we can just get inside that place, then I am sure we can get to the archives and find what we're looking for.'

Andrew sighed and pressed his lips together as his mind went through just some of the virtually infinite number of ways in which this plan could go sideways. And yet, at the same time, he found himself reluctantly attracted to what was on the face of it an utterly mad scheme, precisely because it was mad. Fiona was right. It was so hare-brained that it could actually be possible, although it would require some serious planning. But the prize could well turn out to be worth it.

'You know,' he finally said with a small shake of the head, not quite able to believe what he was about to say. 'This just might be sufficiently insane to work.'

'So you agree?' said Fiona excitedly.

'Well, I agree that it *might* be possible,' said Andrew. 'But I will need to come up with a really good plan first. We're going to need a way in that no one has thought of. And then we're going to need luck. A lot of luck.'

'Great,' said Fiona, as if fully expecting him to be able to produce such a plan. 'The SAS is meant to be able to get into even the most hard-to-reach places, right? And with your security clearance and access to intelligence, I am sure you could get your hands on everything British intelligence knows about that building. I am sure they have spent the past half a century studying every aspect of it and mapping out practically every brick. There has got to be a way.'

'Yes,' said Andrew grudgingly. 'Although, I really can't promise anything. But I will see what I can come up with.'

'Thank you,' said Fiona. 'That's all I ask. And if you come back and tell me it isn't doable, then we'll just have to come up with something else.'

Andrew leaned back on the sofa, draped an arm over the seatback, and regarded her for a few moments as she took a bite of a chocolate cookie. When she caught him watching her, she turned and smiled inquisitively.

'What?' she said, chewing her cookie.

'You know, Fiona,' he said, looking at her with genuine affection in his eyes. 'You're crazy, you realise that, right? Fearless and crazy. But I love you for it.'

'I know,' she smiled, leaning over and giving him a kiss on the cheek. 'I am sure we can do this.'

★   ★   ★

That evening, after spending most of the afternoon at the office at Sheldrake Place making a series of calls and corresponding by email with various contacts he had made through the course of his career, Andrew returned home to Hampstead with what just might prove to be a viable means for them to realise Fiona's seemingly preposterous and reckless idea. Drawing on the full spectrum of resources available to him, as well as getting in touch with old friends in the intelligence community, Andrew had secured a cache of schematics, floor plans, and other information that could conceivably be put together to produce a way into the Lubyanka building on the eponymous square in central Moscow.

The building had served as the headquarters first for the Soviet Union's spy agency, the KGB, and then as the HQ for the Russian Federation's intelligence apparatus and internal state security services, the FSB. For more than a century, this building had been a symbol throughout Russia and the world of the nefarious power of dictatorships, and never in a million years had Andrew thought that he would one day be planning to break into it.

The most useful interior plans for the feared building turned out to have been provided by a double agent who had been a KGB colonel while at the same time secretly working for MI6 in the 1980s. The agent had eventually been caught and executed, but not before providing British intelligence with dozens of reports about the KGB's organisational structure, its chain of command and high-ranking personnel, as well as their individual responsibilities. He had also managed to hand over several schematics showing the interior layouts of multiple KGB facilities in the Soviet Union, East Germany and the other Soviet client states in Eastern Europe, and this included the fortress-like Lubyanka building in the centre of Moscow.

'The building has 8 floors, including the ground floor,' said Andrew as he spread a large sheet of A2 paper out onto the coffee table. 'These are the floor plans, as far as we are aware at this moment.'

'Wow,' said Fiona. 'I can't believe we actually have these.'

'They might not be 100 percent accurate,' said Andrew. 'It is possible that parts of the building's interior might have been changed since the 1980s, but I somehow doubt it. And the basic structure of the interior is almost certainly exactly as it was when it was built in 1897. This is bound to be especially true for the sublevels, which would be particularly difficult to alter since they have a massive building bearing down on them. And according to these plans, those sublevels are where the archives can be found.'

Fiona leaned in over the floor plans and studied them as Andrew pointed to different locations.

'The archives are located right here,' he continued, pointing. 'They are at one end of the lowest of three sublevels, roughly 120 feet below street level. The other end of that level is taken up by the secure bunker for the FSB leadership. That bunker has been built to withstand a nuclear strike on Moscow as well as to serve as a temporary command centre in case of an ICBM exchange with the US.'

'How lovely,' said Fiona caustically. 'I'm glad it never had to be used that way.'

'Now look over here,' said Andrew, tracing a line from the archives along a corridor. 'This level is accessible via a secure lift or a set of stairs from the 1st floor, where most of the offices of senior staff are located. Both will be locked behind gates that are controlled from the main security office on the second floor. It is possible that the lift also requires some sort of punch card key to work. It is a pretty ancient and low-tech type of security, but that's exactly how the Russians like to design things, not least because it's impossible to hack.'

'I see,' said Fiona, studying the plans and committing them to memory.

'But we don't have all of the details,' said Andrew. 'We simply won't know until we get there. And then, of course, we will need to find a way to open the archive doors. It is possible that this can be done from the main security office, but I am not certain about that. We might need some sort of master key. In other words, once we're inside the building, we'll know where to go, but we might need to improvise to actually figure out how to get there.'

'Right,' nodded Fiona. 'That's the archive itself. But how do we get to Lubyanka Square? And how do we get into the building?'

'This is where things get interesting,' said Andrew, pulling a different sheet from his bag and unfolding it on the table. 'This is a map of the greater Moscow area, with the Moskva River meandering through it, and Lubyanka Square is located right here.'

He tapped on a spot on the map and then placed his other index finger far to the west, just outside the main metropolitan area.

'These coloured lines are the Moscow Metro system,' he said. 'There are 17 lines in total crisscrossing the city and spanning just under four hundred kilometres. And as I am sure you already know, they are quite famous for being infinitely more spacious and attractive than their Western counterparts, especially compared with the Victorian London tube network.'

'Yes,' said Fiona. 'I have seen the photos. Those stations are quite spectacular.'

'And out here,' continued Andrew, 'is Vnukovo Airport, which includes a separate complex reserved for use by Russian government officials for both domestic and international flights. It's generally referred to as Vnukovo-2.'

Andrew then pulled another sheet from his bag and unfolded it, but this one was made of thin transparent plastic, and it had its own much less comprehensive network of coloured lines printed on it.

'Now have a look at this,' he said, as he placed the transparent sheet on top of the city map. 'This is the so-called Metro-2 system, and it lies much deeper than the main public metro system.'

'Metro-2?' said Fiona, examining the handful of shorter coloured lines.

'That's right,' said Andrew. 'Its official KGB codename was D-6, which you can see printed up here in the top corner. It is a secret alternate metro system built in the 1950s by Joseph Stalin. The reason for its construction was to insulate the Soviet Union's top leadership in the communist Politburo from the masses, and also to allow them to move around the city safely during a crisis, including in the event of a nuclear war. Now, as you can see, it has only four lines, but they connect all the major state institutions in central Moscow together, such as the Ministry of Defence, the Kremlin and also the FSB building on Lubyanka Square. There are even some indications that there is a station under the suburb of Ramenki which connects to an entire underground city codenamed Ramenki-43. This place supposedly includes a massive wartime command bunker and a shelter for thousands of highly placed members of the communist party who would be able to live there for years if necessary. That is, if the rumours are to be believed. But that part has never been confirmed. Anyway, the rail system is operated with electric battery power so that it was never dependent on power being delivered from the surface, and it uses small carriages since it was never designed to move more than about a dozen or so people at a time.'

'That's really amazing,' said Fiona. 'I have never heard of any of this.'

'I'm not surprised,' said Andrew. 'The Russians have always denied its existence, and they have done everything they could to ridicule and dismiss it as an urban myth concocted by conspiracy theorists. But MI6 has proof positive that it actually does exist, courtesy of our American friends at the CIA and one of the moles they had inside the Soviet Union in the early 1980s. Anecdotally, there was an uptick in public interest in the Metro-2 network a few years ago, and wouldn't you know it, the Russian State Duma then promptly fashioned a new law against entering Moscow's metro tunnels, including some pretty draconian penalties for anyone foolish enough to ignore it.'

'No smoke without a fire?' observed Fiona.

'Exactly,' said Andrew. 'And here's the kicker.'

He traced a finger along a purple line from the Metro-2 station under Lubyanka Square and west all the way out to Vnukovo Airport.

'One of the secret metro tunnels stretches from the government airport complex at Vnukovo-2 to FSB headquarters and then onwards to the Kremlin. And that's our way into the Lubyanka building. If we can find a way to access this purple tunnel at the airport, then we should be able to make our way to the station underneath the FSB building. And that ought to give us a decent chance of getting inside from there.'

'Well, that's assuming there's some means of transportation from the airport,' said Fiona. 'It looks like a long way to walk.'

'Yes,' said Andrew. 'It's about 30 kilometres. So we're going to need to hijack something to get us into central Moscow. But there is bound to be something we can use.'

'Are all these underground tunnels and bunkers really still there?' said Fiona with a note of scepticism. 'The Cold War has been over for decades, and I don't imagine the Russians would have spent much on maintaining such a network during peacetime.'

'That's a valid point,' said Andrew. 'According to our best intelligence, Metro-2 is still operated by the GUSP agency, which is the Main Directorate of Special Programs of the President of the Russian Federation. However, it is likely that these tunnels are no longer in pristine condition, and it may even be the case that some of them are no longer usable. As you might know, Moscow was essentially built on a swamp surrounding the Moskva River, and there are indications that some sections have suffered from water ingress and flooding over the years.'

'Okay,' said Fiona. 'But assuming that we can get to the Lubyanka building, how do we get into it?'

'The Metro-2 line should take us straight there,' said Andrew. 'If our Cold War intelligence reports are accurate, then there is a tunnel leading from the metro station to a sublevel entrance into Lubyanka. And according to these floor plans, it should be close to the FSB leadership's secure bunker on the lowest sublevel where the archives are also located. I am not sure about the precise nature of the doors and security systems there, so we will have to pack some serious kit and then improvise.'

'Right,' said Fiona, as she pondered the suddenly very real prospect of travelling for tens of kilometres along decaying underground tunnels and then breaking into the HQ of Russia's main intelligence services. 'Is there no other way for us to do this?'

'No,' said Andrew, with a brief shake of the head. 'Not as far as I can see. Short of driving a truck full of explosives through the front door or sending in the SAS with a bunch of breaching charges, this is the only way. And we obviously can't draw attention to ourselves. We need to make sure that we stay covert the whole time. As we say in the Regiment. In and out quietly, and then back in time for tea and medals.'

'Except there'll be no medals for us,' said Fiona. 'But I will settle for tea if we can get the transcripts out with us.'

'Good,' said Andrew. 'I've had a chat with Colonel Strickland, and he has managed to pull a few strings in Whitehall and arrange for us to tag along during a scheduled shipment of office equipment to our embassy in Moscow. For fairly obvious security reasons, British diplomats never purchase any hardware in the countries where they are stationed, so it all has to be brought in on flights from RAF Northolt. Everything from PCs to printers to coffee machines to light switches. Nothing is ever purchased locally. Anyway, you and I are joining as extra crew on a government plane to Vnukovo-2. Or at least, that is how it will appear on the flight manifest. Once the plane has touched down there and taxied to the official government terminal, we will then follow the flight crew and walk inside the terminal to the designated holding area where the crews wait to begin the return leg later that evening. From there, we will peel off to locate the entrance to Metro-2 while the cargo from London is being unloaded. I've studied the layout of the terminal closely, and the entrance to the Metro-2 station below the airport appears to be located near a VIP area about thirty metres from a parking hub that is dedicated to Kremlin vehicles. There is a set of stairs and a lift, but we will have to wait and see what the best option is.'

'Alright,' said Fiona thoughtfully. 'You make it all sound so simple.'

'Oh, it won't be simple,' said Andrew. 'There are plenty of things that can go wrong, and we will need to improvise along the way. But this is our best option.'

'Fine,' nodded Fiona. 'When do we leave?'

'The flight is scheduled for late tomorrow afternoon,' said Andrew. 'We touch down in the evening local time, and if everything goes to plan, we should reach the Lubyanka building at around midnight. At that time, there will only be a skeleton crew on duty, including some cleaners. So, we might need to find a way to disguise ourselves as being part of that team.'

'What about the guards?' said Fiona. 'Surely it will be crawling with those.'

'Not as far as we can tell,' said Andrew. 'Again, it's the Lubyanka building, and no one goes there unless they have business to conduct, so security is not nearly as heavy as you might imagine. Of course, there will be some guards, but I don't imagine any of them will be especially vigilant. As security guard jobs go, these are probably among the least eventful in the world. Remember, what you and I are planning to do, no one will expect. And also keep in mind that for the two of us, this is a big deal with a lot riding on it. But to those guards, it's just Tuesday.'

'Good point,' nodded Fiona.

'Anyway,' said Andrew. 'I think I have probably spent all the favours I had saved up with just about everyone I know in order to get this thing set up. So it had better work.'

'We'll make it work,' said Fiona, more hopeful than confident now that the reality of their upcoming endeavour was beginning to assert itself in her mind.

'Listen, Fiona,' said Andrew with a grave look. 'I need to make sure that you understand. If anything goes wrong for any reason, you and I could end up in a lot of trouble, including not coming home again for a very long time. This is serious business.'

'I know,' she said with a sober expression. 'And so was the murder of Ben Ambrose. And of Bateman, for that matter. But we can either sit on our hands and let bad people act with impunity, or we can try to do something about it while also getting to grips with what Rittenhausen is up to. Because whatever that is, it is worth killing for, which means it is nothing good.'

'Alright,' nodded Andrew. 'Just so long as we're clear in our minds that this won't be a cakewalk.'

'Crystal clear,' said Fiona. 'I'm ready. Let's do this.'

Ten

The sun was low in the sky as the small Dassault Falcon 900LX took off from RAF Northolt, headed east, and began to climb towards its cruising altitude. Operated by 32 Squadron, the RAF had renamed the aircraft type Envoy IV, and with its Union Jack livery draped over its rear section and tail, it was used to ferry government officials and diplomats to overseas meetings and events. With a cruising speed of almost a thousand kilometres per hour and a range of more than eight thousand kilometres, the flight to Moscow's Vnukova-2 airport was well within its capability, and the trip was scheduled to take just over three hours.

Upon landing, the Russian authorities would be keen to inspect the delivery to the British embassy, but since the flight was designated as a diplomatic flight, they would have no authority to board the aircraft. The passenger cabin was packed with various boxes and bags full of items required for the continued operation of the embassy. Two Foreign Office staff members who were rotating into the Moscow embassy were also aboard, along with two assistants who would be in charge of loading the various items into a diplomatic vehicle for the journey by road to central Moscow.

Andrew and Fiona were seated next to each other wearing crisp flight crew uniforms, and before taking the opportunity to grab a couple of hours' sleep ahead of their nocturnal undertaking, they made sure that everything they needed was in the two black leather holdalls they would be carrying into the terminal in Moscow.

Having had years of practice going to sleep on planes ahead of missions, Andrew slept for most of the way there after his in-flight meal. Eat when you can. Sleep when you can, as the SAS mantra went. When he opened his eyes again, Fiona had been awake for about an hour, and as he looked out of the window, he saw that it was dark and rainy outside. He peered out through the rivulets of water streaking across the glass as the aircraft descended through the clouds towards Vnukovo-2. In the far distance, he could see the lights of central Moscow lighting up the underside of a thick and leaden layer of low cloud.

Five minutes later, the wheels touched down and cut through the standing water on the runway, sending a plume of spray up into the air behind the aircraft as it braked. Shortly thereafter, the pilot nudged the plane forward onto its stand by the VIP terminal, and then he killed the engines while a couple of Russian border officials approached holding umbrellas. Behind them, the diplomatic vehicle was inching forward in preparation for being loaded up with the delivery from London.

The pilot and the copilot left the cockpit and entered the passenger cabin where Andrew and Fiona got to their feet. They were wearing dark grey overalls identical to those of the embassy staff assistants, and they donned their caps as the door was opened. Then they followed the flight crew and the embassy staff out of the aircraft, descended the steps to the wet tarmac and unfolded their umbrellas. The pilot quickly signed a piece of paper attached to a clipboard that had been handed to him by one of the disinterested-looking uniformed officials. The uniformed man took receipt of the clipboard again and didn't even look at it before turning on his heels and disappearing along with his comrade.

While the two embassy staffers and their assistants began unloading all the boxes from the passenger cabin and carrying them out to the waiting vehicle, Andrew and Fiona followed the pilots into the terminal building. The two men had clearly done this before because they headed straight for a desk behind which sat a bored-looking uniformed Russian border official. The pilot handed him a set of documents, and after checking them silently and then giving them a stamp, he glanced lazily at the four passports that were handed to him. Arranging for the creation of fake IDs for Andrew and Fiona had been a matter of routine for Colonel Strickland, and the quartet were soon waived through towards the lounge where pilots usually waited for any embassy staff rotating out, as well as clearance to return to London. The wordless border guard had barely performed his duty before he packed up for the evening and left his station, leaving the new arrivals to make their own way into the lounge.

As soon as he was out of sight, Andrew and Fiona peeled off carrying their holdalls and headed along several corridors towards the rear of the terminal. It was very obvious from its construction and décor that the building was many decades old, and with its low ceilings, worn linoleum flooring and pale green walls, it looked more like a run-down, underfunded hospital than an airport for government VIPs.

Andrew had memorised its layout, and after a couple of minutes, during which time they were relieved to find the terminal deserted, they found themselves at the end of a wide corridor with a single armoured door located next to the sliding double doors of a lift. Both had been painted a slightly darker green, but that was evidently a very long time ago, judging from the peeling paint, and none of them looked as if they had been used for many years.

'Let's try the lift,' said Andrew.

He pressed the single brushed metal button on the wall with an arrow pointing down engraved into it, but nothing happened. He pressed it a few more times and harder this time around, but still, there was no sign of any movement.

'No power,' he said. 'It looks like this access point has been mothballed.'

'Damn it,' said Fiona with concern etched on her forehead. 'That could mean that the rail tunnels might not be passable anymore.'

'Let's not jump to conclusions,' said Andrew, pulling a lockpicking gun from a side pocket in the trousers of his overalls. 'I should be able to get through this door. It's an old tumbler lock.'

He dropped his bag on the floor, went down on one knee and inserted the tip of the lockpicking gun into the lock. He then pumped the handle several times in quick succession until he could feel that all the key pins inside the lock had been bounced up inside their respective pin channels. At that moment, he twisted the gun, and there immediately followed a satisfying metallic click.

'Done,' he said, picking up his bag and getting to his feet. 'Let's go.'

To their relief, no alarm went off when Andrew twisted the hefty metal door handle and pushed the door open. It squeaked slightly on its old hinges, but within a few seconds, they were through. After donning their head-mounted LED lamps and stepping through into a large and dark stairwell, Andrew then closed the door behind them.

The stairwell's walls had once been painted with the same paint as the corridors in the terminal on the other side of the armoured door, but very little of that paint was now left. Most of it had peeled off, and what remained appeared to have faded into an almost grey colour. In the corners by the ceiling above their heads and running down the walls in strange flowing streaks were large patches of black mould, hinting at the slow but certain defeat of this concrete structure in its battle against nature and time. The air was cool and dusty, and it smelled slightly damp. Leaning out over the concrete railing and looking straight down, Andrew could barely make out the bottom of the central shaft. He extracted a green glowstick from his holdall, cracked it and waited a few seconds until its eerie glow lit up the top landing. Holding the glowstick out over the railing, he then dropped it and watched it fall towards the bottom which appeared to be some thirty metres or ten sublevels below them. As it fell, it lit up each level in turn before clacking audibly onto the floor at the very bottom.

The steps on the stairs were covered in a thin but perfectly even layer of pale grey dust, providing more evidence of the abandoned nature of the place, and as the two of them began descending, the faint echoes of their footsteps reverberated up and down the stairwell like a dry whisper.

'What a place,' said Fiona quietly as she looked around and allowed the light from her headtorch to move across the walls. 'It looks like no one has been here for decades.'

'And that's lucky for us,' said Andrew. 'It means that we won't run into anyone. At least not at this end of the Metro-2 network. Let's head down to the rail station and find some wheels. There's got to be something we can use.'

They continued down the dark and eerie stairwell, and as they descended further, the temperature dropped noticeably, and the air became even more stale and musty. They finally emerged onto a wide but short platform whose ceiling was supported by several riveted steel pillars whose paint had long since peeled off and fallen onto the stone floor below. Adjacent to the platform was a wide tunnel with two rail tracks, and it appeared to have been constructed using huge pre-fabricated, curved concrete sections slotted together every few metres. Overhead and stretching along the ceiling for as far as they could see was a chaotic network of rotten pipes and rickety-looking ventilation shafts. On one side, mounted on the arching tunnel wall opposite the platform, were banks of thick black electrical cables that snaked along like a nest of writhing anacondas.

One of the tracks appeared to be a standard-width track for full-sized rail cars, while the one next to it was significantly narrower with much thinner steel tracks. While there were no carriages on the main track, the narrow track had what looked like a small four-person service vehicle akin to a hand-pumped railcar sitting on it. However, this vehicle did not have any levers to propel it forward. Instead, it appeared to be battery-operated.

'Well,' said Andrew as he stepped out to the edge of the platform and looked across to the railcar. 'That little thing appears to be our only ride. But it will have to do. Let's see if the batteries still work.'

As he climbed down onto the main track and made his way over to the small service speeder, Fiona stood on the edge of the platform, pulled a powerful handheld torch from her holdall, and shone its beam along the rail tracks in both directions. To her left, the wide but dilapidated tunnel seemed to go on forever, eventually disappearing at a point hundreds of metres away in the darkness. However, when she looked to her right, she could see buffer stops, one for each of the two rail tracks, and behind them was a concrete wall stretching up to the curving ceiling. Along the wall were placed several rusty metal cabinets that she assumed contained tools and equipment for maintaining the rail lines, and there were also a couple of shelving units stacked with red metal boxes.

'This is the end of the line, alright,' she said, her voice echoing in the quiet and cavernous space. 'Just like your plans indicated. Let's hope they are just as accurate about the layout when we get into Moscow.'

'There's only one way to find out,' said Andrew as he mounted the dust-covered railcar and switched the power on.

The small control panel with its dials and indicators lit up faintly with an orange glow, and the railcar began emitting a low hum as its headlights came on. Andrew inspected the controls, found the accelerator and the brakes and shifted the small vehicle forward a couple of metres before stopping again.

'It seems to be working,' he said, although sounding unconvinced. 'You can say what you want about the Soviets, but they took pride in building things to last. But I am not sure this battery will. Especially since we'll need to keep the headlights on the whole way. Judging by the speedometer, I am assuming this thing can go about twenty kilometres per hour, it should take us just over an hour to get to the station under the Lubyanka building. I doubt we can do that on one battery charge, so let's see if there are any spares here somewhere.'

He switched the railcar's power off in an attempt to conserve power, and as he dismounted from the driver's seat and used his own handheld torch to walk back towards the buffer stops, Fiona hopped down from the platform and joined him, letting her torch beam fan across the end wall. As the two of them approached the corroded metal cabinets and shelving units, they realised that the red metal boxes lined up there were all spare batteries for the railcar, and they carried back two each to the vehicle and placed them on the empty seats.

'One second,' said Andrew. 'I want to have a look at those cabinets.'

They returned to the end wall and opened up the cabinets one by one to inspect their contents. As the doors squeaked on their rusty hinges, they found that they were mostly empty. However, there were several items that they decided to bring along just in case they needed to do repairs on the railcar. There was a large wrench, a mallet, a couple of screwdrivers, a small packet of spare lightbulbs for the headlights, a small cable snipper and a heavy-duty wire cutter.

'This is useful,' said Andrew. 'We don't want to get stuck halfway there with no way of repairing this old thing.'

Fiona, concerned about losing light in the tunnel, also picked out two kerosene lamps as backups. They looked as if they might easily be much older than herself, but they appeared to be full of fuel. While she picked up the lamps and a large glass bottle with more kerosene, Andrew stuffed all of the remaining items into an old leather kitbag he found lying at the bottom of one of the cabinets, and then they returned to the railcar.

He got back behind the controls and removed a metal panel by the engine compartment to make sure that they had found the correct type of battery. Satisfied that they now had all the power they would need, Andrew mounted the driver's seat again as Fiona sat down in the passenger seat next to him, facing forward. They took off their head torches and began to get ready to move out. Zipping open their holdalls, they each put on what was a combined harness and tactical vest and attached to them the various tools and items that they had brought from London. Among them, Andrew had a sheathed hunting knife and a Glock 17 with two magazines that he hoped he wouldn't need, but it was better to be safe than sorry. Then they got into the two front seats and prepared to move out. Ahead of them lay an almost pitch-black void, and the massive but completely quiet tunnel stretching into the darkness seemed strangely menacing. Only when Andrew switched the headlights back on did Fiona begin to feel as if they just might be able to make it all the way to their destination.

'Let's get going,' said Andrew. 'The clock is ticking, and we need to get this done as fast as possible.'

* * *

Once they got underway, it became evident that the rail tunnel towards central Moscow was practically as straight as an arrow, except for a couple of occasions when it seemed to curve almost imperceptibly to one side or the other. Andrew had been unsure about how fast the railcar would be able to go and which speed the condition of the tracks would allow for. However, as it turned out, the railcar was comfortably pushing 35 kilometres per hour, if the onboard speedometer was anything to go by, and the track sections were clear and straight. The two front-mounted headlights lit up the way ahead of them, and for as long as that was the case, Andrew was happy to keep the speed up. As it moved along the tracks, the railcar was rattling loudly, and every once in a while the metal wheels would squeal for a few seconds before going back to simply rumbling on.

Just as Andrew was glancing at his wristwatch, feeling pleased with their faster-than-expected pace, one of the headlights suddenly winked out. In an instant, the view distance ahead was dramatically reduced, and he decided to come to a full stop to try to fix the problem. Lower visibility meant less time to react in case there was an obstacle on the tracks. As the railcar screeched to a halt, they both dismounted and walked to the front of the vehicle.

'Can you fix it?' said Fiona, standing next to Andrew as he used a screwdriver to dismantle the headlight's metal housing.

'It ought to be straightforward,' he said. 'Hopefully, it is just the bulb that has burned out.'

He opened the housing and replaced the lightbulb, but it did not fix the problem. Then he tried another bulb from their pack of spares, but that too produced no light.

'There must be a problem with the wiring,' he said. 'We don't have time to start taking the whole thing apart. We'll have to continue with just one light. It will slow us down, but as long as the other one stays lit, we'll be okay.'

Fiona eyed the remaining headlight suspiciously but decided not to jinx things by asking what they would do if the other headlight died too. They got back into their seats, and soon they were continuing along the oppressively dark and damp tunnel. Every once in a while, they would drive past partially crumbled sections of the tunnel wall, and the more time they spent down there, the clearer it became to Fiona how this transit system must have been sitting in its abandoned state for decades. Once the Cold War had ended and the threat of imminent nuclear armageddon through the convention of mutually assured destruction had all but disappeared, the Russian leadership had clearly preferred surface transportation to the dark and claustrophobic tunnel. Sitting motionless and peering ahead into the gloom as the railcar sped along the track, its headlights revealing section after dilapidated section of tunnel and the curving walls sweeping by her on either side, she soon felt as if she was falling down into a seemingly endless well. At regular intervals, she had to look down to her lap or to the lit-up railcar instrument panel to re-orientate herself. On one such occasion, Andrew suddenly slammed on the brakes, and her head snapped up to discover that they were driving straight towards some sort of obstacle lying across the track.

'Shit,' said Andrew as he brought the railcar to a stop just a couple of metres from large, jagged pieces of concrete that appeared to have fallen from the ceiling.

They both directed their torches upwards to discover that several of the tunnel's prefab ceiling sections had come loose and had collapsed onto the track. As they had fallen, they had pulled heavy electrical cables free from the tunnel ceiling, and several of them had snapped and were now hanging down towards the track like black lianas from a tree deep inside a jungle.

Examining the broken ceiling more closely, it soon became clear why it had happened. Water ingress was coming through from behind the concrete sections, and over time, they had evidently caused some of the sections to detach and fall. Even now, water was falling down onto the ground by the side of the track like a trickle from a leaking showerhead, and the sound of the drips of water hitting the ground echoed thinly along the tunnel.

'We'll need to clear this,' said Andrew as he approached the obstacle while looking up at the ceiling. 'Hopefully, nothing else will fall any time soon.'

They began pulling pieces of concrete from the pile of rubble that was blocking their way, and they were soon making good progress. The fallen sections had broken into several smaller pieces when they had slammed into the rail tracks, and this allowed Andrew and Fiona to move them by flipping them over repeatedly until they were clear. As they worked, the remaining railcar headlight began to dim noticeably. Clearly, the battery was running low, and they would need to swap it out for one of the spares.

They had almost finished clearing the path ahead when Fiona noticed a strange noise coming from one side of the track up ahead. At first, it sounded like a faint rustling of leaves, but it soon grew louder and became something else. Something strangely organic. And then she saw it. A huge swarm of rats was pouring out of a low, broken semi-circular drain grille about ten metres further along the tunnel. But these were no ordinary rats. They were huge. The size of cats but bulky with short legs, grimy fur and small intense eyes that seemed to glow in the railcar's headlights as they came closer.

Moving swiftly like a single large mass of some strange subterranean being, they flowed out through the grille and curved straight towards the light and the movement they had clearly sensed nearby. As they scurried forward, they emitted a frenetic chittering noise as if in ravenous anticipation of being able to sink their long, sharp incisors into the flesh of fresh meat. No doubt, they were more used to eating waste, carrion and whatever else they could find down here, including the corpses of their dead brothers and sisters, but they also appeared to be more than prepared to attack much larger prey.

Without hesitation, Andrew pulled his Glock 17 from its shoulder holster, racked the slide, aimed and fired several shots towards them. The loud reports exploded through the dank, quiet air in the tunnel as the bullets slammed into the writhing mass of fur, cutting through tissue and bone and ending the lives of handfuls of rats, but it was like trying to hold back the tide with your hands. Oblivious to their fallen comrades, the rats just kept coming.

'Get back into the railcar!' Andrew shouted.

They ran back to the vehicle and mounted it, but when Andrew pushed the throttle forward, the railcar barely moved. Its battery was now so low that it was only able to inch the railcar forward at a snail's pace. Up ahead, the rats seemed emboldened by the sight of their fleeing prey. It was the natural instinct of predators to chase after anything running away. More rats poured from the grille, swelling their numbers to several hundred, and they kept moving inexorably forward, seemingly now committed to trying to overpower the two large creatures in front of them at all costs. As they came nearer, the railcar's remaining headlight all but died, leaving the tunnel in virtual darkness.

'The oil lamps!' said Andrew urgently, putting the pistol back in its holster. 'Quickly.'

Feeling a rising sense of panic, Fiona quickly reached into her holdall and extracted the two oil lamps she had brought from the metal cabinets that were now several kilometres behind them. Andrew took one in his hand and reached inside his pocket for a lighter. Once the lamp was lit, he stood up and tossed it towards the swarm. It sailed through the air and shattered on the rocky ground in front of the rats, and then the kerosene ignited with a whoosh, bathing the tunnel in yellow light. Dozens of rats were instantly set alight, and as they writhed and screeched in panic, Andrew hurled the other oil lamp forward. Like the one before it, it also shattered and sprayed kerosene over a large area which then immediately ignited, burning yet more rats. However, it wasn't enough. The dark mass of hungry creatures kept surging forward, and they were now less than ten metres from the railcar.

'The bottle,' shouted Fiona, reaching into her holdall once more and pulling out the almost full bottle of kerosene.

'Throw it,' said Andrew, once again pulling his gun out. 'Throw it as high as you can.'

Fiona immediately understood what he was trying to achieve, and she held the bottle in her right hand and brought it back behind herself in preparation for her throw. Then she hurled it forward and up, causing it to sail in a long arc towards the front of the army of rats. Just as it passed its apex, Andrew fired four shots in quick succession. At least one of the bullets hit the bottle because it exploded in midair, and an expanding shower of fine kerosene spray fell towards the rats. Less than a second later, it suddenly ignited in a massive airburst explosion that travelled along the tunnel in both directions, almost causing Andrew and Fiona to lose their balance.

Burning kerosene fell like fiery rain onto the rats below, and as they became enveloped in roiling flame and smoke, there was a loud cacophony of furious screeching and squealing as the inferno incinerated them alive. Now in a blind panic, those few creatures that were on fire but still among the living scurried away like tiny torches running through the darkness, and soon the tunnel was quiet apart from the crackling noises of the burning corpses left behind.

'Damn,' said Andrew. 'I've never seen anything like that.'

'Yeah,' panted Fiona, still stunned by what they had just witnessed. 'That was scary. I hope they've had enough.'

'Let's not hang around to find out,' said Andrew, grabbing one of the fresh batteries. 'Could you get the panel for me?'

Fiona knelt inside the railcar and removed the battery compartment's metal cover. Andrew then swiftly detached the old one, tossed it over the side and slotted the new one in place. A few seconds later, the railcar moved forward through the smouldering landscape of dead rodents, and soon it was nothing but a faint, receding orange glow behind them.

★ ★ ★

Around ten minutes after their run-in with the rat army, Andrew glimpsed something up ahead. It was a large, bulky rectangular shape sitting on the right-hand side of the tunnel. Next to it, the tunnel ceiling changed from its curved shape to a square hole. It was some sort of gateway. Only when they drew nearer did he realise what he was looking at.

'A giant blast door,' he said, glancing at Fiona as he slowed down. 'Big enough to seal the whole tunnel.'

'Look,' said Fiona, pointing ahead as the light from the railcar began extending into the space beyond the huge rectangular doorway. 'It's a platform.'

'Wow,' said Andrew. 'You know what this means? This is the Ramenki station. The underground emergency complex built for the Soviet leadership.'

'And there's another blast door at the other end of the platform,' said Fiona, pointing into the semi-darkness. 'This station could be completely closed off from the rest of the network in case of a nuclear war. Perhaps even during a popular uprising. The Soviet leadership was not exactly a popular dictatorship, but they were certainly paranoid, and for all the things you can say about them, they developed a real talent for self-preservation.'

As they passed through the doorway designed to fit the enormous steel blast door that was currently swung aside in its open position, Andrew spotted a rail switch up ahead. It had been placed next to the rail track just inside the blast door, and it looked like it would be guiding them off the main track at a ninety-degree angle and onto a short dead-end track running alongside a smaller platform.

'Damn it,' he said. 'We're about to be shunted onto that other track. I'll have to stop here.'

He hit the brakes, and the railcar came to a stop a few metres before reaching the rail switch. They both got out and walked forward to the switch.

'I don't see a way of moving it to allow us to go straight,' said Fiona. 'There's no lever or anything like that. Maybe it needs power.'

'It probably does,' said Andrew, 'except we don't have a way to get electricity to it. But there has to be a way to move it manually. The whole point of this place is to be independent of the power grid on the surface. We'll have to look around.'

Carrying their handheld torches, they walked along the dead-end track to the short platform and climbed onto it, and only then did they notice another blast door running along the platform wall.

'This must be the entrance to Ramenki,' said Andrew.

It was about ten metres wide and four metres tall, and it appeared to be hinged in such a way as to allow it to swing inward. On either side of it were machinegun nests behind thick concrete walls, evidently built in anticipation of some form of siege. Whether this had been constructed as a last defence to fend off foreign forces or in an attempt to keep out the general population during wartime panic was anyone's guess.

'I don't see any controls for this thing,' said Fiona, placing her hands on her hips as she looked up at the massive steel barrier. 'There's no way we're getting through. It must be operated from somewhere else with hydraulics or electric motors.'

'Not a problem,' said Andrew, pointing his torch off to one side. 'There is a small armoured door over here next to it. It's ajar. It might be some sort of service tunnel. Come on.'

Putting his shoulder to the rusty metal door and pushing hard, Andrew managed to shove it open enough for them to get through. On the other side was a short corridor with another armoured door at the other end, but that one was closed shut. By the looks of it, the small space in between the two doors had functioned as some sort of airlock to make sure that nothing and no one unauthorised ever managed to penetrate into the interior of the Ramenki complex. Andrew gripped the door handle on the second door and pushed it down, but it didn't move.

'Locked,' he said. 'Let me try something else. Step back, please.'

Fiona got out of the way, and he then attempted to kick the door open, hoping that either the doorframe or the lock had corroded sufficiently over the years to allow him to force his way through, but nothing happened. The door seemed sealed shut.

'What now?' said Fiona. 'We need to get in there if we're going to be able to move that rail switch.'

'Wait here,' said Andrew. 'I'll be right back.'

He disappeared out of the airlock and walked back to the railcar, returning about a minute later with a small black cube roughly five centimetres across.

'What's that,' asked Fiona.

'Thermite,' said Andrew, moving up to the sealed door. 'It's like a regular thermite charge, but it sits inside a ceramic shell on five sides. The sixth side is metal, and once the thermite is activated, the molten core pushes out through that metal plate and melts whatever is in front of it. It should work.'

He used an integrated ceramic clasp to fix the charge to the door and then aligned it across the lock.

'Alright,' he said, pulling the pin. 'Let's get out of here. This will get hot and toxic for a few minutes.'

They left the airlock and stepped out onto the small platform as the thermite charge began its violent chemical reaction, turning its interior into a molten mass of metal reaching temperatures of more than two thousand degrees Celsius. As the exothermic process picked up speed, the charge fizzed and crackled, and white smoke started billowing up from the armoured door's lock as it began to melt and disintegrate. About three minutes later, during which time smoke was pouring out of the airlock and flowing eerily along the ceiling above the short platform and the rail track, the charge finally burned itself out. Another couple of minutes later, most of the smoke had dissipated, but as they re-entered the airlock, the air inside was noticeably warmer, and it had an acrid tang to it.

When Andrew examined the lock, there was virtually nothing left of it, and small, charred and deformed metal parts had dropped onto the dusty concrete floor below. However, most of it had melted away and flowed down the side of the door. Putting his shoulder to it, he was able to push it open, and the two of them finally proceeded into what appeared to be some kind of control room. It was roughly four by five metres in size with a low ceiling, and on one side of it was a small dust-covered window that looked out to a large open space. This had to be what was on the other side of the blast door by the small platform. The open space was akin to a courtyard some twenty by twenty metres across, and the ceiling was around ten metres above the floor. It was entirely empty, and opposite the blast door was yet another similar door, also shut tight. Evidently, it was a holding area where people and supplies would wait for the exterior blast door to close before they could be let through the second blast door into the main Ramenki complex.

'This is some serious construction work,' said Fiona as she peered out into the subterranean courtyard. 'It reminds me of the German underground bunkers built during the Second World War.'

'Look at this,' said Andrew, sweeping his torchlight across the opposite wall, on which was mounted some sort of control station with oversized analogue dials, switches and levers. 'This looks like the controls for the blast doors and the rail switches. No power though. And no way of turning it on. We'll need to look for another way.'

Fiona moved over to a set of closed wooden cabinets on the adjoining wall, and as she opened them, she found a large electric lamp made of corroded metal. With a wooden handle mounted on top, it was roughly the size of a large toaster, and it was clear that it was powered by the standard red batteries also used on the railcar, because a battery of that type was already sitting inside it. She picked it up and flicked the switch, and the lamp immediately lit up the room.

'Perfect,' said Andrew, joining her. 'We can put that on the front of the railcar. That should allow us to pick up the pace a bit. Let's see what else is in here.'

Andrew rummaged through the remaining cabinets, and at the back of one of them was a long and thick metal bar leaning against the back. It had a wooden handle on one end, and the other end was shaped like an octagon.

'Bingo,' he said. 'This looks like it might be a tool for manual rail switching. I knew we would find something in here.'

Fiona once again glanced out of the small window, this time letting the powerful light from their newly acquired electric lamp light up the courtyard.

'I wonder what is behind that thing,' she said, looking across to the second blast door leading into the interior of the Ramenki complex. 'What if the rumours are true? What if there is a huge underground city in there?'

'It certainly looks like it,' said Andrew, standing behind her and looking through the window. 'But we can't get in there, and anyway, we don't have time.'

They were moving away from the window and heading for the door when Andrew spotted something shiny hanging on a small peg on the wall by the control station. Seemingly barely corroded at all, it appeared to be a steel punch card the size of a playing card. Andrew walked over and picked it off the wall, turning it over in his hand as he studied it. It had a set of precisely placed holes drilled in a grid-like pattern that appeared random. But it was clear that the holes would allow the card to unlock a door when inserted into an appropriate type of lock. And there was a small piece of text engraved and painted red across its top, next to the hammer and sickle of the Soviet Union.

'Your Russian is better than mine,' said Fiona as she joined him. 'What does it say?'

Andrew wiped the thin patina of dust and grime from the key and examined the text.

Д-6. Мастер-ключ

'Holy crap,' he said as he read the words out loud in Russian, suddenly realising what he was holding in his hand. 'It says 'D-6. Master key'. I think this key opens all the doors in the entire Metro-2 network.'

'Crikey,' said Fiona. 'This would have been a real intelligence scoop during the Cold War. That might come in handy.'

'Definitely,' said Andrew, shoving the punch card into a pocket in his tactical vest. 'Right. The clock is ticking. Let's get moving again.'

A couple of minutes later, they were back outside by the rail switch, where Andrew inserted the long metal bar for manual switching into the octagonal hole and wrenched it from one side to the other. The switch was rusty, and at first appeared to be stuck, but with enough force, Andrew finally managed to make it flip, and it did so with a loud clack that travelled along the empty tunnel in both directions as the rails shifted over, finally allowing them to continue their journey.

'There,' said Andrew, panting as he stowed the metal bar on the rail car in case they would need it again. 'Time to go.'

Eleven

The rest of the journey along the Metro-2 line towards the station below Lubyanka Square took about twenty minutes and passed without incident. At one point, Andrew had to stop the railcar to swap out batteries once more, but they had brought along more than enough to reach their destination. When they finally arrived at the platform under the Russian spy HQ, a rail carriage was parked on the opposite track. It looked like something designed in the 1960s, and it had more than likely been built around that time. With two pairs of seats arranged in rows along a central aisle, the carriage had small square windows, and its exterior was made of slightly corrugated sheets of polished steel that had by now faded and begun to corrode here and there. Its large, dark headlights made it look forlorn as it sat there by itself after what might have been decades of not being used.

Andrew and Fiona dismounted the small railcar and clambered up onto the platform, carrying their holdalls.

Now in relative darkness after having switched off the railcar's headlights, they allowed their torchlights to sweep across their surroundings.

'Over here,' said Andrew, pointing his torch off to their left. 'There's a small tunnel this way.'

They walked along the dust-covered platform and entered a narrow tunnel about two metres across and roughly as high. It was not unlike the standard walkways that connect London tube stations with each other, but this tunnel was only about five metres long, and at the end of it was another armoured door with no visible lock. However, the door had some sort of access contraption integrated into it at around chest height. It consisted of a shallow metal box with a mechanical lever and a small slit whose dimensions Andrew immediately recognised.

'We could probably get through this with another thermite charge,' he said quietly, 'but let's try the punch card key. I also don't want to send smoke up into the stairwell or whatever it is that leads up into the building on the other side of this door.'

He extracted the steel punch card master key from his pocket and prepared to insert it into the narrow slit in front of him. From the looks of it, the armoured door's locking mechanism was classic Soviet design. Sturdy and mechanical, and almost impossible to wear out. No hydraulics. No electric servos. Only cogs and gears designed to translate raw manual power into the slow movement of locking pins and latches. It was low-tech and reliable, and it was impossible to override with modern technology. And as it turned out, it still worked.

When he slotted the master key into the slot in the device, he could feel it slide smoothly in, and through his fingertips, he sensed all the little key pins snapping into place in the key's holes. When the key was all the way in, there was a faint metallic click, and then he gripped the lever handle and pulled it from its upright position. It took some force, but as the handle finally pivoted around its central axis to point straight down, the sound of locking pins retracting from the doorframe sounded through the steel. The heavy armoured door was now unlocked.

'Beautiful,' Andrew whispered as he put the key back into his pocket and reached for his Glock. 'Alright. Listen. Things are about to get serious, so try to stay quiet and alert, okay? We don't know what we're going to find on the other side of this door.'

Fiona nodded silently, and then Andrew pushed open the armoured door to the bowels of Lubyanka.

★   ★   ★

Holding his pistol out in front of himself, Andrew moved through the doorway, with Fiona following behind. They now found themselves inside a short, roughly four-metre-wide corridor whose concrete walls on either side extended up about three metres before curving over to a flat ceiling. Once upon a time, the walls and the ceiling had evidently been painted an insipid green, but the paint had now all but lost its colour, turning instead to a pale grey, and it was peeling heavily in places. It was pitch black inside the corridor, except for the light from their head torches that swept across the walls of the derelict-looking room.

Facing them, directly ahead at the far end of the corridor, were what appeared to be two old elevators. They were embedded into the concrete wall and framed by heavy metal doorframes that were rusting visibly. The one on the left was noticeably smaller than the other, and fixed to the wall above each one was the corroded hammer and sickle emblem of the Soviet Union. Across both elevators were concertina doors pulled shut, and mounted on the narrow wall section between them and reaching down to the floor was a tall but shallow metal box with chamfered corners. As the two of them approached, Andrew recognised the box as being another key card lock.

'Where do you think these go?' said Fiona, peering at the elevators.

'If I were to guess,' said Andrew, stepping closer, 'I would say the large one is the main people transport, and that it goes up to the ground floor. But it might also stop before that on the level where the FSB leadership's secure bunker and the archives are located. The smaller one probably has a more dedicated purpose. But I'm not sure what.'

'They look like they haven't been used for ages,' said Fiona, using an index finger to wipe a thick layer of dust from the top of the metal box.

'Let's try this key again,' said Andrew, stepping close to the thin slit in the metal box and extracting the D-6 master key from his pocket. 'With a bit of luck, we can get straight to the archives from here. According to the schematics, I reckon we should be just below and less than twenty metres away from the vault door.'

As soon as he slid the key into the slit and pulled the lever, there was a series of muffled mechanical clicks coming from somewhere inside and behind the box, as if the elevators were being prepped for usage. Then the lights inside the small elevator on their left suddenly came on. Also lighting up was a small control panel on its inside wall that had a single polished but slightly corroded metal button. However, the larger of the two elevators remained in darkness.

'Well,' said Andrew. 'I guess that makes things simple. There is no direct access to the archives from here. We'll have to use the small elevator and see where it takes us. There's only one button on the control panel, so there is clearly just one stop.'

He gripped the handle on the concertina door and pulled it aside. It squeaked loudly as it moved, making him wonder just how deep beneath the Lubyanka building they were and whether anyone above them would be able to hear the noise reverberating up through the elevator shaft. Fiona pulled up her sleeve and glanced at her wristwatch.

'We're coming up on 1 a.m.,' she said.

'Right,' said Andrew. 'It has taken us longer to get here than I would have liked, so we need to get moving. Come on.'

Carrying their holdalls, they stepped inside and Andrew pressed the button on the control panel. After a couple of mechanical clacks and a disconcertingly long pause, there was a brief hum of electricity, and then the elevator finally began to climb up slowly inside its shaft. Soon, they were travelling upwards at roughly walking pace towards an unknown destination somewhere inside the FSB headquarters. As it ascended, the elevator vibrated and rattled slightly every few seconds, and after about a minute, Andrew felt sure that they were now well above street level somewhere inside the building. Shortly thereafter, the open side of the lift, which until then had shown only a concrete wall appearing to slide ever downward, suddenly became a large wood panel. After another few seconds, the panel gave way to what was clearly a wooden door with a handle, and then the elevator came to a stop with a small jolt.

Readying his weapon again, Andrew placed his left hand on the door handle, pressed it down and pushed open the door. The door appeared to be connected to an automatic switch because as soon as it opened, the ceiling lights came on inside a small room that was roughly two by two metres in size. On the left-hand wall was a large metal rack with several weapons, including what Andrew immediately recognised as being an SR-1 Vektor pistol, which was a 9mm handgun used by the Russian Federation's special forces, the Spetsnaz. Although a thoroughly modern weapon, its design was remarkably similar to that of the trusty old Makarov that had been used by Soviet and Russian spies and military personnel for over half a century. There was also a state-of-the-art Vityaz-SN submachinegun hanging by its shoulder strap, as well as boxes of ammunition and other equipment, including a torch and a black ballistics vest. On the right-hand wall were mounted two tall metal cabinets that appeared to be unlocked. Opposite the elevator was a plain door-sized wooden panel with two brass push plates located on either side of a thin seam that ran down the middle of it.

'What is this place?' whispered Fiona.

Andrew stepped out of the elevator first and moved to the cabinets, carefully opening each door in turn.

'It almost looks like a changing room,' he said. 'A place for some bigshot to kit up with weapons and clothing before leaving the building and heading down to the Metro-2 system.'

'The question is, who?' said Fiona quietly, glancing inside the cabinets to see several very different sets of clothing, from suits to dark green military uniforms and bright yellow workman's attire. 'These almost look like different disguises.'

'The answer will be behind this door,' said Andrew, gesturing to the panel with the push plates and placing himself off to one side of it with his weapon up. 'It's the only way out of here. Ready?'

'Ready,' nodded Fiona.

Gripping the Glock with his right hand, Andrew placed the fingertips of his left hand on one of the brass plates and began pushing. At first, it didn't seem to give at all, but then it suddenly clicked open, and the two sides of the wooden panel swung smoothly open to reveal a large, dimly lit office on the other side. They cautiously stepped inside, realising that what they had just passed through was a false wall designed to hide the small anteroom and the elevator.

'So that lift is some sort of VIP escape route,' said Andrew quietly as he turned to look back into the anteroom. 'A way for whichever bigwig owns this office to get down to the Metro-2 system and out to Ramenki if the proverbial excrement were to really hit the fan here in central Moscow.'

'Authoritarian leaders always have a way out,' said Fiona dryly as they both took a few careful steps inside the office and began looking around.

The office was about ten by fifteen metres in size, and on one of its long walls was a set of four large windows that appeared to be facing out to Lubyanka Square. None of the lights inside the office were switched on, but there was enough streetlight coming in through the windows to faintly illuminate the large space. The other walls were clad in wood panelling that was a rich walnut colour and bedecked with oil paintings of old men in dark suits looking sombre and grave. There was also a section with what appeared to be a collection of framed certificates and diplomas.

In the centre of the large wall opposite the windows hung a huge painted metal crest with the FSB emblem. It consisted of a vertical sword behind a large steel shield that was emblazoned with the two-headed Russian eagle holding a sceptre and an orb. On one side of the emblem was displayed the tri-colour flag of the Russian Federation, and on the other hung the blood-red flag of the Soviet Union, adorned with the yellow hammer and sickle.

The overwhelming impression created by the office and its décor was that they had somehow been sucked into a time machine going back at least half a century. Everything still looked and felt like the 1950s, because the interior of the office had probably changed very little, if anything, since then. For decades, the Soviet and Russian secret services had been both feared and revered to such an extent that no one had seemingly had the courage to change the décor one bit since the building's heyday as the nexus of the dreaded Soviet intelligence apparatus.

Fiona stepped over to the man-sized FSB crest on the wall. Above it was a large oil painting of a man whose image had once adorned virtually every official office in the land.

'Holy crap,' she whispered, glancing at Andrew in disbelief. 'That's Joseph Stalin. And all of these other old men are former directors of the KGB and the FSB.'

'And this place,' whispered Andrew as he looked around in amazement, 'is the FSB director's office. I never thought I'd find myself in here.'

'What about CCTV?' said Fiona, suddenly sounding anxious as she looked around the room, trying to spot security cameras.

'Not a chance,' said Andrew calmly as he walked quietly to one of the windows and peered down onto Lubyanka Square, where the traffic was flowing as normal. 'There's absolutely no way the head of the FSB would allow cameras to record anything in here. We're perfectly safe. At least for now.'

'Wow!' Fiona suddenly exclaimed, struggling to keep her voice down to a whisper.

'What?' said Andrew, turning to see what she had found.

When he looked over at her, he saw her standing open-mouthed with her right index finger pointing at a large sphere in a dark corner of the office.

'Look over here,' she said, sounding stunned as she approached it. 'Do you know what this is?'

'It looks like a globe,' said Andrew. 'Is it a drinks cabinet?'

'This isn't just any globe,' said Fiona. 'This is the famous missing Hitler globe. The one that stood in the corner of his office in the Reich Chancellery in Berlin. So *that's* where it disappeared off to. People have been looking for this ever since the end of the war.'

'How do you know?' said Andrew, moving closer to inspect the roughly one-metre-large painted wooden sphere.

Fiona leaned in and placed a finger on a spot in the eastern part of Africa.

'Only a handful of these were ever made,' she said. 'And we know that Hitler's globe was the only one to reflect the Italian annexation of so-called Abyssinia, which we now call Ethiopia. On this globe, it is correctly labelled as Italian East Africa. So, there is no doubt. This thing used to belong to the Führer. The Soviets clearly took it from Berlin in 1945 and carted it back to Moscow.'

'Quite the war trophy,' said Andrew as he studied it.

"No wonder no one has been able to find it,' said Fiona. 'It has probably been sitting right here in this corner ever since.'

'Alright,' said Andrew, a note of urgency in his voice. 'We need to get on with things and get down towards the archives.'

'Okay,' said Fiona, struggling to tear herself away from the artefact. 'But how? Where do we go from here?'

'Well, since this is the director's office,' said Andrew, looking up towards the ceiling as if recalling something, 'then we're currently on the fourth floor. I memorised the building's layout from those schematics I managed to get my hands on. We should be able to access the sublevels using an elevator at the end of the hallway that is just outside that door. It should be just a few metres along.'

He gestured towards a set of ornate double doors, which he knew led out to a long corridor running the length of the building on this floor.

'The problem,' he continued, rubbing his chin, 'is that the elevator down to the vaults is partly controlled from the security station. And an additional problem is that there are definitely cameras out there in the corridor. So, if one of the guards in the security station happens to be looking at the right screen, we could have a real issue on our hands very quickly.'

'Hey, how about those disguises?' said Fiona, turning to gesture back towards the elevator anteroom. 'We could use those.'

'That might be a good idea,' said Andrew, nodding as he contemplated the idea. 'Let's have another look.'

They went back and opened the cabinets, but it soon became clear that the only plan that had a chance of working was for Andrew to don one of the dark green military uniforms and pretend to be an officer. From the sizes of the various outfits, it was clear that the FSB director was very tall, and if Fiona attempted to wear any of them, she would look so baggy and ridiculous as to be recognised immediately as an intruder.

'I think you might need to stay here for a bit,' said Andrew as he put on the military uniform. 'And I'll have to get to the main security station and neutralise the guards. Hopefully, there's a way to activate the elevator to the sublevels and the doors to the archives from there.'

'Neutralise?' said Fiona hesitantly. 'What does that mean? We were supposed to do this thing quietly without being seen.'

'Rule number one of special forces operations,' said Andrew evenly as he released the Glock's magazine and replaced it with another mag that was loaded with small, yellow dart projectiles. 'Nothing ever goes exactly according to plan. You always end up having to improvise.'

'Right,' nodded Fiona pensively, disliking both the idea of being alone in the FSB director's office and the notion of Andrew somehow neutralising security guards. 'I guess there's no other way.'

'The main security station is on the 3rd floor near the central staircase,' said Andrew. 'Once the coast is clear, you leave this office and join me there. And then you will need to remain there and watch the monitors. You'll be able to see if anyone is heading my way as I approach the archives. We'll stay in touch with these.'

He handed her an earpiece with a short boom mike and then attached an identical device to his right ear.

'Got it,' said Fiona, putting on the earpiece and adjusting the microphone. 'I sure hope this plan will work.'

'The range on these things is several hundred metres,' he said, tapping his earpiece. 'But it might be a lot less inside this building. So, comms might be dodgy at times. Are you ready for this?'

'In for a penny,' said Fiona, with a note of fatalism. 'Let's get this thing over with so we can leave. You look handsome, by the way.'

Andrew looked down at his crisp military uniform and smiled, and then he donned the officer's cap that came with the uniform.

'Thanks,' he said, picking up his holdall. 'Let's go.'

The two of them walked across the office floor and stood by the double doors for a moment while Andrew put his ear to them to listen for movement out in the corridor.

'I think we're okay,' he said, adjusting his cap and the sleeves of the uniform. 'See you in a bit.'

'Good luck,' said Fiona, and then Andrew slipped out into the corridor and closed the door behind him.

★   ★   ★

The long corridor looked very different from the dark walnut-covered interior of the FSB director's office. It was at least four metres wide, with a heavily ornate plaster ceiling that towered over Andrew's head. Every few metres, it was supported by Greek marble columns with richly decorated and swirling capitals at their tops, and the shiny checkered floor was made from large black-and-white marble tiles. Even though no one else seemed to be around, he made sure to stay in character as a Russian army officer. Moving briskly along with his back straight and his shoulders pulled back, the echoes of his footsteps reverberated through the long, virtually empty space. The SAS wasn't exactly known for being big on ranks and hierarchies, but Andrew knew how to project authority when needed.

Just as he reached the wide stairwell at the end of the corridor and was about to turn the corner and head down, a young FSB officer came hurrying up the stairs two steps at a time. The two men almost collided, and Andrew caught the man's eyes scanning the rank insignia on his uniform. As soon as he had done so, he scooted aside quickly and snapped to attention while performing a sharp salute. Then he greeted Andrew and said, 'Good evening, sir'.

'*Dobryy vecher, Ser,*' he said stiffly as Andrew pushed past him down the stairs.

'*Dobryy vecher,*' Andrew mumbled grumpily, lazily returning the salute while making an effort to sound both busy and disinterested.

It appeared to work because as Andrew reached the landing below and turned to continue down the next set of steps, he watched the young officer from under his cap as the man's arm came back down, and he continued to hurry up the stairwell towards the floor above. Moments later, Andrew strode purposefully along a seemingly identical marble corridor on the 3rd floor. The security monitoring station was the second door on the left, and as he approached it, there was no doubt that it was the correct door. It had a small camera mounted directly above it, pointing down at whoever was in front of it, so Andrew had to make sure that his face wasn't visible.

With his officer's cap pulled down low, he swiftly walked up to the door, turned, placed himself in front of it and let the holdall drop onto the floor next to him. Glancing left and right to make sure no one else was around, he then drew himself up to his full height, lifted his right hand and used his knuckles to rap impatiently while ordering the security guard inside to open the door for an inspection.

'*Otkroy dver'! Inspektsiya!*' he called out.

After a few seconds, he heard the sound of shuffling on the other side, and then a click as the door's lock disengaged. As soon as he heard it, he reached inside his jacket and extracted the Glock. No sooner had the lone and somewhat sleepy-eyed security guard pulled the door open and snapped to attention before Andrew fired the pistol and a small dart filled with a highly potent tranquilliser shot out of the pistol's barrel and hit the man in the chest. A split second later, Andrew adjusted his aim and shot the guard in the neck with another dart for good measure. Blinking and looking shocked and bewildered, the guard took a step back and reached up with his right hand to where the dart was now stuck in his neck. He opened his mouth to speak, but by then the engineered chemicals had reached his brain and were rapidly shutting down his entire central nervous system. About a second later, Andrew watched as the guard passed out standing up and then slumped to the floor like a marionette with no strings. He then grabbed his holdall, stepped swiftly inside and closed the door behind him. With any luck, the guard would be out for the count for about three hours, and Andrew dragged him to one side and placed him in a slumped, seated position against a wall.

The dimly lit monitoring station was more or less what Andrew had expected. It was small and had banks of monitors connected to dozens of CCTV cameras placed both throughout the building and on its exterior. Each screen was subdivided into eight smaller squares, and each of those displayed a black-and-white live feed from a single camera. The monitors were mounted on the wall, and in front of them was a desk with two chairs and two computers. This meant that there could potentially be more than one guard on duty this evening, and perhaps the other one had gone off for a smoke and could return any minute now.

Still holding the pistol in his hand, Andrew sat down in one of the chairs and looked at the multiple feeds. Quickly scanning all of them, he barely spotted a soul anywhere in the building. It was the middle of the night, after all, but there would still be guards at various locations, including the ground floor and possibly also in the sublevels or near their access points. It didn't take him long to match the various feeds with his recollection of the building's interior layout and the maps that he had memorised, and he used a couple of sticky notes to mark them out. He also used the computer to find the security system that was capable of remotely locking and unlocking each individual door in the building, leaving open the page that listed all the doors on the sublevels. Then he touched his earpiece.

'Fiona,' he said quietly. 'Are you there?'

'Yes, I am here,' came the reply almost immediately. 'Are you alright?'

'All good,' he said. 'I'm inside the security station. There was only one guard, and he's sleeping.'

'Not permanently, I hope?' said Fiona haltingly.

'Just for a few hours,' said Andrew. 'Anyway, I am looking at all the feeds now, including the corridor on the 3rd and 4th floors, and you are good to leave and come down here now. Second door on the left.'

'Alright,' said Fiona. 'Leaving now.'

Fiona had barely finished her sentence before Andrew could see her on one of the monitors as she left the FSB director's office and began walking hurriedly along the corridor. She disappeared out of shot and then reappeared on a different feed, this time from the stairwell. Then she was on the 3rd floor, and seconds later he opened the door to the security station just as she arrived and slipped inside to join him. She glanced at the unconscious guard propped up against the wall behind the door.

'You're sure he's not dead?' she said, looking concerned. 'It's one thing to break into Lubyanka. It's another to kill guards.'

'I know,' said Andrew placatingly. 'Don't worry. I shot him gently. Now, listen. I need you to sit here and watch the feeds I have marked with sticky notes. They cover my route down to the archives. I have numbered them in sequence, so if you see anyone in a location that I am approaching, you need to let me know ASAP, alright?'

'Got it,' said Fiona, sitting down and adjusting the chair. 'Just hurry. This place is making me nervous.'

'These rectangles represent the various doors and elevators throughout the building, including down on the sublevels,' Andrew said, pointing to one of the computer screens that displayed a set of floor plans drawn with thin coloured lines. 'When I approach these, you simply click them, and they should open.'

'Right,' said Fiona. 'Easy.'

'Oh,' said Andrew. 'I should also tell you, there might be another guard coming.'

'What?' Fiona blurted out incredulously.

'I am not one hundred percent sure,' said Andrew. 'But it is possible there is one more on duty.'

'What the hell am I supposed to do then?' said Fiona with her mouth half open. 'And don't say improvise.'

'You shoot him with this,' said Andrew, placing the Glock with the special tranquilliser ammo on the desk in front of her. 'Two rounds should do it.'

Fiona hesitantly picked up the small and surprisingly light semi-composite weapon and felt its weight in her hand.

'The safety is off,' said Andrew, 'and there's plenty of darts. If anyone comes in here that isn't me, you just point and shoot.'

'Point and shoot,' repeated Fiona, nodding but sounding unconvinced. 'Right. Got it.'

'Alright,' said Andrew. 'I'd better get moving.'

He glanced at one of the monitors and focused in on a square showing the corridor outside the security room. It was still empty.

'See you soon,' he said, picking up the holdall and slipping out of the room, leaving Fiona watching the screens and fingering the Glock nervously.

Realising that she might inadvertently pull the trigger on the weapon, she slid the pistol to her left so that it was still within reach. Then she leaned forward in the chair and began following Andrew from one CCTV square to another as he moved through the building.

Within a couple of minutes, he was back up on the 4th floor, walking past the director's office, and then he reached the elevator that would take him down to the sublevel containing the secure FSB bunker and the archives. He stopped in front of the doors and pressed the button to call it, but as he had expected, nothing happened. It first needed to be activated from the security room. He touched his earpiece.

'Fiona,' he said quietly. 'I am at the elevator. Can you open it?'

'I know,' she said, sounding tense. 'I see you. I've clicked the correct icon, but it is asking for a password. What do I do?'

'Shit,' Andrew whispered. 'Can you activate the sliding doors to the elevator shaft? If you can open them, I might be able to climb down.'

'There's no option to do that,' she said, frustration now spilling into her voice. 'Damn it.'

'Hang on,' said Andrew, pulling a hunting knife from his holdall. 'No need to panic. There's always a way.'

He unsheathed the powerful blade and jammed it into the slit between the elevator's two sliding doors until it was in all the way to the hilt. Then he gripped the handle tightly and twisted it, forcing the two door sections apart by a few centimetres. It wasn't much, but it was enough. He re-sheathed the knife and stuffed it under his belt, and then he wedged his fingers into the small slit and began prying the doors apart. Peering through the slit, he could see an empty concrete elevator shaft on the other side, and cool, dry air was coming through the gap. It took significant force, but he was finally able to pull the sliding doors far enough apart to create a gap wide enough for him to squeeze through.

'Someone's coming!' said Fiona urgently in his ear. 'Stairwell. You've only got a few seconds.'

Realising that he only had one option and that he needed to move fast, Andrew picked up the holdall, jammed it through the opening and let it drop. It took a disconcerting amount of time for it to finally hit the bottom with a distant, reverberating thud.

'Two guards,' said Fiona. 'Coming your way.'

He squeezed himself through the gap and stood on a narrow ledge just inside the elevator shaft while he reached out to his sides, gripped onto the edges of the sliding doors and forced them back towards each other. Gritting his teeth and pulling hard, he finally managed to make the two doors meet and close in front of his face. Panting from the effort but otherwise remaining silent and still, he listened as the footsteps of the guards approached along the corridor. They eventually passed him, and the sound of their footsteps soon began to recede.

He peered down into the gloomy elevator shaft, which was lit only by a set of small service lights mounted above the sliding doors on each level. It was a dizzying drop of at least six storeys to the bottom, and he could only just make out the black holdall that appeared to be lying on top of a cab at the very bottom. Extending down through the centre of the shaft was a thick steel elevator cable that was covered in a thin layer of oil, which made the cable gleam faintly in the dim light.

'All clear,' said Fiona. 'Are you okay?'

'More or less,' said Andrew quietly. 'The good news is that I have a clear path to the archives. The bad news is that it's a long way down. The cab is at the bottom. I'll have to slide down the elevator cable.'

'Be careful,' said Fiona.

'Just keep an eye on the monitors,' said Andrew. 'Find the one by the elevator exit on the archive sublevel. If anything moves down there, let me know.'

'Got it,' said Fiona. 'Good luck.'

Still balancing on the narrow ledge above what would without question be a lethal drop, Andrew managed to slip out of his uniform jacket. He then wrapped it around his hands and got ready to jump. If he missed, he would probably die, but at least he would have only about five or six seconds to regret his decision to come here.

'Who dares wins,' he whispered sardonically to himself, and then he leapt out over the void.

The jump was only about two metres, but given what was at stake if he missed, it felt a lot further than that. His hands gripped the oily cable tightly through the jacket, but the momentum of his body flung him around one side of the cable and almost made him lose his grip. However, he then managed to wrap his legs around the cable, and seconds later, he was corkscrewing down towards the bottom of the shaft. The cable was even more slippery than he had expected, and he had to squeeze tightly with his hands and legs to stop himself from accelerating out of control and eventually slamming into the roof of the cab below with bone-breaking force. As his boots finally thudded onto the top of the cab, he let go of the cable and allowed himself to slump down into a seated position next to the holdall to catch his breath. He then reached up to activate his microphone.

'I'm down,' he said. 'Any sign of guards?'

'Yes,' said Fiona tensely. 'There's one sitting at a desk in front of the vault door to the archives, but he looks like he's packing up. Yes, he's definitely leaving. Don't move. He's coming your way.'

A few seconds later, Andrew heard the cab doors slide open, and then he sensed the cab shift slightly as the guard stepped inside. Moments later, a set of safety clamps next to Andrew disengaged, and then the cab began to move upwards with him on top of it.

'Are you alright?' came Fiona's urgent voice, but Andrew didn't reply for fear of giving his presence away.

As the cab travelled back up the shaft he had just come down, he looked up and peered at the top of it. If the guard was on his way to the top floor, there was every chance that Andrew would end up ground to a pulp between the cab and the steel girders above him. As it turned out, the cab stopped on the 2nd floor, and Andrew felt relief flood through him.

'I'm alright,' he said. 'Do you see the guard on the monitors?

'Shit,' he heard Fiona's anxious voice say, and then the audio was cut off.

'Fiona?' he said after a moment, but there was no response.

Had their communications system died? He waited for another few seconds before trying again.

'Fiona, are you there?' he said, his voice now sounding tense.

Once again, there was no reply, but then, after another anxious twenty seconds or so, the line suddenly crackled, and then Fiona's voice came through.

'Andrew?' she said.

'I'm here,' he said. 'What's going on?'

'Things just got a little dicey,' she said, panting as she spoke. 'We need to hurry up.'

'What happened?' said Andrew.

'The guard from the archive,' said Fiona. 'He came straight here. I had to shoot him with the darts.'

'Is he knocked out?' said Andrew.

'Very,' said Fiona. 'I shot him four times.'

'Jesus,' said Andrew. 'What did you do with him?'

'Dragged him over next to his colleague,' said Fiona. 'You wouldn't believe the body odour of those two.'

'What about the first one?' said Andrew. 'Is he still asleep?'

'Yes,' said Fiona. 'They are both out cold.'

'Alright,' said Andrew. 'Just make sure they don't wake up.'

'How?' said Fiona. 'How the hell do I do that?'

'If they move, shoot them again,' said Andrew. 'Anyway, can you control this elevator from where you are?'

'Hang on,' said Fiona. 'Give me a second.'

She sat back down in the chair in front of the computer screen and found the correct icon for the elevator.

'I still can't get access,' she said. 'I need that password.'

'Alright,' said Andrew, getting back onto his feet. 'I have an idea. I am going to try to get into the cab. Give me a couple of minutes.'

Using his hunting knife to pry open the cab roof's thin metal panels and then employing an appropriate amount of brute force to remove them, he eventually managed to kick his way through the cab's flimsy ceiling. Shoving his holdall through the hole first, he then dropped down inside the cab and stood back up. The control panel gave nothing away with regards to what was on each floor, but he knew where he had to go. He immediately pressed the button for the lowest sublevel, and the elevator soon began to descend. Although the officer's jacket was now streaked with black oil stains, he still put it on, only then realising that he had lost the cap somewhere in the shaft.

'On my way down,' he said into his mike. 'Please keep an eye on the sublevels.'

'Okay,' said Fiona. 'All clear so far.'

As the elevator cab kept descending, he watched the small animated location display, hoping that no one else would be coming into the cab. He was about to congratulate himself on having successfully got past the ground floor when the panel suddenly produced a brief ding and the elevator came to a stop. A couple of seconds later, the doors slid aside. Outside was the large ground-floor vestibule that he recognised from the schematics, and looking in was a single guard carrying a large cardboard box in front of his chest. He stepped inside and gave Andrew a respectful nod.

'*Dobryy vecher*,' he said as he moved inside the elevator cab.

Andrew nodded and grunted, but said nothing.

The guard turned his back to him and glanced down at the control panel. It appeared that he was also heading down to the archives because he merely leaned over and used his elbow to quickly nudge the button to close the doors.

The doors closed and the elevator began descending once again. After a few seconds, Andrew noticed the guard turn his head to one side and look down at the holdall. Then he glanced furtively back at Andrew. His eyes seemed to linger briefly on the oil-streaked uniform jacket, and then he looked up at Andrew's face before turning back and facing forward with an almost imperceptible frown. The eyes of the two men had only met for the briefest of moments, but Andrew's well-honed threat detector was already blaring loudly. The guard was clearly suspicious. The question was whether he was going to do something about it.

Suddenly, the guard let go of the cardboard box, and as it hit the floor, he reached over to the elevator controls and flicked open a small panel behind which was a red metal button with a single word written on it in Cyrillic. Andrew didn't need to be an expert in written Russian to know that this was the security alarm button that would send every guard in the building converging on their position within seconds.

Without hesitation, Andrew launched himself at the guard and barged violently into him from behind while gripping his wrist and wrestling it away from the alarm button. The guard's face slammed into the wall by the control panel, and Andrew heard bones break. With blood gushing out of his nose, the guard attempted to spin around to face his attacker, but Andrew had already wrapped his right arm tightly around his neck and now had him locked in a chokehold. He squeezed hard while the guard's arms flailed around wildly in an attempt to reach behind him. But Andrew was not about to let go, and he maintained the iron-like chokehold for several long seconds until the guard finally began to lose consciousness. His wild movements soon became uncoordinated, then his legs began to give way, and eventually, he sagged to the ground as Andrew guided his limp body down onto the floor of the elevator.

No sooner had he released his grip on the now unconscious guard before the elevator dinged once again and the doors slid aside. Andrew quickly popped open the guard's sidearm holster and extracted the gun. It was a 9mm Grach pistol, which was the standard sidearm for Russia's various military branches, and Andrew flicked the magazine release button to find that it had a full mag of Parabellum rounds. He stuffed it into his belt. Then he poked his head outside into the dimly lit sublevel corridor, and he was gratified to find it empty. Unlike the building up above street level, this part of the Lubyanka complex was much more basic. The rendered concrete walls were painted a pale grey, and the floor was tiled with large, dark slabs. At one end of the corridor, Andrew could see the large blast doors leading into the secure FSB bunker, and in the other direction was the archive's rectangular vault door. Immediately in front of the vault was a wooden desk with an empty office chair, presumably occupied during working hours by whoever was responsible for access to the archives. Straight across from the elevator was what appeared to be a small storage room whose door was partially ajar. He touched his earpiece again.

'Fiona,' he said. 'Have you got eyes on the corridor?'

'All clear,' came Fiona's voice.

'Coming out,' he said.

He reached down to grab the unconscious guard under the arms and began dragging him out into the corridor and across to the storage room.

'What now?' Fiona exclaimed in his ear with a note of exasperation as she watched him manhandle the guard. 'Another one?'

'Listen,' said Andrew as he hauled the guard inside the storage room and let him slump onto the floor. 'I can't help it if these guys keep showing up where I need to be.'

'Fine,' said Fiona. 'Whatever. Let's just get this over with. Get to the vault quickly. I can help you open it from here.'

'Alright,' said Andrew as he left the storage room. 'On my way.'

Twelve

Andrew walked up to the desk and sat down, looking for a way to open the vault. Attached to the underside of the desktop was a slim wooden tray that slid out, revealing a yellow, translucent plastic switch connected to a red metal button.

'Flick the switch, and then I need to activate that button from here,' said Fiona, watching him on the monitor as he pulled the tray out. 'Then you push the button, and that should do it.'

'Got it,' said Andrew, flicking the switch. 'Ready?'

'Ready,' said Fiona. 'Press the button in 3, 2, 1.'

As soon as the yellow switch lit up, Andrew pressed the red button, and the machinery inside the vault door behind him immediately began whirring into action. Moments later, the sound of locking pins disengaging echoed along the empty subterranean corridor, and then the vault door came open with a faint hiss. Amidst the distant-sounding noise of electrical servomotors whirring away somewhere, the door slowly swung out until it was fully open, and Andrew could see the lights inside the archive begin to turn on automatically. Then the corridor was quiet again.

'Good job,' he said, getting to his feet. 'I'm going in.'

Once through the vault door, the archive opened up into a space that was much larger than Andrew could have imagined. Not only did it extend back at least fifty metres, but its ceiling was at least five metres above the smooth, painted concrete floor. Arranged in about a dozen long and straight rows were deep shelving units that towered almost all the way up to the ceiling. Each shelf appeared to be crammed full of dark grey fibreboard boxes with brass label holders, and the boxes were stacked on top of each other in some byzantine system that Andrew was sure only the archivists could make sense of. And judging from the size of the boxes, they were all filled with standard-sized documents. Above each of the long aisles was a line of white, ancient-looking neon tube lights that cast a cold and insipid glow down towards the floor below.

As he moved closer and began walking down the centre aisle, he realised from looking at the labels that everything in there was arranged chronologically by year. Not sure where to start, he walked over to the far left and began moving along the first aisle. As he walked past each section corresponding to a single year, he wondered what secrets were buried in here.

1950: The Korean War. 1953: The agonising death of Joseph Stalin under mysterious circumstances in his Dacha outside of Moscow. 1960: The year when the Soviet Union tested the largest nuclear bomb ever built on a remote island in the Barents Sea far to the north near the Arctic Circle. The so-called Tzar Bomba. 1962:

The Cuban Missile Crisis. 1963: JFK's assassination and the rumoured links between Lee Harvey Oswald and the Soviet and Cuban intelligence agencies. 1979: The ruinous Soviet invasion of Afghanistan. 1986: The historic meeting in Reykjavík between presidents Reagan and Gorbachev. 1989: The fall of the Berlin Wall. This place was a historian's wet dream.

'It's a good thing it's me down here and not you,' Andrew whispered into his mike.

'Why?' said Fiona.

'I would never be able to make you leave,' he replied. 'Still clear outside?'

'Yes,' she said. 'No movement.'

Realising that he had now walked too far, Andrew turned back and found the section for 1961. The year when Pierce Latimer stole and handed over the Farm Hall tapes and transcripts to his Soviet handlers. The section was on a shelf about two metres from the floor, and he had to push a ladder sideways along its rail to the right position and climb up. Examining each of the paper labels attached to the archive boxes took a while since it was in Cyrillic, and he had to spend a few moments on some of them to make sure he didn't mistranslate and accidentally skip the correct box. After several minutes, he finally laid eyes on a label with two words.

Операция Эпсилон

Romanised, this text read '*Operatsiya Epsilon*'. This archive box contained the Soviet documents pertaining to Operation Epsilon. He pulled it off the shelf and climbed back down to the floor. Placing the archive box on top of a stack of other boxes, he opened it up to find a thick pile of documents, some of which were loose while others were kept inside manilla folders or black hardcover binders. One of the binders contained several hundred pages, and it carried a two-word title.

Ферма Зал

'*Ferma Zal*'. Farm Hall. Andrew flicked open the binder and leafed through some of the first yellowed pages, inspecting the typed text as he went. This was definitely what he had come for. These were the original full Farm Hall transcripts.

'Found them,' Andrew whispered into his mike. 'I've got the transcripts.'

'Great,' said Fiona. 'Now, let's get the hell out of here. I don't want to sit in this place for a second longer than I absolutely have to.'

'Okay,' said Andrew, placing the binder back in the box and replacing the lid. 'I'm heading back to the elevator now. We should be able to retrace our steps back to the director's office and take the elevator down to the Metro-2 platform.'

'Well, about that,' said Fiona. 'We certainly could do that, or we could do something a lot quicker.'

'What do you mean?' said Andrew.

'I am looking at the exterior camera feeds right now,' she said. 'And there are several cameras on the roof.'

'So?' said Andrew as he approached the vault door to exit out into the corridor.

'The FSB have a helipad up there,' said Fiona. 'And there's a chopper parked on the pad right now.'

Andrew's first instinct was to play it safe and return the way they had arrived, but the more he thought about it, the more Fiona's suggestion made sense. It was the middle of the night, and if they could fire up the helicopter and disable its transponder, then they could fly unnoticed below both civilian and military radar systems out to the airport in a matter of minutes. But the best part was that it was almost certain that no one would interfere or ask questions. It was all because of a phenomenon that was unique to a society like Russia's, where all power in the country had been captured by oligarchs who maintained their positions through corruption, bribery, intimidation and violence. And in a system like that, anyone who wasn't an oligarch went out of their way to keep their head down and avoid creating any problems or asking any questions. The powerful in Russia were untouchable, and the little people just kept out of the way and avoided getting involved.

What this meant for Andrew and Fiona was that even if anyone noticed the FSB chopper taking off and flying low towards the west of Moscow, if they had any sense, they would rather hack off their right arm with a dull spoon than make a fuss and start asking questions. The safest thing they could do would be to assume that it was simply another case of one of the omnipotent FSB officers or one of the godlike oligarchs carrying out their personal business. And if anyone so much as looked as if they might poke their nose into the affairs of these powerful men, then they were likely to disappear off to some penal colony in Siberia. It was a good plan.

'You know, this just might work,' said Andrew. 'Any guards up there?'

'Not that I can see,' said Fiona. 'And the elevator goes all the way up there.'

'Alright,' he said as he stepped out into the corridor. 'Head for the elevator access on your floor. I should be with you in about one minute. See if you can wipe all the CCTV recordings first. There's no need for us to leave calling cards.'

'I already did that,' said Fiona, glancing at the monitors to make sure that no one was around in the corridor. 'See you soon.'

When the elevator doors slid aside and Fiona spotted Andrew standing there holding the archive box, she hurried inside and shot him a smile as he pressed the button for the top floor.

'Glad to see you managed to get all the way back up here without knocking out any more guards,' she said dryly.

'At least they are still alive,' said Andrew. 'And those darts contain a small amount of a drug that wipes short-term memory, so they probably won't remember anything about what happened to them. The guy in the archives might remember my face, but that won't help them much. By the time he wakes up, we should be in the air. And with no proof, the Russians won't be able to do anything about what happened.'

'I sure hope so,' said Fiona, glancing at her wristwatch. 'I don't want to be on their most wanted list.'

'Hey,' said Andrew, raising an eyebrow. 'This whole thing was your idea. And we got the transcripts, didn't we?'

'Yes, alright,' said Fiona. 'Let's just get out of here before we start celebrating.'

The elevator doors opened on the top floor, and from there, it was one flight of stairs up into a small service structure on top of the FSB headquarters that allowed for access to the roof and the helipad where a black Sikorsky S-76 corporate helicopter was parked. A light rain had now begun to fall over the Russian capital, and as Andrew and Fiona exited onto the roof and hurried along the steel walkway towards the helipad, Fiona glanced at the archive box in Andrew's arms with concern.

'Don't let those documents get wet,' she said. 'They are literally priceless.'

'I know,' said Andrew. 'Could you walk ahead and open the side door for me?'

Fiona did as he asked and rushed up onto the raised helipad, where she gripped the sliding side door to the chopper's passenger compartment and slid it aside. She found herself surprised that it was unlocked, but then she realised that absolutely no one in their right mind would be foolish enough to try to steal a chopper from the FSB. No one except for her and Andrew.

She climbed up into the passenger cabin and waited for Andrew to arrive. When he did, he handed her the archive box, pulled the side door shut, and then climbed up into the cockpit. Fiona used a seatbelt to strap the archive box securely into one of the plush cream leather seats, and then she joined Andrew in the cockpit and slumped into the copilot's seat. They both strapped themselves in, and having flown this type of aircraft before, Andrew began running through the preflight checklist, flipping switches and turning knobs and dials before finally hitting the engine start button.

As the whine from the two turbofan engines rose in pitch and the main rotor began to turn, Andrew used the multifunction display in front of him to enter their flight profile into the navigation computer. He plotted waypoints towards Vnukovo-2 Airport that would allow him to fly close to the ground, skimming over buildings and treetops and weaving between any tall buildings in their flight path. Then he found the switch for the transponder and turned it off. From now on, the aircraft would emit no identification signals to allow anyone on the ground to locate or identify it. All he had to worry about now was to remain low enough to evade radar.

'We're all set,' he said, turning to Fiona as the engines screamed and the rotor blades became a blur overhead. 'All strapped in?'

'Yup,' said Fiona. 'Let's go.'

Andrew pulled back on the collective control stick, and the helicopter began to lift off from the helipad. He used the rudder pedals to rotate the aircraft until it was facing west, and then he pushed the cyclic stick forward, causing the chopper to pitch its nose down slightly and begin to accelerate. Within seconds, they swooped out over Lubyanka Square and continued picking up speed as they only just cleared the rooftops in the area. Within a minute, they were crossing low over the black Moskva River, and then they were racing at breakneck speed over and between buildings, skimming treetops and using parks and other open areas to mask their presence. With a top speed of almost three hundred kilometres per hour, the chopper barreled along and began covering the distance to the airport in a fraction of the time it had taken them to travel through the Metro-2 tunnel.

At one point, Andrew was almost caught off guard by a set of powerlines that rose out of the rainy gloom ahead. By the time he saw them through the windscreen wipers that frantically moved from side to side in front of him, it was almost too late. He pulled back hard on the stick and pitched the nose up. The chopper only just cleared the powerlines, but then an insistent-sounding electronic caution sounded. As soon as he had guided the chopper back down to the nap-of-the-earth flight path, the caution disappeared.

'What was that?' said Fiona.

'We just got spiked by a radar,' said Andrew. 'This thing must have electromagnetic detectors. Handy if you're trying to stay off radar screens.'

'Do you think we were spotted?' said Fiona.

'It's possible,' said Andrew, peering ahead towards the brightly lit airport in the distance. 'But it was so brief that they wouldn't have got a good fix on us. I think we're okay.'

Five minutes later, Andrew followed the flight path south of the airport over a large forested area, from where he was able to approach the commercial heliport near the Vnukovo-2 terminal. With all the lights off, including those in the cockpit and the passenger cabin, he swooped in low and set the chopper down right on top of a large H painted inside the centre of one of the landing pads, and then he immediately killed the engines. Within seconds, the turbofan engines had wound down completely, and roughly a minute after that, the long rotor blades had stopped spinning and were curving down slightly under their own weight.

The two of them exited the helicopter and mounted a small ground vehicle that belonged to the airport maintenance crews. While Andrew drove with the lights off towards the government terminal, Fiona cradled the archive box as if it were her firstborn baby. Soon, they arrived at the terminal apron where the Envoy IV aircraft was parked. They then dismounted the service vehicle and headed inside. There was no staff around except for a couple of cleaners, and the two of them were able to rejoin the flight crew inside the lounge, unseen. Within minutes, the pilot and copilot led them out to the aircraft where the pilot radioed the tower for permission to take off and follow their designated flight path out of Russian airspace to return to the UK. The permission arrived promptly, and half an hour later they were airborne heading west towards the Latvian border. As soon as they crossed over into NATO airspace and headed for the Baltic Sea, Andrew pulled a bottle of chilled Pinot Grigio from the fridge in the passenger cabin, and the two of them then slumped back into their seats, sipping away at the cool drinks.

During the rest of the flight back to London, Fiona was unable to stop herself from opening the archive box and beginning to read its contents. Soon, she had disappeared into her own universe of World War 2 weapons and secret conversations between Nazi scientists recorded at Farm Hall more than half a century earlier. Andrew left her to it and used the opportunity to catch some sleep. By the time they landed back at RAF Northolt, it was early morning, and he felt surprisingly well-rested considering the events of the long night. Fiona, however, was beginning to flag badly. In the car back to Hampstead, she said little as she sat gazing out of the windscreen, and by the time they opened the front door to the house, she was barely able to stand. Without a word, Andrew picked her up and carried her upstairs to their bedroom where he undressed her, placed her gently in the bed and pulled the duvet over her. Within seconds, she was fast asleep.

★   ★   ★

By noon the following day, and after a large breakfast and several cups of strong coffee, Andrew and Fiona were back to sitting in their living room, pouring over the old documents from the KGB archives. While Fiona methodically went through the full and unredacted Farm Hall transcripts, Andrew began examining all the accompanying Russian documents that had been produced after Pierce Latimer's arrival in Moscow in 1961. At one point, Fiona lowered the document she had been reading to her lap and looked at Andrew, her face a picture of amazement and disbelief.

'Wow,' she said, her mouth half open as she shook her head. 'This is really incredible.'

'What?' said Andrew.

'You know how the official story of Operation Epsilon is that the Allies grabbed ten high-ranking Nazi scientists and held them captive at Farm Hall for six months?'

'Yes,' said Andrew, looking mildly perplexed. 'You're not suggesting that didn't happen, are you?'

'Oh, it happened, alright,' said Fiona. 'But listen to this. There weren't ten scientists. There were eleven.'

'I don't understand,' said Andrew. 'What are you saying?'

'What I am saying,' began Fiona, 'is that there was one scientist held at Farm Hall whose very presence there was completely expunged from the official MI6 transcripts. Every single conversation he had with anyone else was simply kept out of the official version. As if he didn't exist.'

'But why?' said Andrew. 'And who was he?'

'His name was Horst Feldmeyer,' said Fiona. 'And he was a senior research scientist and righthand man of none other than Doctor Otto Drexler, the man in charge of Project Omega.'

'Crikey,' said Andrew. 'Drexler's second in command was at Farm Hall?'

'That's right,' said Fiona, leafing through some of the yellowed pages in her lap. 'The other scientists also had several private conversations about both Drexler and Feldmeyer, but none of those conversations ever made it to the official transcripts. But they are right here in these originals.'

'So, what did they say about him?' said Andrew. 'And are there any details about what Project Omega actually was?'

'Yes,' nodded Fiona. 'Various bits and pieces. First of all, the other scientists spoke rather derisively about Drexler, whom they considered to be a maverick, even though he had been personally appointed by Kammler to head up Project Omega. When you read the conversations, there seems to be some envy involved. The whole thing comes across as if there was intense rivalry and competition for resources between Project Alpha, the nuclear bomb project, and the mysterious Project Omega. But it is not entirely clear to me that the scientists working on Project Alpha actually fully understood what Project Omega was even about.'

'Compartmentalisation,' nodded Andrew. 'It's pretty much standard operating procedure in the military. Everything is on a need-to-know basis. And it looks like that's how the Nazis ran their science programs as well. It makes sense.'

'Well,' said Fiona. 'Feldmeyer refused to engage with his fellow scientists and countrymen about any of the details surrounding Omega. It is as if he didn't trust them at all. He might have been worried about some of them switching sides and working for the Allies after the war. And as we now know, that would have been a valid concern, because so many of them did just that. Anyway, from the transcripts, it seems clear to me that Feldmeyer was disliked by the other detainees, and he came across as quite bitter and arrogant. In one conversation, he spoke scathingly about the efforts of the scientists working on Project Alpha, saying that if only the Alpha team had performed its duty and finished developing the bomb, then the Omega team would have secured its delivery anywhere in the world, and Germany would have won the war. According to Feldmeyer, all they needed was a bit more time to perfect the device being built at B8. The only thing that is clear from all of this is that Project Omega involved the construction of a large cyclotron at the Bergkristall facility in Austria.'

'The place where Edward Harding disappeared,' said Andrew.

'That's right,' nodded Fiona. 'Now, on the face of it, that doesn't really appear to make much sense. At least as far as I understand it, and I am not a physicist, cyclotrons are simply nuclear research tools that are used to explore the characteristics of different atoms by splitting them into smaller atoms. You can probably correct me if I am wrong, but it is essentially the same thing that happens in a nuclear fission bomb, right? But without the chain reaction. So, it is perfectly harmless.'

'That's correct,' said Andrew.

'But from what I can gather from the conversations in these transcripts,' said Fiona, 'the Nazi scientists working on Project Omega appeared to have stumbled upon some sort of alternative use for a cyclotron.'

'Any idea what that might have been?' said Andrew.

'Again, I don't fully understand the physics of it,' said Fiona, 'so I can only go by what I am reading here. But there is one particular conversation in the transcripts between two of the more junior scientists at Farm Hall, from which it seems as if Drexler's device was a nuclear weapons delivery system. They mention that its design was based on some sort of accidental discovery involving a cyclotron that had been built using what they call "Wolfram", which today is known as tungsten. It was apparently the result of tiny trace amounts of rhodium contained in the tungsten ore, which caused the cyclotron to exhibit some unexplained effects. Interestingly, the device Drexler and his team were building at Bergkristall was specifically referred to as a 'portal'. That's the precise word quoted right here in this transcript.'

'A portal?' said Andrew sceptically, hesitating for a moment before continuing. 'As in, a portal to somewhere else? Is it just me, or does that sound a lot like science fiction?'

'I agree,' said Fiona. 'It sounds pretty unbelievable, but then most people would have said the same thing about giant V-2 rockets and Me262 jet fighters if you had asked them back in the early 1930s. And yet, less than a decade later, hundreds of those very weapons were bombarding London and shooting down Spitfires over the English Channel.'

'True,' nodded Andrew. 'Perhaps we should be open-minded about this.'

'Think of it this way,' said Fiona. 'What is almost certain, based on what we have discovered, is that the Nazis had developed some kind of nuclear weapon near the end of the war. Perhaps it was a fission bomb like the one produced by the Manhattan Project, perhaps it wasn't, but a nuclear weapon nonetheless. However, as you know better than anyone, the main limiting factor in the deployment of such a weapon is its delivery. The V-2 rockets were very powerful and highly advanced for their day, and they wreaked havoc on London for many months. But they were not powerful enough to deliver a nuclear warhead to London, and the United States was completely out of reach.'

'So, I guess that is where Project Omega's portal technology could come in,' said Andrew pensively, allowing himself to go along with the idea. 'Whatever that actually entailed.'

'Exactly,' said Fiona. 'Now, of course, it all sounds pretty crazy, but that doesn't mean that there isn't something to this whole story. I certainly wouldn't dismiss the idea of a portal, as outlandish as it might sound. I think it is worth remembering that the Nazis poured huge resources into Alpha and Omega. And according to what we have found so far, Alpha almost certainly came to fruition, although not soon enough for the Nazis to win the war. So, it is at least conceivable that Omega managed to do the same. And Feldmeyer's criticism of his scientist colleagues on Project Alpha certainly seems to imply that Omega actually worked.'

'Good point,' nodded Andrew. 'For now, at least, let's assume that Omega was some sort of portal. But why do you suppose MI6 wanted to keep Feldmeyer's presence at Farm Hall a secret?'

'I reckon they simply wanted to conceal his existence from the Soviets,' said Fiona. 'So he never got a mention in the official transcripts.'

'I wonder what happened to him after the war?' said Andrew.

'Well, that's where things take a bit of a dark turn,' said Fiona. 'He never made it out of Farm Hall alive.'

'What do you mean?' said Andrew, looking mystified.

'In early 1946,' said Fiona, 'just a few days before the scientists were to be released and sent back to occupied Germany, Feldmeyer was found dead in his dormitory. Apparently, he had concocted some sort of lethal chemical dose for himself, although no one could ever work out how.'

'Bloody hell,' said Andrew. 'Any doubt about it being a suicide?'

'Apparently not,' said Fiona. 'The other scientists were very shocked and upset. Even if they didn't like the guy.'

'Wow,' said Andrew. 'That's a bit of a twist to the story. At least MI6 didn't have to worry about him falling into Soviet hands.'

'No,' said Fiona, holding up a few transcript pages in her hand. 'But they still ended up getting their hands on these.'

'Yes,' said Andrew. 'Courtesy of Pierce Latimer.'

'Anyway,' said Fiona. 'The story actually gets even stranger than this.'

'Really,' said Andrew. 'How?'

'Apparently,' said Fiona, 'Doctor Horst Feldmeyer's body disappeared from the local mortuary in Cambridge.'

'You're kidding me,' said Andrew. 'It disappeared?'

'Yes,' said Fiona. 'So either Feldmeyer came back to life and walked out of the mortuary never to be seen again, or he somehow managed to fake his own death and escape.'

'That sounds like something straight out of a spy novel,' said Andrew.

'I know,' said Fiona. 'And if he did manage to escape, where did he go?'

'I can't believe none of this has ever been made public,' said Andrew. 'Although if a portal delivery system was ever developed, it would change the world forever, so I guess it is no wonder MI6 did what they could to keep it under wraps.'

'But having said that,' said Fiona. 'If portal technology had been developed at any point, we would almost certainly know about it by now, right? So, can we then assume that it never happened?'

'Well, we can speculate about this until the cows come home,' said Andrew, 'but until we find hard evidence, we should remain open to all possibilities. Anyway, I want you to hear what I found in the Russian files that accompanied the transcripts. There are some pretty amazing things in here as well, including several reports written by agents of the GRU, the foreign intelligence agency of the Soviet military. And they demonstrate a significant interest in Project Omega.'

'Okay,' said Fiona, placing the transcripts on the coffee table and turning to face him.

'Firstly,' said Andrew. 'Everything I have read here seems to more or less corroborate Ben Ambrose's findings. This includes GRU reports written to Stalin in early 1945 about the German nuclear weapons tests where hundreds of Polish POWs were killed.'

'Those reports are in there?' said Fiona, pointing at Andrew's stack of documents.

'That's right,' said Andrew. 'But what is more interesting is that long after the war in 1957, the Soviet scientists tried to replicate the German cyclotron experiment. It happened at a secret test facility deep in the Ural Mountains called '*Vorota*', which means 'gateway' in Russian. It was run by a team of scientists that included several German physicists that the Soviets had captured in southern Germany and Austria in early 1945. The research team was headed up by a German scientist codenamed '*Otkupshchik*', and they were pressing ahead with building a high-powered cyclotron.'

'Just like the Germans did at Bergkristall,' observed Fiona.'

'Precisely,' said Andrew. 'Anyway, during its first test run, the device apparently suffered what was called "an unexplained and catastrophic implosion event". This event annihilated the entire test facility, vaporised everything inside a fifty-metre sphere inside the mountain, and killed all the members of the top science team, including the Germans. The incident left no trace of any of them, the cyclotron, or any of the other equipment. And look here. There's even an old photo attached. It was taken inside the mountain in the Urals.'

He detached the black-and-white photo from under the paperclip with which it had been attached to the document folder and handed it to Fiona. It was grainy and somewhat faded, but it was still perfectly possible to see what was in it. It appeared to have been taken from an underground tunnel that ended abruptly and opened up into an enormous, cavernous space in the shape of a perfect sphere. Several lights trailing black power cables had been mounted on the walls, and there were a couple of uniformed figures walking on the bottom of the bizarre cave, which clearly conveyed the true scale of the surreal space.

'Christ on a bike,' said Fiona, amazed. 'What the hell did this?'

'The device, clearly,' said Andrew. 'But as for exactly how that sort of thing could happen, I have no idea. Anyway, according to these documents, the event caused a temporary collapse of the Soviet power grid in most of the central parts of the Soviet Union, which I have actually been able to verify using other sources.

And it turns out that, as a result of this event, the entire program was shut down and never attempted again.'

'I'm not surprised,' said Fiona, gazing at the photo. 'It's quite scary to look at. In fact, it looks completely unnatural.'

'Wait a minute,' Andrew said, as a thought suddenly struck him.

'What?' said Fiona, looking up from the photo.

'What if the head of the Soviet team was Horst Feldmeyer?' he said, picking up a pen and a piece of paper. 'Look.'

'*Откупщик*', he said, scribbling the name. 'That was the team head's codename. In Romanised form, it becomes 'Otkupshchik' and that means something like tenant farmer, which is exactly what 'Feldmeyer' means in German. His codename wasn't just a codename. It was his *actual* name, except in russified form.'

'Wow,' said Fiona. 'So, Otto Drexler's righthand man somehow ended up working for a Soviet research program tasked with continuing Project Omega's work.'

'That's right,' said Andrew. 'It would make sense. We already know that the Soviets captured lots of German scientists and put them to work in the Soviet Union's various weapons programs.'

'Here's an idea,' said Fiona. 'What if the Soviets managed to somehow communicate with Feldmeyer while he was at Farm Hall? What if they made him a deal to get him out in return for joining the Soviet research program?'

'After everything we have discovered so far,' said Andrew, 'I wouldn't be surprised.'

'Soviet agents could have helped fake his death, right?' said Fiona.

'Possibly,' said Andrew. 'There are various drugs that can induce a person into a state that is difficult to distinguish from someone being dead. There are even some completely natural compounds that can do that.'

'So, the Soviets could have smuggled the drug to Feldmeyer,' said Fiona. 'And then they could have broken him out of the mortuary and spirited him away to Moscow.'

'I certainly wouldn't rule it out,' said Andrew. 'But either way, the Soviet program appears to have ended with his death. When the Soviet prototype of the portal device was vaporised along with him and his entire team inside the Vorota facility, they shut the whole thing down and never went back to it. At least, as far as we know.'

'In other words, this is a dead end,' said Fiona. 'Which makes me wonder. What happened to Doctor Otto Drexler?'

'That is a very good question,' said Andrew. 'And one that this mysterious Ferdinand von Rittenhausen could well have the answers to. He seems to be obsessed with anything connected to Drexler and his work at Bergkristall.'

'So, how are we going to find out what he knows?' said Fiona.

'Well,' said Andrew, looking meaningfully at Fiona. 'Not to put too fine a point on it, but we know where he lives.'

Fiona regarded him for a long moment.

'You want to visit his apartment in Berlin, don't you?' she said.

'That's right,' said Andrew. 'It can't be any more tricky than breaking into the FSB headquarters. So, are you in?'

'Of course I am,' she said. 'If Rittenhausen had anything to do with Ambrose's murder, then we need to get to the bottom of this whole thing and prove it.'

Thirteen

Adam Holbrook was walking along the final stretch of the tunnel leading from the small underground rail station to the test facility belonging to Rittenhausen's estate near Mendoza City. He wasn't exactly sure, but he believed that it had now been roughly a week or so since his arrival here, although he might be off by a day or two. Being injected with a powerful sedative and then kidnapped and transported halfway across the world had caused confusion in his mind, and it had been an upsetting experience, to say the least. And he would be the first to admit that he had more or less lost track of time. Either way, he had now been working long hours for several days to help Rittenhausen's team of engineers prepare the huge ring-shaped device for its initial test run, and it was beginning to take its toll.

As he reached the enormous, circular and well-lit concrete cave, he stopped for a moment to gaze at the device standing at the centre of the cavernous space.

He hated being here, and he fumed about how he had ended up joining Rittenhausen's bizarre pet project, but at the same time, there was no denying it. To someone like him, the device in front of him was a thing of beauty. Towering up around five metres in the centre of the space and surrounded by banks of terminals that looked like something from a NASA flight control centre, it looked like something out of a science fiction movie. But it was a very real, although heavily modified, cyclotron. And whatever its true purpose, Holbrook knew that it was probably going to work when it was finally powered up.

His work here so far had involved a wide range of tasks that the engineers had struggled with, including calibrating the powerful electromagnets for optimal efficiency, troubleshooting unexplained feedback loops in the sensor arrays, and fine-tuning the controlled surge of electricity from the capacitor array. But his main task had been to perform ongoing calculations and high-energy particle simulations to determine the maximum amount of energy in the form of accelerated protons that could be held at a steady state inside the device.

Most of these tasks were bread-and-butter issues for a man like Holbrook, and they were something he had done countless times before at CERN. However, certain aspects of the device's design were definitely unlike anything he had ever seen before, not least when it came to the choice of materials used. He had found himself working to material specifications that didn't seem to make much sense, and that he didn't fully understand. Among them was the realisation that most of the unusually designed cyclotron device's inner toroid-shaped containment chamber had been meticulously constructed from tens of thousands of small tungsten tiles that had been doped with very specific amounts of rhodium. The purpose of this strange amalgam was unclear to him, but it was an exotic choice of materials, to say the least, and it was certainly a departure from what he had been used to.

What he did know was that tungsten was one of the strongest materials known to man. Among all of the non-alloyed metals, it has the highest melting point and the highest tensile strength, but in this particular context, its most important characteristic was its very low electrical conductivity. This meant that the device would be able to maintain control of unprecedented levels of hyper-accelerated positively charged protons inside its circular containment chamber, and that the only limiting factor of the device was the strength of the electromagnets holding the torrent of particles in place as they continuously ripped around the device's centre in a perfect circular orbit.

The use of these esoteric materials had forced Holbrook to deviate from his standard operating procedure in several respects, but he had done his best to compensate with the calibration algorithms and the power management software. And so far, it appears to have been successful. They were now only days away from the first test.

With regards to power consumption, the electricity required for the test was off the charts, and until earlier that day, he had been unsure precisely where it all came from. That was when one of the engineers had told him that Rittenhausen's complex had its own nuclear reactor located in a separate underground facility several hundred metres away. It had been built by a Chinese industrial contractor and was connected to a large subterranean bunker crammed full of capacitor arrays capable of delivering massive but relatively brief surges of power. This was not dissimilar to the setup at CERN, but the notion of such an installation belonging to a single private individual was bizarre and almost beyond comprehension. However, whatever Rittenhausen was trying to achieve here, he was certainly serious about it, and he had clearly poured eye-watering amounts of money into the project.

Now, after several days of slogging away in the test chamber as teams of engineers and technicians worked seemingly around the clock to build the device, Holbrook's frustration and bitterness about his predicament were beginning to boil over. Rittenhausen had not shown his face for days, and Holbrook had eventually walked up to a man by the name of Raul Torres, who was Rittenhausen's head of security. Or, as Holbrook liked to think of him, the chief jailor. Torres, who was a former Mendoza City police chief, was a tall and lean forty-something-year-old man with a broad chest, an angular face, olive skin and a short black moustache. He and his security team wore charcoal-coloured uniforms with large orange patches on the shoulders, and there were always about a handful of them around whenever Holbrook was in the test facility. He and his men never got in the way, and they limited their interactions to escorting Holbrook back and forth to and from the estate's manor house. However, Torres always appeared to look down his nose at Holbrook whenever he saw him, and not just because he was much taller. His demeanour gave

Holbrook the impression that Torres saw him as merely an instrument whose temporary presence had to be tolerated for a while. Someone who was entirely expendable.

During their conversation, Holbrook had impressed with Torres that he now demanded to know directly from Rittenhausen what the project was about and for how long he was going to be held here against his will. He also stated that if answers to those questions were not forthcoming soon, then he would simply lay down his proverbial tools and refuse to continue working, consequences be damned. And by the way, he didn't believe they would dare harm his daughter, since that would simply mean a permanent end to his involvement, and they didn't want that, did they? Checkmate.

Seemingly unperturbed by Holbrook's rant, Torres had regarded him impassively as he spoke, and by the end of his tirade, he had simply nodded and said he would relay his concerns to Rittenhausen. Torres had then waved over two of the guards and told them to escort the professor back to his room at the winery.

And so here he was, inside what was effectively his prison cell, just waiting to see what Rittenhausen would do next. It had only been a few hours since his altercation with Torres, but he was already beginning to feel nervous and regret what he had done. Had he overplayed his hand? Had he now foolishly put Alice in danger simply because of his own stupid hubris about how important Rittenhausen thought he was to the project? He paced the floor of his room, sat down for a few minutes on the bed wringing his hands, and then he returned to pacing.

When he heard the door being unlocked, he thought for a brief moment that Rittenhausen had returned from his trip and had come to speak to him, but he was quickly disappointed when he saw the housekeeper flanked by two guards rolling a small trolley with food into the room. Without a word, the housekeeper then left the room again, and the door was locked. Once more, Holbrook was alone, and he had completely lost his appetite. After a few moments, he almost launched himself at the door to get the attention of the guards and tell them that he had changed his mind and that he was sorry for his outbursts. But he just about managed to regain his composure. Surely, he had some leverage here, so he was going to use it to get what he wanted. There was no denying that it felt like a risky thing to be doing, but it just might be the only language Rittenhausen would understand. Or so he hoped.

★ ★ ★

'Mr. Rittenhausen, sir,' said the voice on the other end of the line, speaking English with a Spanish accent. 'This is Torres.'

'Raul,' said Rittenhausen affably as he reclined in an armchair inside his apartment on Zimmerstrasse in Berlin. 'You said you needed to speak to me. How are things going?'

'They have been going very well,' said Torres, 'until today.'

'What does that mean?' said Rittenhausen guardedly. 'Is the professor causing trouble?'

'He has refused to continue working until he is informed of the goal of the project,' said Torres. 'And he demands to speak to you personally.'

'Well, well,' said Rittenhausen, as if appraising the actions of a young and petulant child. 'He's not exactly in a position to make demands. Surely, he must understand that?'

'I am not sure he does, sir,' said Torres. 'He appears to think he is twisting your arm. I would recommend a much firmer approach. Something to help motivate him, if you understand what I mean.'

'Are you talking about his daughter, Alice?' said Rittenhausen.

'Yes,' said Torres. 'These brainy scientists. They are arrogant. All bark and no bite. Punch them in the face, and they will back down and realise who's in charge.'

'Yes,' said Rittenhausen glibly, sipping from a glass of wine. 'I fear you may be correct. Thank you for your advice. I shall take that into consideration and then make a decision.'

'Is there anything you want me to do about it?' said Torres.

'No thank you,' said Rittenhausen. 'That won't be necessary. Hector and Ernesto are here in Berlin. I can send them to take care of it if necessary. Just make sure Holbrook doesn't leave his room. The last thing we need right now is him finding a way to escape.'

'Don't worry,' said Torres confidently. 'I have two men standing guard by his door at all times. He's not going anywhere.'

'Very good,' said Rittenhausen, putting down his glass on the coffee table in front of him. 'Thank you for the update. I will let you know what I decide shortly.'

★   ★   ★

It was late in the afternoon when Andrew and Fiona stepped out of Berlin's Brandenburg Airport, located some fifteen kilometres south of the German capital. It was still warm, and high above was a small scattering of puffy white clouds that drifted slowly on the gentle breeze. Using his connections inside the British security and intelligence services, Andrew had secured them two diplomatic passes, and this meant that their luggage had not been subject to searches or security scans upon arrival in Germany.

They hailed a taxi from the nearby stand, and soon they were headed north along a motorway through wheat fields and wooded areas surrounding the airport into the suburbs and onwards towards their destination near the city centre. After about fifteen minutes, the three-lane motorway curved northwest around a huge open area just south of the city centre that had once been home to the old Tempelhof Airport. Looking out of the right-hand side window of the taxi across the several-kilometre-wide area that was now open to the public, Fiona turned to Andrew and jerked her head towards the outside.

'Do you know why this airport is called Tempelhof?' she said.

'Tell me,' said Andrew. 'Something to do with a temple?'

'In a way,' nodded Fiona. 'It got its name from the fact that this land once belonged to the Knights Templar. And '*hof*' means 'court'. Isn't that interesting?'

'It is,' said Andrew, peering across the traffic lanes as the enormous grass-covered area swept by.

'It only became an airport in 1923,' said Fiona, whose virtually eidetic memory rarely failed to retain any information she had laid eyes on. 'But then it was expanded by the Nazis during the 1930s. This was all part of Albert Speer's plans for the construction of the new world capital of Germania.'

'Right,' said Andrew. 'I remember reading about that. A case of unbridled hubris, if I ever saw it anywhere.'

'You're not wrong,' smiled Fiona wryly. 'The plan was for it to become the Third Reich's gateway to the world once that world had been brought to submission. During World War 2, it was an assembly site for the famous Junkers Ju-87 dive bombers.'

'The 'Stuka',' said Andrew. 'Those were the really noisy ones, right?'

'That's right,' said Fiona. 'They were actually fitted with propeller-driven sirens called Jericho trumpets under each landing gear carriage. That's what made them produce that terrifying wail as they dived and accelerated towards their targets on the ground.'

'Psychological warfare right on the battlefield,' said Andrew. 'I bet it worked too.'

'There's actually an interesting anecdote about this place that fits with what we have been looking into,' said Fiona. 'You see, during the fall of Berlin, when there were intense bombardments everywhere and tanks were rolling through the streets and the whole city was crumbling into ruins, Soviet troops rushed to occupy this airport. And they immediately began combing through the entire complex, looking for anything related to the Reich's aircraft design and manufacturing processes. Anything that they might be able to bring back to Moscow to help with their own weapons development programs.'

'I didn't know that,' said Andrew, as the former airport disappeared from view.

'And then, of course, after the war,' said Fiona, 'Tempelhof fell within the American-occupied sector of the city. And as I am sure you know, it was the scene of the massive Berlin airlift.'

'Right,' nodded Andrew, casting his mind back to distant history lessons. 'The Soviet Union blockaded the city, right?'

'Yes,' said Fiona. 'I think they claimed that all access by road, rail or river to West Berlin was suddenly no longer possible because of "technical difficulties". But it was all an attempt to force the allies to leave Berlin so the Soviet Union could take over all of East Germany.'

Andrew shook his head and scoffed with a sarcastic grunt.

'Right,' he said derisively. 'That sounds just like something the Russians would do. You can't trust those bastards.'

'That's certainly one way of looking at it,' said Fiona as she glanced at Andrew. 'And you would be in pretty good company thinking that way. Winston Churchill once said. "I cannot forecast to you the actions of Russia. It is a riddle wrapped in a mystery inside an enigma. But perhaps there is a key, and that key is Russian national interests.".'

'Yes, I suppose it always boils down to that,' said Andrew. 'But you could say the same about most other countries, including Britain. Still, I have always felt that there is a particularly dishonourable strain to the way Russia conducts itself. A complete lack of morals. There always have been, and there probably always will be.'

'Said the man who just broke into FSB headquarters,' Fiona said teasingly as she nudged him gently.

'Well, that was different,' shrugged Andrew. 'What we did, we did for a good cause. And technically, all we did was take back what the Russians stole from us to begin with.'

'I agree,' Fiona conceded. 'Those transcripts should never have left British soil. Anyway, we're almost there now. I have booked us a hotel room on Kochstrasse, which is coming up on our left in a moment. Rittenhausen's apartment is just north of here.'

When the taxi pulled up in front of the modern hotel, whose façade was all concrete, steel and tinted glass, the sun was just cresting the rooftops to the west and slowly sinking below the horizon. They carried their bags inside the hotel lobby, and after a quick check-in and a change of clothes, they went back out onto the street and headed for a nearby pizzeria. Wearing a black long-sleeved top and a thin leather jacket, as well as black jeans and trainers, Andrew was carrying a small backpack containing everything he might need for the break-in. He slotted it under the table as they sat down, and then they ordered their food. They had a couple of hours to kill before they could make their move.

'We still don't know if Rittenhausen is at home,' said Fiona. 'What are you planning to do if he's there?'

'I'll improvise,' said Andrew with a wink. 'I might hang around and see if he leaves, or we might have to try again tomorrow. Either way, I'll need a decent amount of time in there, so we will just have to wait until that is possible. But I will keep you updated on the earpiece. Have you got yours?'

Fiona reached into her trouser pocket and pulled out a small, black egg-shaped plastic case.

'Right here,' she said. 'Fully charged. The café on the ground floor closes at 11 p.m., so I will grab a table outside on the pavement and watch the entrance on Zimmerstrasse. If anyone enters the building through the entrance to the apartments, I'll let you know.'

After their pizzas had arrived, Fiona took on a pensive look as she gazed out of the window overlooking the busy street.

'You know,' she said, as she began cutting the pizza on the plate in front of her. 'I've been thinking about something. Why would someone like Ferdinand von Rittenhausen possess dual Argentinian and German citizenship?'

'Good question,' said Andrew, taking a swig of his soft drink. 'It does seem like an odd combination.'

'Well, yes,' nodded Fiona, 'except if you consider what happened to a lot of high-ranking Nazis, including top-level scientists, after the war. Many of them managed to escape capture by the Allies via the so-called 'ratlines' through Italy. And many of those ended up in Argentina.'

Andrew kept chewing as he contemplated Fiona's words. Then he took a sip of his drink.

'So, are you saying that you think Doctor Otto Drexler somehow made it safely to Argentina after the war ended?' he finally said. 'And then his son Maximillian became a natural-born Argentinian citizen, which meant that his grandson Ferdinand was born with an Argentinian passport too?'

'Well, it's at least possibly, right?' said Fiona. 'And Ferdinand von Rittenhausen could then have acquired German citizenship for himself later on. I don't think it is too difficult to get if you can prove your ancestry. And if that is true, then I wouldn't be surprised if he was brought up in Argentina to revere Germany and the Nazis. It's been known to happen. And if I am not mistaken, there are still whole communities living in that country who are all proud descendants of Nazi immigrants.'

'Right,' nodded Andrew pensively. 'I suppose it would fit what we know so far. He is clearly an aficionado of all things related to Germany's inglorious Nazi past. So, perhaps becoming a citizen of the old country makes him feel closer to his illustrious grandfather.'

'The more I think about this,' said Fiona, 'and the more we learn about this man, the more I think that his interest in all this advanced Nazi technology goes beyond the science, as fascinating as that might be even today. I feel like there must be some sort of very personal component to the whole thing as well.'

'Perhaps,' said Andrew. 'It wouldn't be the first time that a spurious historical connection to some distant past glory made people do some very weird things. And in this case, it goes well beyond weird. In fact, it could involve murder, although we obviously can't prove that right now.'

'Hopefully soon,' said Fiona. 'Maybe there's proof somewhere in that apartment that he was behind the murders of Ambrose and Bateman. Have you got the memory stick?'

'In my pocket,' said Andrew, patting his jacket. 'If things go according to plan, anything digital in that apartment will be ours shortly, and Rittenhausen won't even know we have it.'

'Good,' said Fiona. 'We need to find out the truth.'

'And we will,' said Andrew confidently. 'Anyway, what's the story with those ratlines you mentioned? How did they work? And how many Nazis actually managed to escape that way?'

'Well, first of all,' said Fiona, 'they were called ratlines because the high-ranking people using them were just like rats fleeing the sinking ship. In early 1945, Nazi Germany was crumbling before their eyes, and when push came to shove, it turned out that they suddenly didn't actually feel like dying for Hitler and the thousand-year Reich. So they were scrambling for a safe way out of Germany, and swooping to help them was what might seem like a pretty unlikely organisation.'

'It was the Vatican, right?' said Andrew.

'That's right,' said Fiona. 'I don't think most people realise just how cosy the Catholic Church's relationship with the Nazis was. The German Catholic Party had been instrumental in securing Hitler's election to the role of chancellor during his rise to power in 1933. And the very first international treaty that Nazi Germany signed with a foreign nation was the so-called *Reichskonkordat*, which was signed with the Vatican just a few months after Hitler had taken power. Essentially, it said that the church would stay out of politics if the German government allowed the church free reign over the education of children.'

'Lovely,' said Andrew with a note of sarcasm. 'What could possibly go wrong?'

'You might not believe it,' said Fiona, 'but that treaty is still in effect today. At least on paper.'

'I am speechless,' said Andrew with a shake of the head. 'Doesn't the Vatican ever accept making a mistake?'

'Also,' continued Fiona, 'Hitler made quite a big deal about Christian values in his book, '*Mein Kampf*', side by side with his intense hatred of Jews. And as an organisation, the Church was conspicuously quiet about the extermination of the Jews, even though there is ample evidence that they knew full well about the Nazi death camps quite early in the war.'

'It seems utterly mad to me that this was their attitude,' said Andrew, shaking his head. 'What happened to 'love thy neighbour'?'

'I guess that only applied if your neighbour was a Christian,' said Fiona. 'But I think it was a combination of things. Remember, the Church had vilified Jews for centuries because of their rejection of Jesus as the Messiah. And pretty much ever since the foundation of Christianity, the faith has made a point of blaming the Jews for the death of Jesus, which, according to their scripture, is the same as the death of God. So, because of the Nazi efforts to rid the world of the Jews, I think the Vatican saw them as a sort of natural ally, as absurd as that sounds now. For two thousand years, all of the descendants of the Jews were fair game across Europe. That's why all those pogroms happened over and over again for centuries. Every time a country experienced some sort of turmoil, they would simply blame the Jews and start lynching them in the streets. It was literally like a witch hunt. And the sad truth is that the church orchestrated that entire mindset, and they were happy to sit back and let it play out. So when what was a deeply Catholic Germany fell under the rule of a psychopath like Hitler, it was very easy for him to tap into that undercurrent of hatred and to pretend that the solution to all of Germany's problems was to simply get rid of the Jews.'

'Absolutely monstrous,' said Andrew, shaking his head. 'So, that's why the Vatican helped the Nazis escape?'

'More or less,' said Fiona. 'It certainly played a large role. They were also terrified of communism, which, as you know, was never a great fan of religion. And in that, they were joined by the Allies, who actually recruited some of the Nazis as spies against the communists in Europe and South America.'

'Bloody hell,' said Andrew, struggling to take in what Fiona had just said. 'What a mess. And a complete moral vacuum.'

'I know,' said Fiona. 'It was shameful. I don't think the Vatican has ever really reckoned with what happened back then. And it has never properly acknowledged its responsibility for a lot of the top Nazis simply melting away and disappearing after the war and then living out their lives peacefully and comfortably in places like Buenos Aires.'

'Amazing,' said Andrew. 'Anyway, how did the ratlines work, exactly? How did the Vatican manage to pull this off?'

'In short,' said Fiona with a shrug, 'because it was the Vatican. I don't think that anyone at that time could have imagined that it would be the Christians who would shelter some of the worst war criminals in human history. So therefore, no one suspected it until much later when evidence began to emerge that it had happened on a quite massive scale. One particularly strongly pro-Nazi actor in this was an Austrian Catholic bishop named Alois Hudal, who had written a book in 1937 praising Hitler and his national socialist project and railing against Jews, communists and supporters of democracy. After the war, Hudal personally helped hundreds of Nazis escape, including fugitive war criminals, because as he stated after the war, he believed them to be "completely blameless".'

'You've got to be kidding me,' groaned Andrew.

'I wish I was,' said Fiona. 'By any moral standards, this was atrocious behaviour, but the good bishop Hudal was happy to do it because he saw how the Nazis and the Catholic church were on the same side against the Jews. And this sort of thing happened a lot. Almost all of these escaping Nazis crossed the Alps and went via a couple of monasteries in northern Italy, including one in Bolzano, less than fifty kilometres from the border with Austria. From there, they were smuggled to Rome, where the Vatican helped them acquire false identification documents through the International Red Cross, whose leadership was most likely also actively supportive of the ratlines. And then they would finally travel to the port of Genoa, where they boarded passenger liners to Buenos Aires and other places in South America.'

'This is just shocking,' said Andrew with disdain painted all across his face. 'How many of these bastards did the church help to get to South America?'

'All in all,' said Fiona, 'about ten thousand Nazis escaped that way. And roughly half of those ended up in Argentina.'

'But why Argentina?' said Andrew. 'What was so special about that country?'

'Several reasons,' said Fiona. 'South America had more or less managed to steer clear of the Second World War, and most of the countries there were not aligned with either side. At least not formally. However, the Argentinian president, Juan Peron, played a large role in the success of the ratlines. He had spent some time as a military attaché in Italy, where he had met a bunch of SS officers who he became friendly with. He was a big admirer of European dictators like Hitler and Mussolini, and after the war, he called the Nuremberg Trials of Nazi war criminals "a disgrace".'

'What a charming chap,' said Andrew, taking another bite of his pizza.

'Yes, and he was fairly entrepreneurial,' said Fiona. 'You see, once the war had ended, he saw an opportunity to bring German engineers and scientists, especially nuclear scientists, to Argentina. After all, these people were out of a job, and his country needed exactly those types of experts. And many of the high-ranking SS types brought large amounts of wealth in the form of gold bars with them, which Peron obviously welcomed. The fact that he was also staunchly anti-communist and very worried about the spread of communism across the world only made his calculation that much simpler. And on top of all that, countries like Argentina had no extradition treaties with European nations, so the Nazis were able to freely enter and settle there.'

'Including one Doctor Otto Drexler,' said Andrew. 'Brilliant particle physicist and grandfather of Ferdinand von Rittenhausen.'

'Yes, presumably so,' nodded Fiona.

'And now,' said Andrew, 'Rittenhausen appears to be moving heaven and earth to locate and acquire as many documents related to his grandfather's work as he possibly can.'

'It would seem that way,' nodded Fiona. 'The question is, why. What is he planning?'

'Well, with a bit of luck,' said Andrew, 'we'll know more very soon.'

Fourteen

By the time Andrew and Fiona left the restaurant a couple of hours later, the sky was completely dark and overcast, but it was a pleasantly warm evening. There were still cars in the streets and pedestrians on the pavements, but it was now noticeably quieter than when they had arrived.

'Be careful,' said Fiona meaningfully, giving Andrew a kiss on the cheek. 'No crazy stuff.'

'I'll be as careful as I can,' he said, smiling and giving her a hug. 'Just keep an eye on that front door for me.'

'I will,' she said. 'See you soon.'

And with that, the two of them split up. Fiona continued north along Friedrichstrasse for another fifty metres before crossing the road to the café on the corner with Zimmerstrasse where the building that was home to Rittenhausen's top-floor apartment was located. She rounded the corner and sat down at one of the small tables that had been placed by the café on the pavement. It was quite busy, and there were patrons coming and going as well as several other people sitting alone or in groups at the other tables enjoying their drinks and each other's company. As she sat down, she glanced up briefly at the windows on the top floor where Rittenhausen lived when he was in town. She then placed her handbag on the table and extracted her phone while she waited for a waiter to come along and take her order.

Andrew headed back to Kochstrasse and continued along the pavement for about thirty metres until he arrived at a short drive allowing for access to a large courtyard that was located between Kochstrasse and Zimmerstrasse. The courtyard contained a lawn with a large tree along with some bushes and a couple of benches, and on the other side of it were the backs of the buildings on Zimmerstrasse. Directly across from him as he walked in was a sleek and modern seven-storey concrete apartment block with a substantial external metal staircase attached to the rear of the building. The base of the staircase sat inside a metal cage about three metres tall, and the only way to access the stairs from the outside was with a key for a door in the side of the cage facing the courtyard. In truth, though, the metal cage had never really been designed to keep a determined person out, but seemed to have been built mainly as a mild deterrent, and within a few seconds, Andrew had scaled one side of it and dropped down next to the fire escape stairwell on the other.

With his backpack slung over his shoulders, he scaled the stairs two steps at a time and quickly made his way up to the residents-only roof terrace, which thankfully turned out to be empty. From there, he crawled up over the roughly two-metre-tall wall to the roof of the adjacent building which belonged to a hotel. Now some thirty metres above ground, he made sure to stay well away from the edge of the building that was facing the street below to make sure he wasn't spotted. Letting people on the pavement catch sight of someone clambering around on top of buildings at night was an excellent way of drawing attention to oneself.

He soon reached the other end of the hotel's roof, and here he had to jump down two metres to the roof of the old building on the corner where Rittenhausen had his apartment. His feet landed softly on the flat, tarred roof surface, allowing his knees to absorb as much of the impact as possible in order to minimise any noise being heard inside the large apartment that made up the entire top floor. About four metres away from him was one of two large skylights sitting in slightly raised boxes that were fitted onto the roof, and as far as he could see, no light was coming up through them from the inside.

He carefully made his way over to it and peered down. It was dark except for a bit of streetlight spilling in through the windows, but he could clearly make out a very large bed some four or five metres directly beneath the skylight. A bit further back towards the rear of the building, a door was just visible to what looked like an ensuite bathroom. There was no sign of any electrical lights being switched on anywhere. The apartment appeared to be empty. He knelt by the skylight box and touched his earpiece.

'Fiona,' he said quietly. 'I don't think there's anyone here. I am about to enter. Stay sharp.'

'Okay,' Andrew heard Fiona say as the sound of voices and rustling cutlery from the café below came through his earpiece. 'I'm on the pavement with the entrance to the apartments in full view. Please be careful.'

Andrew moved along to the second skylight, which was about ten metres away. When he peered down through it, he saw a sizeable living room with wide wooden floorboards, several large rugs and two plush, upholstered Louis XIV-style sofas next to a coffee table made of brass and white marble. However, the floor directly underneath the skylight was clear. This was going to be his entry point, but first, he had to get through the skylight, which was only openable from the inside. And after that, he would have to defeat any electronic security measures.

He quickly unslung and unzipped his backpack, reaching inside to extract a portable foam cutter that looked like a short, thin icepick with a switch on its plastic handle. He flicked the switch and waited a few seconds for the metal rod to heat up to its maximum temperature of 600 degrees Celsius. Then he got on one knee and pushed its tip through the plastic skylight. The rod slid through the transparent plastic like a hot knife through butter, and then he began to cut. Pushing it along smoothly at about five centimetres per second, it took him only a couple of minutes to slice out a hole large enough for him to fit through. He removed the cut-out section and placed it on the roof next to him. He then pulled a roll of high-strength carbon fibre wire from the backpack and used a steel hook to attach it to the skylight's exterior.

Poking his head carefully through the opening just enough to be able to see inside, he began scanning the room for the alarms and security systems that he was certain would be in there. Before he could enter and begin searching Rittenhausen's place, those systems would need to be disabled, and he had brought with him the tools to do it.

First on the list were the thermal motion sensors and cameras mounted throughout the apartment. There were evidently two in each room, and in the living room, they were mounted in the corners under the ceiling facing the windows. This was a rookie mistake on the part of the installer because the fluctuations in the temperature along with the movement of clouds, leaves and rain outside the windows meant that they would have to be calibrated accordingly. In other words, very slight temperature differences or movements would not be picked up by the sensors, so as long as he moved slowly and only exposed a small part of his body, he should be okay.

Pulling his Glock 17 from the shoulder holster under his jacket, he quickly screwed the suppressor on, and then he reached through the hole in the skylight and pushed his upper body through just enough to be able to see along the underside of the ceiling to the two sensors. Hanging almost upside down through the skylight, he carefully brought the weapon up in front of his face. Being inverted played havoc with his deeply ingrained muscle memory for aiming what was a very familiar gun with a familiar weight and feel, but he managed to use the iron sights to line up the first shot. Cupping his left hand over the gun's ejection port, he then held his breath and squeezed the trigger.

The pistol kicked in his hand and produced a muffled pop as the 9mm bullet left the suppressor at just below the speed of sound. It slammed into the first sensor, shattering its plastic housing amid a shower of tiny electrical sparks, bits of broken electronic components and flakes of plastic falling to the floor. Then the bullet lodged itself in the wall behind what was left of the sensor. Immediately after the shot, Andrew caught the spent casing with his left hand and then immediately switched his aim to the second sensor and repeated the exercise. Remaining immobile for several seconds while waiting to see if he had triggered some sort of alarm system, he was relieved to realise that no such systems had been activated.

Then he turned his attention to the floor. On the skirting boards, every two metres or so were tiny black holes that might have looked like small LEDs installed to provide ambient floor lighting. However, these were not there to make the apartment look sophisticated. They were tiny lasers that shot beams of red light across the floor to receivers on the other side. There were a handful of them, and together they created a grid of beams about three inches above the wooden floorboards, and they would trigger an alarm if broken at any point. The problem Andrew was facing was that they were invisible to the naked eye since they were travelling through clear air.

Andrew pulled a small canister from his jacket pocket and flicked the lid open. Then he activated the nozzle and allowed it to drop straight down onto the floor below. It bounced once and rolled to a stop, and then it began to produce a cloud of white smoke. The smoke was designed to be relatively cold, and that meant that it remained near the floor as it began to spread out across the living room like a cloud of ash spreading evenly down the mountainside from an active volcano. Soon the entire living room floor was partly obscured by the smoke, and the paths of all of the red lasers were shining brightly inside it. Now able to see exactly where the beams were, Andrew tossed the roll of carbon fibre wire through the hole and donned a pair of leather gloves.

'First layer of the security system disabled,' he said into the earpiece. 'I'm heading down.'

'Okay,' said Fiona. 'Everything is looking good down here. Good luck.'

Andrew climbed swiftly through the hole and slid down the wire to the floor below. The expensive and tastefully designed and decorated apartment was even more impressive from down here, and the high ceilings, cornicing and large ceiling roses gave it a sumptuous and elegant feel. However, Andrew wasn't interested in the aesthetics of the place. He was looking for the main security system's control panel, and he had a good sense of where he might find it. Moving cautiously across the floor towards the hallway while taking care not to step on any of the lasers and interrupt the signals to their receivers, he soon found himself looking at the small transparent plastic panel by the front door that contained the apartment's security nexus. He could see tiny coloured LEDs inside it, and there was a small LCD panel showing a pulsating red circle indicating that the system was active. However, getting to it was going to require a detour since there were four thermal sensors in the hallway, and he was concerned that shooting them all would cause enough movement to trigger the alarms.

Instead, he made his way through the large kitchen where there was only one sensor, which he managed to dispatch with a single bullet. Moving along the wall to the hallway, he arrived at a doorway from which he could reach the control panel while still remaining inside the kitchen. The control panel was no doubt tamper-proof, so if he were to try to access it without using the proper procedure, or if he were to try brute force, it would almost certainly trigger the alarm. And if that happened, he would only have a couple of minutes before the private security company or the police would arrive.

However, he had prepared for this eventuality too. Reaching inside his backpack once more, he extracted a black, handheld EMP device about the size of a large mobile phone. Inside was a tightly packed array of high-voltage capacitors connected to a thin metal coil that protruded out from its top. Surrounding the coil was a small parabolic funnel for directing and localising the discharge. Once activated, the EMP device would send a brief but very powerful surge of electricity through the coil, which would then instantly vaporise it and turn it into a plasma. This violent deconstruction of the metal coil would produce a directed electromagnetic pulse powerful enough to fry just about any piece of electronic equipment that wasn't adequately shielded. With any luck, it should be enough to disable the alarm system completely without triggering it. And as far as the private security company's remote monitoring systems were concerned, it would look like a simple power outage.

Releasing the catch on the activation button, he slowly reached out from the kitchen to the hallway and placed the device in front of the control panel with the parabolic funnel pointing straight at it. Then he pressed the button. There was a brief but bright flash of light and a pop as the metal coil vaporised and turned into plasma, and an instant later, the control panel winked out and all the small red LEDs in the thermal and motion sensors in the apartment went dark.

'Security system down,' he whispered into his mike. 'Starting my search.'

'Great,' replied Fiona with a note of tension in her voice. 'Nothing to report from this end.'

Andrew turned around and walked through the hallway and back towards the living room when his eye caught a framed watercolour painting hanging on the wall to his right. A small brass plaque on the lower part of the frame read *'Munich Standesamt – 1910.'* The painting depicted the Munich Town Hall, and it was a fairly decent quality painting, although the colours were somewhat drab and uninspiring. However, it was the name of the artist written in red in the lower left-hand corner that grabbed his attention.

'A. Hitler,' he whispered to himself as he read it. 'Bloody hell.'

Unable to help himself, he touched his earpiece and spoke to Fiona.

'Hey Fiona,' he said in hushed tones. 'You're not going to believe what I just found.'

'What?' replied Fiona, sounding perplexed.

'Rittenhausen has one of Hitler's watercolour paintings hanging here,' said Andrew. 'And I would bet my house that it is an original.'

'Crikey,' said Fiona. 'That man really is a proper Nazi fanboy.'

'Yeah,' said Andrew. 'I'm not sure whether to steal it or set fire to it.'

'Well, it's worth a lot of money,' said Fiona. 'But just leave it. We don't need to draw attention to ourselves.'

'I know,' said Andrew, glancing at the painting one last time before moving on. 'Still. This just seems vulgar. Anyway, I am pushing on. I'll let you know if I find anything interesting.'

Leaving the hallway, he walked back across the living room floor to a large office in the corner of the building. It looked to have been outfitted recently with bespoke white-painted bookcases, large rugs on the floor, a small armchair seating area by a window, and a couple of tall mid-century floor lamps. In the centre of the room near one of the walls was a large, polished walnut art deco desk on which sat a green stained glass Tiffany table lamp, along with a stack of books and a laptop that was flipped open but appeared to be powered down.

The wall space inside the office was taken up by bookcases and several large oil paintings featuring various Alpine motifs, although none of them had been painted by any artist Andrew had ever heard of. On the wall directly opposite the desk hung a large wooden display case containing a vintage imperial German flag. The flag, which had been the official standard of the German Empire around the turn of the previous century, was easily recognisable with its horizontal black, white and red stripes. The white stripe in the middle expanded to a roundel at its centre, and inside it was a crowned Prussian eagle in black and red.

Andrew headed straight for the laptop, sat down in Rittenhausen's leather office chair and fetched a small memory stick from his backpack. He powered up the laptop, but then he interrupted the normal boot-up process to enter the system BIOS and force the computer to load the operating system that he had put onto the memory stick instead of its regular operating system. Within seconds, the laptop had loaded the operating system and was ready to use, and Andrew then executed another piece of tailored software that had been developed by the cyber team in London. Activating it, he was able to bypass all the normal security barriers and access the laptop's hard drive without having to use Rittenhausen's password. Finally, he opened a file browser, navigated to the Documents folder and began copying over all of its contents to the memory stick. The hard drive contained several hundred gigabytes of data, including images, text files and spreadsheets, so it would take several minutes for the process to be complete.

Andrew leaned back in the chair and looked at the ornately designed desk. He pulled out the drawers one by one and found mostly standard office items. However, the lowest drawer on the left contained a small, flat leather hardcase akin to a container for jewellery, but Andrew knew exactly what it was because he had a few of those at home himself. It was a box used to present soldiers with medals. He lifted the box out and placed it in front of him, and when he opened it, his mouth fell open. Inside were three military decorations lying side by side, all of which he knew very well from having studied the many different medals handed out during the Second World War.

One was the easily recognisable Iron Cross, which only a select number of soldiers received, and which even fewer non-military personnel were ever awarded. Next to it was the Coburg Badge, which depicted a vertical sword over a swastika that was ringed by laurels. It had been awarded to participants in a Nazi party rally in the Bavarian city of Coburg in 1922 that had descended into running street battles with communists. The third medal was the '*Blutorden*', or Blood Order badge, which was one of the most prestigious decorations of the early Nazi party. It had only been awarded to active participants in Hitler's Beer Hall Putsch in 1923, and it was highly distinctive with its German eagle on one side and the entrance to the Munich beer hall depicted on the other. Finding it here in this box, Andrew was left with the obvious conclusion that Otto Drexler had participated in the attempted coup against the German state in 1923, and that he had been a recipient of the coveted order.

Andrew was on the cusp of flipping the lid of the box closed and putting it back inside the drawer when he suddenly changed his mind. This was clearly a highly personal item for Rittenhausen, so perhaps it could be used as some sort of leverage if ever the need should arise. He snapped the box closed and placed it inside his backpack, and then he continued searching through the remaining drawers. Finding nothing else of interest, he ran his fingers along the underside of the smoothly polished desk, and on the far left-hand side, he felt his fingertips pass over a small circular indent. Reverting to the same spot again, it was clear that he had discovered some sort of button. Not knowing what would happen if he pressed it, he decided to throw caution to the wind.

'Who dares wins,' he mumbled to himself, and then he pressed it.

The button produced no noise, but instead, there was a small but audible mechanical click coming from the wall opposite him, and almost immediately thereafter, the large display case with the imperial German flag began to travel smoothly upwards along the wall. After about ten seconds, it stopped just shy of the ceiling, having revealed what was clearly a large steel door to a wall safe.

★   ★   ★

Across the capital city, Ferdinand von Rittenhausen was sitting inside an exclusive Michelin-starred French restaurant, enjoying a meal consisting of duck magret with creamed potatoes garnished with cranberry and maple sauce. He was discussing the composition of one of his investment portfolios with his personal banker when his phone suddenly began vibrating and producing a sound that he had not heard in years. In fact, the last time he had heard it was during the renovation of his top-floor flat on Zimmerstrasse. A unique sound that was only used by a single app for a single purpose, it was not a welcome sound, because it was meant to alert him to the fact that the wall display case containing the vintage imperial flag he had acquired at an auction was being lifted to expose his safe.

However, with his mouth full of Château Margaux 2005 and his head full of prospective investment risk estimates, it took him several seconds to compute what the alarm actually meant. He then hurriedly extracted the phone from his jacket pocket and looked at its display, his eyes widening in horror. The alarm system app was displaying a red circle that pulsed aggressively, and underneath it was a piece of text indicating that the wall safe was in the process of being tampered with. He quickly attempted to access the apartment's security cameras remotely, but none of them were working. In fact, the entire security system appeared to be offline. A cold chill ran down his spine. Without a word, he jumped to his feet, almost knocking over the table as he pushed past his banker and rushed towards the door to the street. As he went, he speed-dialled a number that he had called many times before.

'Hector!' he almost shouted as he staggered out onto the street with his suit jacket under his arm. 'Where are you?'

'We are at the hotel, Boss,' said Hector calmly. 'As you asked.'

'Get to the apartment!' yelled Rittenhausen as he began waving frantically to his driver, who had parked about fifty metres away. 'We have intruders. They are trying to get into my safe. Get there now and stop them.'

'Yes, Boss,' said Hector. 'Right away.'

As they spoke, Rittenhausen could hear the sound of both Hector and Ernesto already scrambling to get out of their hotel room, which was about a five-minute drive from his apartment. Then he heard the sound of feet echoing through a stairwell.

'And if they are still there when we arrive?' said Hector.

'Beat the shit out of them,' spat Rittenhausen, spittle flying from his mouth as his black Mercedes came to a halt next to him with a brief squeal of its tyres. 'And then kill them. Just end them. I will deal with the consequences. Understood?'

'Yes, Boss,' said Hector, as Rittenhausen heard the sound of car doors slamming and an engine revving aggressively. 'We're on our way. Three minutes.'

★   ★   ★

Inside Rittenhausen's apartment, Andrew was now standing in front of the newly revealed safe, looking at the black circular keypad for the electronic combination lock that was mounted at the centre of its steel door. Seeing the make of the safe printed in small white letters on the high-tech keypad, he instantly knew what to do and reached inside his backpack for the crudest of tools. A simple flathead screwdriver. He didn't stand a chance of opening the safe's door with it, but it would allow him to apply a much more elegant solution to the problem.

Placing the head of the screwdriver where the combination lock's plastic housing met the steel door, he slammed the heel of his hand onto the end of the tool's handle, thereby wedging the head underneath the edge of the housing. He then used the lever effect to wrench the housing from the door. It snapped and popped as the plastic broke into pieces and came loose, but the electronic components inside were intact. As he lifted the housing away from the door, the wide multi-wire riser cable connecting it to the door's internal electronics became visible. He disconnected the cable from its elongated port and placed the broken housing on a nearby side table. Then he pulled a small brute force codebreaker device from his backpack, selected the appropriate cable from a number of attachments, and connected it directly to the circuit board inside the safe's door via the now empty port.

The safe's electronic combination lock required a 4-digit code to open, which meant that there were 10,000 possible combinations, and the codebreaker device would simply run through all of them until it hit the correct one. As was standard with this particular type of safe, it would allow the user five tries to enter the correct combination and then lock itself after the fifth failed attempt. However, when this happened, the codebreaker device would simply send a pulse of electricity through the cable powerful enough to briefly short out the lock's circuit board. The board would then immediately and automatically reset itself, giving the codebreaker device another five attempts. This process would then be repeated until the correct code was found. With the device capable of running through 128 passcodes per second, it would take it no more than 78 seconds to try all of the ten thousand different possible combinations. As it turned out, it only took about 15 seconds to hit the correct combination, at which point the device produced a beep and showed the four-digit code on its display.

'1-9-3-3,' Andrew whispered to himself with a shake of the head. 'The year Hitler came to power.'

The lock snapped open with a click, and Andrew disconnected the codebreaker and put it into his backpack. Then he pulled the safe's door open. Inside were three shelves, each with different items, mainly documents, and Andrew quickly began flicking through them. The top shelf contained what appeared to be a thin family photo album with a handful of old black-and-white photos of three elegantly dressed people. A man, a woman and a young boy. Looking at the dates handwritten on the back, Andrew deduced that what he was looking at were most likely photos of Maximillian and Magdalena with their son Ferdinand. Judging from their clothes and the setting, including the vegetation and the mountainous backdrop, it had most likely been taken somewhere in Argentina.

On the second shelf were several folders containing a number of old, yellowed technical documents bearing a swastika and the German eagle. There were also a couple of what appeared to be original blueprints for some sort of highly complex circular device consisting of what looked like hundreds of individual components. One of the folders also contained photos of an underground complex containing a large number of hulking machines and other equipment that Andrew had no time to examine right there and then.

On the third shelf was a single item. At first, it looked to Andrew like a small leatherbound notebook, but when he opened it, it appeared to be a diary in binder format with many small A5-sized pages that had been typed up and inserted sequentially one by one. The typeface immediately gave away the fact that they had been typed up on an old-fashioned typewriter before being put into the diary. Flicking carefully through the first few yellowed pages and giving them a cursory look, it wasn't obvious to him who had written it, but what was clear was that it had been written in

German and that all the entries were dated somewhere around the early 1940s.

Deciding that he did not have the time needed to examine all of the safe's contents, he carefully extracted the documents and the diary and placed them inside his backpack. Then he slung it over his shoulder and returned to the art deco desk, where the laptop was still busy copying over the entire contents of its Documents folder to the memory stick. Watching the names of the files being copied as it happened, he caught glimpses of a couple of video files, one of which was named 'Bergkristall – 03-1944.mp4'.

At that moment, he suddenly heard tyres squealing in the street below, and then the sound of rustling came through his earpiece as if Fiona was fumbling with her microphone. When her voice finally came through a couple of seconds later, she sounded as if she was on the verge of panic.

'Andrew!' she said hurriedly while trying to keep her voice down. 'They're on to you. Two men have just arrived in a large BMW. They're coming up the stairs right now. They are carrying guns. Big ones.'

'The men or the guns?' said Andrew, getting to his feet as he watched the progress bar on the laptop screen move agonisingly slowly closer to 100 percent.

'Both!' Fiona said. 'You have to get out of there. Now!'

'Okay,' said Andrew as he yanked the memory stick out of the port on the laptop. 'Leaving now. Stay where you are.'

By "big guns", Andrew assumed that Fiona meant either submachineguns or perhaps shotguns. Either way, it sounded like some serious firepower. In most situations, he would have fancied his chances against two attackers even if they had bigger weapons, as long as he could set up an ambush and lie in wait. However, in this instance, he preferred to get out of there cleanly if he could. If nothing else, then just to ensure that the laptop and the information it contained did not get shot to pieces in a firefight. He would have to bring the laptop with him.

He hurriedly disconnected its various cables and powered it down, and then he flipped it closed and picked it up from the desk. It was too big to fit inside his backpack, so he took it under his arm and headed for the hallway. By the time he got there, he could hear the loud noise of heavy boots thudding up the stairwell as the two men Fiona had warned him about rushed up towards Rittenhausen's apartment. Opening the door and stepping out into the corridor now would be virtual suicide, and there was no time to climb back up onto the roof using the carbon fibre wire in the living room.

Instead, he slipped into the kitchen and crouched low behind a large kitchen island. He would only get one shot at this, so his timing had to be perfect. Within seconds, he heard the electronic lock on the front door beep and snap open, and then the sound of two large men as they barged in and ran across the hallway towards the living room, heading for Rittenhausen's office at the back. As they went, he also heard the distinct sound of them racking the firing bolts on their weapons, and they sounded to Andrew like they might be the Israeli-made Uzi mini submachinegun. It was now or never. He had to get out right now.

Bolting from his crouched position with the small backpack strapped to his back and the laptop under his arm, he sprinted into the hallway and continued through the open front door and out into the corridor. Heading straight for the stairs at the far end, he ran down them several steps at a time, but he was only halfway down to the street when he heard the sound of boots above him. The two men had realised what had happened, and they were now giving chase, rushing down the stairwell as they tried to catch up.

Andrew burst out through the door onto the pavement and headed straight for Fiona, who was still sitting by her table, although struggling to stay where she was. Her instincts told her to get up and join Andrew and flee somehow, but as he rushed towards her, he held up his hand urgently, signalling for her to remain seated. As he sprinted past her, he tossed the laptop into her lap, and then he continued running along the pavement to where a red taxi was parked. The driver of the Audi appeared to have paid a quick visit to a sandwich shop, and he was just re-emerging and walking casually back towards his vehicle when Andrew ripped open the driver's side door and jumped in behind the wheel. As Andrew started the engine, he dropped his sandwich, threw his arms in the air, and yelled something unintelligible as he rushed forward.

Just as Andrew floored the accelerator and swerved out into the road, his two hulking pursuers crashed through the door to the street and stopped as if frozen in place for a couple of seconds as they watched the red taxi race off while putting two and two together.

'*Vamos!*' shouted Hector, and he and Ernesto then bolted for their silver BMW.

They practically threw themselves into the front seats of the muscly SUV with Hector behind the wheel, and then the engine roared to life, and the car shot out into the road and accelerated loudly down the street in pursuit of the taxi. Fiona watched in horror as the BMW almost took out a couple of pedestrians who were forced to run for their lives, and then she looked down at the laptop. She glared at it for a few moments, not sure what to do, but then she raised her right hand and pressed on the earpiece.

'Andrew,' she said. 'They're following you. Silver BMW.'

'No shit!' came Andrew's tense reply. 'They're all over me. Do you have the laptop?'

'Yes,' said Fiona. 'I've got it.'

'Alright,' said Andrew, as the signal began breaking up in tandem with the distance between the two communication units being stretched to its maximum. 'Go... hotel. I... soon as... Okay?'

Fiona managed to get the meaning of what he was saying, and she got to her feet and turned to leave.

'Alright,' she said, sounding worried. 'I am going back to the hotel.'

There was no reply, and her ear was now filled with static noise as her earpiece tried and failed to connect to Andrew's. She was about to head back towards the corner with Friedrichstrasse when she heard another vehicle approach and stop abruptly by the curb in front of Rittenhausen's building. When she turned, she saw a short and stocky, well-dressed man in his sixties with grey backswept hair and a distinctive nose who was rushing from the backseat of a black Mercedes before the vehicle had come to a complete stop. She immediately recognised Rittenhausen from the photo Andrew had shown her, but unlike the photo where he had appeared relaxed and calm, his face was a picture of barely contained fury as he raced across the pavement on his short legs, pushed other pedestrians aside and tore open the door to the stairwell leading up to his apartment. His driver killed the engine, stepped out and hurried after his paymaster with a look of confusion on his face. Then he too disappeared into the stairwell.

Deciding that this was very much her time to leave, Fiona headed calmly back to Friedrichstrasse and turned the corner. She walked past Checkpoint Charlie, where several tourists were busy taking pictures of themselves and each other, and then she continued south along the street to Kochstrasse, where she entered the hotel, headed up to their room and prepared for an anxious wait until she would hear from Andrew again. With two large, mean-looking and heavily armed men chasing after him, she was filled with anxiety and dread about what might be playing out in these very moments somewhere in the city. She opened the minibar and resolutely pulled out a chilled mini bottle of Moët & Chandon champagne. Ripping the gold foil off and wrenching the cork from its neck, she took a large swig straight from the bottle and sat down on the end of the bed, exhaling deeply.

'He'll be alright,' she told herself, willing it to be true. 'He'll be alright.'

Fifteen

Racing north through the night at break-neck speeds along Ebertstrasse and rapidly heading towards the Brandenburg Gate, Andrew glanced in the rearview mirror to see the bright headlights of the silver BMW bearing down on him. He was trying hard to avoid the other cars in his lane as he weaved in and out at speeds far exceeding the speed limit, but his pursuers did not appear to be doing the same. He watched as the driver of the silver SUV behind him shunted a smaller vehicle aside to try to close the gap to his quarry. Sparks flew as it careened across the adjacent lane and sideswiped a parked car, and then it came to a grinding halt as the BMW shot past it.

Covering the roughly 500-metre stretch next to Tiergarten Park, Andrew arrived at the Brandenburg Gate and then suddenly had an idea. The huge neo-classical monument consisted of five open archways with Greek columns on either side, and most of them were blocked by bollards sticking up about a metre from the ground. However, one archway on each side of the gate was clear, allowing for slow one-lane traffic to move through it, but it was still a very narrow space. With a bit of luck, his Audi would just fit through the gap, but the large SUV of his pursuers would not.

He turned the wheel hard, mounted the curb and headed straight for the gap while leaning on the horn to get the pedestrians to get out of the way. Seeing the Audi racing towards the archway, they all scattered and cleared the way amid angry shouts and outbursts at the recklessness of the Audi driver, but when they saw the pursuing BMW follow suit, they simply ran for it.

Andrew's Audi shot through the gap with only inches to spare on either side, and it almost made it out, but because the car was swerving as he entered, its rear end swiped one of the columns as it exited, and sparks burst from the bodywork as it finally cleared the archway and continued onwards. Behind him, the BMW looked as if it was about to attempt the same feat, but then the driver suddenly seemed to change his mind and instead swerved to one side and accelerated furiously towards one of the much wider archways blocked by a metal bollard. Andrew watched in the rearview mirror as the bulky SUV tore through the archway, slammed into the bollard and punched it clean off its mount. The heavy metal rod spun end over end through the air at high speeds and slammed into a parked car, sticking out of the mangled bodywork as the silver SUV tore past.

Andrew picked up speed once more as his Audi accelerated along the tree-lined double avenue, heading due east past the Berlin State Opera on his right and the German Historical Museum on his left. With the

BMW having a much bigger engine, it quickly began gaining on him. By the time they raced across the Schlossbrücke bridge over the River Spree that meandered through the city centre, the distance between the two vehicles had shrunk to less than thirty metres. As both vehicles tore past the statues of Greek gods placed on either side of the bridge, Andrew saw that the man in the passenger seat was leaning out of the window and aiming a weapon towards him. An instant later, the first bullets from the man's Uzi slammed into the rear of the Audi, punching through the bodywork and shattering the rear window. Swerving aggressively to one side and then the other, trying to evade the incoming fire, Andrew almost collided with a van and was lucky not to lose control of the vehicle.

Seconds later, the wild and dangerous pursuit raced past the Berlin Cathedral on the left, and at that point, Andrew realised that the car chase had to end. There was simply no way for him to outrun the much more powerful BMW, and it was a question of time before some other motorist or pedestrian got seriously hurt or worse. He had to stop this now.

Spotting a rail bridge up ahead and seeing a lit-up sign for the Alexanderplatz U-Bahn station on his right-hand side at the next turn, Andrew wrestled the wheel hard to the right. With squealing and smoking tyres, the Audi drifted around the corner and almost sideswiped one of Berlin's yellow trams that had just set off from its stop by the overline metro station. Catching a glimpse of his pursuers in the rearview mirror, he veered across to the opposite side of the street, nearly hitting the tram, and then floored the accelerator until he had reached the entrance to the station. There, he slammed on the brakes and came to a violent stop about ten metres from the entrance. Leaving the engine running and with onlookers watching in disbelief as the chaotic scene unfolded in front of their eyes, he kicked open the driver's side door and bolted from the vehicle.

The BMW came to a screeching halt, and two large men wearing light grey suits cradling black weapons spilled out of the vehicle to give chase as Andrew sprinted inside the station and up the first set of steps on his right to one of the platforms. He had no idea when the next metro train might arrive or where it might be going, and he didn't care. All that mattered was for him to get away safely from the two goons so he could get back to the hotel and to Fiona, who would be worried sick by now.

As he emerged on the platform, sweating and panting with shouts of outrage emanating from the stairs behind him where his pursuers were barging into other commuters and shoving them aside as they ascended the steps, he realised that a metro train was already on the platform, silently waiting to depart. He ran along the platform for another twenty metres or so, and then he bolted for the nearest automatic door and threw himself inside a carriage just as the trilling noise announcing the imminent closure of the doors sounded.

When he turned around to look behind him, he saw the two almost identical goons emerge from the stairs. They looked as if they were in a frenzy, like predators full of bloodlust as they hunted down their prey, and without taking even a moment to look around the platform, they sprinted for the nearest doors which were now closing. Somehow, they both managed to get inside the carriage that was immediately behind Andrew's before it was too late, and then the train began to pull away from the station.

And just like that, the chase was over, at least for now. A temporary pause during which Andrew caught his breath and the other late-night commuters read their books, talked on their phones or took the opportunity to snooze on the way to wherever they were going. With the metallic squeaking of the wheels against the tracks, the gentle swaying of the carriage as the train negotiated a turn, and the automated announcements on the PA system informing passengers of the next stop, it all seemed deceptively normal all of a sudden. The only thing that was missing to complete the picture was elevator music.

Looking towards the end of the carriage, Andrew realised that there was no way for his pursuers to make their way from one carriage to the next, so he was safe for the moment. However, in a few minutes, when they would be pulling into the next station, the two men would swap carriages and come after him again, and then he would be back to square one. His only option was to leave his carriage as soon as possible and come up with another way to get away from the two would-be killers who had already sprayed bullets across traffic on a major road in the centre of the capital.

Feeling the weight and bulk of the Glock 17 under his jacket, his warrior instincts told him to simply face the threat head-on and eliminate it, and he was fairly confident that he would be able to do so. But there was every chance that it would cost the lives of innocent bystanders, if not from his own bullets, then from those of the two goons who looked more like oversized thugs than trained shooters. They would most likely have no qualms about causing the deaths of other commuters, and Andrew simply couldn't risk that happening. He had to get rid of them as soon as he could. And then he would try to either escape or draw them off to a location where he had a better chance of setting the conditions for dealing with them on his own terms.

As it turned out, he only had about three minutes to think about what to do next because the train soon began to slow as it approached the Hackescher Markt station near the river. This station was also raised above street level and was sitting on a large redbrick structure with shops and cafes built into the large alcove-like spaces underneath. As soon as the train stopped and the doors opened, Andrew bolted from the carriage and ran along the open-air platform towards the stairs. Behind him, he heard a woman scream and then the sound of something being dropped and then clattering to the concrete platform. He didn't need to turn around and look to know what had happened. The two goons were already out and giving chase, and anyone in their way was just an obstacle to be shoved aside.

Reaching the wide, dimly lit staircase that led down to an underpass, he took the stairs several steps at a time, sprinted the short distance along the underpass, and took a right as soon as he emerged onto the cobbled street that ran parallel to the station. Glancing over his shoulder as he ran, he saw the two men perhaps fifty metres behind him just as they were emerging from the station underpass. They had their weapons out, seemingly indifferent to the shouts of fear and shock coming from the other commuters.

Laid into the cobbled street surface were tram tracks, and as he ran along, a yellow tram suddenly appeared from under the rail bridge and began curving noisily towards him. He ran straight for it and managed to get behind it before his pursuers could open fire, and then he continued across a small, triangular wooded park to the river. With a bit of luck, the tram would block the path of the two men and slow them down by a few seconds. Across the Spree towards the south stood the Berlin Cathedral with its green corroded copper domes and gilded spires, and Andrew realised that he had now almost made a full circle from when he had first been shot at by his pursuers.

Extending out from the raised quay on the riverbank was a small floating pier, and there was a short set of steps with metal guardrails leading down to it. Bobbing by the pier were three small, brightly coloured boats with outboard engines. They appeared to be pleasure crafts available for paying tourists, but Andrew dispensed with payment and ran down the steps to jump into the nearest one. Yanking the engine cord once, the small engine immediately sputtered to life as he released the mooring rope and pushed off. Cranking the throttle on the steering handle all the way as far as it would go, the engine purred happily as he pushed the small boat out into the river and accelerated away towards the south. Going south meant going against the current of the river, and this would slow him down marginally. However, for the moment, he was more interested in getting behind cover of the concrete foundations of a nearby pedestrian bridge than putting distance between himself and the two pursuers.

Glancing behind him as he ducked low inside the boat, Andrew saw one of the men yanking violently on the starter cord connected to the engine on one of the other boats. The other man had stopped halfway down the steps to the pier, raising his Uzi and taking aim. And then he fired. The mini submachine gun spewed a short burst of bullets in Andrew's direction, but none of them hit their target or the boat he was in. With its ultra-short barrel and complete lack of recoil negation, the weapon had never been designed for accuracy at range. In fact, it was little more than a rapid-fire pistol intended to be small enough to be easily concealed under a jacket and to do massive damage up close. But either the man firing it didn't fully understand its limitations, or perhaps he was just chancing it in case he got lucky. Up on the pedestrian bridge, there were screams as the gunfire erupted, and Andrew then heard the shooter's companion shout something unintelligible as the engine on their boat finally came to life. The two large men then entered the small vessel and continued the pursuit.

By this time, the distance between the two boats was just under a hundred metres, which was well outside the effective range of the Uzi. But the shooter finally seemed to have experienced a constructive brainwave and switched the weapon to single-fire mode, taking potshots at the vessel in front. Andrew heard the individual shots being fired behind him, and he caught one of the bullets smacking into the water just ahead and to one side of his boat. Despite the Uzi's innate limitations, as well as the obvious fact that his pursuers were amateurs with regards to its proper use, he realised that it would be a question of time before the shooter got lucky. They almost certainly carried several spare mags each, so they wouldn't be running out of bullets for a while. Once again, Andrew had to come up with a new plan to try to defeat them, and this time it had to be permanent.

He was now passing the cathedral and heading under another low bridge, and as he emerged on the other side, swerving as much as the small and relatively slow boat would allow in order to avoid the incoming fire, several bullets pinged off the concrete bridge mere metres from him. Another few hundred metres later, Andrew was scanning the river banks on both sides for something that might be able to give him options to turn the tables on his attackers. Shooting back was the obvious answer, but he was down to half a magazine, having never anticipated a prolonged shootout in the middle of the city.

Just as he raised his gaze to peer ahead through the gloom of the virtually lightless river while looking for something to help him alter his precarious situation, another report came from behind, and a bullet slammed into the engine housing mere inches from his right arm. Within seconds, the engine started to splutter and cough, and a trail of black smoke began billowing out of the housing. Andrew could feel the boat decelerate as more bullets hit the water uncomfortably close to him. He had to do something, fast.

He cast his eyes ahead once more, and then he spotted a large building site that was right on the river on his right-hand side. It appeared that whatever structure had been there before had been torn down, and now a new modern office or apartment building was being erected in its place. The plot appeared to have been artificially extended a few metres into the river, and a new, low concrete quayside had been constructed there. Behind it rose the foundations and initial half-finished walls of the first few floors of the steel and concrete building, and there were numerous pieces of construction machinery as well as stacks and piles of various building materials scattered around the sizeable plot. A single floodlight mounted on a tall pole was illuminating the site, and behind it in the distance was a road that ran parallel to the river.

Andrew quickly steered his crippled boat towards the riverbank, and before it had reached the concrete quayside, he was on his feet and leaping out of the front. Landing on the quayside as his driverless boat veered back out into the river and began doing circles, he sprinted for a corner of the building site where there were several large cubes of some sort of cladding wrapped loosely in grey tarpaulin. As he slid down behind one of them and pulled his Glock from its holster, the two pursuers clambered onto the quayside and rushed towards cover behind a tall, cone-shaped pile of sand some thirty metres from his location.

Leaning out and taking careful aim, Andrew fired several shots at the men as they took turns to peek out and fire a quick burst in his direction. None of his bullets connected, and he was now down to less than a handful of bullets. Moving low and crouching behind building materials and machines, he made his way towards the sprawling, unfinished building and slipped inside it behind several bare walls that had been erected on the first floor. They had been constructed from reinforced concrete, and there were long metal reinforcement bars sticking up from several wall sections as they awaited being extended upwards.

Planning to use the high ground to his advantage, he found a staircase leading up to the wall-less first floor of one section of the building and managed to get up there without being hit. The two men were now employing half-decent movement and cover tactics as one of them would sprint forward to new cover while the other laid down suppressing fire. With this technique, they were rapidly closing in on Andrew's position, and he was unable to press his height advantage with so few bullets left.

Taking up a position behind a large stack of bricks that was sitting on a steel pallet near a reinforced pillar on the otherwise virtually empty first floor, Andrew pressed the magazine release button and checked his ammo. Four rounds. It just might be enough if he could get a shot at his pursuers out in the open. Waiting behind the bricks, he heard the footsteps of one of the men coming up the stairs. No doubt, the other was now positioned somewhere that provided a line of sight to the first floor, so Andrew had to stay in cover until he was sure he could get a good shot.

He sat immobile with both hands gripping the pistol as he listened out for the approaching enemy. The bare concrete floor was covered in dust and tiny bits of concrete, and the large man's boots produced a slight crunch as he walked along. Andrew could hear him coming nearer, and when he realised that the man was about to walk past him at a distance of less than five metres, he turned silently and raised his weapon, ready to fire a quick double tap as he had done thousands of times before at the kill house at Hereford. At this range, holding the element of surprise and shooting his favourite handgun, there was no way he was going to miss. The attacker stood no chance.

Leaning his head slightly to one side as he raised the weapon and aligned his eye with the iron sights, he saw the Uzi come into view first, followed by a large man whose muscles bulged under his light grey suit jacket. His head was clean-shaven, he had a small black goatee under his chin, and he had a distinctly Latin look about him. Andrew paused his breathing and squeezed the trigger.

There was a faint muffled click as the pistol jammed, and Andrew could barely believe what was happening. Somehow, some dirt must have entered the weapon, preventing the firing mechanism from working properly and allowing the firing pin to hit the primer on the cartridge. This was a rare occurrence with the Glock 17, but it did happen from time to time, and Andrew responded immediately and instinctively. He rushed forward to get inside the gun arc of the Uzi before the man could swing it around and send a spray of 9mm copper-jacketed bullets his way. Covering the distance in just a couple of seconds as the man turned his head, saw him and realised what had happened, Andrew's shoulder barged into him and knocked him off his feet. As he staggered sideways and began toppling over, he squeezed the Uzi's trigger, and a hail of bullets stitched up along the length of one of the reinforced pillars sending bits of concrete chippings and dust exploding into the air.

When he had launched himself at the man, Andrew hadn't quite realised how close they were to the edge of the unfinished first floor of the building, and the force of the impact sent the man flailing over the edge and down and out of sight. He produced something between a roar and a scream as he fell, but then there was a heavy thud and a grinding crunch, and then there was silence. Two seconds later, Andrew heard the voice of the other man yell at the top of his lungs.

'Ernesto!' he called, as genuine distress came through in his baritone voice. 'Ernesto!'

Andrew took two quick steps forward to look over the edge, and what greeted him below was a gruesome scene. The man called Ernesto had fallen backwards onto a wall and a set of metre-long metal reinforcement bars sticking straight up into the air. The bars had skewered him through his torso and abdomen, and he now seemed to hang in mid-air with his arms and legs splayed out to his sides and his head flopped back as blood trickled from the many puncture wounds and flowed down along the metal bars and onto the concrete wall. With his back arched and the metal bars holding him in place, he coughed up blood that spilled out of his mouth and ran down the side of his face. Then his throat produced a thick, gurgling noise as his final breath left his lungs, and then he moved no more.

As Andrew watched the man's life slip away, time seemed to stand still, but now the other man suddenly opened up with his Uzi, and bullets smacked into the concrete all around him. He threw himself to the dusty concrete floor and rolled behind one of the large support pillars, and by some miracle, he managed to avoid being hit. Slamming the heel of his hand down on top of his weapon, racking the slide and clearing the jam, he waited for the burst of fire to stop. It sounded as if the other man had emptied an entire magazine in his direction, and as soon as it was over, Andrew got up, leaned out, and took aim at the spot on the first floor of a different part of the building complex where he had seen the incoming fire originate from.

He fired two shots, both of which smacked audibly into a concrete wall behind which the man was taking cover, and when Andrew saw him pull back and disappear out of view, he shifted his aim to the single floodlight and shot it out amid the shattering of glass and a shower of electrical sparks.

The entire building site was suddenly plunged into darkness, and he spun around and sprinted for the other end of the unfinished building while trying to keep the support pillars between himself and the shooter's location. Reaching the far end, he quickly crouched low and slid over the edge to drop down to the ground below, and then he used the cover of two large bulldozers to reach a gap in the tall and solid wood board fence surrounding the building site to exit out onto the street. He was fairly confident that he had managed to stay out of sight of the other assailant who had been busy reloading. And if the appearance of the two men was anything to go by, they were very closely related, and Andrew's intuition told him that the surviving member of the pair was now likely too stunned by his companion's grisly demise to continue the pursuit.

Despite the late hour, there was still a fair amount of traffic on the roads, and after a few seconds, Andrew spotted a taxi coming towards him. He shoved his pistol back into his shoulder holster and stepped out into the road to flag it down. Seconds later, he was on his way back across the Spree towards the western part of the city centre and the hotel on Kochstrasse.

Sixteen

When Andrew unlocked the door to the hotel room and walked in, Fiona practically launched herself at him and hugged him tight for several seconds before speaking.

'Thank goodness you're okay,' said she, pulling back and looking up at him. 'I was so worried about you. What happened?'

'Just a minor tour of the city,' said Andrew with an apologetic smile. 'All courtesy of Rittenhausen's two thugs.'

He then proceeded to tell her about what had happened during his roughly hour-long absence. He left out the most gory details of how the man named Ernesto had met his demise at the building site, but he could see from the queasy expression on Fiona's face that she was perfectly capable of imagining the violent course of events that had led to his death.

'Did anyone see you?' she asked, looking concerned. 'I mean, you clearly acted in self-defence, but that doesn't mean the police won't try to find you.'

'I know,' said Andrew. 'We should get out of this city tomorrow morning. You never know if someone like Rittenhausen has connections inside the German police or security services. I think they still tend to recruit their leadership from the top echelons of society, so it is a risk we need to consider.'

'I can't tell you how relieved I am to see you safe,' said Fiona.

'Well, we have work to do here,' said Andrew, squeezing her hand gently and then unzipping his backpack. 'I want to know what is on that laptop.'

'Me too,' said Fiona.

'And we also need to have a look at these old documents and this diary,' said Andrew, extracting both from the backpack.

He handed the folders and the leatherbound diary to Fiona, who took them in her hands with such care that it bordered on reverence.

'Wow,' she said, putting aside the folders and placing the diary on her lap. 'This is amazing. Look at the name on the inside of the front cover. Otto Drexler. Rittenhausen's grandfather.'

'Drexler's diary,' said Andrew, intrigued. 'That could hold the key to what this is all about. My German isn't great, so you should have a look at that and the documents in the folder. I will start to comb through the contents of the laptop. I have a feeling it might tell us a whole lot of interesting things about Rittenhausen.'

'Okay,' said Fiona, making herself comfortable on the bed and spreading out the document around her. 'Let's get to work.'

As she methodically went through all the faded manilla folders and the contents of the diary while taking notes along the way, Andrew sat down at the room's small work desk, flipped open the laptop and powered it on. After a couple of minutes, he had booted it up and bypassed the rudimentary security measures in the same way that he had done inside Rittenhausen's apartment, and then he began going through the entire file structure to tease out anything that might be relevant to their investigation.

After about an hour, during which Fiona came across piece after piece of amazing information contained in the various old documents, she finally couldn't contain herself anymore and turned to Andrew.

'This is really amazing,' she said, looking at him. 'You've got to hear this.'

'What did you find?' said Andrew, sitting up and stretching his back after having been hunched over the entire time staring at the screen as he sifted through hundreds of emails, documents and image files.

'See these,' said Fiona, holding up a set of highly complex printed schematics with dozens of individual components that were all presented in meticulous detail. 'These are nothing less than the blueprints for a portal. And according to some of the other documents here, it can be used to reach across huge distances in an instant to deliver a weapon such as a nuclear bomb. And there would be nothing the enemy would be able to do to stop it from happening.'

'So, those snippets from the Farm Hall tapes were correct,' said Andrew, astounded. 'When those junior scientists discussed this, they were talking about something that was actually being built. Project Omega really was an effort to develop some sort of portal technology. That's incredible.'

'I know,' said Fiona with equal amazement in her voice. 'It sounds crazy, but it looks as if it really happened. These blueprints are extremely detailed. They show the ring-shaped cyclotron device, huge intricate capacitor arrays, blueprints for how to build electromagnets for the portal device, right down to specifications for power cables, couplings and control equipment used to calibrate the magnetic fields. It's all presented here in these documents. And according to some of the document headers, all of this top-secret work took place at the B8 Bergkristall facility in Austria.'

'Amazing,' said Andrew. 'So, what we have here is evidence that Edward Harding was right all along. Even if it sounded crazy back then and it seems like science fiction even now.'

'It does sound completely outlandish,' said Fiona, reaching for the leatherbound diary. 'But it's all backed up right here by Drexler's diary, including how they seem to have stumbled across this technology by accident when they were constructing a large cyclotron for their nuclear research. Listen to this entry.'

```
16th October, 1941.

I have finally secured the funding from
the Reich Army Weapons Agency to proceed
with Project Omega. The initial discovery
```

```
of the experimental cyclotron's effects
on spacetime was entirely accidental, but
it is now clear that the presence of
rhodium in the wolfram from which the
device is constructed causes a previously
unknown and highly exotic new phenomenon.
We have finally been able to verify that
with        a       sufficiently      powerful
electromagnetic      containment       field
surrounding the device toroid, and with a
very large number of protons being
accelerated to relativistic speeds, the
curvature effect that was first observed
in the laboratory at the Kaiser Wilhelm
Institute is real. And in the limit, with
enough power, this could mean that it is
possible to cause a fissure in spacetime
itself. I am almost overcome with awe and
impatience to push the project forward,
but   much   more   research   is   needed.
However, I am extremely confident in my
calculations, and once the device has
been built, I will be able to prove my
theory. I have persuaded Horst Feldmeyer
to join me in the effort. He is very
ambitious, and he has a brilliant mind
for particle physics. Together, we will
make history.
```

'Wolfram was the same as tungsten, right?' said Andrew. 'And traces of rhodium apparently produced some very unusual effects inside the cyclotron?'

'That's right,' said Fiona. 'Effects that somehow affected spacetime, which, as I understand it, is the very fabric of reality.'

'I need someone much cleverer than me to explain this properly,' said Andrew. 'I feel like we're in way over our heads here.'

'We are,' said Fiona. 'And we should find someone as soon as we're done here. Anyway, for more than a year following that particular entry, everything Drexler wrote had to do with the initial construction of the test site inside Bergkristall. It apparently involved huge amounts of equipment and very precise installations of an enormous number of different types of advanced machinery and devices, and the power requirements were just colossal. Drexler went into quite a lot of detail about trainloads of things arriving and being unloaded at the rail station inside Bergkristall, and it was only in early 1943 that he began to write about experiments being carried out. Like this one.

<u>22nd January, 1943.</u>

Today was a truly remarkable day. I have never felt as confident in Project Omega as I do now. The portal has completed all of its preliminary tests successfully, and according to the calculations of myself and Feldmeyer, it should now be possible to reach critical power levels. We have already detected a very small curvature of spacetime in accordance with Einstein's theory of special relativity. We will soon achieve a power output that can fully open the portal and keep it stable for several seconds. If all goes well, our first full transfer test will happen in less than two weeks.

'Einstein's theory of special relativity?' said Andrew. 'How familiar are you with that sort of stuff?'

'Not very,' said Fiona, shaking her head. 'But I do remember once reading something about spacetime curvature, although I can't really claim to understand exactly how it works. But there's another interesting entry here from a couple of weeks later.'

```
17th February, 1943.

I feel as tall as a giant. The first full
test of the Omega portal has been
completed. The cyclotron performed almost
perfectly, and the rift in spacetime
occurred exactly as our calculations had
predicted. The small iron test cube was
successfully transferred to the specified
location using Feldmeyer's new coordinate
system, and we will attempt a much longer
transfer range and a larger cube very
soon. The portal sustained minor damage
during the test, but I believe that with
the required replacement components
already being manufactured at the Kaiser
Wilhelm Institute, we should be able to
perform another test within months.
```

'A successful transfer,' said Andrew, struggling to wrap his head around what he was hearing. 'So they used the portal to make a metal cube travel through spacetime, whatever that actually means, and they managed to make it end up exactly where they intended.'

'It certainly sounds that way,' said Fiona.

'Bloody hell,' said Andrew. 'Forget ICBMs. If what Drexler wrote turns out to be the truth, then this technology would be able to provide instant access to anywhere in the world. That is genuinely mind-boggling.'

'Well,' said Fiona, holding up a hand in caution. 'Not everything went according to plan. There seems to have been some sort of accident several months later. It sounds quite horrific, actually. Listen.'

<u>3rd September, 1943.</u>

```
Disaster has struck. Today we experienced
severe, uncontrolled fluctuations in the
magnetic field generators. The anomalies
escalated and became amplified through
some sort of resonance that spiralled out
of control within a few seconds. The
Omega portal was fully open at the time,
and within a small fraction of a second,
it collapsed violently in on itself. I
admit that I do not fully comprehend the
physics of what happened today, but an
entire sphere of matter inside the test
area was either instantly decomposed into
its basic atomic elements, or it was
transferred through spacetime to an
unknown location. It was pure luck that
I, Feldmeyer and most of our senior team
were outside the void sphere when it
occurred. The entire portal is lost
without a trace. It is as if it was never
there, and several of our test personnel
vanished in the event. But we cannot give
up now. There is too much at stake.
```

'Crikey,' said Andrew. 'That sounded terrifying. And doesn't it sound very similar to what supposedly happened at that Soviet test facility in the Ural Mountains?'

'Exactly,' nodded Fiona. 'It would appear that both Drexler and Feldmeyer dodged a bullet in 1943, only for Feldmeyer to be killed in the same type of event working for the Soviet Union in 1957.'

'Who dares wins,' Andrew muttered morbidly. 'Although this feels like taking that concept to the extreme. Sudden and complete annihilation down to the atomic level of all matter inside a sphere many metres across? I wouldn't like to be anywhere near such a device.'

'Same here,' said Fiona. 'But there's a part of me that understands why Drexler was so excited about this. It would be a completely groundbreaking technology if it could be made to work. And if this diary is anything to go by, then they actually managed to do it again just under a year later. Listen to this entry.

```
12th July, 1944.

Almost a year after the void sphere
event, we have now finally managed to
complete the second portal, and I believe
we have managed to stabilise the field
generators. Today we carried out a test
in which the portal successfully
transferred a metal sphere of the same
size and weight as the nuclear bomb that
Project Alpha is working on. The test
object contained delicate electrical
components and wiring, but preliminary
examinations after the test indicate that
they all survived the transfer intact. We
are now very close to possessing a secure
and stable working portal.
```

'Holy crap,' said Andrew. 'They did it. They actually did it. And Feldmeyer was right about what he said at

Farm Hall. If Project Alpha had managed to develop a working nuclear bomb, then Nazi Germany really could have delivered it to anywhere on the planet and probably won the war within days.'

'It's a terrifying thought,' said Fiona. 'But it obviously never played out that way. Less than a year later, the Third Reich was collapsing around them, and they were scrambling to decide what to do. Here is one of Drexler's last entries from Bergkristall.'

19th April, 1945.

The Reds are coming. We heard yesterday that they have crossed the border from Hungary into Austria three days ago and that they are moving this way. Our armies are scattered, and nothing seems able to stop the Slavic hordes. We must keep our work out of the hands of those deranged communists at all costs. If the primitive Bolsheviks manage to acquire our research, they may well conquer the entire world, and humanity will plunge into darkness for an eternity. This must not be allowed to happen. Feldmeyer and I are doing our best to dismantle the equipment and get it ready for transport out of B8, but we are running out of time, and it seems that there isn't anywhere safe for it to go. We may end up having to seal off all of the entire B8 complex with explosives and pray that the Reds never find the lower levels. The future of the world depends on it.

'I sense a heavy dose of panic in that entry,' said Andrew.

'I can understand why,' said Fiona. 'If the Soviets had reached Bergkristall first, they would have grabbed all the advanced technology they could find, including all the scientists, and then they would have hauled them off to Moscow. And Drexler probably wasn't very keen on that idea. Now, as we already talked about, the Allies actually reached Bergkristall first on the 5th of May 1945, but it was then handed over to the Soviets not long after.'

'And as far as we know,' said Andrew. 'Neither the Allies nor the Soviets found anything at Bergkristall like what Drexler describes in this diary.'

'That's right,' said Fiona. 'All they found were V-2 and Me262 manufacturing plants, but nothing to do with nuclear research or anything esoteric like a portal.'

'Which begs the question,' said Andrew. 'Either Drexler was a fantasist and everything in this diary is completely made up, or what he describes actually happened, and somehow neither of the two victorious sides in the war ever found the test facility.'

'Well,' said Fiona. 'Drexler did write that they intended to blow it up and seal the lower levels. If the portal test facility was located deep on those levels, then maybe it was abandoned more or less intact.'

'You mean to say that it could still be there today?' said Andrew.

'I wouldn't rule it out,' said Fiona.

She picked up the tablet that she carried everywhere and that she had used to do some research while she was going through the diary.

'I personally don't think that the Alsos Mission cleared out Bergkristall,' she said, rotating the tablet so that Andrew could see the screen. 'They only thought they did. You see, the Bergkristall complex may have been built by forced labour, but it was designed by one of Germany's main private construction companies at that time. And since much of that company's archives survived the war, I have been able to retrieve some of the original blueprints for the facility.'

She pointed to a schematic on the screen showing a complex web of interconnected lines in what appeared to be an intricate multi-level grid.

'Look,' she said. 'This is the entire Bergkristall facility. All of these lines represent eight-metre wide, thirteen-metre tall tunnels that are all neatly laid out, and as you can see, there were a lot of them. But more importantly, the blueprints show that the complex spanned several individual levels and not just a single one. Altogether, this means that there would have been as much as forty kilometres worth of tunnels inside that mountain, not the eight kilometres that are often cited as the total length.'

'Wow,' said Andrew. 'How many levels were there?'

'At least two, maybe even three,' said Fiona. 'This thing was much bigger than people think. Have a look at these photos.'

She quickly tapped on a different tab on the browser, which then displayed a website containing a series of black-and-white photos. Several of them showed a sheer rockface at least fifty metres tall with what appeared to be three large tunnels stretching into the mountainside, one above the other.

'These photos were taken around Bergkristall during its initial construction,' she said. 'You can see the different levels here. So even if the official story is that there was only one level, you can see here that that simply isn't true. There were multiple levels, but only the top one was discovered after the war.'

'I'm confused,' said Andrew. 'How on earth did Alsos miss this? How did the Omega Project remain undiscovered after the war ended? Why didn't the Allies or the Russians find any clues to it?'

'Perhaps if they found something,' said Fiona, 'they didn't have a clue what they were looking at. And for Project Omega in particular, according to Drexler, the Nazis either cleared out the facility or blew up the access tunnels to the lower levels. And I am guessing the Russians never bothered to dig them out since they would have assumed that everything had already been taken by the Allies. And if neither of them knew anything about the project, then they wouldn't have known what to look for anyway.'

'But then why haven't people uncovered any of this since then?' said Andrew. 'This is a pretty big deal if it's true. It has been a very long time since then, and as you just showed, some of this information is now out in the open.'

'Apparently,' said Fiona, 'there have been several efforts to look into this before. But every single time, the Austrian authorities have resisted, including on one occasion when they halted an excavation of the shooting range above the Bergkristall complex, citing safety concerns. They know there's more down there, but they quite literally don't want anyone to dig up the past. It was the same thing when the Israelis were attempting to bring Nazi war criminals to justice in the 1960s and 1970s. Time and time again, the Austrian authorities proved themselves remarkably adept at being incompetent and incapable of assisting the effort, so it was mainly left to West Germany to provide actionable information for the Nazi hunters.'

'They've quite literally buried it,' said Andrew.

'That's right,' said Fiona. 'And I think it is partly because they want to leave their embarrassing past behind, and partly because they might think that there is nothing left down there after Alsos and the Soviets had it under their control during 1945.'

'But as we've discussed before,' said Andrew. 'What if that isn't true? What if there are sublevels that the Nazis managed to seal up and hide with explosives, just like Drexler wrote. They might even have poured new concrete over it to make the access points invisible.'

'That could certainly have happened,' nodded Fiona. 'Perhaps they were hoping to one day be able to return and breathe new life into these advanced weapons programs. Can you imagine if there is still something down there? Something that was left behind all those years ago?'

Andrew regarded her silently for a moment.

'That would be quite something,' he then said. 'And I think that could well be the case, considering some of the things I have found on Rittenhausen's laptop.'

'What did you find?' said Fiona.

Andrew picked up the laptop and sat down next to her so that they could both see the screen.

'Look here,' he said. 'I've been looking through his emails, his calendar and a whole bunch of his documents, and I discovered that he has visited Sankt Georgen an der Gusen multiple times over the past several years. And not only that, but he appears to be the sole owner of a property development company registered in Vienna. But this property company only owns a single plot of land, and that plot is located in Sankt Georgen.'

'Really?' said Fiona, intrigued.

'Look here,' said Andrew, showing her a map of the small Austrian mountain village. 'Here's Sankt Georgen, and down here to the southeast is the Mauthausen concentration camp. And up here to the northwest, very close to the edge of town, is the entrance to Bergkristall. This is where groups of tourists are allowed to enter and walk around in a small part of the complex. But several hundred metres further to the north inside a small wooded area on top of this hill, is a villa. This is the villa owned by Rittenhausen's property company, and guess where it sits?

Fiona glanced at him, intrigued, waiting for him to speak again.

'Tell me,' she urged.

'It sits right on top of the small granite mountain inside which the Bergkristall facility was built,' said Andrew.

'So, what does all this mean?' she asked. 'What has he been doing there?'

'Apparently,' said Andrew, showing her a folder with spreadsheets and text documents. 'The villa has been under renovation for almost two years, and I have found paperwork and receipts for lots of building materials and equipment such as cement mixers and reinforcement bars. But there are also documents related to the delivery of a large industrial drilling machine.'

'What?' said Fiona, as a slight frown spread across her face and the puzzle pieces began slotting into place inside her mind. 'Are you saying…?'

Andrew nodded.

'I think Rittenhausen has been drilling down to the Bergkristall complex,' he said. 'Having read his grandfather's diary, it would have been as clear to him as it is to us now that something might have been hidden down there ever since the war ended. A technology that would be unlike anything anyone has ever seen before or since. He wanted to get his hands on it, and I think he bought the villa and began drilling a shaft all the way down to the lower tunnels to find it. That's why he has made all those trips to Sank Georgen. For all we know, he could have already reached the lower levels and found whatever was left there.'

'And that's why he has been hoovering up all those research papers at auctions,' said Fiona. 'Is he trying to make his grandfather's design work?'

'Almost certainly,' said Andrew. 'On this laptop, I found indications that he is constructing something big near his estate in Argentina. There is paperwork and a bunch of emails pointing to huge amounts of industrial equipment being shipped over there from heavy industry firms here in Germany. And at a huge cost. All kinds of stuff that sounds quite familiar now. Dozens of types of heavy electrical cables. Components for large industrial-scale electromagnets. Something called a containment field regulator along with various pieces of measuring equipment and control systems. And I found several summaries written by his employees about a range of test results, although they are highly technical, and they don't make much sense to me.'

'He's really trying to do it,' said Fiona, amazed. 'He's actually trying to build a working portal himself.'

The two of them sat silently for a moment, looking at each other as the full implications of their discovery began to sink in.

'There's no other reasonable conclusion,' said Andrew. 'It would be a huge breakthrough, and he would become unimaginably wealthy as a result. It also explains why he was prepared to go to such extreme lengths to secure all those old documents from whatever source he could find. There are multiple emails here between him and Christopher Bateman about all the auctions Bateman attended on his behalf. Most of the correspondence is about auction lots, shipments of various documents and other things either to Rittenhausen's apartment here in Berlin or to his estate in Argentina, but a couple of the emails also mention Ben Ambrose.'

'Ben?' said Fiona with surprise and an obvious pang of sadness in her eyes. 'What do they say?'

'Bateman simply mentions him in passing a few times,' said Andrew. 'I think it might have been because they were competing for items at those auctions. But Rittenhausen seemed to take an interest in Ben towards the end of their correspondence. And then it appears that Rittenhausen fired Bateman quite suddenly. They seem to have had some sort of falling out, although it isn't clear to me exactly what transpired. But looking at the dates, I can see that it happened just days before both Bateman and Ambrose were found dead.'

'That bloody bastard did it. Didn't he?' Fiona whispered, quietly seething as she reached what was now an almost inevitable conclusion. 'Rittenhausen had them both killed. And he tried to have you killed too.'

'Most likely,' said Andrew, nodding slowly. 'It would fit with everything else we've discovered. Although nothing that is in here constitutes actual proof. There's no smoking gun. At least not in what I have found so far.'

'There might not be,' said Fiona with a small shake of the head. 'But I swear, I can smell these types of evil bastards a mile away, and I am smelling one right now. Rittenhausen is a murdering psychopath, and we need to bring him down.'

'I agree,' said Andrew calmly. 'But one thing at a time. I need to show you something else.'

He opened a document entitled 'Candidates – Particle physicists.doc' and showed it to Fiona.

'Have a look at this,' he said.

'What is it?' Fiona said as she leaned in to study the document.

'This is a list of scientists that I assume has been compiled by Rittenhausen or someone who works for him,' said Andrew. 'All of the people on this list are experts in the field of high-energy particle physics, and they are working for a bunch of top-notch universities and private blue-chip companies all over the world. And at the top of the list is a man called Adam Holbrook. He's a professor at CERN in Geneva. And look. In brackets next to his name, it says 'Priority 1'.'

'Presumably, Rittenhausen is looking to acquire these people's expertise,' said Fiona.

'You could say that,' said Andrew. 'I looked up Professor Holbrook online, and guess what? He is currently missing as of about a week ago. Disappeared without a trace from his home in Nantua just over the border in France.'

'What the hell?' said Fiona, aghast, as she glared at Andrew for a long moment before speaking. 'Am I the only one thinking this was a kidnapping? Or am I now becoming completely paranoid?'

'I don't think you're paranoid,' said Andrew gravely. 'Something definitely isn't right about all of this. This professor, who just happens to be a world-leading expert on cyclotron technology disappears in the same week that Ambrose and Bateman are killed. Then I almost end up getting shot looking into Rittenhausen. And then we find out that he appears to have dedicated himself to continuing Otto Drexler's work on cyclotrons and portal technology, and that he might be attempting to build one himself. None of that is a coincidence.'

'I totally agree,' said Fiona. 'It's all connected, and Rittenhausen is at the centre of this spiderweb. It's obvious.'

'The question is, what do we do next?' said Andrew. 'When I was looking into Professor Holbrook, I had a good look at the CERN website, and I discovered a couple of interesting things. Firstly, he is the main person in charge of the cyclotron that feeds accelerated particles into the LHC, the Large Hadron Collider, which I am sure you've heard about. It's the particle collider CERN uses to smash particles together in order to study sub-atomic particles.'

'Yes, I'm vaguely familiar with that,' said Fiona, 'although I wouldn't be able to explain it to anyone.'

'Well,' said Andrew. 'Holbrook was in charge of the machine that the entire CERN complex relies on for its experiments, and it sounds remarkably similar to what Drexler was working on. The difference seems to be that Holbrook's equipment feeds accelerated particles into the LHC, whereas Drexler's design maintains the accelerated particles inside the device. And that then somehow achieves spacetime curvature and creates the portal that Drexler wrote about in his diary.'

'So that's why Rittenhausen would want someone like Holbrook working for him,' said Fiona.

'Precisely,' said Andrew, holding up an index finger. 'Now, the other interesting thing I discovered on the website was that CERN employs another more junior particle physicist by the name of Alice Holbrook. Professor Holbrook's daughter.'

Fiona turned her head and narrowed her eyes slightly as she looked at him in amazement. He then opened a webpage and showed her the staff photo presented alongside a short bio.

'We need to speak to her as soon as possible,' said Fiona. 'She might be able to help us, and maybe we can help her too. If that bastard Rittenhausen has kidnapped her father…'

'I know,' said Andrew, his eyes steely and determined as he nodded slowly. 'Maybe we can get him back.'

Fiona began rummaging around inside her holdall, eventually extracting Edward Harding's diary and flicking through the pages.

'There's something else I need to tell you,' she said, finding the right page. 'Here it is. Do you recall how Harding described a drop site near Bergkristall that had been identified by one of his German collaborators?'

'Yes,' said Andrew. 'A place to stash something in case he was followed. What did he call it again?'

'KDB,' said Fiona, tapping a finger on the relevant page in the diary. 'And he referenced something about that place being guarded by the shepherds of the mountain dead, remember?'

'Yes,' said Andrew. 'So?'

'I think I have worked out what that meant,' she said, showing him a map of the area on her tablet. 'This is the area where Sankt Georgen is located, and over here is a wide valley with a small stream running through it. Is it about five hundred metres from the entrance to Bergkristall, and it is all very wooded. But as you can see, there is a little clearing with a meadow here, and on the edge of it, just by the road, is a small chapel called '*Kapelle der Bergtoten*'. It means Chapel of the Mountain Dead.'

'Holy crap,' said Andrew as he realised what Fiona was implying. 'This was his drop-site?'

'I think so,' said Fiona. 'It fits in terms of distance from the Bergkristall complex, and the name makes sense too. The question is whether he actually ended up hiding anything there before he disappeared.'

''There's only one way to find out,' said Andrew. 'We have to go there and examine that chapel. But first, we need to get ourselves to Switzerland so we can speak to Alice Holbrook. Her father's safety should be our main concern right now.'

Seventeen

Just a few city blocks away, Rittenhausen was sitting still like a statue at his desk in his office, but inside he was like a furious, roiling storm of wrath. Looking at the gaping opening to his safe, he could barely contain his disgust. The whole apartment felt different now. Somehow violated and sullied by the presence of the intruder. He was incensed that someone had dared to break in, and he was equally disturbed by the fact that they seemed to have gone straight for anything related to his research. No valuables had been stolen, and there were plenty of those around. And now, there was an empty space on his desk where his laptop should have been. Naturally, all of its contents were backed up and safe, but the fact that someone now possessed all of the documents contained on that laptop was unsettling and worrying in equal measure. And whoever had been in his apartment had also stolen his grandfather's medals. It was unforgivable.

Much to his surprise and dismay, he then discovered that the burglar had somehow managed to kill Ernesto. Hector had returned to the apartment several hours later, looking like he would have been prepared to murder the entire population of the capital city with his bare hands if it meant that he would be able to catch the man responsible.

Picking up his phone and peering at the small screen, he tapped the play button on the video captured by the building's CCTV systems mounted on its exterior. He had already watched the recordings several times, but he needed to do it again just in case there was anything he had missed. The footage was black-and-white and not particularly high resolution, but it was clear enough for him to watch the burglar barge out through the door, followed shortly thereafter by his South American close protection duo.

The thief appeared to be a Caucasian, well-built and dark-haired man of average height, and before he had commandeered a taxi parked nearby, he had handed the laptop to a woman sitting by one of the café's tables out on the pavement. Unaware that this had happened, Hector and Ernesto had pursued the man immediately after emerging from the stairwell, and so the woman had been able to simply walk away with his laptop under her arm. He was able to follow her on the CCTV feeds as far as the corner with Friedrichstrasse, but none of the cameras had been able to see where she went from there. About twenty minutes ago, as he scrubbed back and forth on the footage, trying to discern the facial features of the two co-conspirators, he had suddenly been reminded of a message he had received from Grigory Komarov the day before. It was a message that he had read with both surprise and dismay. Incredibly, the oligarch and former FSB officer had notified him that there had been a problem retrieving the Farm Hall transcripts from the FSB archives. According to Komarov, the reason appeared to be that two intruders had managed to enter the archives and steal various documents, including the files related to Operation Epsilon, which also included the unredacted Farm Hall transcripts.

Rittenhausen had immediately sent a message to the Russian asking for any CCTV images that might have been captured inside the Lubyanka building, but so far there had been no response. Komarov was probably lying drunk in a bed with a couple of high-class prostitutes. As far as Rittenhausen could tell, that was Komarov's favourite pastime.

As he sat there and stewed darkly, his intuition was screaming at him that the two break-ins were obviously connected. It was too much of a damn coincidence to be pure chance. This was clearly orchestrated, and the perpetrators in both cases had to be the man and the woman he was now watching on the CCTV footage.

'You little shits,' he whispered poisonously. 'I'll fucking string you up and gut you. When I get my hands on you...'

His phone produced a ding and vibrated for a second. There was a new message. He picked it up and saw that it was from Komarov. The Russian had responded uncharacteristically quickly this time, and Rittenhausen tapped the message to open it. Attached were two grainy images of a man and a woman walking along a corridor that he assumed was somewhere inside the FSB headquarters. The man was wearing a Russian army uniform, and the woman was wearing what appeared to be a dark boiler suit, but from their build and height and the way they carried themselves, there was no mistaking them. This was the same pair who had just violated his personal space and stolen his property, including some of his irreplaceable family heirlooms.

His laser-like stare bore into the phone screen, threatening to melt it with pure hatred, and then he tapped the small icon from the sender and tapped again to initiate a call. It rang twice before being picked up, and in the background, Rittenhausen could hear the tones of some sort of bombastic classical music. Tchaikovsky, by the sound of it.

'Ferdinand, my friend,' rumbled Komarov in his deep, slow voice. 'How are you this evening?'

'I'm fucking furious,' growled Rittenhausen, and then he went on to explain everything that had transpired over the previous several hours.

'I see,' said Komarov thoughtfully, as Rittenhausen heard the sound of the oligarch lighting a cigar. 'That is indeed a problem. And you are sure that it was the same people who entered Lubyanka to steal the transcripts?'

'One hundred percent sure,' said Rittenhausen bitterly. 'And I want them found and dealt with.'

'So, tell me. What are you suggesting?' said Komarov magnanimously, having already guessed the true purpose of his friend's late-night call. 'How can I help?'

'I need a favour from you,' said Rittenhausen. 'I'd like to borrow some of your personal security detail. Two or three of your most capable men, preferably with military and intelligence service training. I need them to find and eliminate the two cretins who stole both my personal property and that of your government. After the incident at Lubyanka, I am sure the Kremlin will be pleased with you when they are both dead. I already have some information to go on, and I have useful connections here in Germany that should make it possible to identify and track them. What do you say?'

Komarov had made up his mind even before the question had been asked, but he paused for a long moment for dramatic effect before speaking again.

'Very well,' he eventually said in his usual lazy drawl. 'I will send you three men. Some of my best. Pavel, Maxim and Artem. They are former Spetsnaz, and they have all worked overseas on undercover missions for the FSB. They are highly skilled.'

'Thank you,' said Rittenhausen. 'I am grateful. I owe you for this.'

'Don't mention it,' said Komarov amiably. 'I scratch your back, you scratch mine. It's business.'

'Very good,' said Rittenhausen. 'When can I expect them?'

'They can be with you tomorrow around noon,' said Komarov. 'And they will bring their own tools. Just tell me where you want them to meet you. They are very loyal and will do whatever you ask. No questions asked. And they will be under your command until you send them back to me. I also have a very skilled hacker on my payroll. The best in Saint Petersburg. I will have him make contact with you. He can be extremely useful. Okay?'

'Excellent,' said Rittenhausen, finally beginning to relax as a plan for retribution began to form in his mind. 'Just have them come to my apartment. I will brief them here. Thank you again.'

'Don't worry, my friend,' Komarov said confidently, and then Rittenhausen heard the distinct sound of the Russian taking a long draw on his cigar. 'Everything will be fine. These boys never fail.'

★ ★ ★

By the time Andrew and Fiona had managed to secure seats on a plane to Switzerland and arrived at Geneva International Airport, it was early afternoon the next day. With much too little sleep after the previous evening's dramatic events, they both felt tired and slightly run over, but there was no time to lose in making contact with Alice Holbrook in person.

The flight took an hour and forty minutes, and Andrew managed to catch a bit of sleep while Fiona sat hunched over the fold-down table in front of her, re-reading Otto Drexler's diary. When they stepped out of the arrivals hall in Geneva and got into a taxi, it was a clear, sunny day. The enormous and sprawling CERN complex was only a ten-minute drive from the airport, and they pulled up in front of the triangular reception building on *Esplanade des Particules* just as a minibus full of visitors arrived. At the same time, several small groups of employees were coming and going from the adjacent carpark as well as the tram and bus stations nearby.

As the two of them headed for the entrance to the reception, Andrew spotted a map of the complex, and he hadn't quite realised just how large and packed full of buildings and facilities it was. Inside the almost two-kilometres-long plot were dozens of different individual research facilities, each housed in large, separate buildings. In addition, there were several employee restaurants, teaching facilities, a recruitment centre, a hotel and even a kindergarten. It was essentially a small city on the outskirts of Geneva, and it was evident that many hundreds of people worked here.

They stepped inside and walked up to the reception desk where they asked the female receptionist to see Dr Alice Holbrook. The attractive blonde informed them politely in a pleasant French accent that it wasn't usually possible to simply come in and see CERN staff without first making an appointment, and that anyway, Alice Holbrook had been at home since her father had vanished about a week earlier. As she spoke, she glanced furtively at her colleague next to her, hinting at the fact that Adam Holbrook's mysterious disappearance had probably been a major topic of local gossip lately.

'Would you be able to get a message to her, please?' said Fiona amiably. 'It is extremely important that we speak to her. It's about her father. We believe we might be able to help.'

'Help?' said the receptionist dubiously after a brief pause. 'How so, if I may ask? And who are you exactly?'

'We are friends of her father,' Fiona said, wincing inside at having to lie but realising it was the only way to get anywhere. 'My name is Fiona, and this is Andrew. I'm really sorry I am not able to tell you more. But if you'll just let her know that we are here, and then ask her if we could please come and see her, then we would be very grateful.'

The receptionist seemed to take a moment to consider what was obviously a heartfelt request, and then she produced a nod and gestured to a seating area by the window.

'If you could please wait for a moment,' she said. 'I will try to call her at home. Okay?'

'Thank you,' said Fiona with a sigh of relief. 'Thank you so much.'

The receptionist smiled courteously and gave a nod as she picked up the phone and appeared to look up Alice Holbrook's number on her computer system. Andrew and Fiona walked over to the sunlit seating area and sat down in a pair of wide, upholstered mid-century armchairs.

'Perhaps we were naïve thinking we could just turn up here and have a chat,' said Fiona in hushed tones as she leaned forward in her chair and folded her hands.

'We had to start somewhere,' said Andrew. 'And I don't think calling ahead would have helped any. I am pretty sure your powers of persuasion made a big difference just now.'

'I hope so,' said Fiona, wringing her hands.

'We need to speak to her,' said Andrew quietly. 'If for no other reason than to warn her.'

'You think she could be in danger too?' whispered Fiona.

'Possibly,' said Andrew quietly, rubbing his chin in an effort to partly cover his mouth as he spoke. 'If we are right and her father has already been kidnapped, then there's a risk it could happen to her too.'

'Good news,' called the receptionist as she walked across the floor of the reception towards them with an affable smile. 'I have just spoken to Alice, and she said she would meet you in half an hour at the *Terrasse le Paradis* in the city. It is a small café just on the river. It's quite easy to find.'

★   ★   ★

Half an hour later, Andrew and Fiona were sitting at a small table for three on the quay that constituted the sunlit place of business for the café, whose name attempted to evoke a small slice of paradise to go with the coffees, pastries and various refreshments served there. It was arranged over a set of wide steps by the quayside, and their table was placed by a swirling cast iron railing. On the other side of the railing flowed the River Rhône that began here at Lake Geneva and then travelled for hundreds of winding kilometres through Lyon, Valence and Avignon before reaching the Mediterranean Sea close to Marseille.

They ordered a cup of coffee each and waited as they watched life go by in central Geneva. After about ten minutes, Fiona was becoming worried that Alice had changed her mind and wouldn't show up, but then a young woman walked purposefully down the steps towards them and sat down in the remaining available chair by their table. Wearing a forest green velour blazer over a pale blue blouse and a pair of dark jeans, she was petite and slender. Her light brown hair was slightly longer than shoulder-length, and she had a pretty face with fine features, a button nose and clear blue eyes that made her look younger than she probably was. She was looking straight at them, and it seemed to Andrew that she was one of those people whose mouth appeared to smile faintly even when her face was at rest. However, the dark hue of the skin under her eyes told a story of too little sleep, and the worry lines on her forehead of a week spent in agony over her missing father.

'You're Andrew and Fiona,' she said as she sat down, making it sound more like a statement than a question.

As she looked at the two of them in turn, Andrew was impressed with her apparent self-assuredness and the intelligence that seemed to radiate from her eyes.

'That's right,' he said. 'How did you know?'

'Beatrice,' said Alice. 'The receptionist. She told me what you look like.'

As she spoke, Fiona spotted a delicate silver necklace with a small 'H' slipping out into view from under her blazer. She pointed to it and smiled.

'Is that an 'H' for Holbrook?' she said.

'No,' said Alice, tucking it back inside the blazer. 'It is an 'H' for hydrogen. The first atom to ever exist in the universe. My father gave it to me. I am his first and only child.'

Fiona shifted uncomfortably on her chair at the reminder of the reason for their meeting here, and she cleared her throat and nodded.

'I see,' she said seriously. 'Well, it is nice to meet you. And thank you for seeing us at such short notice.'

'That's alright,' said Alice, subdued. 'You said you think you know what happened to my father?'

'Well,' said Andrew. 'We don't know anything for certain, but we have a theory. And please forgive us, but it is a bit complicated. We'll try to explain it as succinctly as we can.'

Andrew provided Alice with a brief introduction to the two of them, and then he spent the next fifteen minutes relaying to Alice the events of the past week or so, leaving out some of the precise details about their clandestine activities in both Moscow and Berlin but conveying enough about what had transpired in London as well as their research into the Farm Hall transcripts and the Nazi Alpha and Omega projects for her to grasp the big picture. When Andrew told her about the deaths of Ambrose and Bateman and their mutual connection to the enigmatic Ferdinand von Rittenhausen, her face darkened appreciably, and then she began fidgeting nervously with her hands.

'Have you ever heard the name Rittenhausen before?' asked Fiona. 'Did your father ever mention that name?'

'No,' said Alice, shaking her head as deep creases formed on her brow. 'Never. I think he would have told me if some rich oddball had approached him about his work. He's not really used to talking about it to anyone outside of CERN. Aside from his colleagues, I didn't think anyone knew he existed, which is just the way he likes it. The more he can be left in peace to do his work, the happier he is. I'm a bit like that too, to be honest. We don't really like attention.'

'How did you first realise that he was missing?' said Andrew.

'We were supposed to meet up for a meal like we often do,' said Alice. 'He didn't message me to say he was going to be on time, which is what he normally does, and then he didn't show up at the restaurant. I tried to call him, but I couldn't get through. It's not just that his phone didn't ring. There was no connection at all. It was as if his phone had been switched off. I kept trying all night, but it was useless. In the end, I drove to his house in Nantua, and that's when I found the front door open and the house empty.'

'And no clue to where he might be?' said Andrew.

'No,' said Alice. 'Everything looked normal, except for this.'

She reached inside her blazer and extracted a matchbox. Opening it, she pulled out a small, sealable plastic bag with something brown and cylindrical inside.

'This is a cigarette butt,' she said, placing it on the table. 'I found it next to the doormat by the front door. My father doesn't smoke. Never has. And he never lets anyone light up inside his house either, or anywhere else on the property, for that matter.'

'You think it was dropped by whoever took him away?' said Fiona, before caveating her question. 'If that's really what happened?'

'Yes,' said Alice. 'He would never have allowed anyone to drop a cigarette butt on his doorstep, and if someone had done it while he was out, he would have picked it up and put it in the bin. I am quite sure of it.'

'Can I see that?' said Andrew, leaning forward, carefully picking up the bag and studying the cigarette butt through the transparent plastic. 'You see those dark patches down here? Those are marks from the saliva of whoever smoked this. We could have that looked at and run against Interpol's database. I am sure we could get that done very quickly.'

'That's a good idea,' said Fiona, turning to Alice. 'Is that okay with you?'

'Sure,' said Alice. 'That would be amazing. Thank you.'

'I'll sort that out as soon as we're done here,' said Andrew, putting the bag back in the matchbox and placing the box inside his jacket pocket.

'So, what happened next?' said Fiona. 'After you had been to his house. Did you then contact the police?'

'Yes,' nodded Alice. 'I did that immediately. They sent out some local cops who took a look around and began asking about my father's drinking habits. It was pretty upsetting, actually. They didn't seem to take it very seriously, but they filed some paperwork and said that they would produce a missing person's report if he hadn't turned up after 48 hours. I then drove back to Geneva, but I just knew that something bad had happened. And those 48 hours came and went, and I never heard back from them. I called, and they said that they might consider dredging the lake where he usually goes fishing, but that hasn't happened either. I know that the weather was nice and calm that day, his boat was returned to the marina, and an eyewitness at a restaurant said that he went there for dinner, so he is definitely not in the lake.'

'And he wouldn't have gone off somewhere without telling you,' said Fiona.

'No,' said Alice, shaking her head. 'Not a chance. Something has happened to him, and your Rittenhausen sounds like he could be behind it. I mean, you just said he was probably behind those two murders in London, right?'

'Yes,' said Andrew. 'But for what it is worth, we don't believe that your father is dead. We think he is alive and well somewhere.'

Relief washed visibly across Alice's face as her mask of composure slipped for a brief moment.

'Although, I should say,' continued Andrew, holding up a finger didactically. 'We have no evidence to back that up. Nothing except the fact that Rittenhausen appears to be working on something where your father's expertise would probably come in very handy. And I am absolutely convinced that your father's name was on Rittenhausen's list of scientists for a reason. He's one of the best out there, right?'

'Yes,' nodded Alice. 'I suppose. But what is it that you think Rittenhausen is building? A cyclotron?'

'Or something very much like that,' said Fiona, glancing at Andrew. 'Look, we don't understand the physics of it, but perhaps you can help us. Everything we have discovered so far points to the idea that Otto Drexler was working on portal technology.'

She watched Alice's face and expected to see a dismissive frown, but the young woman simply looked at her pensively and gave a single nod.

'And the ultimate goal for the Nazis,' said Andrew, 'was to use it to deliver nuclear bombs to enemy territories without the need for rockets or aircraft.'

'But is it even possible?' said Fiona, suddenly concerned that they sounded ridiculous saying this to a highly educated particle physicist. 'Everything we've seen so far points to the fact that the Nazis certainly believed that it could be done, and they may even have managed to do it at one of their secret wonder-weapon facilities. But what do you make of this?'

'Okay,' said Alice, shifting in her chair as she gathered her thoughts. 'Portals, or wormholes, as we physicists like to call them, are certainly possible. They are essentially tunnels through spacetime, and they are at least theoretically possible, according to our current understanding of physics. It's just that it requires almost unimaginable amounts of energy to make them happen.'

Andrew and Fiona glanced at each other with mild surprise at the matter-of-factness with which Alice talked about what to them had sounded until now purely like science fiction.

'So, are we talking about teleportation?' said Andrew.

'No,' said Alice, shaking her head. 'Teleportation involves disassembling something in one place and then reassembling it somewhere else. That is not what this is. What we are talking about here is the ability to quite literally step foot through a portal or spacetime tunnel and emerge in a location that is thousands of miles away or even much further. It is called an Einstein-Rosen bridge, and it is an actual physical connection between two completely different locations in spacetime.'

'It sounds crazy,' said Fiona with a half-smile.

'I know,' said Alice. 'But the theory is sound. It comes out of Einstein's equations for special relativity, so theoretically and mathematically, these portals can exist, and they are consistent with the laws of physics as we understand them.'

'But how?' said Andrew. 'How do they work?'

'Alright,' said Alice, now seeming to come alive as she delved into a subject that she was clearly passionate about. 'In order to explain this, you need to understand a couple of things about physics. Like the fact that Isaac Newton got it all wrong.'

'What?' said Fiona. 'Really?'

'Strictly speaking, yes,' said Alice. 'He managed to successfully describe the motion and relation between different physical objects, but he ended up using a sort of shorthand for how the universe actually works. It was a bit like if I gave a mechanical wristwatch to a tribe living in complete isolation in the Amazon jungle. They would eventually work out that the small hand goes around the clockface twice for every time the sun moves across the sky, and that the two large hands divide that process into smaller units. But that doesn't mean they would be able to discern that there is a whole set of interlinked differential gears inside the watch. They would have no way of ever working that out, yet they would essentially have worked out how the watch works, or at least be able to describe what it does. What Newton did was essentially the same. He successfully described basic physics, but with no understanding of fundamental things like gravity. You see, unlike what he postulated, gravity isn't a force that attracts bodies of mass to each other, even though it very much looks and feels that way.'

Alice extracted a pen from the small handbag slung over her shoulder and held it over the table.

'If I release this pen,' she said, and let it go, 'it falls onto this table. It looks like there is something pulling at it. Some invisible force. And so Newton and others invented the idea of gravity as a force. But it turns out to only work on very large scales, and it only *appears* to explain what is happening. His ideas allow us to describe the motion of pens dropping towards tables and planets orbiting stars, but they break down at the subatomic level because they never actually incorporate our true reality.'

'Which is what?' said Fiona, struggling to follow.

'That we live in four dimensions,' said Alice, 'which is what we call spacetime. It consists of our familiar three dimensions plus the time dimension. And as it turns out, spacetime can stretch and bend and curve.'

'I'm afraid you've lost me now,' said Andrew.

'Don't worry,' said Alice, with a kind smile. The human brain has not evolved to operate in more than three dimensions, so it can be difficult to wrap one's head around. I found it tricky at first, too. But have a look at this.'

She pulled a small notebook from her handbag, ripped out a page and placed it flat on the table. Then she pulled the cap off her pen and made two dots a handsbreadth apart, marking them A and B.

'This is two-dimensional space,' she said, giving Andrew the pen. 'It's a 2D representation of our 3D world, but it is just to illustrate. So imagine that this is our reality. Now, what is the shortest distance between these two points?'

Andrew looked at her, slightly perplexed, shrugged and drew a straight line between the two points.

'Correct,' said Alice, 'except there is a shorter route. 'In fact, there is a route where you would travel no distance at all going from A to B.'

Andrew frowned, looking perplexed.

'How?' he said.

'By adding one more dimension,' said Alice. 'Then you would suddenly be operating in three dimensions instead of just two.'

She pushed the ends of the piece of paper towards each other until it bulged up in the middle, aligning them so that the two points A and B were immediately next to each other. Then she pushed the tip of the pen through one side of the paper and out of the other, puncturing it straight through the two points.

'See?' she said. 'I've now connected A and B without travelling any distance at all. And I did this by curving space. With this technique, I can create an instant path to anywhere in the world. So, that's what a wormhole looks like in 2D space, and it is equally possible in 3D space which is the reality that we occupy. All you need to do is curve spacetime so much that it folds in on itself.'

'Is that even possible?' said Fiona.

'You're experiencing curvature right now,' said Alice. 'The only reason the pen seemed to fall onto the table was not because of a force called gravity. It was because mass causes spacetime to curve, and the Earth is so large and massive that it curves space and makes everything fall towards it. Similarly, the sun is so massive that it creates a curvature of spacetime large enough for the entire Earth to fall towards it.'

'So why aren't we plunging into the sun right now?' said Andrew.

'Because we are moving through space at a speed that perfectly balances that curvature,' said Alice. 'It is the same principle at play with things like a space station in orbit around the Earth. If it suddenly came to a stop, it would immediately begin plunging towards the Earth. The only reason it doesn't do that is because it is travelling at around 25 thousand kilometres per hour, which perfectly cancels out the plant's curvature and allows it to maintain a stable orbit. Anyway, the key takeaway here is that if you could somehow create enough curvature in spacetime, then theoretically, you could fold it in on itself to create a physical connection between two points, effectively creating a portal between those two locations.'

'This is all pretty mind-bending,' said Andrew, raising his eyebrows as he looked at the folded piece of paper. 'No pun intended.'

'I know,' said Alice, giving him a small, encouraging smile. 'It's a lot to wrap your head around. But the theory is solid.'

'So, why hasn't anyone done this yet?' said Fiona. 'If it is so straightforward, you would have thought that it had been more or less perfected by now. Especially if the German scientists of the 1930s were virtually there already.'

'The problem is energy,' said Alice. 'I am sure you're both familiar with Einstein's famous equation, $E = mc^2$, where 'E' is energy, 'm' is mass, and 'c' is the speed of light. It basically says that there is a linear relationship between energy and mass. In fact, at the subatomic level, it turns out that the mass of atoms *is* energy, so in a very real sense, mass is interchangeable with energy. This is all part of what's known as the Standard Model of Particle Physics, according to which all subatomic particles are actually excitations in what are called quantum fields. And when those excitations interact with something called the Higgs field, that's when they acquire what we refer to as mass. It's sort of analogous to if you are standing in a swimming pool and you hold out your hand in the water without moving it, then you don't really feel your hand. But as soon as you start moving it through the water from side to side, you immediately get the clear sensation of your hand having mass because it is pushing against the weight and volume of the water. And the faster you move your hand, the more massive it feels. So, conceptually, water is to the hand what the Higgs field is to subatomic particles. Now, in the context of a cyclotron, in order to reach the sort of mass required to actually curve spacetime, you will need almost unimaginable amounts of speed and energy.'

'Yet it seems that the Nazis stumbled on some sort of solution to this problem,' said Fiona. 'Some sort of shortcut.'

'I'm sorry,' said Andrew. 'Precisely what does all of this have to do with cyclotrons? From what I have understood, those machines are used for accelerating particles and then smashing them into atoms to see how they break up. Fission, right?'

'That's right,' said Alice. 'That's the reason they were first invented in 1939, and it is part of what we do here at CERN.'

'And your father is one of the world's top experts in that field, isn't he?' said Andrew.

'Yes,' nodded Alice.

'But as far as you know,' said Andrew, 'is there any conceivable way that a cyclotron could be used to create the sort of spacetime curvature that Otto Drexler was trying to achieve?'

'Well,' said Alice thoughtfully. 'First of all, we no longer use the types of cyclotrons that they would have used during the Second World War. The particle accelerators we use now are called synchrotrons, and they use the same principle but with subtle differences. You see, the problem with cyclotrons is that they have inherent issues with their stability once the accelerated particles reach very high speeds, and...'

She suddenly trailed off as she spoke, and then she blinked a couple of times in quick succession with her mouth partly open as a seemingly crazy idea flashed through her mind.

'Wait...' she said breathlessly. 'Wait a minute.'

Andrew and Fiona watched her silently as she sat there, seemingly frozen to the spot for several long moments while her razor-sharp mind went into overdrive.

'The problem with a cyclotron,' Alice continued, 'is that as it accelerates protons to near lightspeed, which is what we call relativistic speeds, they travel so fast that they actually begin to acquire more mass. It has to do with Einstein's equation again. The more energy, the more mass, because the speed of light is a constant. In the end, the protons circulating inside the cyclotron acquire so much mass that they begin to bend spacetime, thereby creating small gravity wells around themselves. This is a well-known phenomenon that marginally slows down the protons, and that in turn causes them to be out of phase with the oscillating magnetic fields that are controlling them. And this is where the synchrotron comes in. Unlike the cyclotron, it also modulates the magnetic fields to take these relativistic effects into account.'

'I think I just about get the general idea,' said Andrew.

'But,' said Alice, holding up a finger in a professorial gesture that suddenly made the attractive young woman look much older and wiser. 'If you were to simply keep pushing up the energy levels inside a synchrotron without allowing the accelerated protons to be fed out to a particle collider, then with enough speed and enough protons hurtling around inside it, their combined relativistic mass could create a toroidal gravitational field. And if that field was strong enough, if enough protons were accelerated and injected into the ring of the portal, then their combined relativistic mass would eventually become high enough to begin to exert a gravitational effect on spacetime. It could cause it to curve. And at least theoretically, the strength of that gravitational field could then be increased arbitrarily with the amount of energy pumped into the system. And in the limit, spacetime would be folded over, creating something like a portal and connecting two locations in spacetime. I mean... theoretically speaking.'

As she finished her sentence and trailed off, Alice frowned slightly, as if she was not quite able to come to terms with what she had just said.

'If I understand you correctly,' said Fiona, 'then stabilising the magnetic field inside the cyclotron was a major hurdle for the early versions of those machines. But with modern computers and control software, that must be much easier, right?'

'It's a dawdle,' shrugged Alice. 'We have complete control over the fields inside our synchrotrons.'

'So, could a synchrotron be used to perform the task that Drexler attempted to do with a cyclotron?' asked Andrew.

'Quite possibly, yes,' said Alice. 'And they would allow for even more power and a much more stable portal if such a thing is really possible.'

''What about energy consumption?' said Fiona. 'You said they would need enormous amounts to create spacetime curvature, right? Could the Nazi scientists have stumbled on some mechanism to unlock the required quantities for this? Drexler's diary mentions traces of rhodium mixed in with tungsten as the key to making the portal work. Does any of that make sense to you?'

'Not really,' said Alice. 'I have never heard of this sort of thing being done before, but I guess I can't rule anything out. The German scientists were clearly working on releasing the energy stored inside atoms. But I don't know how far they got. What I do know is that the energy available inside the nucleus of an atom is truly immense, especially the strong nuclear force, which is what holds protons and neutrons together. When we are dealing with simple chemical energy such as combustions or explosions, it releases a few electron volts per atom, which is just a measuring unit used by particle physicists. However, when we are dealing with fission, several million electron volts per atom are released.'

'Hence the power of nuclear bombs weighing just a few tens of kilos,' said Andrew.

'Correct,' nodded Alice.

'So it is at least possible,' said Andrew, 'that those Nazi scientists, as they were working on nuclear fission, came across some way of unlocking nuclear forces capable of supplying the energy required for opening a portal.'

'Once again,' said Alice, looking as if she couldn't quite believe what she was hearing herself say. 'Theoretically, yes. It's at least possible.'

'There's something else that we should probably tell you,' said Andrew. 'We have found strong indications that Otto Drexler's righthand man, Horst Feldmeyer, attempted to continue the work on the portal for the Soviets after the war.'

'Really?' said Alice. 'I take it they didn't succeed.'

'That's right,' said Andrew. 'Not if our information is correct. The Soviet program codenamed 'Vorota' ended in a catastrophic implosion event that annihilated a huge spherical section of the inside of a mountain in the Urals. And as far as we understand it, the Soviet Union never tried to replicate it.'

The three of them sat silently for a moment as the implications of Alice's speculation settled in their minds. Andrew and Fiona glanced at each other while Alice picked up the folded piece of paper and slowly rotated it in her hands as if emulating the torrent of protons that just might be able to quite literally open a door to something truly revolutionary.

'What about my dad?' she finally said quietly. 'Is that why he was taken? To help build this thing,

'Most likely,' said Andrew.

'Do you have any idea where he is now?' she pressed.

'Possibly,' said Andrew, keen not to dangle false hope in front of her. 'Aside from his apartment in Berlin, we know of at least two other locations that are owned by Rittenhausen, and your father could be in either one of them. But, as I said earlier. We don't have any hard evidence yet that Rittenhausen is even involved in your father's disappearance. But I will have that cigarette butt analysed as soon as possible. With a bit of luck, the results might point us in the right direction. And we will let you know as soon as we have something.'

'And until then?' Alice said, somewhat despondently. 'Do I just sit here and wait?'

'I don't think there's much else you can do,' said Fiona empathetically, looking hopefully at Andrew but seeing only a plea for patience. 'I'm sorry. I wish there was some way we could help right now.'

'What about you two?' Alice said, looking at them in turn. 'What are you going to do now?'

Andrew gave her a calm but determined look.

'We're going to Austria,' he said. 'Rittenhausen owns a villa near where the Nazi advanced weapons facility used to be. There might still be some clues as to what is going on. It is even possible that this is where they are holding your father. But there's only one way for us to find out.'

Eighteen

With no time to lose, Andrew and Fiona chartered a private flight from Geneva to Austria on a small aircraft. However, before leaving the Swiss capital later that afternoon, Andrew paid a visit to the British Embassy where he arranged for the cigarette butt found at Holbrook's home to be analysed by a local private forensics firm. With the assistance of the embassy, the DNA results would then be sent immediately to Interpol to see if there might be a match in their database. Supposedly, the results should be available within a day or so.

The roughly 700-kilometre flight on the sleek single-engine Pilatus PC-12 turboprop aircraft to the small airport in Linz took just over two hours, and by the time they touched down and taxied to the modest terminal, the warm sun was beginning to set over what at this time of year were the green Austrian Alps. They hired a car at the airport and drove through the city of Linz and across the wide Danube River, reaching the town of Sank Georgen an der Gusen only about half an hour later. The picturesque town lay in a wide bowl in the rolling terrain where two shallow valleys met, and on the way there, Andrew and Fiona spotted several businesses operating in the quarry industry that clearly dominated the area.

They headed straight for the meadow with the chapel, and when they arrived, it was difficult to imagine this place having been the setting of a dramatic infiltration attempt by a British agent during World War 2. The meadow, surrounded on three sides by tall conifers, was carpeted with thick, light green grass that took on a golden hue in the sunset, and it was dotted with hundreds of small white flowers. On the far side of it was the stream, and close to the road about a hundred metres away was the chapel. It was about the size of a small living room and rendered white, and it had a dark and very steeply pitched wooden roof.

'Well, this looks idyllic,' said Fiona, peering across the meadow towards the neat little chapel with distant mountains in the background. 'Let's get close and see what we can find.'

Andrew parked the car on a narrow gravelled layby in front of the chapel, and then the two of them stepped out and entered the chapel. It appeared well cared for with its smooth walls, polished flagstones and an elaborately carved wooden altarpiece directly opposite the entrance. There were a number of different motifs and scenes from the Bible depicted there, and as the two of them stepped closer, Fiona immediately homed in on an intricately carved and painted scene of a group of shepherds standing by a small hut with a group of sheep.

'Shepherds of the mountain dead,' she said, kneeling to get a closer look. 'This must be it.'

'Gently,' said Andrew as Fiona touched the figures and began examining them. 'We don't want to break anything.'

'I won't,' said Fiona placatingly. 'I am being careful. I just need to have a good look around.'

She touched each shepherd in turn and tried to see if they could be shifted or removed entirely. However, they all appeared to have been wedged and glued in place a very long time ago, and none of them moved a millimetre. Then she reached behind the small group of wooden figurines and pinched her thumb and index finger around the edge of the doorframe on the small hut behind them. It moved ever so slightly, and then it suddenly came loose with a faint snap.

'Oops,' said Fiona, thinking that she might have broken it, but it then became apparent that there was a different explanation.

'Look,' she said, turning to Andrew, who was now standing next to her. 'The front of this hut was carved as a separate piece and stuck onto the display. And there is a small space behind it.'

Gently turning and rotating the loose wooden piece, she angled it clear and pulled it away to reveal a cavity that was roughly the size of a large fist. Inside was a small camera with a very short lens. Its aluminium-edged housing appeared to be made from the same dull, black polymer as most early rotary telephones, and it had a layer of fine dust covering it.

'That's an old camera,' said Andrew incredulously, lowering himself onto his haunches next to Fiona.

'Harding must have left it here,' she said. 'And it has been sitting in there ever since. Amazing.'

'And look,' said Andrew, pointing to a couple of dark, discoloured smears on the bottom of the wooden cavity. 'That's blood. When he put it here, he must have been wounded.'

'Crikey,' said Fiona faintly. 'I don't know what I expected to find here, but it wasn't this. We might be looking at the reason Harding was never heard from again. He managed to hide this roll of film, and then he was most likely captured.'

'Probably captured and killed,' said Andrew with a small wince as he imagined the scene that might have played out inside the chapel. 'The standing order for how to deal with spies during wartime would have been to kill them immediately unless they could be interrogated for information. Either way, he would have ended up dead fairly soon after leaving this place.'

'That's really chilling,' said Fiona, reaching for the camera and gripping it gently between her fingertips. 'Do you think someone might be able to develop the film? I'm dying to know what's on it.'

'I'm not sure,' said Andrew. 'This would contain a celluloid film, and I don't think that sort of stuff lasts forever. But we'll bring it with us, and then we can give it a try. Come on. Let's leave. We need to get to Rittenhausen's villa.'

* * *

Using the information obtained from Rittenhausen's laptop, their satnav route took them back through the small alpine town and a short distance further north. It then directed them up along a steep, curving road towards the top of a wooded hill where the villa supposedly being renovated by his property company was meant to be located. As it turned out, the property was situated on a large plot and tucked away amongst dense deciduous tree cover behind a tall, ivy-covered brick wall that appeared to wrap around the entire plot. However, as dusk fell and they stopped for a few seconds and looked through the metal gates, they were able to spot obvious signs of construction activity, including various pieces of machinery and materials. But there was no indication of anyone being around at this time.

'That's definitely the house,' said Andrew. 'That's where the granite drilling equipment was delivered to, according to Rittenhausen's own records.'

'We'll need a way in,' said Fiona.

'Not a problem,' said Andrew, putting the car into gear again and pulling away. 'I'll park up here on the left, and then we'll climb over the wall around the back.'

A few minutes later, as darkness closed in, they were making their way across the forest floor, which was covered by dry, crunching leaves of many different shades of yellow and brown. As they approached the boundary of the property, they could see the roughly three-metre-high perimeter wall cutting across in front of them, and behind it, they were able to glimpse the black-tiled roof of Rittenhausen's mountain villa.

Scaling the walls presented no problem since they were heavily overgrown with thick vines of ivy in many places, and the two of them soon dropped down on the other side and began approaching the main building. It sat inside a small clearing that was slightly raised relative to the surrounding forest, and in addition to a separate double garage located next to it, there were two smaller outbuildings at the back. With its long grass and clumps of tall weeds, the back garden looked mostly like a wild meadow, and there was nothing at the front or anywhere else near the house, which suggested that the villa had been occupied since Rittenhausen had bought the plot just over two years earlier. Whatever had been going on here had happened inside the building.

'Have a look at those double garages,' said Andrew, pointing ahead through the trees as they paused to survey the scene in front of them. 'See anything unusual?'

'Not really,' said Fiona, eyeing them inquisitively.

'The carports are facing off to the side,' said Andrew. 'They usually always face towards the driveway at the front of the house.'

'Why was it built like that?' said Fiona.

'Because this isn't a house,' said Andrew. 'This is just a brick shell for a drill site. The carports are lined up so that heavy machinery can drive straight into the middle of the house without having to turn, and I'll bet you anything there's a drilling rig where the living room should be.'

They cautiously advanced through the remaining trees and approached the front door, where Andrew tried the door handle. Unsurprisingly, it was locked, and when he tried to look in through the tall, narrow windows on either side, he realised that both panes of glass had been sprayed white on the inside, making it impossible to see in. The same turned out to be the case with the windows. After having circled around the perimeter of the building, it was evident that the only way inside that had been used during the supposed renovation work was the double garage. Andrew found a small radio receiver box mounted on the wall next to one of the carports, but without the remote control, there was no obvious way of activating the doors.

Using his screwdriver, he cracked open the plastic housing to expose the electrical wiring, and there was also a small red LED inside it revealing that the receiver still had power. After a few rounds of random trial and error, he found a way to short-circuit the unit, and amid the whirring of electrical motors, both of the doors began to open and retract up under the roof of the garage. Inside was parked a forklift next to a mini bulldozer, and almost the entire back wall was taken up by a pair of large metal cabinets that appeared to contain power junctions and transformers. Connected to the cabinets were thick black power cables that ran off to the right and through a large opening in the wall to the villa's interior.

As Andrew had suspected, there was no trace of this having been a habitable space for a very long time, and the entirety of the middle of the villa, including the first floor, had been converted into one large open space where an industrial drill had been mounted. It reached at least five metres up inside the gutted building, and it was painted bright yellow and looked to be virtually new except for the dust that clung to its every surface. On one side of it was a small metal cab from where the drill operator would have controlled its operation as it worked its way down through the granite.

'Damn,' said Fiona. 'Look at this place. This is surreal. I have never seen anything like it.'

'Me neither,' said Andrew, walking closer to a two-metre-tall steel cube sitting next to the drill at the very centre of the bizarre space. 'It looks like they finished drilling a shaft a long time ago. This must be some sort of elevator.'

Andrew stepped up to examine it, and as Fiona joined him, he gave her a quick glance and a shrug, and then he punched the transparent yellow button on the side of the elevator housing. With a muffled ding, the slightly curved door to the elevator slid aside, revealing a cylindrical cab that was roughly two metres across.

'I guess we're going down,' said Andrew.

'This had better work,' said Fiona. 'How far down do you reckon it goes?'

Andrew tilted his head to one side and thought about it for a moment as he tried to recall how far up the small, wooded mountain they had driven before climbing over the wall and entering the property.

'It could easily be well over a hundred metres down to the tunnels from here,' he said. 'If it is true that the Nazis constructed several layers of tunnels that go even deeper than what is on the official Bergkristall maps, then it could be as much as 50 storeys.'

Fiona swallowed at the thought, and when she looked up at the huge horizontal flywheel, around which was coiled what appeared to be a very long steel cable, she could feel herself beginning to sweat. The inside of the elevator cab suddenly looked very small and cramped.

'I'm not sure about this,' she heard herself say. 'Maybe I should stay up here.'

'Fiona,' said Andrew reassuringly as he stepped over to face her, taking both of her hands gently in his. 'You can do this. I am sure this thing was constructed extremely well, so it will almost certainly be as safe as if you took an elevator in a building somewhere in London. And besides, I need you down there with me. You've studied this whole thing even more closely than I have, and who knows what we might find down there? So we need two pairs of eyes and ears.'

Fiona was looking down at her own hands resting inside Andrew's palms, and after a moment, she nodded slowly a couple of times, and then she looked up into his eyes and gave him a brave smile.

'You're right,' she said. 'We're in this together. Let's just get it over with.'

'That's my girl,' said Andrew, giving her a gentle kiss on the forehead. 'Let's go.'

Nineteen

When the two of them stepped inside the elevator and Andrew pressed the 'Down' button, the slim cylindrical cab shook slightly as the giant flywheel began unspooling its cable and the cab began descending down through the drilled-out shaft. As they started moving, they noticed a small LCD panel next to the door, which read their current depth. There was also a tiny sliver of an opening just above the sliding door, which allowed them to see the inside of the shaft as they travelled. As the cab began picking up speed and the shaft outside the cab slid by, it vibrated and rumbled significantly more than a typical elevator. Every once in a while, the cab went past some sort of stabilising metal ring that appeared to have been placed at regular intervals down through the shaft, and this caused a vibration that travelled up along the cable, which in turn translated into a noticeable judder inside the cab.

It felt like a lot longer, but when the elevator cab finally slowed down and came to a stop, the LCD display showed -173 metres, and the entire trip had taken less than a minute. As the cab stopped and the safety clamps snapped into place underneath it, it took several long seconds for the door to slide aside, and when it finally did, Andrew heard an audible sigh of relief from Fiona, who sounded as if she had held her breath the whole way down.

What greeted them as the curved door disappeared into the slit in the side of the doorframe, was an almost perfectly dark void. All they could see by the light coming from the overhead lamps spilling out into the space outside was dusty and rocky ground that stretched away a couple of metres into the darkness before fading into nothing.

Andrew extracted two torches from his backpack, and as they stepped out onto the floor, their two narrow light cones lanced out and sliced through the darkness, revealing a huge cave with lots of modern tools and equipment. Moving into the centre of the space, the small rocks and pebbles strewn across the solid concrete floor were grinding softly under their feet, and the torches quickly helped them map out a concrete-reinforced cavern roughly twenty metres across. The cave was supported by tall steel pylons that stretched all the way up to the curved ceiling, some ten metres above their heads. On the far side of the space opposite the elevator was an opening that was more or less the size of a set of large double doors. Beyond it was darkness.

'This looks like a staging area,' said Andrew as his torchlight swept across the bare granite wall. 'A place to install the elevator and store equipment. And that opening over there must be where it connects to the original Bergkristall tunnels.'

'173 metres below the surface,' said Fiona. 'We must be a lot deeper than the main entrance here.'

'I think you're right,' said Andrew, glancing at the various pieces of industrial equipment lined up inside the roughly circular space. 'And it looks to me like they brought down and assembled just about everything they could possibly need. Let's see what's here.'

They left the lit-up elevator behind and walked over to some of the equipment arranged along the wall. There were diesel generators, which the drilling crew would have used for their power tools before they could run power cables all the way from the surface. There were large chainsaw-like tools with enormous blades designed to cut through rock. And there were dozens of metal fuel barrels stacked on top of each other, although a quick tap on their exterior told Andrew that only a couple of them still had anything in them. There were also stacks of general-purpose timber, boxes and cabinets full of all kinds of tools such as drills, mallets and pickaxes, as well as a few toolboxes full of items for maintaining all the other machines and equipment.

'It looks like they thought of everything,' said Fiona.

'Let's have a look at the old tunnels,' said Andrew.

They walked across to the wide opening to what they assumed was one of the original tunnels, and when they pushed through the roughly three-metre-long passage that had been created to reach the original tunnel system, they found themselves inside an almost cathedral-like space where the air seemed bone dry and it had a dusty smell to it. The concrete walls of the approximately ten-metre wide tunnel extended vertically up at least fifteen metres after which they curved over to meet at an apex even higher above their heads. There was no way to tell precisely how long the tunnel was in either direction because their torchlights faded away well before reaching the ends. However, every noise they made and every word they spoke seemed to echo for an eternity until finally attenuating into soft whispers in the far distance.

'Oh wow,' said Andrew in a hushed voice, in awe as he stepped out into the middle of the tunnel and directed his torchlight up to the ceiling above. 'This place is huge.'

'And this is just one tunnel,' whispered Fiona, struggling to contain her amazement. 'Imagine this place packed full of V-2 and Me262 assembly lines. It almost beggars belief that those things took place here.'

'I know,' said Andrew, turning around slowly as he examined the smooth tunnel walls. 'And practically all of the V-2 rockets built here eventually fell over London, and the fighter jets from this place flew missions over the English Channel.'

'Any idea exactly where we are?' Fiona said quietly, directing her torchlight along the tunnel and peering ahead.

'We should be near the far end of the complex,' said Andrew. 'At least judging from the location of the villa relative to the main entrance to the complex. So, we are nowhere near the main entrance now. We could be as much as a whole kilometre away.'

'It is absolutely enormous,' said Fiona.

'And this area has laid completely untouched since 1945,' said Andrew. 'That is, until Rittenhausen's crew drilled their way down here.'

'I wonder when they left,' said Fiona with a slightly anxious note in her voice. 'They must have spent a lot of time down here, but it looks like that was a while ago. Maybe they found what they were looking for.'

'Or maybe they'll be back soon,' said Andrew, pulling his pistol from its holster and racking the slide. 'The villa and the elevator still have power, so for all we know, there could be someone down here right now.'

'Look,' said Fiona, pointing off to one side where black cables as thick as anacondas snaked their way along the uneven floor near one side of the tunnel. 'Power cables. Rittenhausen's team must have put those down. Whatever they came here for, these cables ought to lead us straight to it.'

They began following the cables, stepping cautiously and shining their torches to light the way as they headed deeper into the mountain.

'Look,' said Andrew, pointing ahead. 'It looks like there might be a junction up there.'

After another thirty metres of walking through the eerily quiet tunnel where only their own footsteps could be heard reverberating off the seemingly endless concrete walls, they reached an intersection between the tunnel and what appeared to be a smooth concrete road. It soon became clear that the road cut across not just this tunnel but several more on both sides, and at this point, the power cables turned ninety degrees to their left and began following the road.

'This cuts across all the tunnels on this level,' said Andrew. 'So, it probably leads to the main entrance to the complex.'

'It must have been collapsed and concreted over by the Nazis in 1945,' said Fiona. 'That's the only way this place could have remained hidden.'

Pushing onwards, they followed the road for what felt like at least another one hundred metres, and then the vista ahead suddenly changed. Instead of the tall arch of the road tunnel continuing to stretch deeper into the darkness, they suddenly realised that the way ahead was blocked by a set of huge, heavily corroded steel doors. At first, they appeared to be sealed shut, but as the two of them moved closer, they realised that one of the massive hinged doors had been pulled open just far enough for a person to pass between them. Along the edges where the two doors had met, several large chunks of metal were missing, as if they had been cut away.

'Look at those burn marks,' said Andrew, pointing at the cutouts that were discoloured by what appeared to have been heavy-duty cutting rods. 'They cut out the locks to get through.'

The two of them slipped through the gap to find themselves in a short stretch of tunnel perhaps ten metres long. It then opened out into an enormous circular cavern that was at least fifty metres across. As they stepped inside, its size almost took their breath away. The ceiling was like a huge smooth dome curving away high over their heads towards a central apex, and long steel cables with rusty light fittings hung in a grid above them. On the far side of the cavern were a handful of tunnels that looked like dark eyes looking back at them across the gloomy, cavernous space.

'This is amazing,' whispered Fiona.

'This must be it,' said Andrew. 'This must be Drexler's test facility.'

Stepping further into the cavern, their torches swept across the walls and the various pieces of equipment arranged there. Andrew spotted what looked like electricity generators, power switches and several large rectangular machines whose precise nature he couldn't discern, but their switches, dials and handles looked to be from a distinctly analogue age. Then he suddenly saw something glinting on one side of the huge space.

'Look at this thing,' he said as he began walking over to it.

It was a long, black limousine convertible with a shiny Mercedes logo sitting proudly on the front of the bonnet. The black finish on the bodywork was covered by a thin and perfectly even layer of dust, and as they walked over to the vehicle, they could see two small red, white and black Swastika flags mounted on either side of the chrome grille.

'Maybe this was Drexler's private car,' said Fiona. 'Or perhaps it belonged to Kammler.'

Next to the almost pristine-looking limo were two military BMW motorcycles with sidecars, and next to those was a large wooden crate tucked to one side near the concrete wall. Its sides were emblazoned with the German *Reichadler* eagle gripping a swastika wreathed in laurels. Underneath it was depicted a single Greek letter. Omega. When Fiona stepped over and lifted up its lid, she gave a brief whistle and turned her head towards Andrew.

'Have a look at this,' she said. 'Not exactly hidden Nazi gold bars, but still.'

When Andrew came over and looked inside, he saw neat piles of what looked like spare items for the military personnel who would have been in charge of the facility's security. Most of them looked rusty and more or less ready to fall apart. There were a dozen black SS helmets, lots of leather boots, a large stack of rifles which Andrew figured were probably semi-automatic *Gewehr 43* rifles, and several neat piles of uniforms, which would probably disintegrate if they were picked up. There were a couple of compact submachine guns and several boxes with ammunition, and there were also two rusty and diabolical-looking metal implements with large, jagged teeth that Fiona didn't immediately recognise.

'What are those?' she said, pointing at the heavy-looking semi-circular objects.

'Bear traps,' said Andrew.

'We're in bear country?' said Fiona, surprised.

'Absolutely,' nodded Andrew. 'There are hundreds of European brown bears in these mountains. And there would probably have been a lot more of them back then. Traps would have been a very sensible thing for the Germans to have around these parts.'

'What are those?' said Fiona, pointing to a set of four elongated metal cylinders attached to slightly thinner wooden handles.

'Those are stick grenades,' said Andrew. 'The Germans used them all through the war. The British called them potato mashers for obvious reasons. See those cords hanging from the end of the handle? You pull that, and then you have around four seconds to throw it and get clear.'

'Do you think they still work?' said Fiona, eyeing them suspiciously.

'Maybe,' said Andrew. 'But I wouldn't touch them, even though they have already been handled. The TNT inside is still reactive, but it is probably partly degraded by now, which makes it a lot more unstable.'

'Right,' said Fiona. 'Got it. No touching.'

'What do these signs say?' Andrew said as he turned and pointed his torch beam towards a number of signs mounted directly on the granite above each of the small tunnels leading off from the large circular cavern.

Fiona stepped towards the partly rusted signs and used her own torch to light them up, and she noted that the blocky font that had been used to print them was typical of the early 20th century, but they were still perfectly legible.

'*Befeelsraum*,' she said, reading and translating them one by one. 'That's the command centre. *Maschinenraum* means machine room. *Kraftstofflager* is the fuel storage. *Atomtestkammer* is the nuclear test chamber. And here's the one we're looking for. *Omega Testkammer*. Omega test chamber. And look. The black power cables also lead that way. That's where Rittenhausen's team went.'

'So, both the Alpha and the Omega teams were working here at one point,' observed Andrew, turning slowly to take in the vista of the entire cavern. 'This whole place would have been crawling with people.'

'And Edward Harding probably made it all the way down here,' said Fiona as she took a moment to reflect on the history of the cavern. 'It's strange to think that all those events played out right here.'

'Let's get to the Omega test chamber,' said Andrew, as he began walking towards the tunnel on the far left. 'That's why we're here.'

They left the large circular cavern behind and headed along the tunnel, which was about four metres across and three metres high. On the wall were mounted several sets of exposed pipes and old, disintegrating power cables. After about fifty metres, the tunnel opened up into another large, dark circular space, and Andrew realised that the black power cables led to several floodlights that were mounted on tripods inside the cavern. There was also a central control switch on a stand, which he walked over to and activated. An instant later, the entire cavern was bathed in bright white light.

However, it wasn't the cavern itself that caught their attention. It was the large, intricate metal device placed vertically on a metre-high platform at the centre of the space. Studded with numerous small devices and dozens of power cables attached to its perimeter, once upon a time it had been a perfect ring some five metres across, but only half of it now remained.

'Holy crap!' breathed Fiona, awestruck. 'It's Drexler's portal. It's still here. Well, half of it is.'

'Rittenhausen's team must have dismantled it,' said Andrew, stepping closer. 'They probably disassembled it down to its smallest components to understand how it was constructed.'

'And now they are building their own,' said Fiona. 'There's no doubt about it anymore. This place proves it conclusively.'

'I agree,' said Andrew as he climbed up on the platform to get a closer look at the dismembered portal. 'It would have been useful to have Alice with us now. She could probably have told us definitively what we're looking at here. Make sure to take a bunch of photos.'

'Right,' said Fiona, marvelling at the scene in front of them.

The highly esoteric Nazi science that many people had speculated about, and that most people would never have believed actually existed, was right here in front of them in all its dark and menacing glory. She got out her phone and methodically began taking pictures of the entire test chamber. Aside from the now partly disassembled semi-circular portal towering over them on the concrete platform, there was a control station off to one side with a handful of terminals each with their own sets of analogue dials, gauges, knobs and switches, and at the back was a single chair that was raised slightly onto a platform. From there, a person could have overseen the entire control station and everyone working there. This had evidently been Drexler's seat during the tests. There was also a raised metal walkway that wrapped around the perimeter of the space and connected to what looked to be a small enclosed viewing platform. The side of it that was facing the centre of the cavern had a large window, and behind the pane of glass, Fiona could make out what appeared to be a stand for an old film camera.

Andrew stepped right up to the gaping hole in what was now the lower opening of the toroidal portal. Leaning in and shining his torch inside the curving, vaguely doughnut-shaped space, he noticed that the entire interior was made from hundreds, if not thousands, of small metal cubes that had been set into its interior sides. As he moved his torchlight across them, they glinted with a mesmerising hue in varying shades of blue and green, depending on the angle of the light passing over them. From certain angles, the tiny metal cubes almost appeared translucent. He pulled back and began examining the small forest of what he assumed was measuring and control equipment mounted all along the curving exterior of the portal, but none of the devices looked in any way familiar to him.

Jumping back down onto the concrete floor, he realised that beneath the thin layer of dust, it had once been painted white. About ten metres from the portal platform was a small square area marked by lines of black and yellow paint, and in the middle of it was a vaguely bowl-shaped scorch mark. When he ran his fingers across it and brought them up to his face, he could see tiny vitrified flakes of concrete glinting in the light, as if this small patch of floor had been exposed to extreme heat that had been intense enough to turn concrete into miniscule bits of glass.

Once Fiona had finished taking photos of the control station, she circled what was left of the portal and took several shots from as many different angles as she could, and then she moved over to the stairs leading up to the raised walkway. She proceeded up the steps to the enclosed viewing platform, and when she reached the closed door, she placed her hand on the doorhandle, pressed down and pushed.

The door came free of the doorframe and began to open, only to bump into something and stop after about an inch. Something was blocking it on the other side. She gave a small frown and pushed harder.

Whatever was preventing the door from opening shifted marginally, but the door remained blocked. Sensing that she might be able to force it open, she put her shoulder to the door and pushed hard. The door slowly moved open as she gritted her teeth and kept applying pressure, and as she put all her weight into it and groaned from the effort, a pungent smell of decay reached her nose, and whatever had blocked the door seemed to roll aside. As it swung open, it revealed a horrific sight.

Andrew had just stood up when he suddenly heard Fiona scream, and as his head whipped around to look her way, he saw her staggering back a step and burying her face in her sleeve as she turned away and retched. Ripping his Glock 17 from its holster, he immediately ran over and came up the steps to join her by the door.

'Oh my god!' she said, her face a mask of revulsion.

'What happened, said Andrew, gripping her by the shoulders.

'There are dead bodies in there,' she said. 'A whole bunch of them.'

Andrew moved to the door and pushed it fully open, and as he did so, a stench as foul and overpowering as it was familiar immediately hit him. It was the stench of death. Something he had experienced many times before in the field, but which he hoped he would never get used to.

Looking at the scene in front of him through narrowed eyes while breathing through his sleeve, he worked his jaw and then held his breath as he took a couple of steps into the room. Sprawled across the floor were six grown men, each with multiple gunshot wounds. The bodies were swollen, but their dark grey skin was also strangely dried out and papery. They had evidently been dead for many weeks. Despite the large blotches of almost black blood that had soaked through their clothes at the time of their deaths, it was obvious that they were wearing workman's clothes. All but one of the men had on orange overalls, high-vis vests and heavy black boots with metal toecaps. They had also been wearing white plastic protective helmets that now lay scattered around them. Farthest from the door was a man wearing jeans and a flannel shirt with a yellow helmet still strapped to his head. Looking over to his side, Andrew realised that the entire back wall of the enclosed viewing platform was peppered with bullet holes from what had to have been several fully automatic weapons that had been used to execute these men. When he couldn't hold his breath any longer, Andrew retreated out of the room, closed the door behind him and walked down the stairs to join Fiona who was hunched over with her hands on her knees, breathing heavily.

'What the hell was that?' she panted, sounding as if she was going to be sick. 'Who were those men?'

'I reckon that was the drilling crew,' said Andrew bitterly, glancing back up at the door to the viewing platform as he placed a hand gently on her shoulder. 'Those guys provided Rittenhausen with a way down into this place, and in return, he had them herded inside that room and gunned down. Probably to stop them talking.'

'What a fucking psychopath,' she said as she rose to her full height again. 'What are we going to do?'

'I'm not sure,' said Andrew. 'They deserved better than this, but I don't think there's anything we can do about it now. Except to find Rittenhausen and nail him to the wall. There's got to be plenty of evidence here to make a link to him.'

'Who do you suppose did this?' she asked.

'It could have been the two men that were chasing me in Berlin,' he replied. 'Or it could have been a different set of goons. I am sure Rittenhausen has plenty of staff on the payroll who are happy to do as he asks.'

'I want to get out of here,' said Fiona, glancing towards the exit. 'I think we've found all there is to find down here.'

'I agree,' said Andrew, pulling his phone from his pocket. 'I am going to take a couple of photos of those bodies, and then we can leave this place. I would like to see the sky and breathe some fresh air again.'

'Yeah,' said Fiona, taking a couple of steps towards the tunnel leading back to the central cavern. 'We got what we came for. This place is like a tomb. Literally.'

A couple of minutes later, Andrew had returned briefly to the viewing platform and had taken a few photos of the grisly scene, and they were now walking back along the gloomy tunnel with Fiona a couple of metres ahead when she suddenly stopped dead in her tracks as if frozen to the spot.

'What's going on?' said Andrew, coming to a halt and reaching for his weapon.

'Shh…' whispered Fiona, holding up her right hand.

She remained like that for several seconds, but then she lowered her hand again and glanced back at him.

'I thought I heard something,' she said. 'Some sort of faint noise, like a distant rumbling. I don't hear it now. I must have imagined it.'

They returned to the main cavern and crossed over to the massive steel doors leading to the road tunnel. Andrew pushed through the gap first and was about to turn around to make sure Fiona followed safely when he spotted movement out of the corner of his eye. He turned to look, and about fifty metres further along the road tunnel near the first junction leading back towards the elevator, he saw the unmistakable flickering of torchlights coming from somewhere around the corner in the connecting tunnel.

'Someone's coming,' he whispered urgently to Fiona. 'We need to get back inside.'

Fiona was already halfway through the gap and had to change the position of her feet to begin to back up. Once she was clear, Andrew began to squeeze back through the gap, but his backpack got caught on a small edge of the steel door where one of the locks had been cut out by Rittenhausen's team. As he twisted his upper body and reached behind him to attempt to get free, a torch beam suddenly cut through the darkness towards him from the corner up ahead, and then another appeared and was directed straight at him. He finally managed to free himself, and as he glanced back over his shoulder, he saw the torchlights jolt rapidly for a couple of seconds. As they did so, he heard the unmistakable metallic sound of automatic weapon charging handles being pulled and slapped back into place. Then he heard a man shouting words that sounded like they had been spoken in Russian. A split second later, just as he pulled back inside the main cavern, a hail of bullets smacked into the steel door as the two figures opened up with their submachine guns, lighting up the tunnel with the still-burning exhaust gases from their weapons. As deafening bursts of automatic gunfire reverberated through the dark tunnels of Bergkristall, 9mm bullets peppered the rusty door and plinked off the steel to drop onto the concrete floor below.

'Get into cover!' Andrew shouted as he threw himself clear of the gap. 'Behind the limo.'

He and Fiona sprinted for the black, dust-covered limousine and slid behind it. Then Andrew turned and threw his torch in a long arc across the cavern so that it landed several metres into the tunnel that led to the Omega test chamber. As it hit the floor, it spun and rolled out of view, but its light remained on, and it could still be seen from their position.

'Turn off your torch,' he whispered as he crouched back down behind the vehicle. 'We can't take them head-on, so we're going to lure them over there and then try to slip out.'

As Fiona's torch winked out, leaving the cavern lit only by the faint light of Andrew's torch lying inside the connecting tunnel some twenty metres away, he pulled his Glock 17 from its holster, racked the slide and handed it to Fiona.

'Get ready to cover me,' he whispered. 'I'm going for the hand grenades. On my signal, start shooting.'

'Okay,' said Fiona tensely, looking down at the weapon in her hand with trepidation. 'I hope you know what you're doing.'

'It's our only shot,' said Andrew, shifting along the side of the limo towards the large wooden crate nearby. 'Get ready. Don't move and stay out of sight.'

A few seconds later, just as their eyes were beginning to adjust to the darkness, there was a deafening blast and a brilliant flash of light that radiated out from near the gap in the massive steel doors. One of the two shooters had tossed a flashbang through the gap, and the reverberations inside the cavernous space had barely ceased before they squeezed through with their weapons up, ready to engage. Mounted onto their tactical vests were powerful torches pointing straight ahead, leaving both of their hands-free to operate their weapons.

'*Davai, Artem*!' one of the men shouted in a commanding, baritone voice, urging his companion to move fast.

Watching the two men from his concealed position using one of the limo's side mirrors, Andrew could see that they were both large and muscular, but they moved with the slight crouch and distinctive economy of motion and light-footed gait characteristic of men who had received extensive weapons and tactical training. They advanced into the large cavern with their submachineguns pressed into their shoulders, sweeping from side to side as they hunted for targets.

However, seeing no one there and evidently building in confidence after receiving no incoming fire themselves, they pushed further into the cavern and began moving cautiously towards the faintly lit-up tunnel. Andrew's ruse appeared to be working, and as the two Russian men proceeded towards the tunnel, he crept around the back of the limo, moving stealthily as he crouched low behind the two motorcycles with sidecars to arrive at the large wooden crate.

He winced as he lifted the lid, praying that it wouldn't make a noise. With sweaty hands, he managed to lift it up without drawing attention to himself, but when he tried to shift it to one side so he could reach the hand grenades, one of the back corners of the lid slipped and scraped audibly against the crate itself.

'Now!' he shouted to Fiona as he reached inside the crate, grappling for the grenades.

Gripping the gun with two hands, Fiona immediately opened fire at the two men who were now about fifteen metres away, but her aim was off. Despite having taken shooting lessons with Andrew, tension and fear made her lose her bearings and squeeze the trigger too hard as the gun kicked in her hands. Firing one shot after another, the bullets zipped past the two men who were now scrambling to get into cover. Having seemingly already committed to heading for the lit-up tunnel, they sprinted straight ahead while zig-zagging from side to side. One of them managed to swing his submachinegun around and fire off a volley as he ran, and the burst of bullets stitched along the side of the limo, smacking loudly into the bodywork and almost making it out the other side.

Andrew had now managed to grip the leather strap holding the four stick grenades together, and as the attacker's bullets punched into the limo, he pulled the grenades out and threw himself onto the concrete floor. While the two men were dashing for the tunnel, one of Fiona's shots hit the taller of the two men in the leg, and he almost stumbled as he cried out.

'*Suka! Blyat!*' he roared, more in anger than in pain.

'*Pavel!*' the other man shouted as he turned around and laid down suppressing fire at Fiona's position. '*Davai!*'

Bullets shattered one of the limo's windows and slammed into the bodywork mere inches from Fiona's head, and she gasped and threw herself backwards onto the floor next to the vehicle to get into cover. The two men had now almost reached the tunnel mouth, one of them staggering along, the other firing off burst after burst.

Andrew rolled onto his back, yanked one of the stick grenades from the bunch and pulled the cord. Degraded and softened from having spent decades in the cavern, the cord snapped in half.

'Shit!' he growled, pulling another from the bunch and pulling the cord on that one.

This time, the fuse mechanism worked, immediately beginning to fizz and smoke. Realising he now had four seconds to make sure it reached its target, Andrew spun around on the ground and got onto his knees. He then tossed it towards the two men who had almost reached the tunnel. It fell down with a clonk by their feet, and then it simply lay there as the two men continued on.

'Damn it,' Andrew hissed. 'What a fucking time for a dud.'

He pulled the cord on a third grenade. Its fuse instantly began its smoking four-second timer, and once again, Andrew threw the grenade towards the men, this time with more force. It landed about a metre from the limping attacker, who had been hit by Fiona's gunfire, and then it exploded with a deafening boom that lit up the place and seemed to shake the entire cavern.

Unlike their contemporary American counterparts, the German World War 2 stick grenades had not been designed to produce shrapnel when exploding. They were mainly concussion grenades, but their charge of

TNT was large enough for them to cause serious damage to anyone nearby. The taller of the two men was knocked sideways by the blast, and he crashed into his companion but also shielded him from most of the blast. However, the grenade's twisted and razor-sharp metal housing had shot out and ripped through the side of the tall man's neck, and when Andrew raised his head to look, he saw him down on one knee clutching his throat as blood sprayed out between his fingers in sync with the rapid beating of his heart.

'*Pavel!*' shouted the other man again, and then he returned fire once more in Andrew's general direction.

Andrew sensed Fiona scramble around behind the limo, and then he heard the sound of the Glock clicking empty as she tried to fire it again.

'It's out of ammo,' she shouted, as Andrew readied the final grenade and pulled the cord.

It immediately began fizzing, and as he raised himself to toss it, he saw the taller man topple over and fall limply to the floor with a heavy thud, and at the same time, his companion spotted Andrew about to throw another grenade. Andrew launched it, and the man immediately got to his feet and hobbled for the tunnel that might afford him some protection from the next blast. The grenade sailed through the air and landed about five metres behind him, and it remained there for what Andrew was sure had to be much longer than four seconds. Perhaps the fuse was faulty, or perhaps the grenade was another dud.

He barely had time to complete his thought when another explosion rocked the cavern, and he barely managed to duck down behind the two motorcycles. Dust and small flecks of concrete fell from the ceiling directly above the explosion, and the dead body of the man named Pavel was shunted aside by its force. However, the man called Artem had made it to safety, and he was now nowhere to be seen. Realising that the Russian had no idea how many more grenades he had left and that he didn't realise that Andrew had in fact just used the last one, Andrew decided that it was now or never. With no more grenades and no more bullets, they had to get out of there right now. He turned towards the limo, which was now full of bullet holes, and called out to Fiona.

'We are leaving!' he urged. 'Now!'

While Fiona scrambled to her feet behind the limo and made her way crouched low towards him, he reached inside the wooden crate and grabbed one of the heavy metal bear traps. As a weapon, it was crude in the extreme, but it just might slow the attacker down if he decided to give chase. Rushing towards the enormous steel doors, Andrew tossed the bear trap through the gap and practically threw himself in after it to make way for Fiona, who was a couple of metres behind him. Just before launching herself at the gap, she glanced back over her shoulder to see the man called Artem stagger out from the tunnel mouth. He seemed to be limping slightly, and he raised his weapon as soon as he spotted her. Just as she slipped through, a loud boom came from inside the cavern, but this time it wasn't the sound of a grenade. It was the dry, thumping crack of a pump-action shotgun. Andrew recognised the familiar sound of the shooter racking it to load the next cartridge into the chamber, and a couple of seconds later there was another boom and the sound of a dozen steel pellets slamming into the door next to the gap they had just passed through.

'Run!' shouted Andrew as he got to his feet. 'If he catches up, we're dead.'

As the two of them ran back along the road tunnel towards the corner leading to the elevator room, yet another shot rang out. Clearly, the limping shooter did not realise that they had made a run for it, and he was evidently trying to clear the area just beyond the gap in the steel doors. They soon rounded the corner and sprinted for the elevator room, Andrew clutching the rusty bear trap in his hands and Fiona lighting the way.

They covered the final distance to the entrance in about half a minute, rushing inside just as another shotgun blast rang out behind them. Pellets chewed up the concrete a couple of metres away, sending dust and bits of cement erupting from the wall as they narrowly missed their mark. Realising that they would only have seconds to enter the lift and wait for it to start moving, Andrew decided that in this situation, as in many more he had experienced before today, the best defence was to attack.

He considered cranking the bear trap open and placing it in the doorway, but that would be too obvious. However, there was nowhere else to put it and nowhere for them to hide. He frantically cast his gaze across the room but saw nothing that might give them an advantage.

'Hide over there,' he said to Fiona, pointing to the stacks of timber. 'And turn off the torch again.'

'What about you?' she said, pleadingly.

'I'll think of something,' he said, hoping that he would be proven right. 'Now go, before he gets here.'

As Fiona dashed for cover behind the lengths of timber, Andrew suddenly heard the distinctive sound of cartridges being loaded into the pump-action shotgun's tubular under-barrel magazine one by one. And then came the snick-snack sound as the shooter chambered the first cartridge, ready to fire. Andrew now only had a second to come up with a plan, or neither he nor Fiona would leave Bergkristall alive.

Twenty

The former Spetsnaz soldier named Artem stepped closer to the elevator room from which he and his now-dead companion Pavel had emerged about twenty minutes earlier. He placed his feet carefully on the concrete floor, moving cautiously towards the room where he now knew the two targets were hiding, and he winced from the pain in his leg that had been caused by the exploding grenade. Pavel had absorbed most of the blast and almost all of the shrapnel from the old grenade's cylindrical explosives housing, but one of Artem's eardrums had burst, and blood was running down the side of his neck. He had also taken some shrapnel to the leg, and his trouser leg was bloody and clinging to the skin.

He knew that the two targets were in the elevator room because he had seen the man slip inside just as he had fired his shotgun from the hip and nearly hit him. And since then, Artem had not heard the sound of the elevator. They were definitely hiding, and he was going to flush them out one way or another. Once that was done, he would be able to head back to recover Pavel's body and then go back up to the surface to join Maxim, who was standing guard at the top of the shaft inside the villa.

'Come out, little piggies,' he called in a menacing and mocking tone of voice with a heavy Russian accent. 'Uncle Artem is here to make you pay for killing his old friend.'

He waited a few seconds, standing by the doorway and allowing his torch to light up part of the elevator room while he trained his shotgun at the area he was able to see as he leaned to one side.

'Show yourselves, you swine,' he said, hoping to be able to goad his prey, but there was no response.

Working his jaw to try to remedy the discomfort in his bleeding ear and wincing from the pain in his leg, he then stepped forward another few steps, covering every square meter of the elevator room with his weapon as he went. He was using room-clearing techniques that were now almost second nature to him after his handful of years as an elite Russian soldier. As he moved around the doorway and still more of the room gradually became visible to him, he grew in confidence that he was about to spot the two targets any moment now and finally take them out with a couple of well-placed shotgun blasts to their heads. Bonus from Komarov secured.

Taking one final, swift step inside and bringing the weapon to bear on the last section of the room, he was surprised to find it as empty as everywhere else in there. At that moment, he heard a strange sound coming from above his head. It sounded like a steel wire moving rapidly across a piece of metal. When he looked up, it took his brain half a second to make sense of what his eyes were seeing. Coming down towards him, attached to a thin wire looped over a pipe that stuck through the wall, was a large, rusty-looking circular object that looked like it had jagged teeth all around its edges.

By the time Artem realised what it was, the heavy, spring-loaded bear trap was already falling like a stone. Before he could duck or move out of the way, it smacked down onto his head with a clang, the push plate connecting cleanly with his forehead, and then the trigger mechanism broke with a click, after which the two terrifying jagged metal jaws slammed together in a diabolic bite that took his head clean off and sent it falling to the ground. It bounced and rolled, leaving a trail of blood as the bear trap clattered loudly to the floor.

As Artem's headless body slumped to the ground in a crumpled heap, the light from the torch attached to his tactical vest flailed around inside the room, and the shotgun which was still in his hand went off with a thunderous boom that caused dust and debris to fall down from the ceiling. Then his head rolled to a stop with his wide-open eyes staring straight up at the ceiling as blood oozed from his severed neck.

'Oh Jesus,' breathed Fiona queasily as she and Andrew stepped from behind the stack of timber to look at the gory scene on the dusty floor in front of them. 'I think I'm going to be sick.'

'It was either him or us,' said Andrew evenly. 'I won't lose any sleep over this. Let's get back up to the surface.'

'How did they find us?' said Fiona, giving him an anxious look. 'And they sounded Russian. What the hell is going on?'

I guess Rittenhausen has friends in low places,' said Andrew, stepping over to the pump action shotgun and picking it up. 'And he clearly got connections and funds to make that sort of thing happen. We could have been ID'ed at Berlin Airport, and then they could have accessed passenger manifests for flights out of there. Our private charter flight from Geneva to Linz would have given the game away about precisely where we were headed. And for all we know, the rental car has a tracking unit installed, and its central server can probably easily be hacked. It's a brave new world.'

'That's really scary,' said Fiona. 'I don't like being monitored like that.'

'Me neither,' said Andrew, racking the shotgun to load the next cartridge into the chamber. 'But that's the world we live in. Come on. Let's just get out of here.'

★ ★ ★

No sooner had Andrew and Fiona turned towards the elevator that would take them back up to the surface, than its door suddenly slid shut and the cab began to ascend up through the shaft drilled by Rittenhausen's now-dead and decomposing drilling team.

'What the hell is happening?' a mystified Fiona exclaimed as she gave Andrew an anxious look. 'Is this thing on a timer?'

'I don't think so,' said Andrew tensely as the rumbling and rattling sounds of the cab began to recede as it travelled ever higher. 'Someone must have pressed the button up top. Another one of Rittenhausen's goons. Maybe more than one.'

Soon after, they heard the distant sound of the elevator coming to a stop at the surface, and a few seconds later, it once again began its descent.

'Someone's coming down,' said Andrew. 'They must have heard the shotgun go off, and now they are coming to investigate.'

'What do we do?' said Fiona nervously. 'We can't take on another bunch of them.'

'Get behind that stack of timber again,' said Andrew, already moving while cradling the shotgun. 'Our best option is to stay out of sight and hope they move further into the tunnels. Then we can grab the elevator and get back up.'

As they moved behind the timber, he checked to see how many cartridges were now left in the shotgun's under-barrel magazine. There were four. They crouched down in the darkness behind the stack of wood and waited.

'Don't move a muscle,' whispered Andrew as the noise from the approaching elevator rose. 'They'll be here any second.'

The elevator room was now lit up only faintly by the torch on Artem's headless corpse pointing up into the ceiling, as well as the dull orange glow of the elevator call button. When the elevator finally came to a stop, there was the sound of safety clamps engaging, and then the door slid aside. Andrew had positioned himself so that he was just able to see around the corner of the stack of timber, and to his relief, he saw only one man exit the cab. Large and bulky like the two other shooters, he was carrying the compact PP-2000 machine pistol that was standard issue for all Russian police forces. How he had ended up being issued with that weapon was difficult to say, but as with most things in the deeply corrupt and dysfunctional Russia, where there was a will and some rubles, there was also a way.

Emerging cautiously from the elevator cab, the man swept left and right with his weapon as he took a few steps into the room, but then he froze as he spotted the decapitated body on the floor in front of him. It was lit up by the ghostly glare of the vest-mounted torch shining up into the faintly dust-filled air. For several seconds, he stood perfectly still, but then he began backing up towards the elevator again.

Realising that the man might retreat into the elevator and escape up the shaft, thereby leaving Fiona and himself forever entombed deep inside Bergkristall, Andrew knew that he had to act now. He brought the shotgun up and began moving out from the corner of the timber stack to get a clear shot, but before he could line up the bulky weapon, his right boot twisted on the dusty concrete floor, creating a dry grinding noise. The man heard it, turned his head and spotted Andrew, and then he immediately threw himself forward into the room to get clear while bringing his machine pistol around. Pressing the trigger in mid-air, his rapid-fire weapon spewed out a torrent of bullets that peppered the front of the timber stack, causing small wood chippings to explode out of it. It was a badly aimed burst, but it was enough to make Andrew pull back into cover, and that was all the man needed. He hit the floor and adeptly rolled up onto his feet, and then he sprinted for the doorway leading out into the tunnel on the other side of the room. Andrew once again pushed out from cover and raised the shotgun as he moved clear of the stack of timber and fired. The boom of the shotgun exploded inside the confined space like a grenade, but the shot went wide and chewed a chunk of concrete out of the wall about a metre from the running Russian.

'Get into the elevator!' Andrew shouted, and Fiona immediately bolted for the empty cab.

Andrew fired again just as the Russian slipped behind the doorway and into the tunnel, and once again, a couple of dozen steel pellets arrived and took a chunk out of the concrete wall where he had been a split second earlier. Andrew quickly glanced over his shoulder to see that Fiona had made it safely into the cab, and then he began backing up as quickly as he could while still keeping the shotgun trained at the opening to the tunnel directly opposite the elevator. As he moved inside the cab, he fired another shot just for good measure before hitting the 'Up' button. The pellets ripped through the air, passed over Artem's severed head and tore out through the opening to slam into the opposite wall of the tunnel. With just one cartridge left and no spare ammo, Andrew kept aiming at the opening until the elevator doors had slid shut.

The cab began to move back up towards the surface, but almost immediately thereafter, a loud burst of rapid gunfire came from the other side, and in the same instant, the cab's sliding metal door was peppered with projectiles that smacked into it like large hail on a flimsy tin roof. Each impact created a visible dent in the door, but its designers could never have guessed that its thickness would one day turn out to be just enough to stop a dozen 9mm Parabellum bullets from punching through it and killing the cab's occupants.

As the bullets hit and the door deformed, creating small rounded dents, Fiona shrieked and crouched to the floor while cupping her ears. And then it stopped. The cab was now swiftly moving up through the shaft, and they were safe. At least for now.

'Are you alright?' asked Andrew urgently, kneeling and checking her over for injuries. 'Are you hit?'

'I don't think so,' said Fiona weakly, examining herself while bracing for having one of her hands come away from her body covered in blood. 'I think I'm okay. Are you alright?'

'The door ate the bullets,' said Andrew. 'None of them went through. We got lucky here. Very lucky.'

The elevator came to a stop inside the hollowed-out villa, and then the mangled door slid aside. With Andrew stepping out first, holding the shotgun and making sure there were no more armed men waiting for them, they left the cab and headed for the garage where they had come in. No sooner had they stepped out that the elevator sprang back into life and began another descent.

'You've got to be kidding me,' said Fiona. 'Is he coming back up?'

'I think so,' said Andrew. 'He must realise that I am holding his colleague's shotgun and that I am probably low on ammo.'

'How many shots do you have left?' said Fiona.

'One,' said Andrew. 'We need to get out of here now.'

They headed into the garage to find that the Russians had closed them after entering, and they were now locked. At the same time, they heard the elevator flywheel come to a halt, and a couple of seconds later, it once again began spooling up the cable and pulling the cab up through the 173-metre-deep shaft.

'Shit,' said Fiona. 'He's on his way. How the hell do we open this? I don't see a switch anywhere.'

'There is a control box over here,' said Andrew, gesturing to a white plastic box similar to the one mounted on the outside of the building. 'But I don't have time to break it open and short circuit the wiring.'

'What do we do?' said Fiona as panic crept into her voice.

Andrew looked back towards the elevator where the flywheel was still spooling up the steel cable. In a matter of seconds, the Russian gunman would reach the top, and he would no doubt have enough clips of ammo for his machine pistol to be able to simply step out and spray the entire room with bullets. With only one shot left in the shotgun, Andrew could perhaps attempt to find cover somewhere and hope to get lucky and take him out with a single shot. However, this was far from a guaranteed way to come out of this on top. The shotgun was a notoriously inaccurate weapon with heavy recoil, and if he missed, both he and Fiona would be dead a few seconds later.

He glanced up at the flywheel. It was now beginning to slow down as the cab neared the surface. Then he suddenly had an idea. He ran forward towards the elevator, vaulted up onto a stack of cement bags and jumped from there onto the top of the elevator housing. He was now standing next to the large flywheel that had almost stopped moving, and in a matter of seconds, the safety clamps inside the shaft would engage and snap into place, allowing the door to open. He quickly knelt down and placed the muzzle of the shotgun less than a centimetre from the steel cable, and then he turned his head away and pulled the trigger.

The shotgun boomed and kicked back in his hands as it fired, and a fraction of a second later, all of the still tightly packed pellets exited the barrel at virtually the same time, travelling at around five hundred metres per second. At that speed, they carried so much energy that their almost instantaneous collision with the steel cable created such intense heat as to allow them to sheer through the cable and completely sever it. Inside a shower of bright, glowing metal sparks, the pellets ripped the cable in two, and as the flywheel came to a stop, the severed cable disappeared into the elevator housing, where the cab was now beginning to freefall. With nothing to hold it up against the pull of gravity, the cab kept accelerating all the way down through the long shaft, rattling and rumbling ever louder as it continued to pick up speed. By the time it reached the bottom, it was travelling at more than one hundred kilometres per hour, and when it slammed into the granite floor at the bottom of the shaft, its housing pancaked into a crushed and mangled chunk of metal like a can of Coke having been stepped on. During the final few seconds of the lethal descent, Andrew could have sworn that he heard something between a furious animalistic roar and a desperate scream coming up through the shaft. The force of the impact sounded like an explosion deep inside the mountain, and it left

Fiona standing with her mouth open at what she had just witnessed.

'He must be dead,' she said, looking shocked. 'There's no way he could survive that, right?'

'Not a chance,' said Andrew dryly as he climbed down from the elevator housing to join her. 'He's about as dead as they come. Now let's get the hell out of this place. I've had enough of tunnels for one day.'

* * *

After shorting the control box for the garage doors, exiting the garage and climbing over the wall to get back to their rental car, Andrew and Fiona drove down the mountain through Sankt Georgen and headed towards the city of Linz. It was now nearing midnight, and while Andrew drove the car, Fiona used her phone to book a hotel for them in the city centre near the Danube. She also managed to locate one of just a couple of specialist photography shops in the city that advertised services pertaining to old cameras and film. By the time they had reached the hotel and checked in, they were both exhausted, but when Andrew placed his phone on the side table next to their bed, he realised that he had received an email from the British Embassy in Geneva.

'This is interesting,' he said after reading it. 'Remember the cigarette butt Alice found at her father's house?'

'Sure,' said Fiona. 'Any news?'

'The embassy sent the DNA analysis results to Interpol,' said Andrew. 'They ran it through their global database and came up with a name. It matched a sample taken years ago in the city of Mendoza in Argentina from a man named Ernesto Navarro. Same first name as the one I shoved off a building in Berlin. He and his older brother Hector were small-time street thugs in Mendoza before being recruited to work the security detail for, guess who…'

'Rittenhausen,' said Fiona, narrowing her eyes.

''Bingo,' nodded Andrew. 'Got in one.'

'That's our proof,' said Fiona earnestly. 'It shows beyond doubt that Rittenhausen was behind Adam Holbrook's kidnapping, right?'

'Almost certainly,' said Andrew. 'I don't know if it would stand up in court, but it all seems to fit. And it is good enough for me.'

'So, the other guy chasing you in Berlin was his brother Hector,' said Fiona.

'That's right,' said Andrew, thinking back to the wild pursuit through the streets and waterways of the German capital. 'And according to this email from the embassy, Interpol looked into their movements across borders recently, and they were both in London when Ambrose and Bateman were killed. It was definitely them.'

'Bastards,' muttered Fiona. 'At least one of them got what he deserved.'

'We need to tell Alice about this,' said Andrew. 'But I don't think waking her up now is a good idea. We should wait until tomorrow morning.'

'I agree,' said Fiona, looking utterly spent. 'Let's try to get some sleep.'

★   ★   ★

The next morning, they both awoke early, had a shower, and headed down to the restaurant on the ground floor. Two hours later, they had finished their buffet breakfast, checked out of the hotel and driven the short distance to the street where a photography shop that Fiona liked the look of was located. It was on a pedestrian square that was surrounded by imposing five-storey buildings with great archways to small rear courtyards and ornate facades that all had a distinctly Renaissance feel to them.

They entered the shop and were met by a young, bookish-looking man who spoke perfect English and gladly accepted the challenge of attempting to extract the film from the old camera and ascertaining if it was possible to develop it. Carefully turning the camera over in his hands with gleaming eyes as if holding an ancient religious relic, he told them that it might take about an hour for him to open it up and have a go at developing the film. He then helpfully informed them that the café on the opposite side of the square served excellent coffee and apple strudel. Taking his advice, they left him to do his work and retreated to the café, watching the world go by, such as it was in the seemingly sleepy and tranquil city where Adolph Hitler had attended school and spent a large part of his youth. As they sat there, Fiona couldn't help picturing the young Adolph walking across the square they were now sitting on, and she contemplated how no one in that city could have known that the young aspiring artist would one day become one of history's most notorious mass murderers. After a little over an hour, she glanced at her wristwatch just as she was finishing her coffee.

'Right,' she said. 'I am going to head over there and see if he managed to salvage anything. Can you imagine if there are actually still photos on that film?'

'Let's not get ahead of ourselves,' said Andrew with a slight smile. 'I honestly don't think it's very likely, but you never know.'

'Come on,' said Fiona encouragingly. 'Have a little faith.'

'Not my strong suit,' he said with a wink, extracting his phone from his trouser pocket. 'Anyway, I am going to call Alice. We need to tell her what we discovered.'

'Do you think she might be in danger?' said Fiona with a hint of concern.

'I sure hope not,' said Andrew. 'But she needs to know everything we know. And then she can decide what she wants to do about this whole thing.'

'Alright,' said Fiona. 'Let me know what she says. See you shortly.'

And with that, Fiona was off. Watching her walk away across the sunlit square, Andrew speed-dialled Alice Holbrook. She picked up after the third ring, sounding slightly out of breath, and Andrew could hear the sound of footsteps in a stairwell and the rustling of clothes in the background as she spoke.

'Hello?' she said.

'Alice,' he said. 'It's Andrew Sterling. We met a couple of...'

'Yes, I remember,' Alice cut him off, panting. 'Sorry, I am just coming back from the shop. I realised I was out of tea for my breakfast. A minor disaster, as you can imagine. How are you?'

Andrew could hear the smile on her lips as she spoke, and he could easily picture the young physicist they had met what now seemed like many days ago.

'I am alright,' he said. 'I wanted to tell you that we got the results back from the DNA analysis.'

As he spoke, he heard the steady cadence of Alice's shoes as she walked along what he assumed was a corridor leading towards the front door to her apartment. There was some more rustling of clothes, and then the jangling of keys.

'Sorry,' she said. 'I'll just let myself in. Then I can speak.'

He heard the metallic sound of a lock clicking and a door being opened. The sound of her steps changed as she entered her apartment, and then came the sound of the door closing shut behind her.

'Alright,' she said, putting something down onto the floor. 'I can talk now. So, what did the results say?'

At that moment, there was a sudden yelp and the sound of a scuffle as Alice produced a shriek. A loud bash made Andrew instinctively pull the phone from his ear, and then he realised that Alice had dropped her phone onto the floor.

'Alice!' he called out, his intuition telling him that something was terribly wrong. 'Alice, are you there?'

He heard what sounded like a struggle and a man grunting, but after a few seconds, it abated into nothing, and then there was silence.

'Alice!' Andrew called again.

There was more rustling as her phone was picked up, and then came a thick, gravelly voice.

'Little Alice is sleeping,' it said menacingly with a heavy Spanish accent, and Andrew knew immediately who he was speaking to and what had happened. 'And once we're done with her, I am going to do the same to her as you did to my brother. *Hijo de puta!*'

Then the line went dead.

Twenty-One

When Fiona returned to the café, she was beaming with excitement, but when she saw Andrew, her face dropped.

'What's wrong?' she said as she sat down across from him. 'Are you okay?'

'It's Alice,' he said, working his jaw and looking agonised. 'I spoke to her on the phone just now, and then she got jumped by someone. I'm pretty sure it was Hector Navarro. He was inside her apartment, waiting for her. The bastard.'

'Oh no,' said Fiona, instinctively cupping a hand over her mouth before lowering it again and gazing at him. 'What do they want with her?'

'Who knows?' said Andrew tensely with a small shake of the head. 'Probably bring her to Argentina too to make sure Holbrook Senior does as he is told. Or maybe they'll even cajole her into helping him build the portal. But it almost doesn't matter now. This is another kidnapping, and this one's our fault.'

'What do you mean?' said Fiona.

'If we hadn't gone to see her,' said Andrew, 'she might have been fine. We might be the reason Hector showed up at her apartment. She's probably being bundled into a car and driven to the airport as we speak.'

'What are we going to do?' said Fiona.

'There's only one thing we *can* do,' he said darkly. 'We need to get them both back.'

'You mean, we should go to Argentina?' said Fiona.

'That's where Adam Holbrook is,' said Andrew evenly. 'And I'd bet you anything that that's where they are taking Alice. So, that's what we need to do. Alice is in this mess because of us. We have to get them both back.'

'Shit,' sighed Fiona, as the reality of the situation began to sink in. 'I guess you're right. But how? Do we even know where the professor is?'

'I can probably place a few calls and find out,' said Andrew. 'It might take a number of hours, but it shouldn't be too difficult to determine the location of Rittenhausen's winery and get all the intel on it. That has to be where Holbrook is being held prisoner.'

'Right,' said Fiona, nodding solemnly as she imagined the young physicist in the hands of Rittenhausen's men. 'It's settled then. We're going.'

'But first,' said Andrew. 'What did the guy in the photography shop say? Was he able to get anything?'

'Oh, right,' said Fiona, looking down at her hands where she was still holding an envelope. 'I almost forgot. Yes. He said that the film hadn't been exposed, but that the celluloid had begun to disintegrate a long time ago. The image quality is low because of the state of the film, but he was still able to develop the negatives from two frames and produce these black-and-white photos.'

She opened the envelope and placed the two photographs side by side on the table in front of him. Andrew leaned forward and moved them closer to allow him to examine them, and he immediately recognised the setting. They had been taken inside the Omega test chamber in the Bergkristall complex, and they both showed a portal that looked slightly smaller than the one he and Fiona had found the remnants of the day before. The first photo showed a number of technicians walking around the chamber doing various tasks, and the portal itself looked powered down and inert. However, the second photo was very different. In fact, Andrew had never seen anything quite like it.

The entire test chamber was lit up brightly by the portal, and curving out from its edges were long tendrils of bright electrical arcs that extended like coronal mass ejections from the surface of the sun and then returned to the portal nearby. The entire device was lit up with a blinding glare, and the countless thin but brilliant filaments of electricity emanating from it spoke of the immense power it was consuming.

Unlike in the first photo, where it was possible to see through the central ring of the portal, the second photo showed an intense and mesmerising swirl of energy, like a vortex in reality that was itself waiting to suck in anything that came near. Over to one side, some fifteen metres from the roiling otherworldly maelstrom of energy was the control station. Standing tall in the middle of it was a man wearing a white lab coat. He had short, slick hair and thin-rimmed glasses, and he could only have been Otto Drexler. Next to him was a short and similarly clad man, whom Andrew assumed was most likely Horst Feldmeyer.

'This is amazing,' he said with a furrowed brow as he looked up at Fiona. 'These photos show the portal in action. Everything Drexler wrote in his diary seems to be true. He didn't make it up.'

'He certainly didn't,' nodded Fiona emphatically. 'The portal was clearly a working machine.'

'And if they could build it back then,' said Andrew, leaning back in his chair and gazing at the second photo, 'then Rittenhausen can build it now. Especially with the help of someone like Adam Holbrook.'

'We should get going,' said Fiona. 'Back to the airport, drop the car and then catch the first flight to Argentina.'

'Agreed,' said Andrew as he rose from the chair and put the photos back inside the envelope. 'I'll try to get as much intel on Rittenhausen and his estate as I can. We're going to have to make this up as we go.'

'You're probably right,' said Fiona with a thin smile. 'But it wouldn't be the first time.'

★ ★ ★

Rittenhausen had just landed in Mendoza City on his private jet coming in from Berlin. The jet had put tens of thousands of kilometres under its belt over the past day, first transporting Alice Holbrook from Geneva to Mendoza and then returning to Berlin to fly him back to his winery in the verdant foothills of the Argentinian Andes. As the aircraft taxied to its designated parking apron, he lifted his gold-plated phone out of the chest pocket of his tweed suit jacket and swiped his way to the phone number of Grigori Komarov.

'Ferdinand,' said Komarov in his usual affable tone of voice. 'How is everything?'

'Not great,' said Rittenhausen bitterly, hating to have to call the Russian with unwelcome news. 'I fear that your three hardmen are dead.'

'Oh?' said Komarov evenly, not giving away his sentiments. 'Why would you say that?'

'The last I heard from them, they had tracked the two thieves to my villa in Austria,' said Rittenhausen. 'They were about to follow them down into the tunnels and finish them off. But after that, I have heard nothing.'

'I see,' said Komarov, sounding mildly mystified. 'I apologise. I will send you another team. And by the way. A friend of mine at the FSB was kind enough to pass some classified files to me after your contact at the German border force had identified the two culprits.'

'Andrew Sterling,' hissed Rittenhausen, venom dripping off every syllable. 'And his sidekick, Fiona Keane.'

'Yes,' said Komarov. 'But there is more to it than that. It turns out that Sterling is a highly decorated soldier with 22 Special Air Service. No longer active with the Regiment, but evidently still very active nonetheless.'

'Really?' Rittenhausen said as his eyes narrowed. 'Well, I suppose that explains a few things, including the loss of one of my men and three of yours.'

'Mistakes happen,' said Komarov dispassionately, seemingly indifferent to the deaths of three men on his payroll. 'It would seem that my first team badly underestimated those two troublemakers. But now that we know who we are dealing with, my next team will not make the same mistake. Trust me.'

'Good,' said Rittenhausen. 'My sources in Europe tell me there are indications that they may be preparing to travel to Argentina. No prizes for guessing where they will turn up.'

'I will dispatch my team to you as soon as possible,' said Komarov. 'We will get this problem solved once and for all.'

'Thank you,' said Rittenhausen. 'We are about to finalise our work here at the test facility, so the last thing I need right now is a couple of pests running around and causing chaos.'

★ ★ ★

After a couple of hours at the airport in Linz, Andrew and Fiona managed to get themselves onto a flight to Madrid. Having made it to the Spanish capital, they boarded another plane that would take them overnight to Buenos Aires, and once there, they would catch a pre-dawn domestic flight to Mendoza City. The entire trip would take almost twenty-six hours in total, and once they were in the air over the Atlantic Ocean, Fiona used the opportunity to continue studying Otto Drexler's diary and making more notes.

'You've read that thing several times now,' said Andrew quietly, mindful that the lights in the cabin had now been dimmed and that most other passengers were either asleep or quietly watching a movie on their inflight entertainment systems. 'Are you finding anything new?'

'A few things here and there,' said Fiona, turning to him with a tired smile. 'It's just really fascinating. I think I'd like to write a book about this whole thing. There is so much stuff here that I never knew about, and the very existence of the Alpha and Omega projects is obviously not at all well understood by most historians. In several entries, Drexler refers to the competition between German scientists and the arms industry for tungsten, or wolfram, as they called it. I found out that Nazi Germany acquired it mostly from the Galicia region in Spain, where it can be found in small quantities alongside other mined metals such as tin. It was mainly used for manufacturing armour-piercing anti-tank rounds, but Drexler was obviously keen on acquiring it for his own purposes. I also managed to find some quotes from some of the main characters involved that really should give people cause for re-evaluating just how far the Nazi efforts to develop these advanced weapons actually were and how many resources were diverted to it. Here's one by Werner Heisenberg that is related to the nuclear research effort, and it is from the Farm Hall transcripts.'

> "One can say that the first time large funds were made available in Germany was in the spring of 1942, after our meeting with Rust, when we convinced him that we had absolutely definite proof that it could be done."

'Bernhard Rust was Science Minister and a Nazi Party loyalist from the very beginning in 1921,' said Fiona, 'and what Heisenberg said sounds like pretty definitive proof to me that they were very confident in being able to achieve their goals.'

'Is it fair to say that scientists were held in very high esteem in Nazi Germany?' said Andrew. 'It seems to me that they were quite revered and that Hitler saw them as the key to German domination of the world.'

'That's certainly true,' said Fiona. 'Keep in mind that this was a time when many new and completely groundbreaking technologies were being developed. Things like electromagnetism, radios, TVs, radar, the internal combustion engine, mass-produced cars, and even jet engines and rockets. And of course, nuclear research had made advances in the previous couple of decades, often thanks to prominent Jews like Einstein. But there was definitely a real sense that the world stood at the beginning of a brave new world, and that technological advancement held the key to power and to the future.'

'And Hitler was on board with this line of thinking?' said Andrew.

'Not necessarily the most advanced stuff,' said Fiona. 'Only insofar as it could be used for weaponry. But from everything I have read, it is abundantly clear from the many quotes attributed to him that he was more than prepared to completely destroy his enemies in pursuit of his goals. And I have no doubt that if he had acquired nuclear weapons, he would have used them.'

'Of that, I have no doubt,' said Andrew.

'But like I said,' said Fiona. 'Sometimes, it took some convincing. As an example, Reich Minister for Armaments, Albert Speer, believed Wernher von Braun to be what he called "a man realistically at home in the future.". And these two men forged a partnership that was probably rare in the dog-eat-dog world of the Nazi party. Speer said that he really liked mingling with this circle of young scientists, and he remarked that "their work also exerted a strange fascination upon me. It was like the planning of a miracle.". Anyway, Speer was so enamoured with the V-2 program that he wanted to share it with the Führer. So he put von Braun in a room with Hitler and had him show a film of a successful V-2 launch. Hitler famously loved films, and he was by all accounts captivated when he watched the rocket lift off from the launch platform, to the point where Speer later recalled that from that moment on, the Führer was completely won over. He apparently began raving about it being a decisive weapon of war, and how he wanted to use it to hit London as soon as possible. And then he immediately awarded von Braun the honorific title of 'professor', which apparently von Braun later used to lord it over his colleagues.'

'Charming,' said Andrew.

'Yes,' said Fiona. 'But the point of this story is that even as he raved about the rocket, Hitler was concerned with one thing only. That it wouldn't be able to carry enough destructive power. One of the attendees recalled that a strange, fanatical light flared up in Hitler's eyes and that he then shouted at them. "But what I want is annihilation. Annihilating effect!".'

'Bloody hell,' said Andrew.

'It is just to illustrate,' said Fiona. 'Hitler was hell-bent on acquiring the most powerful weapons that could possibly be developed, and he was more than prepared to use them.'

'Well, thank you for just confirming every preconceived notion I have ever had about Hitler and his mental state,' said Andrew, raising his eyebrows. 'He sounds deranged. Like a caricature of a Bond villain.'

'He was obviously a lunatic,' said Fiona. 'But he found ways of convincing people that he was simply doing what needed to be done for them. He very much identified himself with the German people, and in one speech he said, "That you have found me among so many millions is the miracle of our time. And that I have found you, that is Germany's fortune".'

'Well, whatever he was,' said Andrew. 'He was certainly a very skilled manipulator.'

'Very true,' said Fiona. 'There's a quote in 'Mein Kampf' where he essentially says that once he had understood how easily the popular mind could be poisoned, only a fool would blame the victims. In other words, people are so gullible that you can make them believe just about anything. He also used religion for this purpose, saying that he believed his conduct to be in accordance with the almighty creator, and that in standing against the Jew, he was defending the work of the Lord.'

'Did he believe any of this?' said Andrew.

'No one really knows,' said Fiona. 'But I would venture that his deeply Catholic upbringing would have laid the groundwork for him to develop these extreme anti-Jewish views.'

'The whole thing was deranged,' said Andrew, shaking his head. 'Those Nazis sound more like a religious cult than anything else.'

'That's probably a very accurate description,' said Fiona. 'And their particular cult, especially the SS under Heinrich Himmler, bore all the esoteric hallmarks of a religious organisation with its rigid dogma, occult rituals and inbuilt notions of superiority.'

'And Hitler was the high priest,' observed Andrew. 'If not actually a god himself.'

'You could say that,' Fiona nodded, 'although gods don't die, and Hitler eventually did.'

'Thankfully,' said Andrew. 'How old was he when he finally did the world a favour and blew his own brains out?'

'Fifty-six,' said Fiona. 'And towards the end, he fully understood that everything was collapsing around him, and he obviously didn't want to be taken alive by the Russians. But unsurprisingly, he blamed everyone else, and he was full of hate to the last. Listen to this quote from 1945.'

> "I know the war is lost. The enemy's superiority is too great. I have been betrayed. We will not capitulate, ever. We may go down. But we will take the world down with us."

'Once again,' said Andrew, shaking his head. 'Just imagine Hitler in possession of the nuclear ICBMs that were brought into existence just twelve years later, in 1957.'

'It doesn't even bear thinking about,' said Fiona.

Andrew sat quietly for a moment, and then he turned to face her.

'And now imagine someone like Rittenhausen selling portal technology to the highest bidder,' he said ruefully. 'Rogue governments across the world, religious extremist groups, or even terrorists without nuclear weapons but with plenty of other explosives. Or how about using it for the delivery of chemical or biological weapons?'

'It's terrifying,' said Fiona.

'We're going to Argentina to try to locate Adam and Alice Holbrook and free them if possible,' said Andrew. 'But we also need to stop Rittenhausen. People like him cannot be trusted with this sort of technology.'

'I know,' nodded Fiona solemnly. 'If we're right in thinking that Alice has been kidnapped and taken to his winery, then he would probably have had her flown there on a private jet. So, she will have been there for many hours already.'

'We'll have to wait and see what we find once we get there,' said Andrew, nodding pensively. 'But if everything we have discovered turns out to be real and Rittenhausen is on the verge of creating a working portal, we have to find a way to stop him, whatever it takes.'

* * *

Adam Holbrook was in what he had now come to regard as his solitary confinement cell somewhere under Rittenhausen's winery estate. Having not seen the sky for days on end, and despite having followed a regular work schedule before he had put down tools and refused to continue, he had now completely lost track of the days of the week. As time had gone by and he had been left by himself to wait for some sort of response from his captor, Holbrook had begun to doubt the wisdom of his decision, and his thoughts kept returning to his daughter. Would she be okay? Had he put her in danger? Last night, he had been so worried that he had barely managed to sleep.

He had only just sat up in his bed after waking up a few minutes earlier when there was the sound of footsteps in the corridor outside, and then he heard the key being pushed into the lock. When the door opened, the moustachioed Raul Torres walked in first, followed by Ferdinand Rittenhausen. Behind them were two stocky, uniformed guards.

'Good morning, Professor,' said Rittenhausen coolly, taking a step forward as Torres moved aside. 'I hope you slept well. Torres here tells me you're having trouble motivating yourself to continue the work.'

Holbrook slowly got to his feet but remained next to the bed. He didn't trust Torres not to use the black truncheon he was carrying in his right hand.

'I refuse to go any further until I receive guarantees that I can go back to my old life after this,' he said with a demeanour suggesting that he thought he still had some leverage over his captor. 'And I want a guarantee that you will never harm my daughter. We both know that you need me here. That much is clear. Without me, your people won't be able to finish the project. Am I right?'

'You are right,' nodded Rittenhausen with a faint, mercurial smile. 'I do need you. I need you to get back to work and finish calibrating the device. And that's why I have brought a new guest to see you.'

Rittenhausen glanced briefly at Torres, who then gave a nod to the two guards. The two burly men exited the room, and Holbrook could hear the sound of their heavy boots as they walked a short distance along the corridor. Then there was the sound of a door being unlocked, and a few seconds later, the boot stomps returned, but this time alongside an irregular shuffling noise. When they re-emerged in the doorway to Holbrook's cell, they were holding Alice, who had her arms tied behind her back, and he instantly felt his stomach drop and his throat constrict at the sight.

'Alice!' he exclaimed, his voice distraught and trembling as he rushed forward, only to be restrained forcefully by Torres.

Alice was manhandled roughly into the room by the two guards. She was staggering and looking confused, and Holbrook was shocked and deeply distressed at her appearance. Wearing blue jeans and a blood-stained t-shirt, her face was bruised and slightly swollen on one side, she had a large, purply black eye, and her lower lip was split and bloodied. Her long hair was matted and partly hanging down in front of her face, and she was unnaturally hunched over. She also seemed to be limping as she entered on her bare feet. As she peered up at her father from under her brow, she appeared to him as if she had aged two decades since he had last seen her.

'Daddy?' she whispered pleadingly, as if hoping that he would be able to simply make it all stop.

'You fucking bastard!' Holbrook roared.

He turned towards Rittenhausen and attempted to launch himself at him, but Torres swiftly stepped forward, wrapped a thick, muscular arm around his neck and held him back.

'What the hell is wrong with you?' Holbrook croaked as he struggled against the much larger and stronger man.

Taking half a step back in apparent surprise at the sudden and violent outburst from the usually mild-mannered professor, Rittenhausen folded his arms across his chest and gazed coldly at Holbrook as one of the guards released his grip on Alice and stepped forward to help Torres restrain him.

'I think I was right,' Rittenhausen mused as he regarded Holbrook like a biologist might regard a new type of fruit fly he had just bred in a lab. 'Bringing Alice here was an excellent idea. I think this will help you find the motivation you need to finish the project. After all, we're very close now.'

Holbrook breathed heavily and glowered furiously at Rittenhausen as he strained against the two muscly men who were restraining him firmly beyond any possibility of breaking free.

'You're a bloody monster,' spat Holbrook, although a defeated look began to spread across his face.

'I think I'll take that as a yes, then,' said Rittenhausen with a smug look. 'Alright?'

Holbrook panted as spittle dripped from his lip and a tear of anger, frustration and defeat made its way down his cheek.

'Alright,' he finally nodded as his head slumped down towards his chest, his voice now weak and feeble. 'I will do it. Just don't hurt Alice anymore. Please. I'm begging you.'

'There,' said Rittenhausen brightly, as if speaking to a small child. 'That wasn't so hard, was it?'

He then nodded and turned to Torres and the two guards.

'Excellent,' he said. 'Take the girl back to her cell, and then escort the professor to the test chamber. There's a full day's work ahead.'

Twenty-Two

The final stretch on the domestic flight from the Argentinian capital on the Atlantic coast to Mendoza City was close to one thousand kilometres long. When they eventually began their final approach and landed in what was one of the easternmost provinces of the country, they were a mere 240 kilometres from the Pacific Ocean and could practically see the border with Chile across the Andes mountain range. Looking out of the window through the murky dawn, they saw that large parts of the region were covered in hundreds of sizeable vineyards with tens of thousands of neat lines of grapevines.

They touched down at Mendoza City Airport early in the morning, just as the sun was hitting the snow-capped mountain tops in the far distance to the west of the city. Stepping outside the terminal with minimal luggage, they headed for the car rental companies and hired a dark grey, medium-sized but powerful Honda 4x4 SUV.

'First things first,' said Andrew as he put the key in the ignition, started the engine and fired up the inbuilt Satnav system. 'We need to do some recon to get the lay of the land around Rittenhausen's winery. It's in a wide, flat valley to the south, so I'll program the satnav to take us up into some of those surrounding foothills that I spotted from the plane. That should give us a good overview.'

Soon after, he put the car into gear and then they pulled away from the car rental shop and got underway. Around fifteen minutes later, as the first sunlight cut across the landscape and began lighting up the distant Andes foothills and the nearby city, they had made it through Mendoza's modern centre out through the low-rise southern suburbs and into the green, vine-covered countryside. As far as the eye could see, vineyards stretched away in almost all directions, except towards the west, where they eventually became the Andes foothills, framed by tall snow-capped mountains behind them in the far distance. Most of the roads through this wine country were straight as an arrow and lined with tall, slim poplar trees that reached up into the pale blue morning sky.

Following their planned route, they took a right turn and drove along a winding road up into the Andes foothills to the southwest of the city, where Andrew eventually pulled over and stopped the car in a layby on a bend. As they got out, they had the almost six-kilometre-tall peaks behind them in the far distance, and in front of them was a near-perfect view of one of the main wine regions in the country. It was laid out like a dark green carpet that was dotted with the various winery estates that owned and operated the many vineyards, and it was intersected every couple of kilometres by poplar-lined roads. Nearer to their elevated location, the landscape was parched brushland that eventually turned to arid, rocky ground as the terrain began to rise. Andrew got out a pair of binoculars from his bag, and then they stepped over to the metal barrier that separated the layby from a steep hillside leading down into a ravine.

'It's beautiful here,' said Fiona, placing her hands on her hips as they stopped by the barrier.

'Rittenhausen's estate is that one,' said Andrew, pointing to an irregularly shaped patch of land a couple of kilometres into the distance that was enclosed inside an enormous plot full of large separate vineyards.

A substantial white villa and several other smaller buildings were situated at the centre of the irregular patch, all of them with orange terracotta rooftops and surrounded by tall trees. The entire area around the villa appeared to be a well-tended park, and on its southern edge was a large, kidney-shaped artificial lake with more trees on one side. Roughly a kilometre west of the impressive-looking villa, the estate's well-groomed vineyards stopped and became dry brushland, and several hundred metres further west across the arid terrain was a strange and lonely-looking building that glinted in the sunlight. A single dirt road led to it, but there was no hint as to its purpose.

'Quite a place he's got,' said Fiona after borrowing the binoculars and peering at the estate for a few moments. 'He certainly doesn't appear to be short of money.'

'Looks like there's only one road in and out,' said Andrew. 'That's going to complicate things.'

'What is that solitary building out there in the brush?' said Fiona.

'I don't know,' said Andrew, gazing at it. 'We should head down and take a closer look at the area.'

They got back into the car and drove down to the expansive, virtually flat terrain below. Following the main road down the low mountain, they then turned right and proceeded along yet another of the long, straight poplar-lined avenues until they came to Rittenhausen's estate. Unlike most other estates, it was surrounded by a tall fence all the way along its perimeter, and immediately behind that was a row of trees that partly obscured the view. After driving almost a kilometre, they passed the single entrance to the estate, which was barred by a tall metal gate made from swirling, wrought-iron sections made to look like grapevines. Above the entrance was a metal sign into which had been cut the name of the estate. 'Villa Magdalena', it said.

As they went past, Andrew slowed down. Looking through the gate along a narrow and paved tree-lined road, they were able to see the white façade of the main villa. Tucked away into the trees about ten metres from the gate was a guard post, but they were unable to see if it was manned.

'Looks like pretty light security,' said Andrew. 'At least out here on the perimeter. Either that or they like to stay out of sight.'

'I don't imagine they've ever had any unwanted visitors,' said Fiona. 'If Rittenhausen has people like the Navarro brothers working for him, then I am sure the locals stay well clear. And that giant fence pretty much tells you to stay out or else.'

'Let's see if we can get around to the other side,' said Andrew. 'There might be some other way of getting inside that we haven't been able to see yet.'

They continued for another kilometre or so, and then they turned right along another road with the tall fence on one side and an open vineyard evidently belonging to someone else on the other. After almost two more kilometres of unbroken fence, they finally reached the end of the estate and turned right once again. They were now on the opposite side of the estate, and whereas the tall fence continued on their right, their left side now offered an almost unobstructed view across the parched brushland towards the snowcapped Andes mountains far away.

However, through the low vegetation and a much lower chain-link barbed wire fence, they were soon able to see the strange, solitary building that they had first spotted from the hills above. It looked much larger from down here, even though it was roughly two hundred metres from the road. When they reached the dirt road leading to it, Andrew stopped the car, rolled down the window and used the binoculars to peer at it through a gate in the fence.

'What can you see?' asked Fiona.

'It's a one-storey structure,' said Andrew, using his index finger to focus the binoculars. 'It looks very utilitarian, but I can't work out what it's for. It has no windows, but it does have a single, large entrance facing this way. There is a huge array of what looks like large air-conditioning units on the roof, and the whole thing looks to be hooked up to the local power grid.'

'Rittenhausen probably has the local authorities in his pocket,' said Fiona. 'Is it just me, or does the pylon carrying the power cables to this building look new and shiny, but the others look old and corroded?'

'Yes,' said Andrew. 'The one on this plot looks like it was installed recently. The whole thing is bizarre… unless.'

He paused for a moment as he studied the unusual building sitting there at the other end of a dry and compacted dirt track, surrounded by arid, yellow bushes and clumps of long, pale grass.

'What?' said Fiona.

'Unless this whole building has a single purpose,' he said, 'which is to provide fresh air and cooling for some sort of underground facility. If Rittenhausen is building his own portal here, then it is almost certain to be underground.'

'That makes sense,' said Fiona, peering towards the building and then looking at the fence and the gate. 'I don't see any security here.'

'I know,' said Andrew, lowering the binoculars. 'And that might work to our advantage. This could be our way in. If there are air conditioners, then there are vents, and we should be able to use them to get inside the facility.'

'So what now?' said Fiona. 'What do you think we should do?'

'We should wait until it gets dark,' said Andrew. 'Even if they are working twenty-four hours a day, whatever guards they have are likely to be less alert late at night or early in the morning.'

'I'm hungry,' said Fiona, glancing at her wristwatch. 'It'll be noon fairly soon. How about we find a place to eat?'

'Good idea,' said Andrew. 'We might be able to talk to some locals and see what they know about Villa Magdalena. It's worth a shot.'

Ten minutes later, they pulled into the parking lot of an attractive-looking establishment by the name of *Bodega Las Pinzónes*, evidently named after the local finch population chirping happily in the poplar trees surrounding the place. Aside from serving a selection of local wines, it also offered various foods and sold both locally made wine and olive oil in a small shop.

After exiting the SUV, they walked up to the slightly raised wooden porch where a waiter greeted them and showed them to a small table overlooking a nearby vineyard. It was covered with a white tablecloth and already bedecked with three sizes of wine glasses and shiny steel cutlery. They ordered some brunch and then decided to follow the waiter's suggestion and taste one of the white wines, despite the early hour.

After the meal, they went inside to what was more of a local watering hole than the sophisticated eatery the bodega's exterior had led them to expect. There was a long bar running the length of the back wall with a single bartender behind it, and most of the rest of the interior was taken up by small separate wooden booths with seats upholstered with black leather and seatbacks covered in mottled black-and-white cowhides. Some were already occupied by couples, but most were empty, and in addition, there were a few older men sitting by themselves at small tables while they sipped wine from large glasses and smoked cigarettes. Coming from a set of speakers was what might have been the latest in Argentinian pop music, but neither Andrew nor Fiona had ever heard it before.

They selected a booth and went up to the bar to order another two glasses of wine, this time a red variety made with the local *Criolla Grande* grape. The bartender, who was a man in his mid-twenties wearing black trousers, a white shirt and sporting short black hair, made a show of opening the bottle for them and allowing Andrew to taste the wine before they took receipt of it. Once Andrew had swirled the small taster around in his mouth and decided that it was more than passable, he nodded affirmatively at the bartender and placed his glass back on the counter.

'Very nice,' he smiled, and then he leaned forward slightly and spoke softly. 'Say, would you happen to know who owns the Villa Magdalena estate?'

The bartender took a moment to regard Andrew and then Fiona, and then he shrugged before replying.

'I'm not sure, sir,' he replied in English with a faint Spanish accent and a slight shake of the head. 'It's not my business.'

'So, you don't know?' said Andrew. 'Have you ever heard the name Rittenhausen?'

'No,' said the bartender dismissively and a little too quickly. 'I don't know him. Can I get you anything else?'

'No, this is fine for now,' said Andrew, about to press on with his questions, but he had barely completed his sentence before the bartender turned and moved to the other end of the bar, where he began busying himself by polishing wine glasses that didn't need polishing.

Andrew gave a shrug as he glanced at Fiona with one eyebrow slightly raised, and then he picked up the wine bottle with one hand and the two glasses with the other. The two of them then sat down in their booth, and Andrew poured them both half a glass of the Criolla Grande.

'Well, that was awkward,' said Fiona quietly, picking up the glass and sniffing the rich aroma.

'Fishy is what it was,' Andrew replied, mirroring her. 'This guy obviously knows exactly who Rittenhausen is. You could see it in his eyes. I am sure everyone in the valley knows, and we're less than two kilometres away from Villa Magdalena.'

'Is he scared?' said Fiona.

'Perhaps not scared,' said Andrew, swirling the wine inside the glass as he contemplated the slightly odd encounter. 'But something tells me that it's better for people not to show too much interest in Rittenhausen and what he does around here. I guess it makes sense.'

'How do you mean?' said Fiona.

'Well,' said Andrew. 'If he is connected to the local criminals, which his hiring of people like Hector and Ernesto Navarro suggests, then it would probably be sensible not to get on his bad side.'

'I guess so,' said Fiona, raising her glass. 'Anyway, cheers, and good luck to us.'

'Cheers,' he said, raising his own glass and clinking it gently against hers. 'We might need it.'

Over at the bar, one of the old men was sliding onto a stool and waving at the waiter, and as he did so, he looked in Andrew and Fiona's direction. He looked to be in his mid-seventies with wrinkled, weathered skin and thick, black but greying tousled hair, and even from a distance, it was obvious that he had somewhat of a brandy nose. He was wearing a loose, blue and black checkered flannel shirt, worn and faded jeans, a pair of brown cowboy boots and a shabby, wide-brimmed felt fedora with blotchy grease stains from where it appeared to have been handled countless times.

As the man placed his elbows on the counter and shifted forward on the stool, the young waiter arrived to take his order. Soon, a new glass full of red wine was pushed across to him, and he grasped it around the stem and raised it to his rosy nose. Then he glanced briefly in the direction of the two foreigners sitting in the booth behind him and to one side. After another few minutes, during which time he drank half of the wine in his glass, he finally dismounted the bar stool and walked towards Andrew and Fiona's booth, the heels of his boots connecting audibly with the wooden floor.

'I think we're about to meet one of the locals,' said Andrew quietly as he raised his glass to his mouth.

'Who?' said Fiona, but before Andrew could reply, the old man was next to their booth.

He stood there for a moment, looking at both of them in turn, and then he walked over to an empty nearby table and dragged over a chair. Sitting down and placing his glass on the booth's table, Andrew and Fiona watched him silently, unsure how to react to this uninvited guest.

'*Buenos dias*,' said the man politely with a heavy accent, once again looking at them in turn and giving them each a nod in greeting. 'My name is Juan Fuentes.'

Andrew and Fiona glanced at each other uncertainly. Perhaps this was the standard way for locals to casually introduce themselves to perfect strangers, or perhaps this man had something important on his mind.

'*Buenos dias,*' said Andrew in his best Spanish in a polite but somewhat halting way while giving the man a nod. 'Is there something we can do for you, *Señor* Fuentes?'

'I have a friend,' said Fuentes cryptically, before embarking on what felt like a very long pause before speaking again. 'On old friend. His name is Garcia. Alberto Garcia. He lives not too far from here.'

Fuentes waved vaguely towards the outside, and then he took another gulp of his wine. Smacking his lips, he then looked at Fiona with his old greying eyes, and then he returned his gaze to Andrew.

'He's an old friend,' Fuentes repeated, pausing again and gazing emptily out of the window as if he was contemplating deeply his own words. 'You want to know something about Villa Magdalena? About *Señor* Rittenhausen?'

In almost perfect sync, both Andrew and Fiona involuntarily leaned forward and looked intently at the old man.

'We do,' said Andrew softly, his eyes performing a rapid scan of the room. 'We would really appreciate any information you have.'

'What can you tell us about him?' said Fiona. 'How long has he been in this area? What does he do around here??'

Fuentes held up a hand and lowered his face slightly, as if admonishing them both to let him finish.

'You should speak to Alberto Garcia,' he said quietly. 'This is not my business. But if you can help him, I will help you and tell you where he lives.'

★   ★   ★

Alberto Garcia lived in a small ramshackle house on a plot no larger than two or three acres with a dozen rows of grapevines. The plot was a couple of kilometres from the bodega, and it was dwarfed by Rittenhausen's enormous estate, which was only a few hundred metres away. When Andrew parked the SUV and he and Fiona stepped out of the vehicle, they heard a dog barking, and soon a powerful-looking white dog came running out from behind the house. It was an Argentinian mastiff called a *Dogo Argentino*, and it looked to be in its prime at around a handful of years old. Known for being a very loyal companion and an excellent guard dog, the dog ran towards them, barking loudly as Andrew turned calmly to Fiona.

'Just stay there,' he said steadily as Fiona froze by the side of the car. 'Don't move.'

The white, muscular guard dog raced directly towards Andrew, and as it closed in on him, he turned towards it with his arms hanging down along his sides while he showed the animal his palms.

'Hello buddy,' he said in a calm and friendly tone, keeping the strain out of his voice despite the sight of the formidable canine coming straight at him.

The dog came right up to him, almost skidding to a halt as it panted loudly and produced a deep and intimidating growl. Then it sniffed one of his hands, and he could feel the hot, damp breath on his skin.

'*Baltasar!*' came a gruff, commanding voice from inside the house, and it was followed by a high-pitched double whistle. '*Ven aqui!*'

The dog immediately turned around and jogged back towards the house, seemingly no longer regarding the two newcomers as a threat. Emerging onto the porch was an old man wearing a shabby brown jumper over an open-collared blue shirt, faded denim dungarees and brown leather cowboy boots. He had long grey stubble and a weathered face that spoke of a life lived mostly outside under the unforgiving Patagonian sun. In his large, calloused right hand, he was holding a glass of red wine, and a lit cigar protruded from the centre of his mouth, from which small puffs of smoke emanated when he spoke.

'*Le gustas!*' he called with a faint note of surprise as he regarded Andrew before switching to heavily accented English. 'He likes you. You are English, yes?'

'That's right,' said Andrew. 'How did you know?'

'I know,' shrugged the man, coming to stand in front of them as he picked the cigar from his mouth and regarded them with his dark eyes. 'I can tell.'

'My name is Andrew, and this is Fiona,' said Andrew, turning to one side and gesturing towards Fiona as she stepped forward. 'Are you Alberto Garcia?'

'*Sí,*' nodded the old man reticently, the inflexion in his voice making it sound like a question. 'I am Alberto.'

'We're sorry to show up unannounced,' said Fiona. 'We spoke to a man called Juan Fuentes at the Bodega Las Pinzónes. He said he was a friend of yours.'

Alberto nodded sagely as he listened.

'You spoke to Juan?' he said, raising his glass towards his mouth. 'Why? Juan does not like tourists.'

'We're not tourists,' said Andrew. 'We are here about Ferdinand von Rittenhausen.'

At that, Alberto's glass stopped moving, and he seemed to freeze for a moment, the glass hovering near his mouth and the eyes in his heavily lined and weather-beaten face narrowing slightly as he regarded Andrew.

'Señor Rittenhausen,' he said evenly, without a hint of emotion. 'Do you know him?'

'We know *of* him,' said Andrew. 'We know things about him that make us concerned. And I wouldn't exactly say that we are on friendly terms. His men tried to kill us a couple of days ago.'

Alberto's gaze remained fixed on Andrew's eyes for a moment, as if interrogating them for truthfulness, and then he shifted it to Fiona, who looked straight at him and gave him a quick nod to confirm. He seemed to contemplate Andrew's words for a while longer, and then he began to turn around.

'*Por favor*,' his baritone voice rumbled, gesturing towards the porch and a small table with three chairs. 'Come and sit.'

The three of them sat down at the table, and Alberto reached into a small wooden crate by the wall to extract a bottle of red wine. Then he went inside and returned a few seconds later with the open bottle and two more glasses in his hands. The white, jowly dog with the thick neck and pointy ears had now laid down on the porch, placing itself next to what appeared to be Alberto's usual chair.

'What's his name again?' asked Fiona, looking at the dog. 'He's beautiful.'

'Baltasar,' replied Alberto as he sat down and began pouring. 'He is a loyal friend. And he keeps people away. But you are good with dogs.'

He glanced briefly at Andrew with a look that seemed to convey genuine respect, as if the disposition of a dog towards a man was a measure of his character, and perhaps it really was. Hearing his name, Baltasar lifted his head off the floor and looked up at Alberto, who reached down to ruffle his ears in a way that seemed second nature and didn't require him to look. Then the canine companion placed his head back down on the wooden floorboards of the porch, snorted once, and then proceeded to calmly sniff the air, the tip of his nose twitching every few seconds.

'I will speak with you because Juan sent you,' said Alberto, and as he spoke, Fiona sensed decency and kindness in him despite his gruff exterior. 'He and I have known each other since we were 'muchachos'. Young boys. We used to play up on those hills.'

He pointed into the distance at a range of hills about a kilometre to the west.

'Thank you,' said Andrew. 'We really appreciate it.'

'Tell me,' said Alberto. 'You say Rittenhausen tried to kill you. Why?'

Andrew and Fiona exchanged a quick glance. They both understood that they had to level with the old man if they were going to have any hope of him being frank with them about Villa Magdalena and Ferdinand von Rittenhausen.

'We believe that he had one of our friends murdered back in London,' said Andrew gravely, looking straight at Alberto, who sat leaning back in his chair with his right hand resting near the edge of the table, gripping his wine glass. 'He is probably also responsible for at least one other death there. And his people have come after us for trying to find out what he is doing. We barely walked away alive.'

Taking turns and complementing each other's accounts along the way, Andrew and Fiona then proceeded to tell Alberto about the events of the past week or so, including the murder of Ben Ambrose and Christopher Bateman, and the dramatic events that had unfolded in Berlin, Austria and Geneva. To the best of their ability, they also conveyed in rough strokes what Rittenhausen had been researching and what he might be trying to build. By the end of it, Alberto was gazing past them and into the distance with a hard thousand-yard stare as he raised his glass to his mouth and then almost emptied it. He placed it back on the table and licked his lips.

'And you think Señor Rittenhausen is holding this man Holbrook and his daughter at the winery?' he said, seemingly disinterested in whether or not Rittenhausen might be building some obscure device at his estate.

'We do,' said Andrew. 'And we mean to get them out.'

'Is there anything you can tell us that might help us do that?' asked Fiona.

Alberto pursed his lips and poured himself some more wine.

'Señor Rittenhausen is not a good man,' he said sagely. 'And it would not be the first time he has treated people badly.'

'What do you mean?' Andrew said, finally picking up his own glass and joining Alberto in drinking.

'A few weeks ago,' said Alberto, 'some of the locals found a young woman by the side of the road near his estate. She had worked at Villa Magdalena as a housekeeper for about a year, and she had been beaten and abused by Rittenhausen's head of security. A man called Raul Torres. But when the police came, they gave her back to him. He told them that she is one of his relatives and that she has psychological problems. But that is not true. I know. The woman is called Gloria, and she is my niece.'

'What a bastard,' said Andrew, shaking his head in disgust.

'Is she back there now?' said Fiona.

'*Si*,' nodded Alberto gloomily. 'She's too frightened to leave. I get a message from her sometimes on my phone. She is very scared and unhappy there, but she needs the money. And I think they are preventing her from leaving.'

'And the police are doing nothing?' said Fiona.

'*Bastardos*,' grunted Alberto, rubbing his index finger against his thumb. 'Rittenhausen pays them, so he and his men can do whatever they want. To her and to me too.'

'What do you mean by that?' said Andrew. 'What did Rittenhausen do to you?'

Alberto gave a bitter shake of the head, and then he produced a long exhale. He raised his gaze to the tops of the poplar trees swaying gently in the breeze, and then he cleared his throat and sat up in his chair.

'This house,' he said, gesturing to the old, rickety building behind them. 'This was a shed, but I had to move here when Rittenhausen bought my winery.'

'You had a winery?' said Fiona.

'Yes, of course,' nodded Alberto. 'It was not big, but it was mine, and I made good wine there. But one day, it was burned to the ground. And then I was forced to sell it.'

'How could you be forced?' said Andrew. 'Were you evicted?'

'Evicted. Yes,' nodded Alberto darkly. 'I was kicked out by the local… how do you say? *Municipio.*'

'Municipality,' Fiona jumped in. 'The local authority.'

'*Si,*' said Alberto, placing his hands flat on the table in front of him as he recounted what was clearly an upsetting course of events. 'One day, they come to me, and they say my land is toxic. Heavy metals.'

'And was it?' said Fiona.

'*Completamente absurdo!*' Alberto grunted derisively, waving a hand as if to dismiss the idea. 'No. It was not. It was just farmland. Only grapevines. But there was nothing I could do. I was forced to sell it to the local governor's office for a very low price, and then they sold it to Rittenhausen. Now, it is part of the Villa Magdalena estate. I tried to make a protest in front of the mayor's office, but I was thrown in jail for three days by the police. They told me I was disturbing the peace.'

'That's outrageous,' said Fiona, looking appalled. 'Can't you challenge that decision?'

Alberto shook his head dejectedly and gave a small, derisive chortle.

'I don't have much money,' he said. 'It would be very expensive. And I would lose. It's all… *finito.*'

He waved dismissively again and took another gulp of his wine, and then he shook his head once more, pressing his lips together as he tried to swallow his bitterness and pride along with the red wine.

'Where was your house?' asked Fiona.

'To the west of the Villa Magdalena estate,' said Alberto. 'It is all overgrown now. It looks like a desert. But I have seen some strange things going on there since Rittenhausen took it from me several years ago. I saw lots of people coming and going for many months. There was some big construction work going on until a few months ago. Since then, no one goes there, except a maintenance crew every couple of weeks.'

'Any idea what they were building out there?' said Andrew.

'No,' said Alberto, 'but it has nothing to do with wine or farming. That's for sure.'

'I'm pretty sure we drove past it earlier today,' said Andrew. 'It's the plot with a new building packed with air-conditioning units, right?'

'Yes,' said Alberto. 'I don't understand. I thought he wanted to make his own estate bigger to make more wine, but he put my property behind a fence and built that strange building. It makes no sense. But they are *Alemanes*. Who knows why they do what they do.'

'*Alemanes*,' repeated Fiona. 'Germans.'

'*Sí*,' said Alberto, nodding sagely, as if simply by mentioning them by name, Fiona had just confirmed everything he was thinking. 'There are many of them here. They think all of this land is theirs. They own the businesses, they pay the politicians, and they make sure the police never cause them any trouble. It has been like this for over a hundred years. We can do nothing.'

Alberto sighed, lifted his glass again and hesitated for a moment, and then he took another gulp.

'How do you know who burned down your house?' said Fiona. 'Did you see it happen?'

'I did not see,' said Alberto. 'They are cowards. They started the fire when I was at the local market. But I am sure I know who they are. Hector and Ernesto Navarro. *Animales*. Criminals from the city.'

'Well,' said Andrew. 'You don't need to worry about Ernesto anymore. He was the one who didn't get to leave Berlin alive.'

'Good,' grunted Alberto with a nod and a grimace. 'But his older brother Hector is here now. I saw his car yesterday. You should be careful.'

'What kind of car is it?' asked Andrew.

'A Porsche,' said Alberto. 'White. Very fast.'

'We'll keep an eye out,' said Andrew coldly. 'I have unfinished business with him too.'

'So, you want to go inside Villa Magdalena and get Holbrook and his daughter out?' said Alberto, regarding them with a hint of scepticism. 'They have many guards there.'

'Yes,' said Andrew. 'That's why we're here. Perhaps we can help Gloria too. And we will deal with the guards one way or another if they get in our way.'

'I would be very grateful if you could help her,' said Alberto. 'Gloria is a good person. She has a good heart. Let me find a picture of her for you.'

Alberto got to his feet and disappeared into the house where he rummaged around in a drawer. A couple of minutes later, he came back and placed a small passport photo on the table in front of them. Its colours were somewhat faded, and its corners were slightly dog-eared, but the image of the attractive young woman was clear to see. She looked to be in her late twenties with slightly curly, brown shoulder-length hair, and her face was lit up in a smile with perfect teeth and small laugh lines by the edges of her dark, almond-shaped eyes.

'This was Gloria a couple of years ago,' he said.

'She's gorgeous,' said Fiona. 'Poor girl.'

'We'll do what we can,' said Andrew, lifting his eyes from the photo. 'We'll find her, and we'll get her out of there if at all possible.'

'Thank you very much,' said Alberto, bowing his head in gratitude.

'You have my word,' said Andrew, giving Alberto a determined nod.

But...' said Alberto slowly, evidently chewing over an idea as he spoke. 'Maybe you need some help?'

'What do you mean?' said Andrew. 'Are you offering to assist us?'

Alberto grunted and put down his glass on the table. Then he rubbed his stubbly chin for a moment before spreading out his rough hands and glancing over his shoulder at the house.

'I am an old man, and I don't have much to lose anymore,' he said, initially sounding dejected, but then his eyes revealed a spark of resolve as he went on. 'But if you can get Gloria out and kick Rittenhausen in his *cojones*, then I will do whatever I can to help you.'

Twenty-Three

Ferdinand Drexler von Rittenhausen was in his office inside Villa Magdalena, swirling brandy in a snifter glass as he listened to one of his technicians relay how Adam Holbrook had applied his newfound motivation to the work in the test facility. The previous evening, after presenting the scientist with his daughter and using her to persuade Holbrook to continue, Rittenhausen had finally revealed to him the true purpose of the huge device sitting at the centre of the underground facility.

Holbrook's eyes had widened in disbelief as he took in the seemingly absurd idea of constructing a portal capable of generating an Einstein-Rosen Bridge, but then Rittenhausen had shown him the theoretical work of Otto Drexler from more than half a century ago. Flicking through page after page of Drexler's original notes and calculations, Holbrook appeared to have begun changing his mind. He had then rushed to a whiteboard in an observation room inside the facility, where he had spent a couple of hours furiously writing equations, deriving complex mathematical expressions and results, and then finally, using Einstein's field equations to verify that neither Drexler nor he were in fact crazy. A carefully calibrated and vastly overpowered particle accelerator could trap a mind-boggling torrent of protons and then accelerate them to a fraction below the speed of light. In theory, this would increase the mass of those protons to the point where they would produce a gravitational effect that could curve spacetime around the centre of the device. And according to Holbrook's own calculations, this had the potential to create a temporary but stable portal connecting two points in spacetime.

Once Holbrook had arrived at this result, he had slumped down in a chair in the observation room and stared silently out at the portal through the toughened glass window for a long time. The technician, who had accompanied him during this revelation of the device's true purpose, and who was now sitting across from Rittenhausen, relayed how Holbrook had appeared shocked and even disturbed by his own findings, but that he had eventually got to his feet and resumed his work.

'Very good,' said Rittenhausen, nodding. 'When can we expect our first live test?'

'In a matter of hours,' said the technician confidently.

He was a lanky man with small eyes, pale skin and medium-length blond hair, and he was wearing a white lab coat over a blue shirt and dark tie.

'All of our monitoring software is pointing in the same direction,' he continued. 'Holbrook's work on the magnetic field algorithm will allow us to contain the proton stream and accelerate it to the required levels without causing any damage to the portal itself. The path for an Einstein-Rosen bridge now lies open to us.'

'Excellent,' said Rittenhausen with a nod, after which he emptied his glass. 'That will be all.'

The technician immediately rose to his feet, nodded respectfully and turned towards the door.

'Oh, and one more thing,' said Rittenhausen. 'Tell Torres to move Ms. Holbrook to the observation room. I want her father to be able to see her at all times. Just in case he tries something stupid, like attempting to sabotage the portal before the test. You never know with narrow-minded idealists like that.'

'Certainly, sir,' said the technician, and then he left the room.

When the door to his office had closed, Rittenhausen leaned forward over his desk and carefully leafed through the old notes, schematics and equations that his grandfather had produced inside Bergkristall. Turning the pages with the reverence befitting of an ancient foundational religious text, he gazed with admiration at the complex equations and marvelled at how his ancestor had managed to use one of Einstein's most significant results to quite literally open the door to a whole new realm of physics. Not only was it breathtaking, but it was about to make him one of the wealthiest and most powerful men in history.

He lifted his head and looked across to the oil painting hanging on the opposite wall. It was a portrait of Otto Drexler that he had commissioned about ten years earlier after first realising what his grandfather had been working on. Ever since then, it had loomed over him as a permanent fixture in his office and a constant reminder of what he was working towards.

Looking up at his esteemed and brilliant grandfather, Rittenhausen found himself pondering what it must have been like for him to be forced to abandon his life's work in the spring of 1945, when the Allies were approaching from the west, and the Soviets were closing in from the east. According to his now long-dead father Maximillian, *'Opa'* Otto had followed the ratline from Austria through a monastery in northern Italy, after which the Vatican had facilitated a safe onward journey to Argentina. Once there, his grandfather had moved south and as far from the Atlantic coast as he could get, finally settling with his wife Magdalena in what was then a very rural backwater of the country.

Mendoza City was at that time home to only a fraction of the population living there now, and when the Germans fleeing Europe after World War 2 had arrived, they had soon begun to quietly take control of the entire region. Welcomed by President Peron, they carried with them wealth, skills and education levels that were orders of magnitude higher than those of the local population, and it made that tight-knit group of foreigners unstoppable. Either setting up or taking over existing businesses and running them very efficiently, their success soon allowed them to outcompete the locals and obtain political influence which in turn only further strengthened their power. Within decades, anything worth owning was owned by them or their descendants, and the regional criminal prosecutors and police force were entirely in their pockets, and so it had remained ever since.

Sadly, however, Otto Drexler had died only a couple of years after arriving in Mendoza and building Villa Magdalena and its vineyards. The cause was still a mystery, but Rittenhausen suspected that he had eventually succumbed to the effects of radiation, which were not well understood at the time. Not long after, Magdalena had joined him in the afterlife, passing the estate to their only son, Maximillian, or Max, as he was known locally.

Max had eventually married a young woman named Hilda, who was from one of the other influential German families around Mendoza, and together they had raised their son Ferdinand to admire and revere their German heritage, not least the thousand-year Reich that almost was. After what was initially a very conventional upbringing amongst the powerful families of the region, Ferdinand had one day stumbled across some of Otto Drexler's notes inside one of his father's desk drawers. This had been the beginning of his multi-decade journey to fulfil his grandfather's dream of converting his theoretical groundwork into a working Einstein-Rosen Bridge. A portal with the potential to usher in a whole new reality. And the rest, as they say, is history.

Rittenhausen swivelled in his chair and opened an app on his PC that allowed him to remotely monitor everything that was going on inside the underground test facility roughly one kilometre away. Inside the subterranean chamber, people in white lab coats were busy tinkering with the portal's sub-components, setting up new banks of monitoring equipment, using consols to operate a multitude of control software, and preparing the newly installed glass tank. Filled with water, the cube was three metres on all sides, and it was going to serve as the destination for the object they were about to send through the portal. If all went according to plan, the solid carbon sphere would pass through the portal and instantaneously appear inside the centre of the water tank. Rittenhausen felt a shiver run down his spine. The magnitude of what he was about to achieve could not be overstated. This was quite simply history in the making, and the accolades and riches that would result from it would be his to claim.

A firm knock on the door pulled Rittenhausen out of his expectant reverie, and he swivelled to face the door and called out.

'Enter!' he said, leaning back in his chair.

The door opened, and three large men walked in. One sported a short, full beard, while the other two were clean-shaven. They were all wearing boots, dark trousers and black t-shirts displaying their bulging biceps, and strapped to their torsos were black shoulder holsters with pistols. The bearded man heading the group, who was slightly taller than the other two, moved confidently towards Rittenhausen's desk where he stopped, flanked by his two companions.

'Ah!' said Rittenhausen, giving them each a quick glance before his gaze settled on the bearded man, who was clearly the top dog. 'I have been expecting you three. You must be Viktor.'

'I am Viktor,' rumbled the bearded man in a thick Russian accent as he gave a brief nod before jerking his head to one side and then the other while introducing his two comrades. 'This is Stanislav, and this is Bogdan.'

Stanislav was leaner than the other two, and he had a calculating look about him that made Rittenhausen feel vaguely uneasy. Like a hungry hyena eyeing a juicy antelope through the undergrowth. Bogdan was the shortest of the three, but he was built like a tank, and his hands looked to Rittenhausen to be the size of two tennis rackets. These men were exactly what he had been hoping for when Komarov said he would send another team. With Komarov's first team now almost certainly dead at the hands of the same man who had killed Ernesto Navarro in Berlin, Rittenhausen wanted a serious security detail around him, especially if the two thieves were planning to come here. Relying on a bunch of mean-looking but unskilled local hoodlums with guns from Mendoza City was no longer an option.

'Well, I am very pleased to meet you,' smiled Rittenhausen, sitting up in his chair and folding his hands on the table in front of himself. 'Thank you all for coming.'

Viktor gave a shrug of his broad shoulders and replied in an even and monotonous tone of voice.

'Komarov says to go,' he said. 'We go.'

'Right,' said Rittenhausen with a thin smile, realising that he was never going to get scintillating conversation out of the trio. 'You three are here to keep me safe. Alright? Now, Komarov told me that you guys are his best men, so here's what I want from you.'

★   ★   ★

As night fell, Andrew and Fiona were getting ready for their attempt at covertly entering the portal test facility through the ventilation shaft coming down from the solitary structure on Alberto Garcia's former plot. They were hoping that whatever activities were going on down there would fall quiet late at night. With a bit of luck, this would allow them to make their way from the facility along what had to be an access tunnel back to Villa Magdalena, where they assumed both Adam and Alice Holbrook were being kept. Andrew was wearing his small black backpack with tools and items that he thought they might need. In addition, Alberto had given them a large leather holdall with various tools from his toolshed.

Hours earlier, Andrew had enlisted the help of a friend from his investigative unit's cyber team back in London to dig up as much information as possible about the construction of Rittenhausen's luxury villa. However, all that was available from the firewall-protected servers of the construction firm were plans and drawings for structures above ground. No plans for anything below ground could be found, and the hacker had concluded that either those plans had been permanently erased, or the construction work had been carried out by Rittenhausen's own employees. Either way, Andrew and Fiona were going in blind, and they would have to make it up as they went.

Driving with the headlights off and using only the light of the half-moon in the starry sky, they approached Alberto Garcia's old plot and pulled over by the entrance. When the SUV crunched to a halt on the gravel in front of the padlocked chain link gate, Andrew stepped out carrying the leather bag. He pulled out a large bolt cutter and snipped the metal chain locking the gate. The padlock clonked onto the ground, and then he pulled the chain free, tossed it into a bush and pushed the gate open. Getting back into the car, they drove slowly along the uneven dirt track leading up to the lone building where Andrew allowed the SUV to roll to a stop behind some bushes and out of sight of the road.

The building was roughly thirty metres on all four sides, and when they exited their vehicle, they could hear the whisper of fans coming from the large array of air-con units mounted on top of its flat roof. Emanating from the building itself was a muffled, multi-layered hum produced by the machinery working inside. There appeared to be only one way in, and it was a single wide metal door with a brass-fronted cylinder lock. Andrew opened the boot of the car and extracted a crowbar from the spare wheel compartment in the boot. He jammed its tip between the lock and the doorframe, and then he wrenched the door open amid metallic creaking and snapping noises. While it came away from the doorframe and small pieces of the mangled lock fell to the ground, Fiona kept watch but saw no movement along the main road.

Resulting from the force of habit more than anything else, Andrew extracted the old semi-automatic Walther P38 that Alberto had given to him from his jacket pocket. One of almost 1.5 million units produced in Germany during World War 2, Alberto had bought the slightly scuffed 9mm weapon from a man at a flea market after his old property had been burned down. More than likely, it had been brought to Argentina by one of the fleeing Germans shortly after the end of the war, and judging from the fact that it was in almost mint condition, it had most likely spent the intervening decades lying in a box in someone's attic before finally being sold off as a near-antique curiosity. It was, however, still perfectly serviceable, as Andrew had discovered during a quick shooting trial at the back of Alberto's house. The only downsides were that it did not have a suppressor, and its magazine only held eight rounds. He had brought along another handful of cartridges from Alberto's illegal stash, but he was hoping that he wasn't going to need them. With a bit of luck, and exploiting the fact that the guards were going to be less than perfectly alert at this late hour, they just might be able to make their way inside and free the two captives and possibly also Alberto's niece without firing a single shot. Andrew knew from sometimes bitter experience with the Regiment that no plan ever survived contact with the enemy, but as long as they were prepared to improvise, having a plan and working towards a goal was a lot better than just winging it.

Andrew pulled open the door to the building, and when the two of them stepped inside, they were met by a cacophony of whirring and humming noises coming from a handful of large, hulking ventilation units sitting inside the dark space like huge organs deep in the bowels of a gigantic metal beast. Once the door was closed behind them, Andrew hit a light switch on the wall, and the large room was lit up brightly by banks of fluorescent lamps mounted under the ceiling about four metres above their heads. Emanating from the top of each ventilation unit was a large metal duct that reached up and penetrated the ceiling, connecting to the air-con units on the building's exterior.

'Wow,' said Fiona as she surveyed the noisy, whirring collection of large machines. 'That's a lot of air being cooled and pumped down into the ground.'

'And that can only mean one thing,' said Andrew. 'Whatever facility is down there must occupy a huge volume to require this much fresh air. Let's get to work.'

He stepped up to the nearest machine and flipped open the transparent plastic cover on its integrated control panel. Then he hit the large red stop button, and within a few seconds, the fans inside the machine had fallen silent, and its fan blades had stopped spinning. He then used the crowbar to loosen one of the metal panels making up the ventilation shaft that curved out from the machine and extended down into the concrete foundations of the building. Once he had pried it loose and created a narrow gap, he was able to grip the edge of the panel with his fingers and rip it off, creating a square opening that was roughly half a metre on either side.

'There,' he said. 'That should be just big enough for us to squeeze through. Let me have a look inside.'

Sticking his head through the opening and using a torch, he was able to see that the cylindrical ventilation shaft extended straight down towards the bottom.

'It's about fifteen metres straight down,' he said, turning to Fiona. 'Alberto's rope should be plenty long enough.'

Fiona reached inside the holdall and pulled out a thick, blue coiled-up nylon rope, which she handed to Andrew. He used a noose knot to tie it to a heavy-duty bolt attached to the bulky ventilation machine's cast iron exterior, and then he tossed it through the opening, after which it uncoiled itself as it dropped down through the shaft.

'Alright,' he said. 'I'll go first. Are you sure you're up for this? I know you're not a fan of small spaces.'

'Sure,' said Fiona with a quick nod, sounding somewhat less than convinced. 'I'll be okay.'

'Good,' said Andrew, wrapping the top of the rope around his lower arm. 'Just wrap the rope around your right arm like this, and then squeeze with your hand to manage your speed. Use your feet to press against the sides as well. That will give you more control.'

With his torch strapped to his chest and holding onto the rope with his right hand, Andrew climbed up and stuck his feet through the opening, allowing him to sit on the edge. Then he pushed himself inside, splayed his legs out to get a purchase on the inside of the shaft, and then he began lowering himself down. Fiona stuck her head through the opening to watch him descend, and as she did so, she saw that the nylon rope was already fraying slightly on the sharp metal edge of the vent opening.

After about a minute, Andrew reached the bottom of the shaft and found himself in a small space that continued on into a horizontal, rectangular vent system. The first long section of the vent that he was able to see was almost a metre wide, but it was less than half a metre in height. This meant that if they were going to continue through there, they would need to go down onto their fronts and crawl.

'Are you okay?' Fiona called, her voice reverberating down through the metal shaft.

'All good,' Andrew replied, indicating to his right with a slight chopping motion. 'The vent goes on in that direction. You can come down.'

Fiona gave him a thumbs up and pulled her head back out of the opening, giving the frayed bit of the rope a suspicious glance. It looked like it was going to hold. She then gripped it and coiled it around her arm the way Andrew had shown her, climbed up on the edge and wriggled herself through to press the soles of her trainers against the inside of the shaft. Holding on to the rope with her right hand and still gripping the edge of the opening with her left, she took a deep breath, and then she let go with her left hand and swapped over so she was now holding onto the rope with both. At that moment, her left foot slipped on the smooth steel of the shaft's interior, and she let out a yelp and hung there for a couple of seconds, clutching onto the rope while her feet scrambled for purchase. Once she had regained it, she began lowering herself slowly down towards the bottom where Andrew was waiting.

'Are you alright?' he asked.

'Yes, I'm fine,' she said, panting as she looked up through the dark tunnel to see the light from the shaft's opening above her. 'Are we all the way down?'

'I think so,' said Andrew, gesturing to the horizontal vent next to him. 'We're probably at the facility's ceiling. But we'll have to lie down and crawl from here.'

Fiona sank to her haunches and looked into the horizontal vent, wondering if she had made a big mistake following Andrew down here. But then she took a deep breath and steeled herself.

'Fine,' she said with a brief, determined nod. 'Let's continue.'

'I'll head in first and see if it's stable,' said Andrew. 'Stay here until I signal you. We don't know what's below this vent.'

Moving on his front, he began crawling inside the metal vent, and as he did so, he could feel it flex slightly under his weight. Crawling along at a slow and steady pace while alert for any sounds or sensations that might indicate that the vent was about to break open and drop him onto whatever was down below, he could hear the low-pitched hum of some heavy machinery that sounded like pumps, and he could feel a vague vibration coming through the sections of sheet metal from which the vent was made. After about five metres, he spotted a grille in the floor of the vent roughly five metres ahead. It was square and almost as wide as the vent itself, and a dim light seemed to be coming up through it. As he approached, the humming noise increased in intensity, and he also picked up the faint scent of ozone in the air, indicating that there was some sort of high-voltage electrical process going on nearby.

Upon reaching the grille, he turned off his torch and moved up close to it, taking care not to put any weight on it in case it might suddenly detach from the vent and fall down into the space below. Looking down through the slits in the grille, he saw a huge rectangular room some fifty by eighty metres in size, and it was at least ten metres from his vantage point down to the concrete floor below him. However, it was not the size of the room that took his breath away. It was the large and instantly familiar object sitting in the middle of it.

It was almost certainly the case that hardly anyone would have been able to recognise the roughly twenty-metre-wide domed cylinder protruding from the centre of the cavernous space. However, to someone like Andrew, who had spent years studying and staying abreast of threats from various weapons of mass destruction, there was no doubt in his mind as to what he was looking at.

'Holy shit,' he whispered, turning his head towards Fiona. 'There's a nuclear reactor here.'

'What?' said Fiona, sounding incredulous while trying to keep her voice down. 'What the hell is Rittenhausen doing with that?'

'Electricity,' Andrew replied. 'That portal of his needs massive amounts of power to operate, so this must be where he gets it from.'

'This would have cost billions to build,' said Fiona. 'And it must have taken years.'

As he gawped at the enormous room, trying to take in what he had just discovered, he also noticed that there was no sign of any workers there. He began moving his head around so as to be able to clearly see the rest of the reactor room through the narrow slits, and he spotted several other large pieces of heavy industrial equipment, including what appeared to be a heat exchanger positioned in one of the corners of the huge space. The vent he was inside was running under the ceiling along one of the walls, and it continued straight ahead and appeared to be passing directly over the heat exchanger. This gave him an idea.

'I'm going to move to the other end of this vent to try to open a grille there,' he said. 'I think we can get down that way.'

'What about me?' said Fiona.

'Move up to where I am now and keep watch,' said Andrew. 'If you see anyone, let me know.'

'Alright,' said Fiona, moving down onto her front and slowly beginning her crawl through the narrow, claustrophobic space.

While she made her way into the small space, gently putting her weight on the bottom of the suspended vent, Andrew pushed further along it, passing two more grilles and eventually arriving at a third that was directly above the top section of a large rectangular heat exchanger, where steaming hot water from the reactor was transferring that heat into a different set of pipes connected to turbines, which then generated electricity for the entire subterranean complex.

As he looked through the grille, he began to wonder how the reactor might be employed for powering the portal. Nuclear reactors produce very stable levels of power, and even a relatively small reactor like the one in this room would be capable of supplying enough electricity to power thousands of homes if it was ever put to that use. However, as far as he understood it, the very nature of particle accelerators, and even more so of the portal, whose basic design characteristics had been explained to him and Fiona by Alice Holbrook, required a relatively brief burst of vast amounts of power that a standard nuclear reactor was simply unable to produce. In other words, Rittenhausen's test facility had to encompass some sort of additional facility for storing and then releasing the energy in one massive surge.

As Fiona approached him, he pulled his hunting knife from its sheath and used it to pry open the grille.

It was fixed to the vent with small bolts, but using the knife as a lever, he was able to pop them loose, lift the grille up through the hole, and place it slightly further along the inside of the vent. Just as he stretched to place the grille, the section of the vent holding his weight suddenly jolted and flexed disconcertingly, producing a rumbling metallic warble.

'Stop there,' Andrew called back to Fiona as he showed her his palm. 'This section of the vent is unstable. You'll need to wait for me to climb down.'

'Okay,' said Fiona, immediately stopping and then remaining still. 'What can you see?'

'There's a big heat exchanger directly underneath this vent,' he said. 'We'll climb down onto it, and then make our way down to the floor at the back of it. I haven't seen anyone here yet, but there must be people working here twenty-four-seven. And there has to be a control room somewhere.'

'Won't they have CCTV?' said Fiona.

'Maybe,' said Andrew, 'but it is probably directed at the equipment. We might be able to slip through here undetected, and then hopefully there is a way through to the test facility and then the villa.'

'It feels like threading a needle,' said Fiona, her brow furrowing with a look of concern.

'I know,' said Andrew as he moved up to the hole where the grille had been, preparing to slip through. 'But it's still our best shot at getting to Holbrook and his daughter without anyone seeing us. Get ready to follow me down.'

Sticking his head through the opening to make sure no one was around, Andrew then pulled his knees up to his chest and pushed his feet through. Then he gripped the edge of the vent and allowed himself to slip down and out of the vent. Hanging by his fingers a couple of metres above the heat exchanger, he let go and landed on top of the solid metal casing of the large humming machine. He immediately pulled out the Walther P38 and thumbed the safety off. Lying down flat on his front, he moved out to the edge and made sure that the coast was still clear. Then he signalled for Fiona to come down.

She swung her legs through, and as she slid down through the opening, she used one hand to pull the loose grille with her and place it back over the hole as neatly as she could while hanging by one hand. Then she let herself drop, landed cat-like next to Andrew and immediately went prone.

'Nice work,' said Andrew. 'Well done. Now, let's get off this thing and find the way to the villa.'

Twenty-Four

Alberto Garcia walked out of his house with Baltasar by his side and headed for his two sheds. Slung over one arm was a shotgun that he had used to hunt quail in his younger days, and the left pocket of his dungarees was bulging with high-velocity shotgun cartridges designed for fast birds. The smaller of the two sheds contained all of his many tools, and it was from here that Andrew had selected a handful of different pieces of equipment for his and Fiona's mission several hours earlier. The second shed was much larger, and whereas most men might have kept a beloved car in such a space, Alberto stored the only piece of farm machinery that he had managed to salvage from his old house after the fire. A cherished old tractor. It was a dark green 1962 Massey Ferguson 35, which, for its relatively minor size, was a powerful little beast, and it had served him well ever since he had bought it. Designed and built to last, its diesel engine had worked flawlessly for decades, and the only things he had ever been forced to swap out were the tyres, but even then, this had only happened once. Whether the trusty old machine would make it back to the shed in one piece later that night was still an open question, but even if it didn't, it would be a small price to pay for the prospect of seeing Ferdinand von Rittenhausen being given a serious kick in the balls. And to Alberto, the appearance of Andrew and Fiona represented the best prospect of that happening ever since that diminutive, jumped-up little vinegar-brewing *Aleman* had taken his livelihood from him.

Slinging the shotgun over his shoulder, Alberto unlocked the heavy and slightly rusty padlock that was keeping the shed's double doors locked. He then pulled at both doors and allowed them to swing fully open. Sitting inside the darkness, lit only faintly by the moonlight and the light coming from the open door to his house, was the green tractor that almost always put a smile on his face when he looked at it. How such a small, inanimate object could seem so alive to him was a bit of a mystery, but perhaps it was its large, round headlights that looked like eyes or its perennial readiness to work hard. Maybe it was its somewhat temperamental performance in very cold weather unless treated in a particular and gentle manner. Or perhaps it was its apparent loyalty and refusal to quit, even many decades after it should have outlived its usefulness and given up the ghost. Either way, he loved the little machine, and he suddenly felt that there was probably nothing the world could throw at it that it wouldn't be able to survive.

He walked inside the shed and mounted the tractor, put the thin metal key in the ignition, depressed the clutch and turned the key. The starter motor turned over laboriously three times, sounding as if the machine thought it was too late in the day to begin work, but then the diesel engine suddenly sprang to life, sending a plume of grey smoke out of its exhaust, after which it settled down and began chucking away as it idled happily.

Alberto made sure the smaller gearstick was set to 'Low Gear', and then he put the regular lever into 1st gear and slowly released the clutch. The tractor trundled forward, and once it was clear of the shed, he then backed it up towards a rusty 3-furrow plough sitting next to the shed, positioning the tractor so that its three-point hitch was aligned almost perfectly with the metal pins on the plough. Leaving the engine idling, he hopped off the machine and walked back around one of the large rear tyres to complete the attachment. Once done, he climbed back up into the driver's seat and engaged the hydraulic lifting mechanism.

The mechanism had only just finished lifting the plough up to its elevated position when a set of powerful headlights swept across Alberto's gravelled front yard. As he turned his head, he was blinded by the bright lights, but the engine of the vehicle arriving immediately gave away who it was. The purring, impatient-sounding V-6 engine was that of a Porche 911, and the driver could only be Hector Navarro.

With his hands still on the large steering wheel of the Massey Ferguson, Alberto froze in the driver's seat as the Porsche came to a stop directly in front of him at a distance of less than ten metres. He could hear the muffled thumping of music coming from inside the vehicle, and for several seconds, nothing happened. Then the driver's side door opened, and a large, muscular figure wearing a light beige suit stepped out. Alberto grimaced and squinted as he tried to look at Hector's face, but as the thug stepped forward and stood in front of his car, whose engine was still running, all Alberto could see was the dark, faceless silhouette of the man who had taken everything from him.

With faint swirls of dry dust moving in the air in front of the Porsche's headlights, Hector stood with his feet planted half a metre apart, his hands placed on his hips, and his chin raised as he looked at the old man.

'*Hola, Viejo!*' called Hector coarsely, using the slang term for an old-timer. '*Buenas noches.*'

Alberto couldn't believe it. Not only was Hector turning up here as if nothing had happened, but he had decided to do so just when he was about to...

A sudden chill ran down his spine. Had Hector somehow got wind of what was about to happen? Had someone been watching him and seen Andrew and Fiona come to his house? He didn't have to wait long for an answer.

'You had visitors, old man,' said Hector, using the crass local dialect that gave away his upbringing on the mean streets of Mendoza City. 'Do you know who those people really are?'

Alberto said nothing but just sat immobile on his tractor and stared at the silhouette in front of him. Several long seconds ticked by, during which time Hector looked like he was expecting some sort of response, but Alberto remained silent.

Hector tilted his head slightly to one side and reached inside his suit jacket with his right hand. It emerged a couple of seconds later holding a large, heavy-looking pistol, which he immediately pointed straight at Alberto. The old man's knuckles turned white as his fingers gripped the steering wheel tightly, and his jaw was clenched as he stared down the thug. But there was no way he was going to let this sewer rat intimidate him. Not anymore.

'Listen to me now, my friend,' said Hector with menacing calmness. 'You are going to come down from that old pile of junk, and then you will tell me what you three were talking about. *Comprende?* I am going to count to three, and if you have not come down, then you'll lose your stupid old head.'

Alberto's breathing was quickening, and his mouth turned into a narrow strip as he pressed his lips together in barely contained fury. He stared straight at where he knew Hector's eyes to be, and then his left hand moved to the switch controlling the tractor's large headlight. Then he produced a quick whistle. What felt like only an instant later, the white, growling shape of Baltasar bolted up alongside the tractor and launched himself through the air towards Hector Navarro. At the same time, in one swift movement, Alberto flicked the switch for the headlights, pressed down the clutch and shunted the gear lever into 2nd gear. As soon as he felt the lever slot into place, he immediately released the clutch, and the tractor leapt forward.

With Hector's face now lit up by the headlights, Alberto could clearly see the shock and surprise on his face. Shock at finding himself suddenly vulnerable, and surprise at the old man in front of him not folding and complying in the way that he was used to people doing when he beat his chest and waved his gun around.

Blinded by the headlights and caught off guard, Hector never managed to get a shot off before Baltasar reached him and barged straight into his chest, snapping at his throat. An instant later, the dog was gone, and Hector instinctively threw himself to one side to get out of the way of the oncoming metal beast. By the time he landed painfully on the gravel and rolled out of the way, the small front wheels of Alberto's tractor had mounted the bonnet of the white Porsche, and a second later, the farming machine had driven up onto the German sportscar, crushing much of its bodywork as its headlights exploded and winked out. Before Hector could fully take in what was happening, the Massey Ferguson was driving off the other end of the car, and then Alberto dropped the plough. The three large steel blades slammed down into the soft, curved sheet metal and began carving one huge furrow through the plush upholstered interior.

Only then did Hector regain his composure and get back on his feet. Still clutching his pistol, he staggered upright and threw up his hand to fire at Alberto, who had yanked the gear lever into neutral and was now lifting himself out of the driver's seat to take cover. Hector only managed to squeeze off a single badly aimed round when Baltasar emerged like a white missile streaking through the cool night air. With his powerful jaws open and his jagged teeth gleaming in the light, the dog had timed the jump to perfection. His jaws clamped down around Hector's wrist, and the thug produced a panicked roar as the dog bit down hard. With upwards of 500 pounds per square inch of pressure, or similar to the hydraulic system lifting the tractor's plough, Baltazar's sharp back teeth cut through the skin, sliced Hector's tendons, and crunched straight through his wrist bones, severing the hand from his arm. As Baltasar landed, the bleeding hand was still in his mouth, but the gun fell out of it and onto the gravel. Hector let out a bloodcurdling scream as he watched the blood squirt out of the stump where his hand used to be. As he fell to his knees clutching the stump, he caught sight of Alberto moving behind the tractor's large rear wheel, and then he launched himself towards his pistol. Ignoring the mind-numbing pain of his injury, he managed to scrabble forward and pick up the pistol with his left hand, and as soon as he had swung it around to point at the tractor, he began firing a hail of bullets towards it. 9mm projectiles slammed into the tractor's bodywork, and one or two of them even hit the engine, but none of them did any material damage. After only a few seconds, the magazine was empty, and Hector grimaced and grunted in pain as he reached for the spare mag that was sitting in his belt. However, all he ended up doing was shoving his bleeding stump onto his shirt, and he roared in pain and frustration as blood soaked through his expensive clothes.

Still holding the gun in his left hand, he used it to try to reach for the magazine, and he managed to extract it from his belt. He pressed the magazine release catch on the pistol, and the empty mag clattered to the ground. He then tried to load the fresh mag into the magazine well by holding it in his teeth, but the mag merely slipped out and fell onto the gravel.

At that moment, out of the corner of his eye, he spotted two old cowboy boots enter his field of vision. When he looked up with a deranged and furious look on his face, he saw a disturbingly calm-looking Alberto standing there with his shotgun cradled in his hands and a snarling Baltasar by his side, his own hand still in the beast's blood-smeared mouth.

'*Chamaco*,' said Alberto icily, using the slang term for a kid. 'You took the most important thing from me. My purpose. Now I have nothing.'

Hector grimaced and grunted derisively as he glared through the pain up at the old man.

'I am glad I took your shitty winery from you,' he hissed. '*Hijo de pu…*'

Before Hector could finish the insult, a loud boom rang out across the nearby vineyards, and a tight group of shotgun pellets exploded out of the barrel, covering the distance to Hector's head in a fraction of a second and taking it clean off. His headless body remained upright for a brief moment, but then it toppled over onto the ground as blood continued to ooze out of the severed neck for about a minute, but then even that stopped.

'You don't get to insult my mother,' he said, spitting on Hector's body.

He stood over the last of the two Navarro brothers for a long time, contemplating all that had led up to this and what this killing might mean for the future. But in the end, he decided that none of that mattered now. He then turned around and looked at the smoking carnage of the Porsche, and he glanced once again at the body of the dead and mutilated thug. Then he turned to regard the tractor, whose indomitable engine was still ticking over, and whose headlights were still shining brightly. That was the moment when he decided that the little machine needed a name, and he knew exactly what to call it. '*Valiente*'.

★   ★   ★

Emerging from behind the huge heat exchanger inside the reactor room, Andrew and Fiona approached a central walkway that was suspended about a metre off the floor and orientated along the length of it. The tall cylindrical reactor itself was towering over them, and Fiona couldn't help but feel that somehow the radioactive materials inside it were pushing out through its exterior and permeating the entire room. Logically, she knew that almost certainly wasn't true, but her fear of harmful radiation was deep-seated, and despite realising the room was almost certainly perfectly safe to move around in, she couldn't wait to get out of there.

With Andrew out in front, holding the Walther P38 in his right hand, ready to engage, they moved along the walkway and approached a set of open double doors that led to a long rectangular corridor with walls painted dark grey. Next to the doors on the wall was a clothes rack with several sets of white lab coats and a couple of orange hard hats. They both slipped into a lab coat and picked up a helmet from the rack. At least from a distance, this might help them blend in for long enough not to be noticed by guards or other people working in the facility.

The dark grey corridor was lit by a series of wall-mounted lights, and at the far end of it, some thirty metres away, were another set of identical double doors.

'We need to move through this,' said Andrew. 'It's the only way out of here.'

'What if someone comes the other way?' said Fiona.

'Then we'll improvise,' said Andrew.

Moving swiftly but without running, the two of them advanced through the corridor and arrived at the second set of double doors without incident. Andrew pushed up to stand close to the doors and nudged one of them open a crack, allowing him to see into the next room. It looked nothing like the reactor room. It was marginally smaller with the same high ceilings, but it was filled across eight levels with hundreds of metal cylinders arranged in groups of six, all of which were connected to massive power cables that curved up under the ceiling and disappeared into the wall at the far end of the room.

'What do you see?' said Fiona, coming to stand close behind him.

'I think this is a giant capacitor array,' said Andrew. 'They use the nuclear reactor to charge it up, and then they rapidly discharge all of that electricity through those huge cables to power the portal for a short time. That would fit with what Alice told us about how that thing is supposed to work.'

'Is there anyone in there?' said Fiona.

'Yes,' said Andrew, leaning to one side to be able to scan the whole room. 'There's a couple of scientist types walking away from us along the centre aisle. And it looks like there's some sort of control room up on the wall to our right. I can see three people behind the glass. One of them looks like some type of uniformed guard. I am sure there are more than one. Oh, and I see a large countdown timer up on the far wall.'

Fiona moved closer and peeked through the gap past the capacitor arrays to the other end of the room, some forty metres away. Above yet another set of closed double doors was a large digital display with red numbers counting down one second at a time.

'00:08:32,' said Fiona. 'Eight and a half minutes until… what?'

'It might be counting down to a test of the portal,' said Andrew. 'Shit. I thought this place would be deserted by now.'

'Looks like they picked tonight to run a test,' said Fiona. 'It's going to be crawling with people. Should we abort?'

'No,' said Andrew. 'We're committed now. It's now or never. But we need to get past the test chamber so we can reach the villa, and we can't do that with people up in that control room. They'll see us walking through here, and they might realise that we don't belong here.'

'Is there another way?' said Fiona.

'I can't tell from here,' said Andrew, peering along the centre aisle as the two figures dressed in lab coats disappeared through the double doors. 'But maybe we won't need it.'

'What do you mean?' said Fiona. 'How are we going to get past?'

'I am going to hit the control room,' said Andrew. 'Make sure no one there can raise the alarm.'

'Alright,' said Fiona as she adjusted the orange hard hat that was slightly too big for her head. 'Just be careful.'

Andrew slipped out of the corridor and into the capacitor array room, walking purposefully along the centre aisle as if he had done that thousands of times before. As he walked away, Fiona was watching him nervously through the small gap between the double doors. When he was halfway along the centre aisle, he took a right turn up to a single door directly below the control room windows. When he walked through it and disappeared from view, Fiona exhaled deeply in an attempt to calm herself, and then she directed her gaze up towards the window, where she could just make out a couple of people moving around.

*   *   *

Inside the portal test chamber, Adam Holbrook was manning the central control terminal, surrounded by a small team of technicians who each had their own very specific responsibilities regarding systems monitoring and software management during the upcoming test. The enormous cavernous space hummed with noise from the many pieces of high-powered equipment installed there, and the portal stood in the middle of it like the ring of a giant. All of its sub-components were activated, and a perpetual sequence of blue lights was running along the inside of it, indicating the focal points of the magnetic fields that would shortly be trapping and accelerating huge amounts of protons to mind-boggling relativistic speeds.

Rittenhausen had ensured that there were a handful of his uniformed guards placed in various locations inside the test chamber, and immediately behind Holbrook was the head of security, Raul Torres. The professor glanced surreptitiously back at him. He was a brute of a man, physically strong and loyal like an attack dog. But much worse than that, he had eyes that glinted with ill-concealed malice, and the covetous way in which he had regarded Alice had sent a cold shiver down Holbrook's spine.

He glanced up at the large digital timer sitting on the wall just below the observation room. It was now just over seven minutes until the test would commence. Looking through the large glass panes into the observation room, he could see Alice standing by the window, surrounded by two guards wearing the now familiar dark grey and orange uniforms. Even from down here on the floor of the test chamber, he could see the bruising on her face, and it was clear that she looked anxious and distraught. Next to her was Rittenhausen with his new squad of three mean-looking Russian guns for hire. The muscular trio were wearing black t-shirts and ballistic vests, and they each carried a shoulder holster with a pistol strapped into it. The implication was clear. If he didn't do exactly as he had been told, or if the test failed because of him, Alice would pay the price. Feeling a pit of foreboding darkness gnawing at him somewhere deep in his stomach, Holbrook produced a heavy sigh and worked his jaw as he tried to mobilise all of his self-restraint. He had to remain calm and continue focusing on the upcoming test.

'Attention all personnel,' said one of the technicians into a microphone, his voice amplified through all the speakers in the entire subterranean complex. 'Portal test commences in seven minutes. Portal test in T minus seven minutes.'

Holbrook tried to shut down his own emotions as he stared at the multiple displays in front of him showing telemetry data from the portal, the capacitor array and the nuclear reactor. Everything looked nominal, and he then began to punch in the optimal values for the magnetic field generators. Once they were set, he signalled for the rest of the team to perform their final diagnostics routines. He desperately wanted this test to work, not because he wanted to have any part in Rittenhausen's deranged plans, but because he needed to have his daughter back. More than anything, he just needed her to be safe. And if that meant going along with this test, then so be it. More than ever now, he realised that she was the only thing in this world that truly mattered to him.

Twenty-Five

With his P38 in a two-handed grip out in front of himself, Andrew moved cautiously and quietly up the stairwell, checking corners carefully as he went. As he neared the top landing where a door led into the control room he had observed from below in the capacitor array room, he double-checked his pistol to make sure there was a round in the chamber and that the safety was off.

He moved up to stand next to the door behind which he knew there was at least one armed guard in addition to two scientists. With his eyes narrowed as he exhaled slowly through his nose, he pulled back the hammer on the pistol and focused his mind in preparation for the breach, and then he gripped the door handle with his left hand and pushed open the door. Now practically on autopilot, and with the speed and aggression that had been instilled in every fibre of his body since his time in active service with the Regiment, he burst into the room with the pistol raised, moving quickly and ready to fire at any threat at a moment's notice.

'Nobody move!' he shouted, pointing the gun at the control room's three occupants and using his voice to intimidate them. 'Hands above your heads.'

The two scientists by the control terminals, who had been busy overseeing the huge capacitor array, did little except turn their heads and raise their hands nervously into the air. However, the guard in the grey and orange uniform was less compliant. As soon as he heard Andrew's voice, his right hand reached down to the sidearm attached to his belt. As he turned to face the intruder, Andrew could see in his eyes that he fancied his chances against what looked like a civilian holding an ancient pistol. Dropping to one knee as he pulled the pistol from its holster, thereby betraying the fact that he had at least some firearms training, the guard then brought up the weapon to aim and fire, but he never got close to pulling the trigger.

Even before the weapon left its holster and came up to point at him, Andrew had clocked the movement in the guard's shoulders and right arm, and he was ready. His weapon arced around and aligned with the man's centre mass. Then Andrew pulled the trigger three times in quick succession, and the P38 barked angrily every time. The trio of 9mm bullets smacked into the guard's chest, causing his arms to flail as his body was pushed back over his feet, sending him thudding heavily onto his back. His legs spasmed a few times, and he rasped for breath as his chest heaved and his back arced. Then a protracted gurgling noise emanated from his throat, after which he finally lay still.

'*Madre de Dios!*' one of the scientists whispered with a trembling voice, invoking the Virgin Mary, as he and his stunned colleague turned to look at the dead man on the floor behind them. 'Please. Don't shoot. We just work here.'

'So did he,' said Andrew coldly, taking off his hard hat, jerking his head towards the dead guard, and then pointing the pistol back at them. 'Take off your coats. I need to make sure that you're not armed.'

The two men instantly sprang into frantic action to comply with the order they had been given, at which point Andrew once again raised his voice to the commanding tone he had used countless times with new recruits in the SAS.

'Slowly!' he said. 'I don't want to shoot any of you unless I really have to.'

The two nervous scientists froze for a brief moment as they exchanged glances, and then they slowly continued taking their coats off, dropping them on the floor and turning around slowly to allow Andrew to verify that they presented no threat. With their hands still above their heads, they finished a full rotation and came to a stop, anxiously eyeing the guard, who was now lying in an expanding pool of his own blood. It was clear that the only thing the two men were in possession of was a mortal fear of the intruder turning his gun on them too.

Without lowering his weapon, Andrew then moved sideways towards a small seating area by the back wall consisting of a small sofa, two armchairs and a coffee table next to a water cooler and an instant coffee machine. There was also a floor lamp with a long power cable coming out of the wall. He bent down and pulled the plug from the socket, and then he ripped the power cable out of the lamp. He then threw the length of cable to one of the scientists and pointed at his colleague.

'Use one end to tie him up,' he said. 'Arms behind his back.'

The two scientists immediately complied, and a few seconds later, one of them had his hands tied behind his back. Andrew then used the other end of the cable to secure the other man's hands in a similar fashion, and then he tied the two together. It was likely that they would be able to wriggle out of their restraints given enough time, but Andrew felt confident that such an act was the very last thing on their minds at that moment.

He ordered them to sit down on the floor with their backs leaning against each other, and then he walked over to the dead guard and plucked the pistol from his hands. It was a modern semi-automatic SIG Sauer P226 with which Andrew was very familiar since it was part of the standard kit in the Regiment. He released the magazine to discover that, unlike the Walther P38, this pistol had been chambered for the 0.40 Smith and Wesson cartridge. Being larger and weighing almost fifty percent more than a 9mm Parabellum, it had considerably more stopping power, but at the cost of fewer rounds in the magazine. However, the mag was full, which meant that there were 15 rounds in the gun. He then decided to search the guard and found a full spare magazine in his belt, which he stuck into a back pocket.

Getting back up, he walked over to the control consoles by the window overlooking the capacitor array room and leaned forward to study them. They displayed a multitude of readouts from different instruments and pieces of equipment, and they included a graphic representation of all of the capacitor arrays and their individual charge levels. From the data on the screens, it was clear that the entire array was fully charged and prepped to deliver an enormous surge of electricity. In other words, the complex system that had been built to power the portal was like a bow with its string drawn. It was ready to fire.

He then turned towards an open gun cabinet that was mounted on the wall next to the door. It contained three black M16 assault rifles that were sitting in a rack, ready to be pulled out and used. He picked one from the rack and pressed down on the two takedown pins on one side to separate the lower receiver from the upper receiver. Then he grabbed the charging handle, extracted the bolt carrier and picked out the firing pin retainer. The firing pin promptly dropped out of the back of the bolt carrier and into his palm, and he put it in his pocket. A few seconds later, he had repeated the exercise with another M16, and now none of those two weapons would fire, even in the unlikely event of the two scientists suddenly changing their minds and deciding to put up a fight. Picking the third rifle from the gun cabinet, he then walked back over to the two men, who sat watching him silently with faces that told him that they were prepared to do just about anything to be able to leave the control room alive.

'Do. Not. Move,' Andrew said, giving them a hard stare and then deciding to hoodwink them. 'If any of my teammates see you in those windows, they'll use their rifles and your heads to play whack-a-mole. Is that clear?'

'Yes,' both of the men said in unison, nodding their heads vigorously.

'And once I am gone,' continued Andrew, 'you'll have no recollection of what I look like. Also clear?'

More nodding.

'Good,' said Andrew. 'Now, all you two have to do is sit here and be quiet, and nothing will happen to you.'

With those words, he left the control room carrying the M16 and headed down the stairs to meet up with Fiona again. At that moment, the disembodied voice on the speaker system once again sounded throughout the test facility.

'Portal test commences in three minutes. Portal test in T minus three minutes.'

★   ★   ★

Driving along under the moonlight on one of the narrow poplar-lined roads that cut through Mendoza's wine region, Alberto steered the old Massey Ferguson through the night with its headlight switched off. Flakes of white paint still stuck to the blades of the raised plough at the rear of the tractor, but its job for this evening was not yet done. With Baltasar running along by his side, his loaded shotgun slung over his shoulder, and the cool evening air moving through his hair and filling his lungs, he felt more alive than ever, despite the risk of what he was about to do.

He took a right turn at a higher speed than he would normally have done, and the tractor wobbled slightly but stayed on the road. Then he yanked at the throttle again and picked up speed once more. A couple of minutes later, he arrived at the gates of Villa Magdalena, where, instead of slowing down, he switched on the headlight, veered off the road and crashed right through the tall fence to Rittenhausen's estate.

With its large rear tyres digging into the ground and continuously propelling it forward, the small tractor seemed unstoppable as it tore through the fence as if it wasn't even there. Driving over its remnants and tearing it into pieces as it went, the tractor continued into the vineyard on the other side, and then Alberto did what he had dreamt of doing ever since that day when Hector and Ernesto had torched his home and his livelihood. He gunned the throttle to full, reached down to the handle by his left side, and then he released the plough.

As the tractor roared along through the vineyard, the one-tonne heavy metal farm tool slammed down onto the ground, where it immediately dug itself in. As the tractor continued barreling through the neat rows of grapevines, it ripped up the soil and turned it over, leaving three deep furrows cutting through the neat vineyard. When Alberto neared the fence on the far side, he lifted the plough out of the ground, swung the tractor around and then lowered the plough again. Soon, surrounded by a cloud of dust and flying debris from the torn-up vines, he had carved several deep gashes across the vineyard, wrecking hundreds of expensive plants as he tore mercilessly through the winery's most prized assets.

Suddenly, a floodlight was switched on near the villa a couple of hundred metres away, and it was soon followed by another. Within seconds, they had both been directed towards Alberto and his tractor, and then two pickup trucks parked by the villa suddenly roared to life. Switching on their headlights, they immediately began making their way out of the main driveway along a dirt track towards him.

Upon seeing them, Alberto steered the tractor away from the cars in a way that would allow him to circle back towards the villa, and after another minute or so, he tore through the neatly manicured hedges making up the perimeter of the villa's gardens. The plough made short work of the immaculate laws and neat footpaths as it tore straight across them, and a few moments later, the tractor had crashed through the hedge on the other side and continued its rampage through another vineyard.

Sitting at the wheel with a wide grin on his face, Alberto was loving every second of it, but then the shooting started. The first he knew of it was when a bullet smacked into the rear left metal wheel guard and ricocheted off into the night sky with a loud whine. Alberto ducked down as low as he could but continued steering the tractor in a wild and unpredictable pattern through the vineyard. As much as he had enjoyed his wanton act of destruction and sabotage, he knew that it would soon be time to retreat if he was going to have a chance at getting out of there alive. As he approached the estate's perimeter fence, he reached down to the lever by his side and got ready to lift the plough back up. Once he was back outside, he would detach the plough, switch off the headlights and disappear into the night.

★   ★   ★

Andrew and Fiona moved swiftly along the centre aisle in the capacitor array room, heading for the closed double doors at the other end. Tucked under Andrew's lab coat along his right leg was the loaded, approximately one-metre-long M16 assault rifle that he had pulled from the gun cabinet. They inched open the doors to find a small empty space from which two tunnels with curved ceilings roughly three metres above the floor led off in two separate directions. Affixed to the wall were two metal signs. One read 'Portal Test Chamber', while the other read 'Transit System'.

'We're close,' said Andrew. 'The transit system must be what they use to go back and forth between here and the villa.'

'Let's push straight ahead to the test chamber,' said Fiona. 'If they are about to conduct a test, the professor is bound to be there.'

'Good point,' said Andrew, pushing the door fully open. 'Let's try to find some sort of vantage point.'

With Andrew in front cradling the M16 and Fiona following close behind, they proceeded straight ahead along the tunnel leading to the test chamber, and after about fifteen metres, it made a ninety-degree turn to the right, after which a stairwell led up what seemed to be about one floor. Then it turned left again, after which they were met by a closed door that was painted dark red, and as they approached it, the now familiar voice came over the speaker system again.

'Portal test commences in two minutes. Portal test in T minus two minutes.'

Andrew stopped at the door, reached inside his jacket for the SIG Sauer P226, and handed it to Fiona along with the spare magazine.

'Take this gun,' he said. 'The safety is here, and the mag release is there. Point and shoot.'

Fiona took the heavy steel and aluminium pistol and shifted it from one hand to the other to feel its weight. Then she looked at Andrew.

'I really hope I won't have to use this thing,' she said with a hint of trepidation and anxiety in her eyes.

'Me too,' said Andrew. 'Think of it as a parachute. It's better to have one and not need it than to need it and not have it. Ready?'

'Ready,' nodded Fiona.

He gripped the door handle, pulled the door open a crack, and found himself looking across a metre-wide, raised metal walkway. It had guardrails along the edge, and beyond it, he could see down into an enormous circular space built from concrete. Above them was a huge dome studded with hundreds of lights that were attached to the curving ceiling. Roughly ten metres below the walkway and placed in the middle of the concrete floor was a ring-shaped contraption roughly ten metres across. Made from some type of metal, it was sitting on a raised concrete platform, and it looked to be crammed full of electrical instruments and components that all had multiple wires looping out from it. Although familiar in shape to what he and Fiona had found inside the test chamber in Bergkristall, it was clearly a much more advanced piece of equipment. More importantly, it was pulsating slowly from lights mounted on its circumference, and along its inside edge ran a rapid sequence of lights that circled the entire ring every few seconds.

Directly in front of it was a mobile walkway similar to those allowing passengers to board an aircraft. It was mounted on a large, hydraulic-operated metal lattice arm, at the end of which stood a technician wearing a white lab coat. He appeared to be checking a dark spherical object, which Andrew assumed was about to be sent through the portal. The sphere had been placed on a small ramp at the end of the walkway, from which it would most likely be shot into the portal once it had been activated.

'Look at this,' whispered Andrew, scanning the huge cavernous space. 'Rittenhausen's portal facility.'

'It's so much bigger than the one we saw in Austria,' said Fiona, craning her neck to look down at the portal. 'This is an incredible place.'

There were about a handful of uniformed guards spread throughout the chamber, and near the far side was what appeared to be the rail transit system that provided transport back to Rittenhausen's villa. Next to the rail was a short platform, and a small white-painted carriage with capacity for about eight people was parked there. Directly in front of the platform and down on the test chamber floor was a control station manned by three people in lab coats. One of them was Adam Holbrook, and off to one side, flanked by two large men wearing black t-shirts, slacks and carrying assault rifles, was Ferdinand von Rittenhausen.

'That's Professor Holbrook,' Andrew whispered, pointing through the narrow gap between the door and the doorframe. 'And Rittenhausen is with him.'

'And Alice is over there!' Fiona exclaimed, trying to keep her voice down.

Andrew had been so focused on the sight of the portal, Holbrook and Rittenhausen that he had completely missed that directly across from their position was a set of three large windows behind which was what looked like a glass-fronted meeting room. It contained a long table with chairs, but there was also a set of larger chairs lined up so that anyone sitting in them could look out of the windows and down into the chamber. Alice was standing by the window with her hands tied together in front of her, and she looked like an empty shell of the spritely young woman they had met in Geneva mere days ago. Her head hung low on her chest, and her hair looked tousled and unkempt, and even from across the test chamber, Andrew could see bruising on her face. Towering over and standing directly behind her was another large black-clad thug with an assault rifle. From his position, Andrew could see that the walkway in front of him curved around the wall of the chamber roughly ten metres above the floor and continued all the way over to near the windows behind which Alice and the thug were standing. Along the way, there were a couple of closed red doors similar to the one they were hiding behind, and there was another door just metres from the three large windows.

Suddenly, several of the guards appeared to become jittery, and one of them, who looked to be some sort of team leader, swiftly moved to Rittenhausen's side and spoke into his ear. Rittenhausen looked agitated and issued an order, after which the team leader, followed by the other uniformed comrades, all headed up the stairs to the transit system platform where they entered the small carriage.

'It looks like Alberto came through for us,' said Andrew, glancing at his wristwatch. 'The timing couldn't have been better.'

Down on the test chamber floor, Holbrook had turned to see what the commotion was all about, and Rittenhausen immediately marched up to him and seemed to fling a bunch of angry words at his face. As he did so, he gesticulated up towards Alice standing behind the window with the menacing shape of the goon behind her. Holbrook clearly got the message because he nodded and turned back to focus on the telemetry displayed on the control console in front of him.

The disembodied voice suddenly rang out once again, and the sound reverberated loudly through the gigantic man-made concrete cave as the mobile walkway began retracting away from the centre of the portal.

'Portal test commences in one minute. Portal test in T minus one minute.'

'What do we do?' whispered Fiona anxiously. 'The test is about to start.'

'We can't do anything about the professor right now,' said Andrew, 'but maybe I can get to Alice.'

'You're just going to walk over there?' said Fiona incredulously.

'Everyone in this chamber is focused on that portal,' he said. 'No one's going to pay attention to a man in a lab coat walking along this walkway. At least, I hope not.'

The voice on the speaker system returned.

'Portal test in T minus thirty seconds.'

'Whatever you're planning to do, you need to do it fast,' said Fiona. 'We're running out of time.'

'Alright,' said Andrew. 'Here goes nothing.'

He rose to his full height, tucked the M16 back inside his lab coat, pulled his shoulders back and adjusted the hard hat. Then he opened the door and slipped out onto the walkway. Down below, the lights on the inside edge of the portal were now spinning faster and faster. At the same time, the air inside the test chamber began to fill with a strangely disorientating mix of a deep hum and a high-pitched warble that kept rising as the light sequence sped up. When Andrew was roughly halfway along the walkway towards the door leading to the room where Alice was being kept, small flashes of light began to emanate from inside the centre of the portal as if manifesting from thin air and sending brief bursts of pure white light out in all directions inside the chamber.

'T minus twenty seconds.'

Andrew reached the red door, placed his hand on the door handle and pushed inside. As the door swung shut behind him and the bearded thug turned his head to look at the intruder, Andrew silently took several steps inside the room to get away from the windows. In one fluid movement that lasted no more than a second, he then ripped his hard hat off, flung open the lab coat, lifted up the M16, pressed it into his shoulder and aimed it squarely at the chest of the large man. However, the black-clad goon had somehow sensed that something was wrong, and as Andrew's weapon came out from under his lab coat, he grabbed Alice by the back of her neck, moved swiftly to one side, and pulled her roughly in front of himself, causing her to produce a startled yelp. Using the young woman as a human shield, the hulking man then smirked as he brought up his own weapon to point back at the armed trespasser.

'You're too slow for Viktor,' he grunted in a heavy Russian accent as a sneery smile spread across his face.

As he spoke, he was backing up against the window, looking briefly over his shoulder to glance down into the test chamber, where the portal was now resembling a roiling vortex of swirling light, and brilliant tendrils of electricity began shooting out from its perimeter and curving back towards the device.

'T minus 10. 9. 8…'

Suddenly, Alice raised her head to look straight at Andrew. From the look on her face, she clearly recognised him instantly, and then she spoke in a voice that was almost chillingly calm.

'You know what we physicists like to say?' she said, glancing sideways towards the window behind her. 'Gravity is a bitch.'

Andrew immediately understood what she meant, and he watched as Alice surreptitiously brought her left hand up to her chest with her thumb, index finger and middle finger outstretched. As the voice on the speaker system continued to count down towards zero, Alice retracted one finger for each second.

'3. 2. 1. Initiate.'

At that moment, Alice's legs suddenly folded beneath her as she allowed her body to slump down towards the floor. The muscular Russian thug still had a firm grip on the back of her neck, but even he instantly lost the battle against gravity as he failed to keep her upright.

As a brilliant flash of light suddenly exploded out from the centre of the portal down below, Andrew pulled the trigger, and the M16 rattled off a rapid three-round burst of gunfire that tore into Viktor's chest. Two of them smacked into the ballistics vest and jolted him backwards, while the third bullet zipped past the edge of the vest and slammed into the top of his sternum, ripping through his windpipe and spine before exploding out the other side and shattering the window directly behind him. The force of the three impacts was enough for him to release his grip on Alice and be shoved back hard, and if the window had still been intact, it might have stopped him. However, with the glass having been turned into hundreds of shards glinting in the light, the momentum of his body carried him out through the opening. Andrew was now already moving towards Alice to make sure that she was unharmed. At the same time, Viktor tumbled out of the opening and continued down, falling roughly ten metres to the floor below where his head smacked violently into the concrete, cracking his skull as a spray of blood shot out onto the floor nearby.

The brilliant flash that had temporarily almost blinded everyone inside the test chamber had been caused by the dark carbon sphere being shunted into the centre of the whirling portal, instantaneously being transported to a location about ten metres away. Now that the portal had powered down and returned to being an empty ring, its high-pitched whine falling and receding in intensity, all eyes inside the test chamber had been directed towards the nearby cube-shaped water tank where the carbon sphere was now floating exactly in the middle of it. After a few seconds, it slowly began to sink down towards the bottom, but by then Rittenhausen and his staff had realised that one of the three Russian close protection team members was lying dead in a pool of blood surrounded by glass shards some twenty metres away.

Everyone inside the test chamber directed their attention towards the missing window above, and after a couple of seconds, Andrew suddenly emerged with the M16 pressed into his shoulder, aiming at the group of people below. He was about to shout a command for Rittenhausen to step forward and then for Professor Holbrook to move clear of the two technicians by his side, but he never got that far. Upon seeing their dead team leader on the floor, the other two seemingly fearless Russian thugs, Stanislav and Bogdan, whipped out their Vityaz-SN assault rifles and opened up on Andrew. He barely had time to duck down and roll away from the opening where the window had been before a hail of 9mm copper-jacketed projectiles peppered the exterior concrete wall and the ceiling inside the observation room. The loud barrage of gunfire caused the two technicians to flee, and they immediately began running up the stairs towards the transit system's platform where they piled into a carriage that then sped away. With his hands covering his ears and his mouth open in panic, Rittenhausen threw himself underneath a control console with a terrified wail as the shooting continued and a barrage of fire ripped through the ceiling of the observation room and shattered its remaining windows.

Suddenly, a handful of single shots rang out from across the test chamber. Stanislav seemed to twitch, and then he raised his right hand towards the side of his neck. Blood was spurting out, and as he turned in shock towards the location of the other shooter, blood began to bubble out of his mouth, and he suddenly spluttered as he fell to his knees.

Bogdan spun around and spotted the slightly-built blond female crouching by a door up on the walkway on the opposite side of the chamber. As soon as he did so, he swung his weapon up and released a torrent of bullets towards her. It was a minor miracle that she had managed to hit Stanislav from that distance using only a pistol, but he was going to make sure it was the very last thing she ever did. As the hail of bullets peppered the concrete walls around her, she scrambled to turn around and get inside the doorway, but Bogdan now had her in his sights. Flicking the assault rifle back to single-fire mode, he aimed, felt the tension on the trigger and squeezed. A single shot rang out across the huge test chamber.

The lone bullet coming from the observation room window above hit Bogdan in the side of the head, tore through his skull and exploded out of the other side, sending a burst of brain matter and bone fragments spraying across the floor next to him. At the same time, his head instantly jerked to one side and his legs gave way under him, and then he slumped down onto the concrete in a heap, his weapon clattering harmlessly to the floor.

Still with the M16 pressed into his shoulder, Andrew immediately took the iron sights off the falling body of the Russian thug and quickly scanned the rest of the room for threats. Not taking his aim off Rittenhausen, who was still cowering behind a control console, Andrew then shot a quick glance towards the red door by the walkway across the chamber. To his immense relief, he saw Fiona's head appear from behind the doorframe, her hand raised in a simple thumbs-up gesture. Then he returned his attention to the control station below.

'Rittenhausen,' he called out, pointing the M16 directly at him. 'Stand up and step out onto the floor with your hands above your head.'

At first, Rittenhausen did not move, but then Andrew shifted his aim slightly to one side and fired a single shot that slammed into a control console and sent electrical sparks flying and bits of glass and plastic raining down onto the podgy man below.

'Alright!' shouted Rittenhausen. 'Alright, you English dog. I will come out.'

Wriggling and getting to his feet in an ungainly manner, the portly man staggered out from the banks of consoles and stopped about five metres away, standing with his hands on his hips and looking defiantly up at the man who had managed to almost single-handedly ruin his life-long dream.

'Well done, you little bastard,' he sneered, venom dripping off every syllable. 'You've managed to stop the inevitable march of science for a little while. I hope you're proud of yourself.'

'Professor Holbrook,' Andrew called down, ignoring Rittenhausen's outburst. 'Are you able to stand up, please?'

At that moment, Alice appeared next to Andrew, wiping a lock of matted hair from her forehead.

'Daddy?' she called. 'Daddy, are you alright?'

'I'm okay!' came the reply from under a console, and then Adam Holbrook got to his feet and stepped away from the control station. 'A tad discombobulated, but okay.'

Without another word, Alice suddenly ran for the stairs that led from the observation room down to the test chamber, and a few seconds later, Andrew watched her sprinting towards her father and throwing her arms around his neck, nearly causing him to lose his balance.

'I'm alright, Sweetie,' he said softly as he held her in a tight embrace. 'I'm alright.'

Fiona had now emerged from her vantage point at the other end of the chamber, and soon she was in the observation room with Andrew.

'Everything okay?' he asked her.

'Sure,' she shrugged, flicking her hair with affected dismissiveness. 'I've been shot at before.'

Andrew gave her a quick smile and a wink.

'Would you mind going down there and pointing that gun at Rittenhausen?' he said. 'I'll cover you from up here, and then I'll join you.'

'Okay,' said Fiona, heading for the stairs.

A couple of minutes later, Rittenhausen had been restrained with his hands behind his back using Alice's leather belt. Adam and Alice Holbrook were standing by the main control console, examining the telemetry data and looking at the readouts from the test that had just been completed, both of them barely able to comprehend what had just happened. Fiona kept her gun trained on Rittenhausen, and after eyeing her for a brief moment, he took a defiant step towards her and sneered.

'You morons have no fucking idea what you've just done,' he hissed in a low rasping voice as his eyes flashed and he bared his teeth.

'Shut up, you bastard,' said Fiona icily. 'You murdered Ben Ambrose and Christopher Bateman. And you had an entire drill crew killed inside Bergkristall. What kind of monster are you?'

'Oh,' said Rittenhausen, raising an eyebrow. 'So, you *did* manage to find a way in there.'

'I am just glad you won't be able to abuse this technology,' said Fiona. 'People like you shouldn't be allowed to make those decisions.'

'Really,' said Rittenhausen scathingly. 'Well, then who should? People like you?'

'No,' said Fiona. 'People who know what the hell they are doing. People whose moral compass isn't spinning aimlessly like yours is.'

'That's cute,' scoffed Rittenhausen. 'The moral high ground. Always the last refuge of naïve do-gooders like you.'

'Just shut your mouth,' said Fiona. 'I don't want to hear another word from you.'

'Alright,' sighed Rittenhausen, turning around to face the control station where Adam and Alice Holbrook were standing, and then he suddenly raised his head and spoke in a loud and commanding voice as if addressing a person. 'Portal main control! Emergency protocol 'Kammler'. Location One. Initiate!'

Immediately, the portal began powering up, emitting a climbing, high-pitched whine combined with a rising warble as the speed of the light sequence on its interior edge quickly sped up. At the same time, the electrical arcs began forming around its perimeter, and the metal lattice arm with the mobile walkway began moving back towards the portal, its end lining up with the centre of the rapidly forming vortex of swirling light.

With his hands tied behind his back, Rittenhausen suddenly bolted for the mobile walkway with surprising speed and agility, and before Fiona could react, he was halfway to the steps leading up to it. As he did so, Andrew turned around to see what was happening, and he almost began to give chase. But it would be no use. He would be unable to catch up with Rittenhausen before he was at the portal. From Andrew's perspective, the swirling vortex quickly began to coalesce into something strangely familiar. It was like looking through a liquid, deformed and vaguely spiral-shaped window into a space beyond. A space that looked unmistakably like an office. And that's when it hit him. Rittenhausen had programmed an emergency protocol that would allow him to escape from the test chamber in an instant by using the portal itself. As soon as he reached the end of the walkway, he would leap through the portal and end up inside his office in Villa Magdalena, and from there he could easily escape with his entourage of guards. Andrew raised his M16, aimed and placed his index finger on the trigger, but then he hesitated. He had no idea what might happen to the portal if he fired into it or if he accidentally hit its sensitive, high-energy components. Was it possible that it might result in some sort of catastrophic failure that would annihilate all of them?

Adam and Alice Holbrook had watched the scene play out from the main control console, and as soon as Rittenhausen had called out his voice command and the portal had begun firing up, the displays on the console lit up and showed rapidly rising energy levels inside the reactor, the capacitor arrays and the portal. All of the telemetry was deep into the red, but it appeared that whatever the Kammler protocol was, it had been designed for such a rapid surge.

When Alice saw that the swirling vortex was beginning to form an image of the office inside Villa Magdalena, she immediately realised what was about to happen. As Rittenhausen covered the last few metres before reaching the end of the walkway, her fingers danced across the console, re-selecting the portal's exit point, then accessing the power management menu and tapping through options to reach the emergency portal shutdown section. As she looked back up with her index finger hovering above the emergency shutdown button, she watched as Rittenhausen pushed off from the walkway and sailed through the air towards the swirling portal that was now his only escape route.

At the exact moment when Rittenhausen's body began passing through the portal and instantaneously crossing the Einstein-Rosen Bridge to his office more than a kilometre away, Alice let her finger drop onto the console. With the power to the portal cut from one instant to the next, the bridge collapsed, and the connection through spacetime ceased to exist. The fabric of reality snapped back to its normal state, instantly slicing Ferdinand von Rittenhausen's body in half from the top of his skull down to his crotch. One half of him continued through the air and landed in an ungainly, oozing, bloodied heap on the concrete floor on the other side of the portal where it rolled and slushed along, leaving a red trail across the concrete. The other half instantaneously appeared inside the cube-shaped water tank, where it floated in a gory spectacle as it slowly rotated and coloured the water red and cloudy as blood and intestines cleaved in half oozed out.

Fiona's left hand involuntarily flew up to cover her mouth as she lowered the SIG Sauer and turned away in revulsion, but Alice just stared impassively at the water cube as it turned ever more opaque.

'Good bloody riddance,' she whispered icily.

'Holy crap,' said Andrew, struggling to believe what he had just seen, and then he called out to the others. 'Everyone alright?'

'Yes,' came the reply from Professor Holbrook.

'Never better,' said Alice, her eyes still fixed on the water cube.

Fiona, still with her head down, her hand across her mouth, and her blond hair partly obscuring her face, gave a thumbs up and produced a muffled sound that sounded vaguely like the word 'okay'.

'Alright,' said Andrew, fetching his phone from a pocket and finding a picture that Alberto had sent to him. 'Let's call the transit and get to the villa. We need to find Gloria. I have her picture here.'

'Right,' said Fiona as she stood back up and began walking towards him. 'But just wait a minute. Before we go, I have an idea about how to get rid of the remaining guards.'

'Alright,' said Andrew. 'What is it?'

'There are security cameras in here,' said Fiona, pointing up towards several locations on the walls of the test chamber where small black cameras had been mounted. 'If we take over the cameras and zoom in on what's left of Rittenhausen as well as his three Russian bodyguards, I think the guards would probably scarper. I can't imagine any of them would be prepared to enter a firefight and defend a man who is already lying dead in two different places ten metres apart. It's not like they are going to get paid ever again.'

'Good point,' said Andrew. 'Professor Holbrook. Do you think you could make that happen?'

'I should be able to do it,' said Holbrook, moving to one of the consoles and accessing the security systems. 'Give me a few minutes.'

'There's something else we need to do,' said Alice gravely as she came over to join Andrew and Fiona.

'What?' said Fiona.

'It's about that implosion event in Russia,' said Alice. 'We need to make the same thing happen here.'

At that, Adam Holbrook lifted his head and looked their way.

'What?' he said, sounding both surprised and incredulous. 'But we can't do that. This is an incredible discovery. Think of what it could do for the world.'

'It could bring an end to the world,' said Alice evenly, turning to look at him. 'Dad, I know you're excited about this, and so am I. But just think about this for a moment. If this technology gets out, there is no telling what it will be used for, but it almost certainly won't be anything good. As a weapons delivery system, it will be unmatched and completely terrifying. It's one thing for countries to have thousands of nuclear warheads sitting on top of ICBMs pointing at each other, but at least with those, you can see them coming. And that means that there will be a retaliatory response, and that's the only reason there hasn't been a nuclear war yet. Mutually assured destruction, remember? But this portal will wipe all of that away. There will be no warning. No way to avoid it suddenly happening. The first country or the first terror organisation to get their hands on this technology will be able to annihilate anyone anywhere with impunity. The human race simply isn't ready for something like this. We just can't handle something like this responsibly.'

Professor Holbrook was looking at his daughter with a strange mix of emotions. He felt a deep and glowing pride welling up inside him because of her heart and her intellect. Yet at the same time, there was something inside him that was shouting for him to find some way of continuing the work on the portal. This incredible technology that he had never thought would be possible. However, the more Alice spoke, the more he understood that she was right.

'Dad,' she continued softly. 'You know I'm right about this. We have to do this. We have to end this right here, right now.'

The professor bowed his head. She was right. He knew there was no good argument he could present that would be able to counter the case she had just laid out. The portal was too dangerous to be left in the hands of any creature as prone to being governed by its emotions as human beings. In the wrong hands, a simple flash of anger could lead to the end of human civilisation. It was a no-brainer. The portal and the entire complex had to be destroyed.

'I agree,' he finally sighed. 'It has to stop here.'

'Can you do it?' Andrew said, looking at Alice. 'Can you trigger such an implosion event?'

'I think so,' said Alice. 'We pump continuous power from the reactor through the capacitors into the portal until it is at a sufficient level to initiate a portal opening, and then we disrupt the magnetic field stabilisers in such a way as to achieve self-reinforcing resonance inside it. Within a couple of minutes, that should lead to a runaway process that results in the containment fields rupturing and exactly the sort of implosion event that happened at the Vorota facility.'

'Professor?' said Andrew, turning his head towards Holbrook, who then nodded.

'That should do it,' he said. 'Just as long as we are well clear of this place when it happens.'

'Alright,' said Andrew. 'Let's do it. But give me five minutes. I need to pick up a couple of technicians from the capacitor array room. I told them they would be safe there, and I don't intend to leave them.'

While Andrew headed back to fetch the two men who turned out to have been true to their word and had remained seated on the floor the whole time, Adam Holbrook piped a live feed from the test chamber back to the villa and made sure it appeared on all CCTV monitors as well as all the TVs throughout the huge sprawling villa. The feed showed a zoomed-in image of the concrete floor where all three Russian hired guns lay dead, along with both halves of Ferdinand von Rittenhausen. He also added a small piece of text saying that everyone in his employ should now consider themselves fired. If the guards had any sense, they would vacate the property immediately.

Alice spent a few minutes prepping the algorithm that would push the portal over the edge into self-destruct territory, and then she came over to join Fiona just as Andrew reappeared with the two technicians, whose heads hung low and who looked thoroughly beaten and more than compliant.

'Are we all set?' he asked as he walked them towards the transit system.

'Everything is ready,' nodded Alice. 'I've set up a timer. Critical overload should happen in ten minutes, plus or minus a few seconds. And then there will be nothing left of this whole place except an empty sphere.'

'Alright,' said Andrew. 'Let's get back to the villa ASAP. You and the professor should head for the airport immediately and get on the first flight back to Europe. Fiona and I still have something we need to do. Now, let's get the hell out of this place before it implodes.'

Twenty-Six

A couple of minutes later, Andrew and Fiona, along with Adam and Alice Holbrook and the two captured technicians, had boarded the small white rail carriage and were on their way back along the subterranean track towards Villa Magdalena. The smooth concrete tunnel that it travelled through was straight as an arrow and well-lit the whole way, and it felt more than anything like a modern transit system between airport terminals.

As expected, when they arrived at the short platform directly underneath Rittenhausen's villa, it turned out to be completely deserted, and this also proved true of the stairwells, the elevator system and the rest of the house once they arrived up at ground level. Like rats fleeing the sinking ship, everyone appeared to have abandoned their posts once they had realised that the captain was dead and lying cleaved in half inside the test chamber. Loyalty, it seemed, was a monetary phenomenon only, and when the small group stepped outside onto the gravelled driveway that was surrounded by perfectly maintained gardens, all that greeted them were the soft symphony of cicadas and the occasional call of an owl.

'You should get moving towards the airport,' said Andrew, looking at Adam and Alice. 'Fiona and I have something we need to do before we can leave.'

'Thank you,' said Alice, gripping Andrew's hand in hers. 'For everything. I'll never be able to repay you.'

'You don't have to,' said Andrew. 'We just did what needed to be done. No need to thank us.'

'That may be so,' said the professor, giving Fiona a hug and placing a hand on Andrew's shoulder. 'But you still have our profound gratitude for ending this nightmare. I can't wait to go back home and spend a day out on the lake again. Perhaps you two would like to join sometime?'

'Perhaps,' said Andrew. 'Thanks for the offer, but right now we have things to do here.'

He gestured to the handful of expensive vehicles parked nearby.

'You should pick one of those cars and head out,' he said.

'He's right,' said Alice, turning to her father. 'Come on, Dad. Let's go.'

'Good luck,' said Andrew. 'And take good care of each other.'

Alice and Fiona exchanged a brief hug, and then the two scientists got into a low, sleek Mercedes convertible and drove off into the night.

'What do we do with these two?' said Fiona, gesturing towards the two bound technicians with her pistol.

'Maybe we should just let them go,' said Andrew.

'What?' said Fiona, glancing at him sceptically.

Andrew stepped over in front of the two men and regarded them for a moment. Both of them had heard what he had said, and they allowed themselves a defeated but hopeful glance at the man in front of them holding an assault rifle.

'You two have a choice now,' said Andrew, his voice carrying a sinister edge as he moved up close to them, ripping their photo-adorned name tags from their chests and inspecting them briefly.

'Kühn and Birkner,' he read, looking back up at them with a hard stare. 'Consider yourselves lucky to be alive. You saw what happened to Rittenhausen and his thugs. And if you look around, you'll notice that everyone else has run away with their tails between their legs. So, the best thing you two can do now is to go home and thank your lucky stars that your families didn't end up having to bury you this week.'

The two men glanced fretfully at each other with apparent contrition.

'And if you have any sense,' continued Andrew darkly, holding up the name tags in front of their faces to make his point, 'you'll never ever talk about anything that happened here in this place. Wherever you go, I will be able to find you. Do you understand what I'm telling you?'

'Yes,' said one of them, nodding enthusiastically.

'Perfectly,' said the other, bowing his head.

'Good,' said Andrew. 'Now, get behind the wheel of one of those other cars and get out of here. I am keeping these name tags. Don't ever give me a reason to look at them again.'

There followed more vigorous nodding from both men, and then they shuffled over to the nearest car, got in and drove off in a hurry, seemingly concerned that the gun-wielding Englishman might suddenly change his mind.

'Wow. You should have become a gangster,' said Fiona, stepping up next to Andrew as they watched the headlights of the car travel to the end of the long avenue and disappear. 'You're terrifying when you want to be.'

He shrugged and glanced at her with a brief smile.

'I'm prepared to shoot the bad guys if there is no other option,' he said evenly. 'But I prefer not to. If a few words can sort things out, then that's a much better deal in my book. Come on, let's head downstairs and find Gloria. Alberto said that the servant's quarters are down there.'

* * *

Andrew and Fiona headed back inside to the large, opulent foyer of Villa Magdalena and then proceeded down a separate stairwell towards the servant's quarters. Moving carefully while cradling the loaded M16 in case there were stragglers down there, Andrew emerged into a corridor, followed closely by Fiona, who was gripping the SIG Sauer with both hands. Advancing through the corridor and checking each of the small bedchambers on either side with the fluidity of someone who had practised room clearance for decades, Andrew made sure that all of the rooms were empty.

By the time they reached the end of the corridor, he suddenly heard shuffling inside the last room. He moved cautiously up to the door, signalled for Fiona to stay back, and then swept through the doorway and inside the room with his weapon up and ready to engage. The small room was empty, but then he heard movement inside a closet next to the single bed. He proceeded up to it, reached out for the handle with his left hand and yanked the door open.

Sitting inside on the floor was a young woman with short blond hair wearing a maid's uniform, and she shrieked in panic and recoiled away from the door, kicking her feet as she scrambled further back into the closet. Once she was all the way inside with her back pressed against the wall, she held up her hands in front of her face as if to ward off an incoming blow, whimpering as she did so.

'*Por favor,*' she sobbed as she begged to be left in peace. '*Déjame en paz!*'

'It's alright,' said Andrew, immediately crouching in front of her, placing the M16 on the floor as he showed her both of his palms and proceeded to tell her that he was a friend of Gloria's. '*Soy un amigo de Gloria. Todo está bien.*'

The young woman haltingly lowered her hands and peered up at Andrew and then over his shoulder as Fiona emerged with her palms showing as well. As the young woman lowered her hands to her lap, they revealed a pretty but bruised face. There was swelling around her left cheekbone, and there was a cut next to her right eye.

'It's ok,' said Fiona softly as she approached. 'Do you speak English?'

The woman nodded silently, glancing briefly back at Andrew before returning her gaze to Fiona.

'What's your name?' said Fiona gently.

'Esmeralda,' said the woman weakly.

'We're here to help,' said Fiona empathetically, as Andrew moved aside. 'Are you hurt? What happened to you?'

With tears forming in her eyes, the woman nodded as her right hand came up to touch her bruised cheek.

'*El jefe de seguridad*,' she said. 'Raul Torres. Chief of Security. He took Gloria. My colleague. She resisted. He beat her. Then I tried to stop him, but he beat me too. *Bastardo*.'

'Esmeralda, where did he take Gloria?' said Andrew. 'Do you know?'

'His home, *probablemente*,' said Esmeralda. 'Not far from here. It's a big house behind a fence. *Señor* Rittenhausen made him rich, and now he thinks he can do whatever he wants. He is a very bad man.'

'Why did he take Gloria?' said Fiona, fearing the answer she might receive.

Esmeralda looked up at her, and then her eyes darted fleetingly towards Andrew, as if nervous about how to phrase what she was about to say. She swallowed and returned her gaze to Fiona with a pained expression.

'Gloria is very beautiful,' she finally said. 'He will do bad things to her.'

Andrew's jaw clenched visibly as she spoke, and he lowered his head for a moment. When he glanced back up, Fiona was looking at him over her shoulder with a look that spoke volumes. The two of them exchanged a silent agreement before Andrew spoke again, this time with cold determination in his eyes.

'Tell us where Raul Torres lives.'

* * *

Half an hour later, after a quick text message exchange with Alberto, Andrew had recovered the silver SUV rental car and met up with the old man at his modest home. At the same time, Fiona was now driving one of Rittenhausen's luxury cars on her way to deliver Esmeralda back to her parents' house, where she lived. After a quick war council, Andrew and Alberto then set off to find Raul Torres.

Within less than ten minutes, they had arrived at a small, arid plateau up on one of the nearby hills, from which there was an uninterrupted view of the entire wine region. Rittenhausen's head of security turned out to be living in an ultra-modern, cubist house with white-rendered exterior walls and huge windows sitting in black steel frames overlooking the valley below. The building was set back about fifty metres from the road on a modest plot, and Andrew parked the SUV out of sight behind some bushes a bit further along the hillside road. The two men then stepped out, Andrew carrying the SIG Sauer and Alberto cradling his old shotgun.

The two-storey house had a large, lit-up infinity pool at the back, and it was surrounded on the other three sides by a lawn that was in the process of being watered by an automatic sprinkler system. All the windows were dark, except for two on the top floor, but the curtains were drawn, so they were unable to see inside. However, they could hear loud rock music playing.

A tall, thick hedge had grown up to envelop a chain link fence that ran along the perimeter of the plot, and as Andrew and Alberto approached the front gate, they were met by an electronic locking system that required a code to open.

Andrew considered climbing over the gate, but there was a chance that it might trigger the alarm, so instead, the two of them proceeded along the outside of the tall hedge to where the hillside dropped away towards the valley below. They were then able to inch along the house's massive concrete foundations and climb up over the edge of the infinity pool. From there, they could see the lit-up floor-to-ceiling windows on the first floor, and they were able to walk along the side of the pool to a narrow veranda that was separated from the building's interior by a set of sliding doors. The doors were pulled shut, but when Andrew gripped one of the handles and began to pull gently, the door slid aside swiftly and silently, allowing them to enter the house on the ground floor.

The interior was all shiny stone, glass and steel, and it had the minimalist furnishing that led Andrew to believe that Torres had hired an expensive interior designer to create the perfect bachelor pad for him. The aggressive-sounding rock music was playing throughout the house, and they were unable to hear any sounds or voices anywhere.

The two men moved quietly towards a set of steps leading up a long, straight stairwell to the first floor, but as they began to ascend, they were suddenly filled with a new urgency as a female voice cried somewhere up ahead. This was followed by a sequence of inaudible words that were almost drowned out by the music, and then the baritone voice of a man shouting angrily and a clearly audible slap. Andrew glanced back at Alberto, whose eyes told him that the old man was about to come apart at the seams with a volatile mix of barely contained fury and fear as his white-knuckled hands gripped the shotgun. Deciding to dispense with the covert approach, Andrew began moving swiftly up the steps, racking the slide of the SIG Sauer and flicking the safety off.

They emerged on a wide landing, from which a corridor stretched off to one side. The corridor had several doors spaced roughly equidistantly along its walls, but only one of them was closed. This had to be where Torres was holding Gloria. As they pushed up towards the door, another cry came from inside, and Andrew then picked up the pace, moved in front of the door and kicked it as hard as he could. His boot slammed into it next to the lock, and it flew open, with small pieces of lock and doorframe flying off into the room beyond. Using his forward momentum, Andrew continued through the doorway with his weapon up and ready to engage the violent head of Rittenhausen's security, prepared for the fact that Torres almost certainly had some sort of firearm close by at all times.

With Alberto following close behind, Andrew advanced into what was a large bedroom. There was an enormous king-size bed with an upholstered headboard on one side of the room, a three-person sofa on the other, and tall floor-to-ceiling windows straight ahead. Gloria was sitting on the end of the bed with her arms tied behind her back, her legs pushed together and the front of her maid's uniform ripped open, exposing her bra and her chest. She had a terrified look on her face, and she was grimacing as if in anticipation of being struck again. Standing over her next to the curtains that had been drawn across the window was a bare-chested Raul Torres wearing only his dark grey uniform slacks and a pair of black boots, and in his hand was a bottle of Jack Daniels that was half full. A maniacal grin had spread across his face, but it instantly froze as the door exploded open and crashed into one of the walls, breaking a large mirror.

'Don't fucking move!' Andrew shouted as he moved aggressively up to stand about three metres from Torres, whose wild eyes looked as if he had been doing several lines of cocaine. 'Take a step back, or I'll drop you right now!'

Torres seemed to need a couple of seconds to process what was happening, but then he took an unsteady step back while turning towards Andrew with his muscular arms hanging down his sides and his broad chest rising and falling as he breathed heavily. Alberto's face was now a picture of homicidal fury, but as he moved forward to stand next to Andrew with his shotgun in his hands, a confused and terrified Gloria turned her head towards them. As soon as she spotted Alberto, she leapt off the bed, pulled the front of her dress back across her chest and rushed towards him. She reached him in a couple of seconds and launched herself into his arms as he held her tight and spoke softly to her.

'*Chica*,' he whispered, telling her that everything was alright and not to worry. '*Todo esta bien. No te preocupes.*'

'Alberto Garcia,' said Torres disparagingly, swaying slightly as he spoke, his eyes rolling vaguely in their sockets and his nostrils flaring. 'Why must you always be a nuisance?'

'This is the end of the road for you,' said Andrew icily. 'Your boss is dead, and there is literally nothing left of Rittenhausen's crazy project. It's all gone.'

'So what?' Torres said, slurring his words slightly and raising his arms out to his sides. 'I have plenty of money.'

He turned his head towards Gloria, shot her a leery glare, and grinned.

'And plenty of women,' he continued. 'I don't need that old goat anymore.'

At that, Alberto got to his feet, gently releasing the embrace of his niece. Holding the shotgun in his right hand as it hung down along his leg, he stepped closer to the tall, bare-chested man with eyes that burned with hatred.

'You people,' he said with chilling menace. 'As soon as you get money, you think you're better than everyone else. You think you can do anything you want.'

Torres shrugged dismissively and snorted.

'That's because we can, old man,' he said.

As he spoke, he tilted his head slightly to one side as if explaining something to a child, but at the same time, his hand was moving slowly towards the small of his back where a pistol was concealed.

'This is something you will never understand,' he continued, his hand now almost closing around the pistol grip. 'Money is power. And power lets you do whatever you want. That's the way the world is. Look at your niece. If I want her to be mine, I can make her mine, and there is nothing you can…'

Torres never had a chance to react when Alberto's shotgun suddenly boomed and kicked as he pulled both triggers at once. The report was deafening inside the bedroom, and the recoil almost knocked the weapon out of the old man's hands. In that same instant, two sets of steel pellets tore through the air at supersonic speed, slammed violently into Torres' broad chest, lifted him off his feet and shunted him through the shattered glass behind him where his mutilated body flailed down into the infinity pool below with a loud splash.

With smoke still rising silently from the two barrels, Alberto stood immobile for a few moments, breathing heavily as his burning fury began to leave his body.

'It's over,' said Andrew, placing a hand gently on the old winemaker's shoulder. 'He's gone. He can never harm anyone again.'

Only then did Alberto seem to relax as he lowered the shotgun, and the tension in his shoulders melted away. Then he tossed the weapon onto the bed and turned around. He suddenly looked exhausted as he raised his head and regarded Andrew for a moment.

'Thank you for what you did,' he said.

At that, Gloria got back onto her feet, gripped Andrew's hand, and squeezed it gently as she looked up into his eyes.

'Thank you so much,' she said. 'You saved me.'

'No,' said Andrew with a calm and reassuring smile. 'Your uncle's the hero here. And scum like Torres deserve everything that's coming to them. As far as I'm concerned, he just did the world a favour. Now, let's get you two out of here.'

EPILOGUE

LAKE NANTUA, FRANCE

The late afternoon sun was glinting off the tranquil mountain lake as the quartet allowed the rowing boat to drift gently along. It had been two weeks since the news of an unusual earthquake in the Mendoza region had hit the wires in Argentina. An investigation carried out by the central authorities in Buenos Aires had speculated that a poorly understood geological phenomenon had caused an enormous underground cavity to form south of the city, possibly as a result of subterranean aquifers flowing under the region for tens of thousands of years. The investigators had concluded that the cavity had finally caused almost an entire vineyard to collapse into a giant sinkhole, but thankfully there appeared to be no casualties. Mysteriously, however, the vineyard's owner had disappeared without a trace, and none of the locals had proven to be of any help in the efforts to locate him. It was as if he had vanished into thin air.

'So, the entire complex was wiped out in the implosion?' said Fiona as she leaned back in the small rowing boat and adjusted her cap.

'Yup?' said Alice. 'Once I knew how much power was being channelled into the portal during its operation, I was able to calculate the radius of an implosion event for that specific portal.'

'You've always been so much cleverer than me,' said Professor Holbrook, smiling tenderly at his daughter. 'I just couldn't be more proud.'

'Oh, stop it, Dad,' said Alice, returning his smile with a hint of embarrassment. 'There's a reason why Rittenhausen kidnapped you and not me. You're the cornerstone of the whole of CERN.'

'Either way,' said Andrew, lifting his small, stocky bottle of French lager. 'You're both back where you belong. That's all that matters.'

'Exactly right,' said Alice, lifting her own bottle and clinking it against his. 'Thanks to you and Fiona. Cheers, both of you.'

'Cheers,' said Fiona, bringing her bottle close to the two others as the tiny wavelets lapped gently against the boat.

'*Salut,*' said Holbrook Senior, pointing towards the restaurant on the leafy east shore of the lake. 'Now, who's hungry? There's a great place to eat just over there on the lake shore.'

Andrew gripped the oars and turned the small boat around, and as his long strokes pushed the vessel smoothly across the calm surface of the water towards the restaurant, the sun dipped below the peaks to the west, marking the end of another day.

NOTE FROM THE AUTHOR.

Thank you very much for reading this book. I hope you enjoyed it. If you did, I would be very grateful if you would give it a star rating on Amazon and perhaps even write a review.

I am always trying to improve my writing, and the best way to do that is to receive feedback from my readers. Reviews really do help me a lot. They are an excellent way for me to understand the reader's experience, and they also help me to write better books in the future.

Thank you.

Lex Faulkner

Printed in Great Britain
by Amazon